Devil's Midnight

devil's midnight

Yuri Kapralov

Akashic Books
New York

Published by Akashic Books
Originally published in hardcover by Akashic Books in 2003
©2003, 2005 Yuri Kapralov

Layout by Melissa Farris and 450
Back cover portrait of the author by Max
Ukraine map by Sohrab Habibion

ISBN-10: 1-888451-88-2
ISBN-13: 978-1-888451-88-7
Library of Congress Control Number: 2005903221

Akashic Books
PO Box 1456
New York, NY 10009
Akashic7@aol.com
www.akashicbooks.com

For Vera and Anatoli and the millions who perished in this,
the bloodiest, most brutal war in Russian history.

THE STORY TAKES PLACE IN THE FOLLOWING LOCATONS:

- •Kiev under the Bolsheviks and the Whites
- •The Central Russian front near Kursk
- •The Great Red Offensive and the battles involving the armored train "Our Homeland" along the Kursk-Zhigri railway line
- •The Asian front, the Khara Khum desert east of Krasnovodsk
- •The provincial town of Sumy, northern Ukraine
- •The last days and the fall of Odessa
- •The luxury liner "Catherine the Great," en route to Novorossyisk
- •The town of Armavir, North Caucasus
- •The port town of Novorossyisk

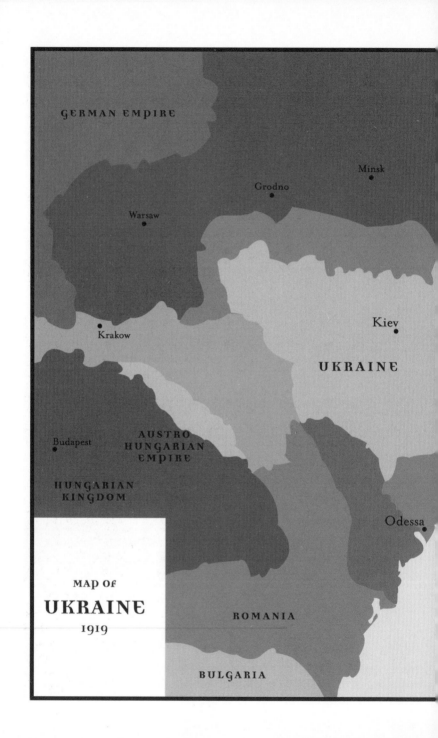

GERMAN EMPIRE

Minsk

Grodno

Warsaw

Krakow

Kiev

UKRAINE

Budapest

AUSTRO
HUNGARIAN
EMPIRE

HUNGARIAN
KINGDOM

Odessa

MAP OF
UKRAINE
1919

ROMANIA

BULGARIA

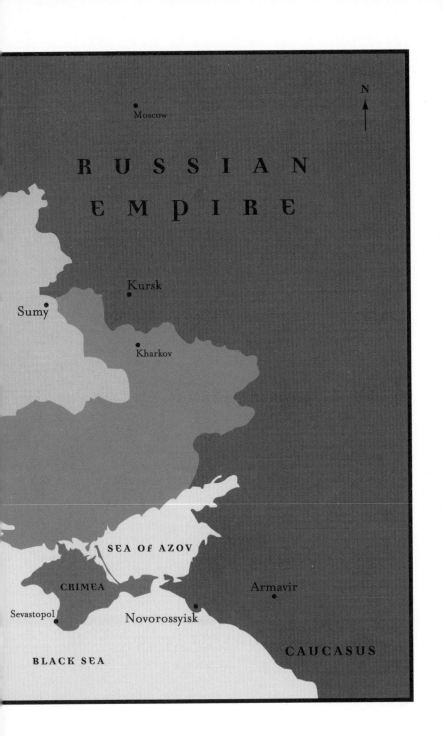

A **long gray line** of several hundred Red soldiers stood silently on the unused railroad track overgrown with weeds, near the charred remains of the water tower. Their rifles and carbines, thrown to the ground just minutes before, were being collected by two elderly railway workers who simply dumped them into a two-wheel cart one of the workers was pushing. They came to the Maxim machine gun, too heavy to lift, and stood, not knowing exactly what they were supposed to do.

No one was guarding the prisoners. A group of them, taking advantage of the situation, cautiously crossed the ditch behind the water tower and ran toward the few houses with boarded-up windows and the apple trees beyond. After they disappeared among the trees, there was a short burst of machine-gun fire and a few rifle shots. Several Cossacks raced by on their small horses.

The sleepy iron monster resembled a giant caterpillar: dark-green, covered with the need of cannons and machine guns. The armored train "Our Homeland," with the new white, blue, and red banner of the Volunteer Army on its command turret, stood on the main track, suddenly awakened.

Its forward cannons roared simultaneously; flame and smoke filled the air. About half the prisoners, thinking that the firing might be directed at them, fell to the ground. The windows of the tin yellow station house were shattered by the blast, and at least a dozen hens and roosters flew out of it and ran in terror—some toward the armored train and some toward the prisoners.

Four very young Volunteers immediately jumped off the armored train and chased and caught most of them. They handed the chickens to their very happy comrades and went to examine the machine gun. No good—the lock was missing and the feeder was jammed. "Climb back in." An officer standing under the banner waved to them with his binoculars. "The track is clear, we're rolling out."

The monster leaped forward amidst a river of sparks and black smoke toward the city of Kiev, less than ten kilometers away.

BOOK ONE

Kiev
August 1919

"**This was** A MAGNIFICENT PARK BEFORE THE REVOLUTION. So very well kept. The emperor himself walked down this alley in 1914. Shame, shame." An old man with a battered briefcase shook his head in sorrow as he brushed the broken bottles, empty tin cans, crumpled newspapers, and mountains of sunflower seeds off the bench. He took off his thick glasses and wiped them, put them back on the tip of his red nose, and cautiously sat down.

The shabbily dressed Ukrainian peasant woman to whom he was complaining walked out of the park and crossed the street. *So far so good,* the old man thought. He opened his briefcase and took out Merezkovski's *Christ and Antichrist*. With his thick book, glasses, wellworn blue jacket, and neatly trimmed white beard, he looked like a retired professor enjoying the bright summer morning. At least, he hoped he did. It took Yuri Skatchko over two hours—and all the skill he had accumulated in his brief but memorable career as the leading actor, director, and janitor of a small theater on Podol—to apply the facial makeup alone. But those skills had been acquired in another life, and quite another universe.

Perhaps the professor could not sleep last night because of

the artillery fire. His book seemed to close by itself, and he appeared to others to be dreaming. Death. The end. Period. Loss of body, thoughts, feelings. How many times had he faced death during these two brief months? How many of his friends went into that dark void with bullets in the back of their heads? Is there anything beyond this darkness, the river which even the ancient Egyptian kings had to cross in their narrow boats . . . another beginning? Today, tomorrow: another spring. Victory! Resurrection!

On a bench across from him a large sailor and a young woman were locked in a passionate embrace. The sailor wanted more than just an embrace. He tried to drag her toward the bushes, but the woman resisted. He let her go, stood up, and looked around, angry. The woman hurriedly left. The park was nearly empty. Near the pond two Oriental men were arguing. Next to them: another couple, another embrace.

The sailor stretched, took out a pouch of machorka, and rolled himself a Goat's Leg. He then searched his pockets for matches. No matches!

"Give me a match, Granddad," he growled at the professor. He walked over and grabbed the old man by the collar. "Wake up, bourgeoisie, or I will cut your throat."

The professor appeared startled, frightened. "I do not have matches, dear comrade . . . I do not smoke. Perhaps you too should quit, it is not healthy—"

"What? Are you lecturing me?" The sailor swore, and took a shiny Finnish knife out of his boot, then thought better of it. Why kill the old fool? He put the knife back, grabbed the professor's book and briefcase, and threw both into the pond, where they landed in the murky water and then slowly sank. The professor looked crushed. The sailor walked out of the park. Before crossing the street, he turned around and showed the professor his fist.

A middle-aged man with a black beard lazily followed the sailor. He stopped by the professor's bench for a few seconds, looked the old man over very thoughtfully, then walked away. When the bearded man finally left the park, Yuri Skatchko, age twenty-eight, promoted this week to full colonel in Denikin's Volunteer Army, and the commander of the most powerful White underground organization in Red Russia, sighed a deep sigh of relief.

No more stupid masquerades, no more acting in this life-and-death theater of the absurd. The nightmare, the incredible tension and nonstop work of these last two months—and especially these past three weeks—was almost over.

Possibly as early as this evening, the White army would take the city.

The large sailor who had threatened him, posing as one of the prosecutors of the dreaded Kiev Cheka, was in reality a former naval officer and one of Yuri's most trusted agents. During their altercation, a folded piece of thin paper had found its way into Yuri's pocket. On it, in clear hand, were the names and addresses of all Cheka agents the Reds were leaving behind to set up their underground. This was a great victory indeed. Now he, too, should be leaving.

Yet the morning was still so pleasant, so fresh, even the sporadic booms of the artillery fire failed to break the lazy, intoxicating serenity. Yuri closed his eyes.

The past three weeks had been especially difficult, because Yuri's immediate commander had been summoned across the front by Denikin—an idiotic order that had weakened the organization more than Cheka. Yet the organization had sur-

vived, in part due to Yuri's superhuman efforts. Just yesterday, the planned evacuation of the families of leading
Communists via the Dnepr flotilla had been sabotaged. Not a
single ship had been able to sail; not one engine was working.
And after the chief mechanic had been arrested and shot, the
Reds discovered that the boilers were beyond repair. The supply ship loaded with ammunition and four brand new cannons
had sailed—right into the Whites' hands. Almost one thousand
officers had been saved in a pre-dawn raid on the Cheka
annex. And there had been many more victories, large and
small. Yet the losses were heavy. Nearly one hundred members
of the organization had been shot in the past two days alone,
as well as hundreds of innocent people.

Yuri suddenly opens his eyes. "You fell asleep," rings the
alarm clock in the back of his mind. "You fell asleep and you
are not allowed to sleep!" He notices that the quiet park is now
in turmoil: screams, whistles, commands. Two Oriental men
run past him, hurriedly throwing some packages into the
nearby bushes. Soldiers, sailors appear, red armbands, bayonets.

He slides the flat black Colt out of his pocket, and it falls
softly onto the uncut grass behind his bench. He walks carefully toward the side entrance, his escape route, a hole in the
wrought-iron fence. *I must have slept at least fifteen minutes,* he
thinks, amazed. A few more steps and he is free . . . Not so
easy.

"Turn back, Grandpa, right now." A very young, happy
voice. A red-haired lad with a carbine. Smiling.

"Dear comrade, what is this?"

"Cheka. You too must come with us. Don't ask me why.
Orders."

"But my family, they will be so worried."

"Relax, you will be home soon enough. We shot everybody who needed to be shot yesterday. Faster, faster!"

About fifty people are being herded to the Cheka, a gray three-story building. At the entrance stands the familiar cream-colored limousine and two armored cars.

Commissar Volkov, Yuri thinks, *that smart, dangerous cat. He only has a few more hours and he is still in the game. And why not? Why not spread your net in the last moment and see what swims in. Clever, damn it!* The second floor, again so familiar: the long corridor, the uncomfortable wooden benches. Only a question of hours now, perhaps less. And then the dark cellar, blood on the walls, one well-placed bullet in the back of the head. *No time to torture anyone today, comrades, you have almost run out of time.* And outside so close, so very close. Boom, Boom! Heavy guns from the armored train. *Ours must already be in Slobotka.*

Yuri sits down in the corner so that he will be one of the last people called into Volkov's cabinet.

The commissar is very busy and does not waste much time. Three, five minutes a person. Most people are freed. The two Oriental men do not return. Goats and the sheep. One door of Volkov's cabinet leads back into life, the other . . . forget the other.

Eh, had the White Guard Brigade acted more decisively, we would have already taken the city.

About a dozen women are brought in. They are crying, arguing, begging. They have come to inquire about their husbands and fathers and brothers. One sits down next to Yuri—one of the most beautiful women he's ever seen. She speaks softly about her father who was arrested last night. Some important railroad official and an American citizen. How could they? What will happen to him?

Last night? The red-haired young soldier is now standing

near Volkov's door. *Last night? "We shot everybody who needed to be shot yesterday."*

The woman has incredible eyes, the color of ancient gold. She is somehow familiar. Where has he seen her? Has he ever seen her, or has she simply walked onto the wrong stage? This is, after all, still his theater of the absurd and macabre. Nothing matters, except for death. Not even the thin paper with the neat handwriting which they did not find when he was searched for weapons, not the pair of golden new shoulder patches with two red lines and crossed cannons which he had sown into the lining of his blue jacket, not his disguise. Least of all, his disguise. Had the Red soldiers been less drunk, they would have looked at his hands and shot him already.

He listens attentively to the beautiful woman, nods his head, promises to help.

Commissar Volkov jumps out of his cabinet. "Get these women out of here!" he screams, a high falsetto. "Send them to wash the floor of our barracks. No more talk that we are retreating. Our fortress city will never fall. We are strong, we are winning!" He runs back into his office.

Nerves, comrades, nerves. Yuri shakes his head. Volkov looks like he too has not slept for an entire month. *Too much blood, comrade, too much cocaine.* A tired-looking soldier enters his cabinet and comes out with an empty pitcher of water. He pauses to talk with the red-haired guard. They are laughing, talking about women.

Yuri listens to a loud and wonderful machine-gun serenade, so close, so very close. *Perhaps there's a hope.*

"Granddad," the tired-looking soldier calls to him, "go next door; they have a barrel of clean water. Fill this pitcher . . . for comrade commissar. Tell them Trofim sent you, and hurry."

"Certainly, dear comrade." *Anything to escape that familiar room.* Cobwebs on the yellow curtains, rusty bars on the long-unwashed windows. A huge oak desk, empty except for a revolver and a shiny metal box filled with cocaine. Behind the desk, an apparition, a snake that is almost dead, its hissing so very, very familiar. *One step, two. Is that a blood stain on the stairway? On the white wall? Red on white? Insanity, fantasy, reality, what difference does it make? White on red?*

Colonel Skatchko, not the captain, please notice this colonel, the biggest fish, the Moor, is this not your code word for me, comrade Commissar Volkov? And you are letting me swim away. Reality? Fantasy? Death? Life? White? Red?

Yuri bites his lower lip and spits out the blood. In the underground, during the most dangerous raid, when Cheka agents burst in the room with their revolvers, he calmly blew out the candle and began shooting them, whistling the old Scottish ballad: *"You'll be the first one . . . to ride out the squall . . . the stronger your nerves are . . . the nearer the goal."* The goal? So easy. Out, out to freedom, to fight, to die perhaps, but not here.

Caution. Nerves. Do not walk too fast, you are an old man.

Down the stairs, every step an eternity, every foot weighs a thousand pounds. In the vestibule another tired-looking soldier is talking to a sailor. *Good.* Nobody looks twice at the old professor with an empty pitcher who walks hurriedly—a walk of an energetic young man—across the street. *The stronger your nerves are.* Only the cream-colored limousine and an old truck being loaded with wooden boxes.

Shrill whistles inside the building. *Soon,* he thinks. *The smart cat will realize. Very soon.*

Too late, comrades, too late! A narrow alley, the familiar boarded-up cellar window. Off with the makeup. A new set of clothing. Worker's overalls, cap with a red star on it. Heavy boots. Small revolver goes into one of the boots, the Nagan in one of the pockets of the overalls. He tears the lining of the blue jacket and retrieves his two gold shoulder patches. *Cannot stay here. The houses will be searched.* Another yard and another. The sound of a siren not so far away. The yellow shadow of Commissar Volkov's limousines in the narrow streets. Soldiers, sailors, bayonets. *Too late, comrades, too late.*

So close though. Must keep on running. Volkov knows these streets as well as I do. Another backyard, high brick fence. Shouts in the street— aeroplane! aeroplane! A proud steel bird with a three-colored emblem on its wings. A long machine-gun serenade and then another. Behind the tall fence, a small cemetery, a few trees, and a tiny wooden church. Six bullets in his Nagan, five more in the small revolver. Ten for them, one for me.

In the church, a few people, an old priest, and a deacon. Funeral service.

Yuri sits down in the corner, far away from the door, under an icon of some barefooted Russian saint. The floor feels cold and comforting. His eyes are closing; the wheels of some strange train are rolling in his head. *The stronger the nerves are . . .* He lies down on the floor. *They will think that I am distraught, that I am praying.* Praying? *The stronger . . .* The hand around his Nagan is beginning to lose its grip. *The nearer the goal . . .* The beautiful young woman with her strange golden eyes, so familiar, so far, far away . . . *Will she ever find her father?* *"We shot everybody . . ."* Not everybody, you haven't shot me. Time has run out for you, Volkov, you smart, smart cat. Will your claws reach into this church? Not very likely now—you better run while you can.

It doesn't matter anyway; this time I am ready. Why does the floor suddenly feel hot as coals, and why am I still trembling? Ridiculous! The giant wheels, the cannons, and the sparks, they must disappear. Sounds? Only the sound of the wind. White clouds moving fast over the flames. So hot. The last cloud gone, the soft gray mist settles over the river. Now it feels comfortable. I can breathe again. Stars. Silence.

The barefooted Russian saint steps out of his icon and leans over Yuri. "You do have strong nerves." He shakes his head and laughs.

waking up HAD NEVER BEEN EASY FOR ALEXEY Lebedev. This morning it was nearly impossible. Nightmares mixed with the artillery fire: the fear of being shipped to the front, the desperation of being trapped, helpless. He had to escape. The seven months under the Bolsheviks—the dreaded Cheka and the dreary reality—were almost over. Another dawn, another life was coming; perhaps as early as today. Yet the fear remained. And the dreary reality: the army greens, the cap with the red star, the empty headquarters of the Garrison Regiment, the silent telephone, the high-pitched, catlike screams of the deserters being shot in the courtyard under his window.

Reality. This morning the artillery barrage was so close and so intense that Alexey, navigating across his room, stumbled over his mother's old easel and almost fell.

"What are you doing?" His sister Lucy, sleepy, stood in a long nightshirt and watched him from the door of her room as he tried to regain his balance. "Go back to sleep."

"Easy for you to say." Alexey rubbed his eyes. "Our devil Kuzmenko shot six more deserters yesterday. Shot them himself. Bastard loves it."

"He's probably already run away. I watched them during the night. Trucks, cannons, their whole army must have gone by."

She might be right, he thought. *Besides, I can't leave her alone. God knows what can happen. To hell with Kuzmenko and the regiment. To hell with reality.* "I am staying, Lucy," he replied, "and going back to bed."

This time it was a wonderful, pleasant dream: white sands and the blue, warm water of some tropical lagoon, sensuous breezes, faces of beautiful women, euphoria. But, too soon, the reality intervened once again. Two young soldiers were loudly arguing with Lucy at the front door.

"Just give it to him, girl," one of the soldiers insisted, pushing a slip of pink paper toward Lucy. "These are orders, very important, we are from Cheka . . ."

"I don't care if you're from the moon; my brother is not home, I am telling you." Lucy refused to accept the paper.

"Then call your mother."

"I don't have a mother." She wanted to tell him that her mother was shot last year by the Moscow Cheka, but she bit her tongue. "Go away. Let me get some sleep."

The soldiers whispered among themselves.

"Listen, girl." One of them had a thumbtack and he pinned the pink sheet of paper to the door. "If your brother doesn't show at the regiment, he'll be arrested and shot. Don't think we are leaving. We defeated Denikin's bands yesterday. No more evacuation. Tell him that."

"Go to the devil!" Lucy slammed the door. One soldier shouted an obscenity, but they quickly departed.

"You're not going, are you?" Alexey was already dressed. Red star armband, uniform.

"I am. What if Denikin is really thrown back? They will definitely shoot me. And then you'll be all by yourself. I will be careful, very careful. And I do have a contingency plan." He kissed her, and they embraced. On the way out, he touched the framed photograph of his mother and father, looking, as he always did, at a blue semi-abstract painting, one of his mother's last canvases, hanging over the old couch in their living room. The blue sky outside the window matched the blue in the painting, and somehow Alexey felt that, no matter what, this would be an extraordinary day. He tore the stupid piece of pink paper off the door. It contained the usual warnings: "Failure to comply . . . death by firing squad." What a nice pink color, though.

It was a fifteen-minute walk from his house to the regimental headquarters. There were soldiers in the streets, but no civilians. Some skeletons resembling horses dragged wagons overloaded with furniture. Alexey was so preoccupied he was almost run over by an armored car that appeared out of nowhere and roared north. There were no guards at the entrance, and Alexey was about to turn around and go home when he heard the familiar, "Alexey Sergeevich—I am so relieved that you came. And on time . . ." This was the voice of his immediate supervisor, Fokin, a good simple man, a village teacher, and a Communist. "I have to leave for an hour or two . . . on orders of the regimental commander, of course."

Of course, thought Alexey. *Another rat jumping ship. In his case, however, it's understandable. If the Whites capture him, they will hang him. Why did he join the party anyway?* Yesterday it was Slava Finkelstein and Boris who ran off, today it is Fokin. Now, Lebedev is left, an idiot still sitting by a telephone that never rings. *I'd better put my contingency plan into action and get the hell out of here.*

Here was a completely empty room on the second floor. The old furniture and filing cabinets had been evacuated two weeks ago. Let the White bandits get their own old chairs and desks. The only item that remained was a black telephone on the windowsill.

Alexey sat next to it and looked into the courtyard.

Cobblestones, yellow walls, boxes with ammunition, an empty wagon. No sign of life. Perhaps they did run away.

The silent telephone finally rang. Alexey shuddered and picked it up.

"Listen, student." This was the devil himself speaking—Kuzmenko, the commander of the regiment. So he was still here. "Listen good, we beat Denikin last night. Where is Fokin?"

"He went out on your orders, comrade commander."

"My orders?" Kuzmenko swore long and hard. "Look out your window." He abruptly hung up.

A few minutes later, Alexey heard the familiar screams and howls. He saw soldiers and bayonets and Kuzmenko waving his huge Mauser. Two deserters, badly beaten, were left near the yellow wall. One of the men tried to cover his face with his hands as if to ward off bullets, the other stood resigned to his fate, blood dripping from his nose.

I cannot watch it anymore. Alexey turned away from the window. Shots, screams, silence. Then Kuzmenko's basso: "This will happen to all who dare to flee!" Sounds of the boots, voices, silence. Another hour goes by. Nothing happens. And there is no artillery fire. *Bad omen. Perhaps they did win. In any event, I cannot take it any longer.*

Contingency plan. Instead of going into the street and risking being picked up and put against the courtyard wall, Alexey would walk downstairs, through the kitchen, the staff cafeteria, then the storage room. Behind the storage room was an empty lot overgrown with weeds, and an alley. If he managed to cross the lot undetected—and it was a matter of only ten, fifteen seconds—he would be home, safe and sound. Alexey had lived in Kiev all his life and knew the backyards like the palm of his hand. And he could also hide out at his friend Petia Ovcharenko's house, if need be.

If Slava Finkelstein, who actually was arrested once and spent a few unpleasant nights in Cheka, had the guts to desert and not be scared of Kuzmenko . . . I am going.

Alexey starts for the door. Suddenly, it flies open and the room is filled with about a dozen screaming and crying women escorted by two sailors with rifles. They are from Cheka.

"What am I supposed to do with these women?" Alexey asks in astonishment.

"Anything you wish, comrade clerk," one of the sailors says, winking. "Anything, just sign this paper. These are the bitches of the counterrevolutionaries we arrested last night. Commissar Volkov sent them to wash barrack floors to show them that we are strong, we are winning." The sailors laugh and depart. Alexey remains standing like a pillar of salt, his mouth hanging wide open, looking at one of the women—so beautiful, a lovely vision that he feels he has seen somewhere, perhaps in a dream.

Ah, this is all a dream anyway, he hopes. *It will disappear as soon as I blink a few times.* He blinks, but the women are still screaming, begging, and arguing.

Finally, the vision speaks: "Dear comrade, please let us go, we have done nothing wrong."

Alexey is hypnotized by the two large golden eyes, so strange, so seductive. He is now sure he has seen the woman somewhere before. Where? He cannot believe his own words: "Yes, go, please go, all of you, and please hurry before someone stops you."

The women run out. The one with the golden eyes pauses, comes toward him, and kisses him hard on his lips. Then she too hurries outside. Perhaps all of this is a hallucination. If so, why does he still feel her kiss? Why . . . He slaps himself on the fore-head. Of course. The vision, of course! A small cinema on Podol. His arm around Musenka, his friend and sometime lover. On the screen: the beautiful, tormented geisha. Yet her eyes are anything but Oriental. They mesmerize the audience. And when she removes her garments and walks into the sea, loud gasps and applause . . . Nata Tai, the greatest Russian film actress, the idol of millions. Far more famous than Vertinski, than Lenin, than Vera Holodnaya. Nata Tai, a woman of hundred of legends, rumors, mysteries. Nata Tai, who disappeared a year or two before the February Revolution. Here? In Kiev—not in Paris, not in New York? And she kissed Alexey Lebedev, one of her loyal fans. And why? Because he granted her a small favor. Lucy would never believe him when he got home. Home?

Alexey jumped up again as the telephone rang for the second time. "Student?" Kuzmenko roared, "You did not run away? You saw what I do with deserters? Now, these bitches from Cheka. Bring them to me immediately or you'll answer with your head." He added a few obscenities and hung up.

Alexey's reaction was swift. The stairs, the cafeteria, the kitchen, the storage room, the weeds, and the alley, the back-yards, and freedom. And just as he was approaching his own house, there was a happy artillery barrage and a series of explosions. *I hope they've leveled the barracks.* He tore the red star off his cap and threw it on the ground.

Lucy was not surprised to see him so early. She had a visitor, Petia Ovcharenko, an awkward, nearsighted young man, Alexey's friend and former classmate, and an incurable pessimist. Both he and Lucy were red-faced, excited. Alexey noted that one of the two bottles of red wine they had hidden since the days of German occupation was open, and at least half was gone. *Hmmm, they drank it directly from the bottle. So unciv-*

ilized. Alexey had known for sometime that Petia had an eye on Lucy. *Well, she is almost eighteen. So if she wishes to say yes, that is up to her; she is old enough.* Alexey brought three glasses and filled them. They drank the wine and he cleared his throat to tell them about Nata Tai.

But Petia spoke first. He gave an assessment of the military situation: The Ukrainians, pushing from the west, were already within city limits. They had at least one cavalry division and an armored train. The Whites, pushing from the south-east, were somewhat delayed because, in a last desperate attempt to stop their advance, the Reds had thrown everything they had against them—an entire infantry division and some internationalist units.

"Kuzmenko told me the Whites were defeated."

"Nonsense. But they are mopping up here and there and that's what delayed them. They will enter the city today."

"How do you know all this?"

"I have my sources." Petia tried to sound as important as he could. He had actually overheard the conversation of two women rolling a small cart loaded with vegetables they hoped to sell to the Whites who were already in Slobotka.

If this is so, Alexey thought, *and the Ukrainians will enter the city before the Whites . . . that is bad news. Hmmm. Free independent Ukraine? And Russia, one and indivisible? Can they ever coexist? Not very likely. But then, anybody is better than the Bolsheviks.* "Hmmm." Alexey cleared his throat again. "Of course, you will not believe me, but make a guess . . . Who did I see today? One clue: Who is the most glamorous, the most beautiful, the most mysterious woman in all of Russia?"

"You should eat something with your wine." Lucy went to their tiny kitchen and came back with a boiled potato and a few slices of cucumber. "Eat." Alexey ate.

"Well?"

"Well what?" asked Petia.

"Who is the most beautiful woman in Russia, and please don't tell me it is my sister. She is very pretty, but beautiful she is not."

"Thank you very much." Lucy stuck her tongue out at him.

"You mean somebody we do not know? A singer perhaps . . . an actress . . . ?"

"I know." Lucy jumped up. "The one and only Nata Tai. You saw Nata Tai?"

"Not only did I see Nata Tai, she kissed me—kissed me rather hard."

"Alyosha, Alyosha." Lucy shook her head in bewilderment. "Are you feeling quite well?"

Alexey opened the last bottle of wine and refilled the glass. "I too thought she was abroad—Paris, London, the Riviera . . . I feel quite good, never better." He drank and waited for them to reply.

"I believe you." Petia was thoughtful. "But only the part that you had seen her. I don't know what she is doing here, but I myself saw her walking on Krestchatik. She is in Kiev." He lowered his voice as if afraid that someone would overhear him. "Nata Tai and the entire cabal."

"The what?" *How wonderful,* Alexey smiled, anticipating another one of Petia's hot gossips.

"Yes, yes." Petia hurriedly drank his wine. "Last Friday, I was walking past the Cheka—brrr, I am trying to get past it as fast as I can—and who comes out surrounded by the sailors? Not arrested, she was in command . . . We just spoke of beauty. Who is the ugliest woman in Russia—pardon—one of the ugliest? A clue: the ugliest pianist? The one who looks exactly like a vampire and probably is one?"

"Stacy Averescu!" Alexey exclaimed.

"You are so right. And a few days ago, I saw Oleg Baclanov, their priest, I suppose. And I am not talking about masons or any of our secret societies . . . They are out-and-out Satanists!"

"So what does it have to do with Nata Tai?"

"You never read," Petia was excited, *"Before the Revolution? Cinema Vérité? Rumors and Facts,* any of them?"

Alexey shook his head. He never had the time to read any of those tabloids. He was too busy trying to survive and graduate. And he graduated, in part, because Petia's father, a respected professor, had pulled some strings.

"I did read something," Lucy said. "Some scandal?"

"So," Petia was beaming, "the famous pianist Stacy Averescu—the Romanian Vampire—was, believe it or not, Nata Tai's lesbian lover, ugly or not! And she is a Satanist, everybody knows it. And now she and Oleg and . . . others, are here, in Kiev . . . and what do you suppose they are doing here?"

"I have no idea." Alexey wondered if there was anything else to eat in the house.

"I do not have a precise idea," Petia confessed, "but they must have a purpose."

"Do we still have some bread? I am terribly hungry."

Lucy went back into the kitchen, brought a square chunk of stale black bread, and cut it into three equal parts. "Let us change the subject," she begged. "Let us talk of love, freedom, love, Petia." She sat next to him on the sofa and winked at her brother.

Alexey refilled his glass and took it with his piece of bread to his room. It was getting dark. He looked out of his window at the sunset—orange and purple—and at their small vegetable garden over which Lucy labored so hard, as had his mother.

Now they had fresh tomatoes, though not as many as they thought they would, several cucumbers, and, amazingly enough, a whole bunch of eggplants. He thought again of how thrilled he had been by Nata Tai's kiss. It was the most remarkable day after all. What seductive, amoral, and totally bewitching eyes that woman had. One kiss, but what a kiss. *Perhaps I will have an affair with her. These days anything is possible. Why would she ever be interested in me, though? Why is she here anyway?*

Alexey remembered her first big role: a young harlot in *The Pit*. What a scandal that was. The church, the censors, the press. He saw that film four times. *Eh, and I almost did not recognize her. And why could we not get together? My mother and father were about as opposite as people can be. My father with his ancient languages and cultures and my mother exhibiting with Malewich, Popova, Kandinsky—a free thinker. And dead. At least the father died four years ago, that wound was healing.*

His mother? Alexey simply refused to believe it at first. An issue of *Pravda*. Back page. A long list of the counterrevolutionaries executed for taking part in an uprising . . . Vera Ivanovna Lebevdeva, an artist . . . What an ending. Alexey was in pain, physical pain, for several weeks. Lucy took it better than he did. *Oh Lucy,* he thought, *say yes to Petia tonight and enjoy yourself. Who knows what tomorrow will bring? And I will dream of something impossible. Gold on some distant shore, gold in those distant eyes.*

The wine was beginning to work. It was now pitch dark outside. No artillery fire, no machine-gun fire. Silence. Alexey said a short prayer for his sister and began drifting into his land of wonders, the land where the people were decent and love was like a beautiful woman, like a butterfly in Lucy's vegetable garden, so fragile and delicate, so easy to catch, so easy to crush.

That was VERY DECENT OF THE YOUNG CLERK TO LET US *go,* Nata thought. *What next?* She felt so exhausted and worn-out, she simply sank down on the steps of some dilapidated house and watched the never-ending procession of horses and wagons and the gray, sad-looking soldiers with their rifles and knapsacks. *I must do something.* But again, what? Going over to Stacy's apartment and begging her was out of the question. Besides, Stacy was somehow connected to Cheka, and perhaps even with her father's arrest. Oleg too refused to help.

It was so very bizarre, her friends turning viciously against her just when she needed them most. Perhaps—on second thought—there was an explanation. Their motive could have been revenge. Their turnaround had begun when Nata's father arrived unexpectedly from Moscow to complete some unfinished business in Kiev, less than two months ago.

Nata adored her father. He had always helped her, and his help was gentle, subtle, loving. When Nata was seriously addicted to morphine, he had spent days and nights at her bedside at Dr. Sevarious's famous sanatorium near Moscow. He had tried to talk her into going back to America, where she could continue her career in film. "Leave this insane, tragic country," he had begged her time and again. But the Bolsheviks were already in power and he was an irreplaceable railroad specialist. And the railroads were the only thing that held the country together. He was told that he could leave as soon as the Civil War was over. He was offered a huge salary and an apartment in Moscow, and his house in Kiev was returned to him. He sent Nata to Kiev, hoping that it would be easier to leave from there. Indeed, there had been an opportunity for her to leave only four months ago, but by that time she was being amused and entertained by Stacy, Oleg, and their friends. There were "artistic evenings" at her house, orgies, and some morphine and cocaine. And, for the first time, she had not followed her father's advice.

When her father walked into the house two months ago, he saw a sight he had not expected to see. Drunken poets and musicians in the living room, and upstairs, and in her bedroom . . . Nata did not wish to even remember. Her father, a handsome giant of a man, born and raised in Montana, took Oleg Baclanov by his belt and threw him out of the house. Two or three poets and artists who did not want to leave on their own had the same experience. He then told Stacy to leave. Getting rid of her proved to be difficult. Stacy threw a fit of monumental proportions with curses and threats and wild accusations. She attacked Nata's father with a small but sharp knife that she carried and cut both his hands. In the end, she too was thrown out bodily, screaming terrible threats and obscenities. Nata had telephoned her the next day to apologize, but she would not listen.

Nata's father, Bill Taylor, had explained to her again and again that these people were dangerous. Not by themselves, but together: They were all members of a powerful group of devil worshippers, a group whose tentacles manipulated not only behind the scenes of the current terrible events, but also reached far outside of Russia. That he did not know what they were doing in Kiev, but whatever their purpose, they should never come to their house. And Nata should not see them at all. Three days later, Nata went to see Oleg at his apartment. This was the second time she had gone against her father's advice.

Nata remembered her mother only vaguely, a beautiful, high-strung Russian woman who, in her youth, was also an actress. Both her mother and her small brother had been killed in some mysterious, unexplained accident in Manchuria in 1905, at the Tzetzekar railroad station, where her father was the chief engineer working for the Russian-Chinese railroad system. By the time Nata became Russia's top film star in 1915 and '16, Bill Taylor had also made spectacular advances in his career, and held the post of the deputy minister for transportation. He had never remarried and Nata often wondered why. A complex man, she thought, a genuine adventurer with quite a few secrets of his own.

He was warned by friends at least a week ago that the Kiev Cheka was planning to arrest several railroad officials. Most of them immediately went into hiding and urged Bill to do the same. He wouldn't hear of it. He was an American citizen and the one key specialist they needed. Bolsheviks are realists, he insisted. He did advise Nata to leave Kiev temporarily and go to the provincial town of Sumy where he had a summer home. And, for the third time, she had not taken his advice.

And just last night: drunken sailors, stench of sweat and machorka, bayonets, abyss.

There are several explosions very close, followed by machine-gun fire. Nata stands up, bewildered, disoriented. *I must go to my house. Where else can I go?* But that path too is cut off.

In front of her house idles a cream-colored automobile,

the same one that had stood in front of Cheka. On the steps of her house, three sailors are smoking their Goat's Legs, passing around a bottle of vodka.

Sailors and bayonets . . . They came to arrest me. Fortunately, they are not looking in my direction. Nata turns around fast and starts walking away. She hears a sharp whistle but keeps walking, faster and faster. She hears: "Stop, or we will shoot." At the same time there is a shadow in the clear sky and many voices shout, "Aeroplane, aeroplane!" Deafening machine-gun fire erupts everywhere. Something bright explodes nearby—a bomb? A grenade?

Suddenly, right in front of her, two horses and a red-faced soldier on a wagon. The wagon overturns, the horses fall down on the sidewalk, and the soldier flies across the street and smashes his head on the pavement. "Run, run," someone screams, "flee for your lives!" and people begin running in all directions. A tall, thin priest appears out of nowhere. He grasps Nata's hand and, pushing her through a narrow gate, points her to an old church, almost invisible behind the trees and bushes.

"Run, run with God."

God? Nata tries to reply that she doesn't believe in God, but the priest is no longer there. She stands by herself in a strange yard. She can still hear the commotion and the explosions and machine-gun fire, but here, behind this tall fence and the wooden gate which is now bolted—another world. She runs across the yard toward the trees and the church and falls, exhausted and frightened, on the dirt floor near the wall covered with icons. The service is over, there are only a few people in the church, mostly old women.

Not far from her, a man in coveralls lies facedown on the floor. Nata thinks perhaps he is dead, but he is breathing. She touches his shoulder, and he cries out and sits up. He is so handsome, and there's something odd about him too—something almost familiar.

There's a faint smile on his face, and he speaks to her like an old friend. "Were you able to find out anything about your father?" Nata is stunned. She never considered herself a serious actress. She was a fantasy, a dream of love, sex, adventure. But she had known many great actors and actresses, and this worker's makeup was phenomenal. A history professor?

She shakes her head in admiration and answers as if she also were an old friend. "No, I did not."

"So you came to pray?"

"No, I don't know how to pray. I came to hide; I was followed . . . Oh, what difference does it make? Tell me something, do you pray? Do you search for that very precise something . . . the *most important* thing in your life? The meaning of your whole existence? I am going insane, I know . . ." She reaches for his arm and squeezes it, then recites: "Someone so faceless, so evil, is throwing the comets of empty lives at us . . . We must forget about *most important*. The *most important* does not matter." Her face is now next to his. "This was written by a repulsive, shallow man who wanted to put the period in the very beginning. Do you understand me? I loved his words though, the words were beautiful. Really. Really, why not end all of it? Why can't we put the period at the very beginning? If that *most important* really exists, it's not what we think it is . . ."

"I do not understand you." The worker touches her hair, strokes her head. Her hair appears a flaming red in the candlelight. He whispers, "For me, these are the *most important* in my life right now." He reaches in his pocket and takes out a pair of golden shoulder patches. They are pretty. Two red stripes and a pin with two cannon barrels, crossed, shiny.

"Colonel Yuri Efimovich Skatchko, at your service . . . for me, Russia, our victory." He suddenly grabs her and roughly pushes her down on the floor.

He is going to rape me, Nata thinks. *Here? In the church?*

Three figures are outlined in the entrance. Sailors, bayonets. "They came for me," Yuri whispers, "do not move."

She sees the revolver in his hand. *I must tell him he is mistaken. These sailors came for me.* But everything is happening so very fast. Explosions, screams, and the whole world turns upside down.

Nata is now a small girl being rocked to sleep by her father on the veranda of their summer home in Sumy. The nightingales in their apple orchard are singing her a lullaby. Reluctantly, she opens her eyes. She is crying and trembling. The handsome worker is holding her. His eyes—two black shiny coals—so close, so concerned. *Who is he? A soldier, a magician?* He keeps saying, "Stop, stop, you are safe."

It's the same old church. Only a few candles are still burning. There are other workers sitting near the two of them on the floor. They are armed. Revolvers, rifles. Another worker appears with a tin cup filled with water. Nata drinks, stops crying.

"Porutchik Shebeko, Staff Captain Gorlin, Cornet Nikulin." Yuri introduces some of his comrades. "Where do you live?"

"I . . . can't return."

Yuri smiles. "They have all left, run away, gone . . . and they are not coming back, ever. But it could be dangerous for you to walk home alone. It's evening already. Perhaps I can escort you?" He whispers at length to his officers and they leave. Only the two of them are now in the church: an eerie feeling. *I must visit this church again,* she thinks. Only three candles are burning in front of a large icon of the barefooted Saint Seraphim of Sarov.

"Come." He touches her arm. She notices the bodies of three sailors near the entrance. It is dark, the stars are our. No people in the streets, an unusual tension, silence.

"I hope the next time we meet it will not be an adventure film or a metaphysical drama punctuated by gunfire." He holds her tight by her waist and she wishes so very much that he would start kissing her right now, this very moment.

They do kiss by her door. Nata tries hard to pull him inside her house. She whispers that more than anything else, she would like to make love to him. The entire night. He politely refuses. Please. No. He gives her a small revolver, tells her not to hesitate using it. Does she know how? Yes, she is a very good shot. As he's walking away, he half turns and asks her her name. She is excited, she feels a delicious shiver run up and down her entire body. Almost as if agreeing to a first date, worried and anxious, she shouts, "Nata!"

In the safety and comfort of her bedroom, Nata drinks champagne, looks into the darkness of her window, listens to a few single shots now and then, to short bursts of machinegun fire. No artillery booms tonight. She thinks of how she felt so sexually aroused in the church, walking with her magician. A long lost feeling. A wonderful feeling. Infinitely better than being aroused mechanically, as she had been, these months, these years. *And he is so handsome,* she cannot get his face out of her mind. More handsome than Sobinov, or Valentino, or Douglas Fairbanks, all of them put together. And so stubborn. She could not remember any man saying no to her. And what an actor . . . such dark skin, too.

This is silly. She refills her glass. *Me? How many hundreds of men and women have I had affairs with, and here I am, like some schoolgirl falling in love for the first time. In the middle of this war, and with someone I do not even know. Someone who just refused me so he could go and fight this idiotic war, and die perhaps. Free Russia and all that. And yet I have never seen any Russian man as dark-skinned as he. He must have Saracen or African blood in him. And he's so brave.* She remembers, before collapsing, how she had seen him calmly shoot at the sailors and toss a grenade that one of the sailors had hurled at them out of the church. *He is so young, and a colonel! I know generals who are cowards. Stop,* she thinks. *I must calm down. Here I am drinking champagne and fantasizing about someone I do not know, and my father is perhaps in mortal danger. But I must sleep or else I am not going to be of use to anybody. Tonight I must sleep. There is absolutely nothing I can do tonight. Tomorrow, the world will change.*

Nata gets off her bed and goes to her bathroom where a small kerosene lamp is still burning. She looks at herself in the mirror, opens a drawer, and takes out a flat box containing a few ampules and a syringe. She breaks one of the ampules and watches the gold liquid fill the syringe. She almost does not feel the sting of the needle going into the inner part of her thigh. She sits beside the mirror for a minute or two. She thinks that, aside from being her lover, Yuri might be useful in trying to find her father. *After all, in the new world, tomorrow, my handsome colonel will be a very important man. What an incredible day this was.* Her eyes are now closing, a pleasant warmth spreads over her body. She turns off the lamp, falls onto her bed. She thinks for a moment of the very young clerk who looked at her so adoringly before letting her go. *He was handsome too, but so different. He must have seen my films.* She smiles and stretches. She feels good now; the morphine is weaving its magic.

At exactly ELEVEN THAT VERY NIGHT A MIRACLE occurred: The electricity was turned on. Usually, it came on for only an hour or two earlier in the evening. Perhaps the workers at the power station had decided to celebrate the Bolsheviks' retreat. Thousands of fireflies on the dark meadow, the street lights here and there along with the Kreschtik, a few on Funducleevskaya and Bessarabka, in the Czar's Garden, along the river, and even as far as Podol.

Two of these fireflies threw their pale lemon light along the bronze of the Stolipin monument and further toward the Duma, illuminating an odd group of characters, mostly middle-aged and elderly men who appeared to know each other.

The murmur of hushed elderly voices: "Anton Ivanovich, my dear, are you still alive? . . . Stepanich was shot by the Bolsheviks . . . Artem strung up by the Petlura, they thought he was a Jew, idiots . . . And both Vova and Goga were hung by the Germans . . . Ah, Yakov Moiseevich, you too are still amongst the living . . ." The group moved cautiously, slowly, closer and closer toward the ornate door. These people were members of the last freely elected city council, and in a time "between the rulers" such as now—the time of total confusion—they courageously met and tried to set up some orderly transition of power to protect the citizens from robberies, rapes, and other crimes, and to safeguard the utilities and hospitals.

As they neared the entrance it opened wide, and Pavel, the

well-liked caretaker, greeted them warmly and invited them in. Minutes later, in the brightly lit main chamber, everyone was happy and relaxed. Behind the podium, the mayor sat alongside the newly elected commandant of the city, Colonel Kuzik. There were more than two dozen deputies in the chamber. Few Ukrainians were present, for some reason. And, for obvious reasons, the left benches, normally occupied by the Bolsheviks, were empty.

During emergencies, Colonel Kuzik, by profession a doctor and an examiner at the city morgue, a sharp-nosed, melancholy individual, always got himself elected as the commandant. He would then don the appropriate uniform. If the Bolsheviks were going to enter: an old leather jacket with a red armband. If the Ukrainians: an embroidered shirt with yellow and blue ribbons. If the character of the forthcoming rulers was hard to pinpoint, but in any event, they were not Bolsheviks, the armband would be white. For a day or two afterwards, Kuzik would sign his proclamations accordingly either Comrade Kuzik or Ataman Kuzik, or, if it was difficult to foretell who would be firmly in the saddle, simply Commandant Kuzik. Once the new rule was established, Kuzik would collect his money and return to his job at the morgue.

Tonight is different. Less than fifteen minutes after Kuzik is elected, Yuri Skatchko, wearing a dark brown tunic with his new shoulder patches and the order of St. George awarded to him in 1915 when he commanded an artillery battery on the Austrian front, proudly enters the chamber. He is accompanied by six of his officers, some with rifles and revolvers. They walk right up to the podium.

He asks permission to address the gathering and permission is granted. "Yakov Moiseevich." He salutes the mayor.

"Esteemed members of the Duma. I have the great honor to inform you that the Volunteer Army is at this time in control of the city, and that Staff Captain Gorlin," he introduces a tall officer next to him, "has been appointed to the commandant of the city."

"The second," somebody snickers. Loud applause from the right, lukewarm applause from the center, and derisive hoots and whistles from the Ukrainians.

"Dear Yuri Efimovich," the mayor replies, "it is, of course, wonderful news for all of us that the Volunteer Army is firmly in control, but I would like to hear something from the Ukrainian commander as well . . ." He stops, his thick glasses nearly sliding off his nose. A loud argument has erupted at the entrance, and three characters, dressed as if they were members of some Ukrainian dance company, walk toward the podium. Yuri knows one quite well—Roh Rafalski, the commander of the Ukrainian underground. Rafalski does not ask for permission to speak.

"There are no Whites in the city," he screams, "and we are already at the freight station! Our scouts are already in the city, and will be here in a few minutes. I was appointed commandant by Petlura himself, and I am the real commandant here."

"The third!" someone exclaims.

"Get out of here," Yuri growls. "We already have a commandant."

His officers raise their rifles, and the Ukrainians pull out their revolvers. Curses. Clown! White dog! Escalating with obscenities.

"I will whistle and one hundred lads will run here at once," threatens Roh Rafalski.

"Until then, I am throwing you out!" screams Yuri.

"Gentlemen, gentlemen . . . let us behave like gentlemen."
The mayor is afraid that a serious scandal is about to erupt.

Suddenly, someone screams, louder than the others, the terrible, frightening words: "Bolsheviks! Here! Now!"

Everyone rushes toward the windows. A small unit is approaching the building: about fifty horsemen with rifles and a torn red flag which looks black near the dimly lit bronze statue of Stolipin, carts with women and machine guns, two field cannons, tired infantrymen.

God! Oh God Almighty! is the prayer of the people inside the chamber, Ukrainians and Jews and Russians. *Please, please let them go by, do not let them stop.* But the unit stops in the square and at least a dozen horsemen ride to encircle the Duma to prevent anyone from escaping through the side and back doors.

Yuri, his officers, Roh Rafalski and his lads, and even two students with white armbands who were guarding the entrance, have melted, vanished through the cracks in the walls and under the floorboards. No one is sitting behind the podium now. Both the mayor and Commandant Kuzik sit right in the middle of the empty rows of the far left.

Fifteen men and two women led by a thin sailor, all heavily armed, enter the chamber. The two women in the procession drag a snub-nosed Maxim machine gun on two small wheels. The sailor walks up the podium. Everyone notices that his walk is unsteady, that he has a square unshaved face, and that he can't stop yawning.

He clears his throat, spits twice, and looks over the gathering with a heavy, sleepy gaze. Grimly, he pushes the podium aside and gets right to the point. "I am the commander of the special battalion attached to the Red Banner Odessa fighting group. My name, remember my name," he raises his voice, "is

Semen Titov. As far as I know, my battalion is the only fighting unit in the city. Therefore, I am also the commandant of this city . . ."

"The fourth," someone groans.

"Therefore . . ." The sailor sticks his thumb in one of his nostrils, takes something out, looks at it thoughtfully, and flicks it on the floor. "Therefore," he suddenly screams at the top of his lungs, sending shivers down the spines of his captive audience, "after I learned of the meeting here of some citizens calling themselves the Duma . . ."

We are lost, everyone thinks. *They will shoot us down in our seats.*

"I am . . . turning over all power to this Duma . . . and leaving this city according to my orders. Long live our great socialist Revolution!"

A few deputies shout a weak hurrah, a few others applaud, everyone lets out a great sigh of relief.

The unit departs. The square is empty; pale lemon light shines on the lonely bronze.

Yuri had watched the preceding drama with some sense of amusement, even humor. He had been reasonably well hidden behind stacks of old chairs and curtains on an unused stairwell leading to the balcony, and from his vantage point he could easily have shot the sailor and the middle-aged man standing next to him who was probably the political commissar of the unit. Yuri simply could not believe that these worn-out soldiers had come to fight, or even to execute the members of the Duma. This was a lost unit, and theirs was a lost cause. It was an interesting spectacle though, good for an entire act in this much-prolonged absurd play that should have ended hours ago.

His officers climbed out of their hiding places, and both the mayor and Commandant Kuzik returned to the podium. No one could find a trace of Roh Rafalski and his lads. From then on, the deputies were agreeable, and since the Ukrainians did not return, the power was divided betweeen the city council and Yuri's organization.

Yuri himself felt as exhausted as the Red sailor. And he had to prepare a briefing for General Offenberg, the commander of the White Guard Brigade, in the morning. Standing in his hiding place, both his revolvers still trained on the space vacated by the sailor and his soldiers, all he could think about was Nata. Of course, he had realized as soon as he left her that she was Nata Tai. He had seen a few of her films. It was just so improbable: Nata Tai, here, in the middle of the Civil War? And no one even recognized her. She had stopped making films two years ago because of some scandal, and these days people avoided looking at the faces of other people anyway. Still, he felt very strange: disturbed, bewitched, still hearing her voice.

He stayed at the Duma long after everyone else had left. His officers came, a steady stream. Good news and bad. The arsenal had been captured intact. The Bolsheviks had mined it, but they had done a sloppy job, and the mines were disarmed. The Ukrainians were going to enter the city first, beyond a doubt. Their armored train, "Free Ukraine," was already at the freight station. The Garrison Regiment barracks, badly damaged by the artillery fire from the armored train "Our Homeland" had been captured by the Volunteers' organization, as had two warehouses still containing large amounts of food and ammunition.

Around six in the morning, Yuri stretched out on the floor and asked Porutchik Shebeko to wake him up at precisely seven-thirty.

As early as it was, there were people in the square. And since Yuri was wearing his tunic with shoulder patches, he was besieged by well-wishers and people complaining that after the Volunteers had disarmed the Jewish self-defense organization on Podol, they had had at least six robberies. The bandits were finally caught and dealt with, severely, but citizens were still frightened and demanding protection. A funny-looking man ran up to Yuri and followed him, talking rapidly about the need to declare Kiev a free city such as Hamburg or Lubeck: "The Volunteers can stay at Slobotka, the Ukrainians on Podol, and the city will be neutral territory."

Yuri smiled. "I love it, a fine idea. Go share it with the Ukrainian commanders, and if they do not hang you, come back and we'll discuss it in more detail."

In his limousine, a blue Packard left behind by some important commissar, Yuri felt dizzy. *What is the matter with me? The stronger your nerves are . . . nerves . . .* "Shebeko, you drive, drive very slowly, I desperately need more sleep."

He woke up as they were driving parallel to the railroad track. A strange, magnificent weapon stood poised for action: dark green armored boxes and turrets, long barrels of cannons, narrow slits and protruding needles of machine guns. It was the armored train "Our Homeland"—the name written in black Slavonic letters underneath the white, blue, and red emblem.

"Naval guns," Yuri commented with admiration. "Long distance field cannons and a Howitzer too. A fine combination."

General Offenberg, the commander of the White Guard Brigade, embraced Yuri as an old friend. "I served in the same division with your uncle . . . St. George, first class?" He touched Yuri's order. "From what I am told, you deserve another. Come, let me feed you." He led Yuri into a room where three tables were put together. Around the tables sat the officers of the White Guard Brigade, some already quite drunk.

On the table was a sight to behold. Yuri had not seen so much food in his entire life. There were two suckling pigs, various fish in aspic, black and red caviar, cutlets, fried chicken and ducks, mountains of sausages and fresh fruits and vegetables, and at least a dozen bottles of vodka, cognac, and champagne. A large blond woman sat on one of the officers' laps with a guitar. Another young woman, dark-haired, very pretty, was kissing a young cornet.

After the introductions, the general sat Yuri beside him and ordered one of the soldiers who was acting as a waiter to fill his plate. He opened a bottle of champagne. "To Kiev, the mother of all Russian cities," the general proposed.

Officers stood up. "To Kiev."

As he was eating, Yuri hurriedly tried to brief the general on the situation and the urgent need to advance into the city. "The brigade must act now," he stressed. "Otherwise there will be street fighting with the Ukrainians, many casualties." The general listened with his eyes half closed, nodding his head from time to time. He drank another glass of champagne and urged Yuri to do the same. There were now sounds of a marching band outside. They looked out the window.

A unit composed entirely of young boys—some, it appeared to Yuri, not older than twelve—was marching by in tight formation. *So this is the Guard Brigade?* He remembered the huge, tough guardsmen from the Great War. Yet these boys were disciplined, and they marched well. As they neared the window, they began singing a song Yuri hadn't heard before:

> *Bravely, we will go into the battle*
> *For holy Russia.*
> *And all as one will give*
> *Our young blood . . .*

So these were the boys who fought their way from the Caucasus to Dnepr, he thought. *They fought the battle-hardened Bolshevik internationalist units, the mercenaries, sailors, and everything the Red Hydra was able to throw at them—fought outnumbered and outgunned. And they won. And perhaps the time is not so very far off when instead of Kiev, they will be marching with the Russian tricolor banner under the Kremlin walls, under the golden domes of Moscow.*

After the boys came the Cossack cavalry, another unit of infantry, an artillery battery . . . Yuri was so moved, he was on the verge of tears. And he was proud too. Proud that he was a part of this movement, that he too would march some day soon on the Red Square. He felt the general's hand on his shoulder.

"My automobile is ready, colonel. Please ride with me, we will both accept keys to the city."

⁂

Peace. Happiness. Loud music. Two flags hang from the balcony of the Duma building: the blue and gold flag of the Independent Ukraine, and the white, blue, and red of Russia, the one and indivisible. Behind their flags sit two old generals: General Offenberg, bald, pale, with a neatly trimmed beard, and Nechai-Lisenko, the Ukrainian commander, with a lock of white hair falling on his purple face and a large mustache à la Taras Bulba. Behind each general stands an archangel: Yuri Skatchko and Roh Rafalski. A bright image of peaceful coexistence.

The mayor finishes a long and pointless speech to a large crowd of citizens who have gathered in the square. A diplomat to the end, he gives each general one key to the city. In the square, the Ukrainian orchestra strikes up another march. There are more and more Ukrainian soldiers and horsemen, and only one part of the Volunteer Army—eight horsemen—an island surrounded by the Ukrainians, who are holding their new blue and yellow flags and waving them in tune with the march.

General Offenberg had known Mishka Lisenko when they were both cadets in the military academy and they shared the same desk. *Mishka has done well for himself,* he thinks. *His land and estate are well inside the Ukrainian territory and he is a corps commander with Petlura. And I am only a brigade commander . . .* For a few moments, he relaxes and remembers how he and Lisenko spent summers together, before the Great War, before any revolutions. He almost wants to say, *"Eh, Mishka, why do we sit here? Let us go drink vodka."* But then the music becomes offensive. Offenberg sees his own ransacked and burning mansion near St. Petersburg, the bodies of his daughter, his grandchildren lying in a common grave. And the most important thought—that to restore Russia, to once again take possession of his vast lands, to avenge the deaths of his loved ones, he must ruthlessly brush aside whoever stands in his way—Nechai-Lisenko, Bolsheviks, anyone.

In the pocket of Offenberg's tunic, a top secret order—clear, to the point—signed by Denikin: *"Do not enter into any negotiations with the Ukrainians; Kiev must be ours. We must slap the hands of Petlura. We are sufficiently strong for that."* A new officer arrives and whispers something into Offenberg's ear.

Yuri hears only: ". . . ready as of . . ." He does not know about the secret order in the general's pocket, or the fact that the two commanders have known each other for so long. He does know that this idyll is not going to last very much longer.

A huge new Ukrainian orchestra squeezes into the plaza, followed by a cavalry unit. The horsemen are carrying blue and yellow banners tied to their lances. The plaza is now a sea of blue and yellow.

"Glory to Mother Ukraine!" someone screams.

"Glory! Glory!"

"Death to Moscovite imperialists!" shouts another voice.

"Death! Death!" from hundreds of young throats. A few civilians begin to leave.

"Down with the Moscovite flag!"

"Down! Down!" agrees the sea of blue and yellow.

A small man standing next to Roh Rafalski rushes past Yuri and tears down the three-color flag. It falls slowly on the pavement and lies there. Silence. Many more couples and civilians hurriedly leave. His fists clenched, Yuri rushes at the small man.

"Colonel, do not make one move," Offenberg hisses. Yuri stops, perplexed. Offenberg slowly stands up.

"Citizens!" he shouts. "You have just witnessed how our glorious banner, the symbol of great Russia, was dishonored by dirty hands." He takes out a white handkerchief and waves it in the air. Immediately, the Volunteer patrol rides off. Someone folds and takes with him the Russian flag. Most of the civilians leave. The Ukrainian orchestra strikes up another march. "Glory, glory to Mother Ukraine!" shout the horsemen.

Suddenly, much louder than the music and the shouts—the machine-gun fire. The square is covered with bluish smoke. And into that smoke, with wild whistles, howls, and terrifying screams—sounds such as no one has ever heard before—races a horde of Cossacks waving their swords. For a few minutes the plaza is a churning sea, a whirlpool of yellow, blue, lances, musical instruments, uniforms, women's dresses, bloody Cossack swords, people running in all directions.

And it is over. Several dozen bodies and a few dead horses remain in the square around the statue of Stolipin. The Ukrainians are gone. The Cossacks gallop somewhere on their fast, small horses. Across the plaza run the Volunteers of the Guard Brigade. A few of them stop, drop to one knee, fire their rifles at something or someone, and run again.

Nechai-Lisenko, his hands shaking, stands up. Roh Rafalski unhooks the Ukrainian flag, folds it neatly, and hands it to the small man who tore down the Russian flag. The Ukrainians leave in stony silence.

Offenberg once again feels the urge to stop Lisenko and say, *"Mishka, let us go . . ."* Then he sees the incredible hatred in Mishka's eyes, the colorless eyes of an evil old man.

"Colonel." He turns to Yuri. "There is no reason for us to remain here. Show me our new headquarters."

In a small decrepit house near the railroad settlement, two men are watching the running Ukrainian infantrymen through the cracks of a boarded-up window. One man is very young with a gentle, sensitive face. He is Vanya Zorin, a member of the Russian Communist Party since he was fifteen. The older man has an angular face, a very high forehead, a thin nose, and thick lips. His eyes are wide open; he is perspiring. He is Anton Volkov, one of the three top commissars left in the city to organize the Red underground. Formerly of the Kiev Cheka, Volkov has the reputation of being ruthless, cunning, and completely without pity. To Vanya, he is a best friend and mentor.

"Forgive me." Volkov smiles. He takes out a small tin box and pours some white powder on the palm of his hand. He quickly inhales. Vanya does not mind; he knows Volkov's only weakness. He continues to watch the now empty street. He hears whistles and screams. A group of Cossacks waving their swords are racing somewhere at an incredible speed.

"Look at them go," Vanya exclaims in admiration. "White guards, elki palki!"

Volkov is not impressed. He looks at Vanya with love and affection. "Remember always, the one thing that is very important—perhaps most important—only those with nothing to lose will win . . . and we have nothing to lose."

"I know we will win." Vanya nods his head. "Though, I think not because we have nothing to lose, but because our cause is just . . ."

There are two rapid knocks on the door, followed by seven more at even intervals. Volkov takes out his revolver and Vanya cautiously opens the door. A large man wearing a railroad conductor's uniform walks in. He is tired and depressed. He sits by the table. "Do you have any vodka?"

Yes, they have half a bottle, but no cups. The conductor drinks all of it. "Volkov," he slams his fist on the table, "we have been betrayed."

Silence.

"Do we know who betrayed us?" Volkov asks very quietly.

"Maybe somebody does; I don't. I was ordered to warn you that the Moor has all of us like baby chicks in his hand."

"The Moor?" Vanya asks.

"Our code name for a most dangerous man. Ironically, he should be fighting with us, not against us." Volkov is thoughtful. "I had him several months ago, an artillery captain and a hero of the Great War. Good proletariat background. His father, Ukrainian, was a railroad worker. His mother, an Ethiopian woman, worked as a maid in the house of Homenkos, our millionaires. They both died when the Moor was a boy. His father, somewhere in Manchuria, in a railroad accident in 1905, and his mother, that same year from cancer, here in Kiev. He was brought up and educated and, of course, indoctrinated by his Uncle Egorov, who is now Denikin's right hand . . . Perhaps not his own uncle, just someone wealthy taking pity on the poor orphaned boy—who knows—and I had the Moor, not once . . . I had him twice. The second time I had him was yesterday . . ."

"All this is well and good, comrade Volkov," the conductor is now impatient, "but this is not the time for discussions. You must flee, and do so immediately."

"Please let me see your mandate."

The conductor gives Volkov a thin strip of white silk on which some numbers are typed in black ink.

"What do we do?"

"You have to cross the front line and go into the Irpen forest to join the Odessa group. Me? I have to warn Kuzmenko and other comrades. Then . . . who knows." He stands up.

"How much time do we have?" Volkov seems badly shaken by the news.

"It appears we don't have any time at all. Listen."

They all stand still and listen to the motor of an approaching automobile.

At the freight station, the Ukrainian armored train "Free Ukraine" erupted in flames. Mortally wounded by the armor-piercing shells of "Our Homeland," it stood helpless, rocked by loud explosions. The conqueror stood a few hundred yards away and it too was wounded. One of the shells from the Ukrainian train had scored a direct hit on the command turret of "Our Homeland," killing its commanding officer—whose head was completely severed in the blast—the second in command, the artillery officer, and two Volunteers. One of its forward cannons was also damaged in the battle.

Suddenly, a huge explosion lifted three cars of "Free Ukraine" clear off the track. They fell on their sides, dragging the locomotive with them. It was over. "Our Homeland" rolled back another hundred yards and its crew watched the few Ukrainian soldiers run and roll on the ground, trying to get out of their uniforms which were on fire.

"Why did we have to do it?" a young Volunteer who was standing near one of the machine guns of "Our Homeland" asked. No one answered.

⚜

The Red Odessa fighting group was a swarm of locusts devouring everything in its path. Four thousand undernourished Black Sea sailors, dressed in rags, several hundred women, the survivors of defeated internationalist units, and even some civilians. They fought their way across the entire Ukraine in a circle of fire. Most of their artillery was left behind, their ammunition was almost gone, and yet, like the locust, they were unstoppable. Not the Ukrainians, not the white clouds of shrapnel from the armored train "Our Homeland," not the

Don Cossacks on their small horses, not the boys of the Guard Brigade, nor the battle-hardened officers of the Special Battalions could stop this swarm, this flood of people and the horse-drawn wagons, from pouring across the railway line west of Kiev and into the dark depths of the Irpen forests.

One of their wagons was unique. Made as an armor-plated cage with only a small opening at the very top, it was drawn by six healthy horses and guarded by two dozen Chinese soldiers who did not speak Russian. This wagon had a priority status, even over the wagons loaded with the wounded. Special orders from the Ukrainian Bolshevik troika—Latis, Peters, and Voroshilov—were specific: This wagon must reach the safety of the forest. At night, the sailors heard the strange songs of the Chinese, as well as alien sounds coming from inside the wagon itself, frightening and inexplicable.

Soon after the Odessa group began to rest and lick its wounds in the safety of the forest, after the contact with the main Red forces was established and food and ammunition had arrived, an incident took place which no one could explain. And it involved that very strange wagon.

During an unusually severe summer storm, at night, amidst a solid sheet of hail, the sounds from inside the cage were heard again. They grew in intensity and were so frightening that the sailors nearest to the wagon ran away and some of them fell dead. After the storm, a gruesome discovery was made. The Chinese soldiers had all been murdered and horribly mutilated, with their limbs and even their heads torn away from their bodies. The wagon appeared as if it had exploded from the inside. And it was empty.

The commander of the Odessa group, a powerfully built sailor named, appropriately, Heavyweight, shook his head in wonder and ordered that everything be kept secret. The remains of the Chinese comrades were buried in an unmarked grave.

Heavyweight was relieved that the whole matter of the wagon was over. The rumors and tensions it had created among his men and women, especially those who were superstitious, were undermining the group's morale. Too bad the Chinese comrades departed this world in such a nasty way. But then, he had seen so many dead bodies just in the past month, that it really did not matter.

What did matter was that he had to reorganize and prepare for an attack. *Now is the perfect time,* he thought. The White front was so thin and stretched out, and was still busy fighting some Ukrainian units. The city of Kiev sat practically unprotected. *One swift blow, unexpected and deadly, and it will be ours. And with Kiev back in our hands, the Whites' much heralded march to Moscow will come to a grinding halt.*

kiev
september 1919

fresh evening AIR. A FEW STARS ALREADY VISIBLE.
Yuri inhaled and exhaled as fast as he could. The air, so
wonderful, so clean, could not help him though, he still felt
nauseated. He lit a cigarette. He had to get that stench of
decomposing bodies out of his nostrils, his mind. Such an
ordinary light blue house on the edge of the railroad settlement. Sunflowers by the entrance and in the basement . . .

"How many?" he asked his aide Shebeko, who was emerg-
ing from the basement door, coughing and holding a handkerchief to his face.

"Five. That is all, five."

"Identified?"

"Yes, all engineers." Shebeko too was gasping for air.
"Obviously the work of the Railroad Cheka."

"Bill Taylor one of them?"

"No, but his assistant Mankovsky, God rest his soul; he is
there."

Yuri watched as the soldiers began carrying out the bodies
wrapped in gray blankets and loading them on a small truck.
Something else caught his attention. A huge dark shadow was
moving slowly toward them on the railroad track directly

behind the house. Two barrels of the forward naval guns, the black boxes, and the needles of machine guns, other cannons. The same monster he saw when he was riding to meet General Offenberg. Again he experienced the strangest premonition: that somehow this iron monster would become a part of his life. And why not? He did not belong in the counterintelligence. He was an artillery officer, not an interrogator or an executioner. Enough of cellars large and small, of the countless bodies, of the horrible stench. Enough cat-and-mouse games with Bolshevik agents. Kuzmenko, Volkov, Abrikosov, all the others; let them rot in hell. And Nata? Nata too must be forgotten. He watched the sea of sparks as the shadow picked up speed and was gone.

A large black automobile stopped next to the truck holding the bodies. The officer who was driving, the tall and very thin Captain Sobolev, came up to Yuri and saluted respectfully. "General Prince Orechov-Maisky requests the pleasure of your company, for dinner, tonight. In fact, the sooner the better. I have the prince's limousine . . ." Sobolev made a movement with this hand that could be interpreted as, "Follow me."

Yuri remained where he was. He first thought of telling Sobolev to go to hell and to take the prince with him. Orechov-Maisky, who had arrived from the Crimea only two weeks ago to be Yuri's commanding officer of counterintelligence, was already being a pest. Sometimes a helpful pest, but a pest nonetheless. On second thought, he felt hungry, and the prince's dinners were real feasts.

"Do you need me for anything?" he asked his aide.

"We're finished for now . . . unless you want to resurrect a few of them." Shebeko nodded his head toward the bodies in gray blankets that lay on the back of the truck. "I am going to change and go get drunk."

"Good health," Yuri replied, then followed the thin officer into his car.

"Some cognac, colonel?" Sobolev offered him a bottle and Yuri drank. It tasted good; he was losing the odor of death.

"Tell me this, Sobolev, do we have only one armored train, 'Our Homeland,' operating near Kiev? Are there others?" Yuri knew that Sobolev was a walking encyclopedia of numbers and events, and that he could also recognize just about every Red agent on sight. "At the moment, only 'Our Homeland,' and it too will soon be transferred to our main front—Kursk perhaps—and the Second Armor Detachment. We are expecting six tanks and a light armored train, 'Honor of the Officer.'"

Not much help if the Odessa group decides to attack, Yuri thought. *And the Red underground is becoming increasingly active, perhaps already planning an uprising.* He drank a few more swallows of cognac and looked out the window.

The city has changed so much in these few short weeks, he thought. *Like a forest after a rain. Almost as if there were no war.* Between the Nikolaevskaya and Luteranskaya he could see a sea of officers' caps—all colors—well-dressed women, the huge round lights of the cinemas. At the Corso: Vera Holdnaya and Runich in *By the Fireplace*; at the City Theater: Sobinov in *La Traviata*; on the other side of the street, a huge lighted advertisement, "Brothers Dubiner, ready-made suits," next to a delicatessen with chocolate mountains and bottles in the window. By the Cinema Express there was a line two blocks long; the canvas at the entrance read, *Mysteries of New York* and showed a horribly mangled hand reaching for a screaming blond woman who was about to jump from a tenth-story ledge onto a fast-moving train. From the open windows of Café Paris, the sounds of the Romanian gypsy orchestra. Theater farce—comedy, naked women—another long line. Horse-drawn carriages, automobiles, and everywhere hats with ostrich feathers, cockades, the gold of the shoulder patches, mustaches, painted faces, and lights—bright, long-forgotten lights.

"Who commands 'Our Homeland?'" Yuri asked, as if in a dream.

"No one, as far as I know." Sobolev seemed only mildly interested. "They lost three top officers fighting the Ukrainians and, I believe, none of them have been replaced . . . Colonel, could you perhaps give me a taste of that cognac . . . We have arrived."

Prince Orechov-Maisky lived in a well-guarded three-story house of the Bessarabka. A well-preserved man of sixty-five, tall and handsome, he led Yuri to his den where a small dining table was being set for two. The den was a large, carpeted room with a billiard table, three chess tables of various sizes, a large couch with a green velvet cover, stuffed heads of lions and leopards on the walls, and watercolors of pyramids. It had the feel of a museum, and the prince in his dark blue smoking jacket was a knowledgeable guide. Yuri couldn't help but smile and shake his head.

"Forgive me, Yuri Efimovich, at my age, I do value comfort. Perhaps you will too, in time."

"I dare say, Prince, I do not expect to live that long." Yuri sat down on the soft couch, and immediately a waiter appeared. He held a tray with two tall glasses containing green liquid a shade lighter than the couch.

"Nonsense, you shall have a long and happy life. Let us drink to that . . . and do not call me Prince, Vassili is sufficient."

The glasses were refilled, and the conversation—more of a monologue—that followed concerned the prince's travels, and his descriptions of the women he encountered from Africa to Malaysia, to Japan, to the Amazon. The food was far better than the monologue, in Yuri's opinion. It was relatively simple this time, but delicious. Grilled steak with mushrooms, fresh vegetables, salad, and red wine. The steak was thick and rare, and for a moment, Yuri hesitated before eating it. Blood. Blood everywhere. After seeing what the Bolsheviks had done in the Cheka basements and the city jail, he could not touch any food for three days. Now it did not seem to matter.

Orechov-Maisky caught his hesitation and smiled knowingly. "I too, Yuri—may I call you Yuri?—have seen more blood in my lifetime . . . One reason I am here is that I was almost shot by the Bolsheviks in Kislovodsk in 1918 and, after my escape, I became interested in their cause." He paused, and they both ate in silence. After they finished, he asked, "Have you ever read *Das Kapital*?"

"No, and I do not have any intention of reading it," Yuri replied.

"Quite regrettable, a remarkable work. The Bolsheviks wish to conduct an experiment . . ."

"Excuse me, Prince . . . Vassili. I have seen the results of that experiment already. Large cellars, small cellars, barns, riverbanks. Just today, five bodies, only five, the smallest amount yet. And tomorrow, I have to drive to the catacombs near the Lavra where, I am told, they've massacred at least a hundred monks and priests. You will excuse me if I do not wish to read *Das Kapital* . . . and perhaps it is time for me to leave." He stood up.

"Please stay, please, do not be angry." Yuri sat down. The prince offered him one of his cigars. They both lit up, smoked, and studied one another.

"Who are you fighting for?" The prince dropped his cigar into a malachite ashtray. His blue eyes were now cold, demanding.

"I do not understand . . ."

"You are fighting Bolsheviks, of course, at least you think

you are, and you are brave and very resourceful . . . but who are you really fighting for?"

"For Russia, for the Russian people, for my country, the country which I happen to love with all my heart."

"You are a romantic, colonel." The Prince laughed. "A true romantic. These are abstract terms. Country. Religion. Tradition. People. Who are you specifically fighting for?"

"Just your average decent citizens, many of whom have already been tortured and murdered by these devils." Yuri began to feel a sharp dislike for this polished braggart. *Why is he here?*

"I am here," the prince was suddenly very serious, "because I am very good at what I do, and I also feel some pity for your average citizen, if not for the so-called 'Our Country.' One country to me is as good as another . . ." He yawned.

Yuri stood up again. "Thank you for the dinner."

"My pleasure." The prince too stood up. "We must do it again, and very soon . . . Devils, did you say? Do you believe in the devil, colonel; do you believe in God?"

"More than anything else, Vassili, I believe in our cause, in Russia. And I believe God is on the side of the Russian people, on our side. Yes, to that extent, I believe in God."

"And in the devil?"

"No, I do not."

They shook hands. Captain Sobolev was already waiting in the doorway. "May I drive the colonel to his apartment?"

"Yes, please," Yuri replied. "How long have you been with the prince?"

"Almost eleven years."

"And you have accompanied the prince on his travels?"

"Some of them."

Yuri decided to let it go. Sobolev was clearly uncomfortable. There were still crowds of people in the streets. Lights, theaters, as if there were no Bolsheviks. *And why not?* Yuri thought. *People need to relax, to laugh, to forget about tomorrow.*

His apartment was a two-room suite in the former Hotel Belgrade, currently used by the officers from the counterintelligence and the Second Hussar Regiment. In the smaller room, on a cot, Porutchik Shebeko was fast asleep and snoring from time to time. Yuri noticed a familiar blue envelope on his desk, the strong scent of her special perfume, jasmine and possibly roses . . . He tore it open and read: *"Dearest, I must see you tonight. Please come, please. All my love, Nata."*

He reached in his drawer for the bottle of vodka, thoughtful. For the past four nights vodka had served as his sleeping medicine. Only four nights without Nata and he wanted to touch her again so badly. She was an affliction, an addiction worse than morphine, and yet she must be forgotten.

I cannot win. Yuri winced and took a long pull on his bottle. I will destroy myself if I keep on seeing her, and I will destroy myself if I keep away from her. He had slept with many women in his life, he thought. Almost married one after the war, a pretty green-eyed actress, Lida. Another actress. Those had been the good times. He organized a small theater after each performance. He gave away his revolver, swore that he would never again fight anybody, for any cause. One dreary winter evening, they came for him. Red stars, leather jackets, revolvers, bayonets.

The cat-and-mouse games had begun. Wet cellars, shots, groans. Volkov's insane face in the shadow, always in the shadow, the box of cocaine on his desk, and the Nagan.

"You are our enemy," Volkov had insisted.

"I have done nothing to you."

"Yes, yes, but potentially. Our obvious enemies we can liquidate . . . we do liquidate. The potential enemies are more dangerous. But you are an artillery officer . . . and your background . . ." The cat-and-mouse continued. He was placed against the wall twice.

My nerves were strong even then. Yuri drank some more vodka. *An artillery officer, had I served in the cavalry, it would have been all over.* The night he was released, a warm spring evening. In his pocket, an order to go to the Military Commissariat for transfer to Moscow . . . *A mistake, Comrade Volkov, a big mistake. You let a mouse out, and the mouse became a cat, and this cat is not going to let you out of his claws. Nata again. She too has claws—sharp, merciless claws. Such an interesting dark side to this woman. But I cannot see her tonight, in any case. An important operation is scheduled for four in the morning. We will finally capture Kuzmenko. There's the real devil in human form. How many innocent people has he killed? How many times has he escaped the rope? Not this time, this time that noose is tight and my claws are strong.*

Yuri reached for his telephone. Cries. Accussations. Tomorrow. Definitely. Absolutely. Another night, the brass bed, the beautiful sensuous body, the golden eyes, trusting and deceiving. Tomorrow night. And between the present and Nata's bedroom, between the desires and dreams, there was an empty bottle of vodka, the hard blanket of duty and honor, and an eternity passing through the blink of an eye.

Tonight, the vodka did not help. Eternity or not, there were too many thoughts, too many doubts, and his mind, racing for answers, came up only with more questions. Why, for example, would the Reds leave Kuzmenko behind in the first place? Yuri had heard many Kuzmenko stories, most had to be taken with a grain of salt. How Kuzmenko led a unit of practically unarmed peasants against the White armored train. How he was wounded eighteen times and his comrades dragged him through the Don Steppes and across the front line. How he tore the throat of the officer who was about to hang him with his teeth and escaped again. How he killed one of his wives in a jealous rag. How he had a harem, recently, in the basement of the Garrison Regiment . . . He was a legendary drunkard and brawler, a sadist without a drop of compassion for another human being, a killer who liked his work, but not a good commander. Even his pal Voroshilov only gave him posts that were safe and away from where he could do real damage. So why have him work in the underground?

"Shebeko," he woke up his aide, "get ten Volunteers. Revolvers only. And dynamite. In ten minutes. Let's get the bastard right now."

"Do you think we have a traitor among us?" Shebeko pulled on his boots, rubbed his eyes.

"I hope not." The thought had occurred to Yuri a few times in the past two weeks. Too many changes in personnel. But it did not matter who it was or even whether there was one. He had to do his part, and it included keeping the opposition off balance. This was how he got Volkov and Abrikosov, and now he would get Kuzmenko. And not only Kuzmenko. He was furious that Stacy Averescu and her friend Oleg Zorin had surfaced as long-lost friends of General Tichomirov, the recently appointed military governor of the Ukraine. He had direct evidence and witnesses linking Stacy to the Kiev Cheka. His case against Zorin was somewhat weaker. Yet Zorin was wearing a lieutenant's uniform, and Yuri knew that he had never been in the army. This alone was reason to arrest him.

To hell with politics. To hell with the fact that the city now had two rulers, General Bredov, the front commander, and General Tichomirov, the military governor—and with the fact that they hated one another more than the Bolsheviks. If he could not arrest Stacy and Oleg, he would simply tell Shebeko to get two trusted Volunteers to kill them. Blood for blood, that is what Volkov used to say, and he was not altogether wrong.

"We are ready, colonel." Shebeko had his sleepy Volunteers wait in the hallway. "Do we shoot to kill?"

"I will give two bottles of vodka to whoever kills him."

Kuzmenko was hiding out in an old three-story apartment house on Panovskaya. He was supposed to be in a room on the ground floor, in the rear. The house was surrounded, but Yuri knew that quite often these old houses had underground passages. In this case, the only underground passage that would make sense should go to an adjacent house, a two-story wooden structure with a gambling establishment on the first floor. On the second floor was a bordello with a room for opium smokers. Yuri had that house surrounded as well. He also posted two Volunteers across the street and one at the intersection. The heavy wooden door was bolted and there was no need to go through it. Kuzmenko's window was boarded-up. As soon as Yuri nodded his head, Shebeko placed a stick of dynamite under the boards and lit the fuse.

The explosion blew away the boards and window frames and part of the wall. They were inside in a matter of seconds with guns and bright kerosene lanterns. The front room was empty. The whole house was searched top to bottom. Only one other room in the house was unoccupied, on the second floor. The candle had been recently blown out; the bed was still warm. On the night table, there was a closed book, *Red on*

White, by Sir Arthur Conan Doyle, in English. *How appropriate.* Yuri noticed an unusual bookmark. A crumpled piece of paper with a crude pen drawing of a funny-looking Russian Chort . . . a Russian *devil.* Horns, hooves, even something resembling a tail. He thought about taking it, then decided against it, placing the drawing back in the book and leaving it on the table. He felt sure Kuzmenko had been here only minutes before. *Everybody told me he was illiterate. And he is reading in English? Interesting.*

The underground passage was found, and it did lead to the next building. Everyone in the building was arrested, even the prostitutes and the opium smokers. Twenty-eight people were marched to counterintelligence, where they were separated into three groups: the officers and Volunteers caught in the raid, the women, and the civilians. Yuri questioned the military men and released all of them. The women were searched and also released. The civilian group of eighteen people—a few small-time merchants, three Ukrainian farmers, some students, and several speculators—were ordered held in a large room under the guard of the junkers. Yuri decided to take his time with them. He was sure one of them was Kuzmenko. He also knew that besides Kuzmenko, at least one of the other students could be a Red agent. This was going to be a very long night.

"Shebeko," he begged, "not vodka; get me a bottle of good cognac."

"Perhaps you want me to part the Red Sea, too?" Shebeko grumbled.

A few minutes later, Yuri poured the golden liquid into a clean glass. Gold. Nata's eyes. *How much I love this insane woman.* He poured some more and drank it. Now he felt ready. The cat in him had awakened. "Shebeko," he purred, "bring in the first student."

Alexey believed THAT SOME DAYS IT WAS DEFINITELY not worth it to get out of bed. His dreams had been so vivid, so exciting. One in particular had him sitting on a beautiful riverbank, feet dangling in the cool transparent water, when suddenly he had no feet, they were dissolved, gone, and yet the surrounds were pleasant and serene and there was no cause for alarm. A strange-looking bird then walked over and began a long discourse about the Paris commune and the death of Robespierre. It was boring, but an old gypsy woman who happened to be walking by chased the bird away and tried selling him some fish stew. He did not have any money to pay for the stew and felt bad about it. He did not have any pockets either. And the stew was strange. The fish was still alive and swimming past the onions and carrots. *What's in a dream?*

Now, sitting on the filthy floor in a large room of the counterintelligence, guarded by the grim-faced junkers with their rifles and bayonets, he felt his legs were lost once again. This time perhaps permanently dissolved. *What an idiot,* he thought of himself. *Two minutes away from my own house, and I had to cross the Panovskaya when I could have gone around safely, across our own backyards.* He had even seen the people being led out of the buildings by the soldiers. But what he did not see was the Volunteer standing at the intersection, who had arrested him for violating the curfew. Now he was stuck among the Bolshevik agents and speculators, and being in counterintelligence was not much better than being in Cheka. *What next? A dungeon?* He hoped he would be given an opportunity to contact his friends who could vouch for him—contact his sister, at least. What rotten luck. And just when he was beginning to do well. Just when . . . Suddenly, a long cry of anguish was heard, punctuated by a shot.

"God rest his soul," one of the Ukrainian peasants whispered, and crossed himself. Two speculators next to Alexey began talking rapidly in their own jargon. *So unpleasant,* he thought, *our liberators shooting people right in this building?* There were two officers and four Volunteers among those arrested. They were being questioned first. The minutes dragged on, very, very slowly.

Alexey thought about Nata. She was responsible, in part, for his being here tonight. Responsible for radically changing his life; lifting him, one day, high above into the clouds, to her very real paradise, then dropping him down, into some bottomless pit, a pit of pain and confusion. *I must stop seeing her,* he swore time and time again. And yet, each time the fluttering little butterfly, Matilda Franzevna, Nata's housekeeper, would arrive with another one of Nata's blue, heavily perfumed envelopes, his heart and his mind would melt. And once again he'd go to her, like a lamb to slaughter.

The first note had been rather formal:

> *Dear Alexey Michailovich,*
> *A mutual friend gave me your name. I am having a few people for supper tonight and would love to see you.*
>
> *Yours,*
> *Nata Tai*

*p.s. I think of you often and wish to thank you once again
for releasing me on that fateful day.*

One the other side was Nata's address, and in that same strong handwriting, *"Please come,"* underlined.

This was a time for joy, a time for change. Alexey was still without a job and Lucy's salary was barely enough for food. Petia Ovcharenko's father had promised to send him a few students for tutoring, but nothing had come of it. Another almost sure job, as a law clerk for a noted attorney, had also evaporated. Law? What law? There were no laws anymore, and not much justice either.

The evening was magical. At exactly seven he pressed the brass bell next to the oak door of a handsome townhouse on Luteranskaya. Matilda Franzevna, the mischievous butterfly, opened the door and looked him over, her eyes twinkling with approval. He looked good in his cream-colored jacket—freshly shaven—and Lucy had even cut his hair.

What luxury. The parquet floor was so shiny it reflected the crystal of the chandeliers. On the walls were Renoir, Degas, Matisse, and some Russian artists, Levitan, Popova . . . In another large room, a white piano, flowers, sofas, armchairs, a few men. Matilda Franzevna introduced Alexey and left him. Nata was nowhere in sight. A waiter appeared with a tray of glasses filled with champagne. Alexey sat down on a sofa, cautiously, not far from a friendly overweight gentleman smoking a long cigar. Amazing luck—one of the wealthiest men in Russia was looking for someone to tutor his nephew. Alexey was offered a great salary and a free meal. Every evening a shiny gray Benz would be waiting for him, and every evening a package would arrive for him—perhaps a bottle of wine, some sausages or ham, even imported chocolate prepared by

Homenko's housekeeper for his sister. Farewell poverty and misery . . .

Aha, he noticed, *they've started questioning civilians. Perhaps I will get home before morning.* Someone sat next to him on the floor— a crumpled blue jacket, a mustache—perhaps a salesman. He reeked of garlic, and Alexey began slowly to move away when he heard: "Student." The one word froze his entire being. "Student, turn away from me." A softest whisper: "They will let you out soon. Go to my wife, Mariinskaya, fifteen, top floor, Antonova. Tell her I am caught and to go to Semen." Silence.

"But I did not recognize . . ."

"Prisoners, silence!" one of the junkers screamed, not at Alexey but at the two speculators who were still chattering away.

"Listen, student, there is a colonel inside who will know in three seconds who I am. Do not betray me. Do this, or you are a dead man, and your sister is a dead girl." And he moved away.

Alexey's heart was pounding so loudly that the small porutchik by the door had to repeat, "You, in the gray suit, follow me." A carpeted hallway, soldiers with revolvers.

"Here, please." In a small waiting room, the porutchik searched Alexey. "No weapons," he addressed someone behind the partition of matted glass. "Sit down here." There was only one chair. The officer went behind the partition.

There was a conversation there between a clear, confident baritone and an almost inaudible tenor. Baritone: "You are maintaining that you are a fourth-year . . . chemistry, yes. Your documents are quite in order; I am well familiar with the signature . . . Allow me two, three more questions, routine . . . Incidentally, could you give me the formula for nitroglycerine . . . What? You don't remember . . . Who read you the inorganic chemistry . . . Kviatkovsky, of course, but was it father or son? Son? Of course, father would not let you pass the first year without . . . Shebeko, bring me the next one."

The small porutchik led Alexey behind the partition. A young colonel, whose dark face was somehow familiar, was thoughtfully smoking a papirossa. Across from his desk sat a blond man in a gray suit holding a green student's cap in his long white fingers. The man appeared very nervous, even frightened.

"Do you know this man?" the colonel asked Alexey.

"No."

"And you?" he asked the blond man.

"No." The man shook his head, reached for a handkerchief, clean and white, and wiped the sweat off his forehead.

"Take him away," the colonel ordered. The blond man stood up. As he was leaving, the colonel pointed his finger at him and said, "You really should be more prepared, comrade. Especially if you are working with students' documents . . . Shame." And to Alexey, curtly, "Sit down."

Alexey sat and waited. The colonel poured himself some cognac from the bottle next to an open file on his desk. He looked at the cognac but did not drink. For a moment or two he studied Alexey's face. He yawned twice. "Your documents." The interrogation was about to begin.

"How long have you lived in Kiev?"

"All my life." Alexey smiled and the colonel smiled too.

"Did you serve in the Red army?"

"Yes, in the Garrison Regiment. I deserted . . ."

"Who was your lecturer . . . Roman Law?" The colonel yawned again, and this time he drank the cognac.

"Petr Ivanovich Sorokin. And one semester . . ."

"Are you by any chance related to Vera Lebedeva?"

"Yes. I am her son." This time Alexey thought he saw a genuine smile on the colonel's face.

"I believe in time she will be recognized as one of Russia's leading artists. When you get home, please give her best wishes from one who greatly admires her work. Yuri Efimovich Skatchko, at your service." Yuri stood up and offered Alexey his hand. Alexey too stood up and shook it.

"Have I said anything wrong?"

"I cannot give her your best wishes, colonel." Alexey was badly shaken by the colonel's outburst. He had to force every word slowly, and the words were hollow, meaningless. "My mother was shot by Bolsheviks . . . Cheka in Moscow, last year."

"Shebeko," the colonel shouted, "another glass!" He was now completely different: a friend, concerned, compassionate. He forced Alexey to drink two glasses of cognac. "I must ask you this one question." He was almost apologetic. "Who is your tailor?"

"My what?"

"Excuse me—your suit—where did you buy it?"

"Buy it? I didn't buy it . . ." Alexey was now thoroughly confused. The suit was a gift from Nata, a peace offering after a frightening and wild night, the first night he ever spent with her—the first and almost the last.

"I have a very good reason for asking you this." The colonel was insistent.

"A . . . good friend gave me this suit."

"What a good friend to give you such an expensive present. May I have the name of your friend?" Yuri's black eyes burrowed hard into Alexey's face, watching his every expression. "Please?"

"A . . . lady I know; we are not really such good friends, I . . . we just met, really . . . three weeks ago."

"Name," the colonel reminded him, "her name."

"Nata Tai." Alexey took a deep breath and saw astonishment on the colonel's face, but only for a moment.

"Thank you, Alexey Michailovich." He stood up and again shook Alexey's hand. "Excuse me for keeping you so long. This matter with your gray suit . . . the Reds must have a warehouse full of gray suits somewhere in Moscow and they often issue them to their agents . . . Sad, but true. So, my best to you. Shebeko! Next."

Thoughts, dreams, memories; those days and nights, they were all irrelevant. Thank God, there was a bottle of wine at the house: thick, red, wonderful Crimean wine. *Another night like this and I will be ready for the front.* At least there you have an enemy: you shoot, you run. Here it is like walking blindfolded in a minefield. And Lucy was still out. That new development bothered Alexey. The last few nights she had come home at five in the morning. She was not at Ovcharenko's, not with Ninochka Reich.

Another unanswered question straight out of *Mysteries of New York . . . Why don't they do a revival of Nata's films?* he wondered. *They were so much better than what was currently showing. Nata . . . Musenka, Kuzmenko. That colonel, Yuri something . . . His hard black eyes. So amazing, he knew my mother's work. Why is it so amazing? I know I have met him somewhere, perhaps before the Revolution, when life was slow. Gray suit? The first suit I ever had. That night, the first night, waiting for Nata in her bedroom. Champagne and more champagne. Almost daybreak. And then she appears, a witch from hell.* Alexey shuddered and drank more wine; drank greedily, out of the bottle, spilling some on his bed. *What was she trying to do—bite through my heart and devour it?* He felt under his left nipple. *And that dagger she was swinging—what a nightmare!* His favorite cream-colored student jacket, torn to shreds. Blood everywhere—his blood. She did cut him twice, but missed his heart.

"Natochka, Natochka," Matilda Franzevna kept screaming, "stop, you're on a binge!" Binge? It was a rampage. Managed to cut her servant too, the old Semen, before Matilda Franzevna stuck that syringe into her arm.

And afterwards, as if nothing had happened: "I have shown you a glimpse of hell. Let me now show you a little bit of paradise. My favorite part of it." And she did. And what a place it was; he could live there forever.

Now, instead of my jacket, this gray suit. And all the Bolshevik agents are wearing gray suits this year. Wonderful. And Musenka is a strange one. Her husband is out of town; she invites me in and nothing ever happens. Alexey was moved, though, when she told him for the first time why she married the man more than twice her age. After her father died, Musenka went through such hard times, washing clothing for her landlady, almost becoming a prostitute. She married for security, only now there was no such thing. *We are all candles flickering near the eye of a hurricane. Scores of empty lives, as Nata would say, hurtling through the darkness of space. Security? What a joke. And getting home from Musenka's house—being arrested—that's security? Well, it could have been worse. I could still be there . . . or shot.*

Another night at Nata's. Thirteen people, their hands on top of a round table. The light is turned off. Stacy Averscu's nasal, unpleasant voice: "What is your name, ghost?"

"Acropis," the table answers.

"Who are you?"

"I am a leader."

"Will the Volunteers win?"

"No."

He was a rude ghost, everyone agreed to call another one. The table began to rock . . . "Mankovsky," the table said. Nata gasped.

"Have you died?" Stacy was now uncertain.

"No, no."

"Were you killed?"

There was a loud crash, and the light turned on. Petia Ovcharenko tried to excuse himself: "I just leaned a little, just a little . . . and it broke."

Nata ran upstairs. Stacy followed her. At least that night Alexey was driven home. *Where is Lucy? It is morning already.* He heard the bells of the first streetcar. Six-thirty. She had to be at work in three hours.

Lucy did not come home until a few minutes past noon. She sat on her bed and cried and let him embrace and console her. Between her sobs she told him that she had quit her job at the gymnasium and was working as a nurse at the field hospital of the Second Hussar Regiment. Last night, they sustained terrible losses. The Reds launched a series of nighttime attacks north of Fastov. And they were successful.

"I work in the ward with the most seriously wounded. Alyosha, you cannot even imagine the horror. Thirty-two wounded arrived yesterday evening. Only one of them was still alive when I left. There's slaughter only twenty kilometers away—a whole squadron of Hussars that counterattacked was annihilated, to the last man. And here, all we care about are naked women, music, *Mysteries of New York,* truly a feast in the time of plague. And all the officers here, on our streets, where do they come from? What do they do?"

A loud knock on the door: Homenko's unfriendly chauffeur. "Hey, teacher, do you think I have all day? Next time you wait for me outside."

Outside? Alexey hadn't even shaved yet. "Listen, *you* wait outside. And you wait until I am ready. Or else you drive back to Sergei without me." Alexey slammed the door in his face.

"Go, Alyosha, go. I will be here when you come back . . . We will have time to talk."

⌇

The gray shiny Benz, the unfriendly chauffeur, the happy, friendly doorman. Homenko was in his library talking to someone on the telephone. He motioned for Alexey to wait. "I have something for you, a little bonus, rather a sign of my appreciation. Seryozha really likes you." And he was gone.

Alexey stuck the envelope in his pocket and went to see the kid. Seryozha was twelve, bright, shy, sometimes very funny.

"Do you know what happened to my uncle?"

"No idea, I just saw him. He gave me . . ."

"I know what he gave you, two hundred in pound sterling. Do you know why?"

"Because I am so good with you?"

"That is part of it . . . but I think we shall be leaving soon. My uncle has a villa somewhere in the Caucasus. So we will travel there first, and then abroad. Too dangerous here; the Bolsheviks tried to assassinate him. There was a colonel here, earlier, from the counterintelligence, a dark man. He discovered the plot and arrested this commissar."

"What does this have to do with me?"

"My uncle wants you to travel with us, as my tutor, companion. And the money is really a bribe. To make you more agreeable."

"This is too fast for me. Listen, Seryozha, I haven't slept all night . . . I have problems at home. I need some sleep, badly."

"You can use my bed, I shall read something. Tell me, though, are you still in love with Nata Tai?"

"What?"

"Everybody is in love with her. My uncle, generals, that colonel from counterintelligence. I saw her in *The Star of the Orient.* I love her too. Of course, I am too young to really get to know her."

"You certainly are." The kid's bed was so soft and comfortable; as soon as Alexey's face touched the pillow, he was in another world.

Another supper WITH PRINCE ORECHOV-MAISKY.
This time fresh steamed sturgeon in some delicious pink sauce
that tasted somewhat like almonds, sweet peas with scallions,
tiny white potatoes. Pinot Chardonnay.

Tonight the swords were drawn. In the corner of the
prince's den sat Sobolev, alone, with a bottle of vodka and a
glass. *Why,* Yuri thought, *does the prince need a witness? Is he afraid
that I may get out of hand and strangle him perhaps, or shoot him?*

Cigars, green liquor, a careful, conservative opening: "I
have underestimated you, Yuri, and I am both very pleased
and angry about it."

"You cannot be that angry at me, Vassili, you just fed me so
graciously."

"I am very angry at you. If it weren't for your uncle, I would
consider bringing charges of insubordination and reduce you
in rank."

Yuri laughed. He did not mean to, and he only laughed for
a moment or two, yet he saw the hatred on the prince's face, a
man so accustomed to command, to having his way, in everything, his entire life, so self-centered, so contemptuous of
everyone. For one brief second the prince's mask was torn off,
and it was Yuri's laughter that removed it. "Excuse me, Vassili,
who were you thinking of reducing me to, and may I ask for
what?"

"Do not be insolent." The prince's mask was back on; he

was beaming and sophisticated, a generous man of the world. "I do have a serious bone to pick, several bones as a matter of fact. Bone number one, here." He pushed toward Yuri a note signed by General Tichomirov, with his personal stamp. Yuri quickly read it. It was a complaint, stating that a certain colonel in counterintelligence was trying to besmirch the name of the internationally famous pianist, S. Averescu, a close personal friend of the general and her companion, Lt. Zorin, an officer of the general's staff. It went on to say that to link Mademoiselle Averescu to any Bolshevik activity was preposterous and that he, the general governor, vouched for her innocence. *I will have both of them killed,* Yuri decided.

He felt now that he had split into twins, sitting next to one another, both acting independently. One twin was correct and eloquent and would hold the prince and his sword away. The other twin was ready for action, decisive action, ready to cut through the chitchat, to find out exactly what game the prince was playing and to beat him at it.

"So," the pleasant twin began, "if Tichomirov objects, he can have both of them. I pass."

"Good. These people, Stacy Averescu, her friends, I knew them from St. Petersburg. They could be very dangerous, but they are not Bolsheviks . . . They have what I would call their own line. Now, what about that operation to take Kuzmenko?"

Aha, thought the wicked twin. *That's the real reason I am here, you polished bastard. You did not like me going in four hours earlier. Why not?*

"I was tipped off that Kuzmenko might disappear." The good twin smiled.

"Let us stop playing games, colonel, you're speaking to another professional. Why did you do it without notifying me? Are you so sure we have a traitor among us?"

It would not surprise me at all, the wicked twin snickered.

"Traitor is a strong word, general. But there were one or two things that made me wonder."

"Such as what?"

"Volkov, for example. Why was his sentence not carried out? I might add, over my objections. That man should have been hung two days ago."

"It was done on my orders and I had my reasons."

"Yes, your Excellency, I know it was done on your orders. As to your reasons, I can only speculate." *Nata got to that general,* the wicked twin whispered. *She struck a deal with the old fool.* "May I have some cognac, Vassili?" That was the wicked twin. The prince nodded to Sobolev and he quickly swam out of the room.

"You are underestimating me now, colonel. Yes, the most beautiful and irresistible Nata Tai, who also happens to be an old friend of mine from St. Petersburg, approached me on Volkov's behalf. It seems someone from the Bolshevik underground contacted her and told her that her father is alive and in Gomel. And, if she manages to keep Volkov alive for a few days, her father will remain alive. Volkov dies, her father dies."

"I have been through this with her too." The good twin was tired of being good. "And I told her that her father is probably dead. And if he were alive, they couldn't make a deal like this anyway. Their communications are practically nonexistent; their organization in the city is hanging by a thread, or worse. It was simply the advertisement and the reward that she placed in the papers that gave some commissar an idea."

"Nevertheless, blackmail is a potent psychological weapon. I agreed to help her because by doing so, we can further infiltrate the Red underground. I have a man arriving here tomorrow who is absolutely the best agent we have ever had. And it was on this man's recommendation that I postponed Volkov's execution."

Sobolev reappeared with cognac and glasses. The prince did not drink. Yuri downed two glasses, one for each twin. "Another bone?" he asked, though he knew already that this was where the prince's sword would strike at his heart.

"If you were simply Colonel Skatchko, hero, of course; but, then, we have far too many heroes—I would have dismissed you this morning. I am a realist and, in my position as the commanding officer of the Kiev counterintelligence, I have to be a diplomat. Tichomirov wants you out; I want you out. I think that you are now on the edge of being burned-out. Such is the nature of our work. Many good officers cannot take working in counterintelligence . . . But General Egorov, your very own uncle, is Denikin's closest advisor. So, I dismiss you, and two days later I myself might be packing for a trip to my palace in Gurzuf . . . and I am not ready to do so."

Why not? the wicked twin wanted to know.

What's the difference? Let us strike a bargain with him, the good one suggested. "You are quite correct, Vassili. General Egorov and I worked in the Kiev underground, and he would have your head unless you could produce a good, good explanation. And you do not have one. Now, what do you propose we do?"

"Do you know General Belousov?"

"I most certainly do."

"He is at present time the commander of the Second Armor Detachment, our main armored force pushing directly on to Moscow. The armored train 'Our Homeland' is being transferred to him, to Kursk. They have a vacancy for an artillery officer. General Bredov asked me to find someone. I have recommended you."

Yuri poured himself more cognac and drank it slowly. He noticed that the prince was getting agitated, looking at his wristwatch. *He wishes me to leave; the audience is over. Sturgeon for this last supper?*

"Let me sleep on it, Vassili," said the reasonable, good twin.

"By all means, by all means. We will work out the details tomorrow. I must caution you though, as an artillery officer, you will be taking orders from another colonel or even a captain—you are technically the third officer in the chain of command on the armored train."

"I understand." He drank another glass of cognac, and another. Handshakes, smiles—the swords are put aside, for the moment.

"Come, Sobolev, drive me home." On the dark stairway he almost ran into a woman hurriedly walking past him. Her face was covered with a veil. Drunk as Yuri was, he could not mistake her perfume—so strong—jasmine and possibly roses. The woman was Nata.

The leaves were turning bright yellow and orange. The summer was like a woman tired of caresses, sleepy, resting for a few moments, satisfied, breathing the apples and pears, smiling at the children playing along the riverbank, at the lovers on the benches of the Tsar's Garden, at the old woman selling her greasy prioshki by the entrance.

How much the park had changed in such a short time. No more empty bottles and cans and oceans of sunflower seeds and the torn issues of *Pravda* flying in the breeze around the pond. An old man was planting roses, assisted by two young men with rakes and shovels. The bushes were trimmed. *How strange,* Yuri thought. *Nature changes only at precise intervals, and always so slowly. Not so with human beings.* Yesterday, he was a different man. Yesterday he would not look at the changing leaves, breathe this smoky, intoxicating air of the early fall, stand and look at this bench. "Shebeko, come here. This is where I sat when they caught me. Look, they've actually repainted it." He wanted to walk all the way to where the alley ended and look at the magnificent view of the Dnepr and beyond. Not much time though. Not very much time for anything.

Back in the automobile, with Shebeko driving him to the freight station, he remembered the backyards and the safe houses, the cellars, the old wooden church on Podol, their meetings, Egorov's house on Shuliavka, the black Bible near the general's narrow cot. The beautiful ancient city where he lived most of his life was moving back in time, out of his life, perhaps forever. The woman he loved so much, with eyes like the changing leaves, she too was already far in the past. Perhaps she existed only in his imagination, a long, long time ago.

At the freight station, he embraced Shebeko, then kissed him three times, and both men crossed one another.

"I will look for you on the Red Square." Shebeko grinned.

"By St. Basil's Cathedral." Yuri lifted his knapsack and walked across the railroad tracks toward the dark green caterpillar, past the guards, and into its belly.

Alexey arrived AT NATA'S HOUSE EXACTLY AT EIGHT. Matilda Franzevna winked knowingly and pointed him toward the stairs, to her bedroom. On her brass bed, as she had promised, Nata lay completely naked, her body in stark contrast to the black silk sheets. A thick, rough-looking horsewhip lay beside her.

Her lips and nipples were painted a bright red. She jumped off the bed with the whip in her hand, stood before him, and handed him the whip.

"I have been so wicked," she whispered, licking her lips with her tongue and stroking her erect nipples. "So bad, I must be punished. You must beat me, without mercy." She turned, laid on her stomach, and buried her head in the pillow.

She is bad, Alexey agreed. *If she wants me to do it, I will do it.* He gave her bottom a tentative whack. It left a red mark.

"Harder, Alyosha, harder," she moaned. He hit her a few more times, the last time so strong she cried out and jumped up.

"My breasts now, I painted them just for you, my breasts." Alexey hesitated. "Now! Remember the first night, remember how I scratched your nipples and bit you and . . . almost murdered you?" Alexey hit her twice on her breasts, then put the horsewhip aside.

She reached up and kissed him, her mouth covering his,

her tongue probing, and her hands frantically undressing him, pulling him on top of her, making sure that he was inside her just as her tongue was deep inside his mouth. "Alyosha," she half-whispered and half-moaned, "you must believe me. I love you, in my own way, I love you and I am insane and I love you . . ." He was on top, and then she was on top, and she introduced him to positions and variations he had only read about and considered pornographic. Somehow, with Nata, nothing was dirty or against any religion. Things he had never even considered experimenting with, especially with a goddess, felt natural and exciting. He was worn-out first. She decided to let him rest.

"Have some champagne, Alyosha, I am not ready yet." He drank and watched her play with the whip, and even this did not seem to be indecent. In fact, it was erotic as hell. He finished the champagne and was again on top of her, and she too was on top of him, and it went on until he felt completely drained. He had no sense of time or space, his body was on fire, his mouth parched.

"Alyosha." She caressed the inside of his ear with her tongue and then around his ear, down his neck. "Have you ever had any morphine? Do you want some? I have morphine. Oh, you will love it. I do it so well, you will not even feel the needle . . . You watch me do it first, then you decide. I have some cocaine too, but cocaine is not good for a man; it makes you impotent and I still have plans for you, the night is young, my love, my friend. Oh, it is so much more important to be a friend than to be a lover, don't you think?"

"I suppose." Alexey thought that judging by the way she had behaved the first night, it was certainly safer to be her friend than her lover. It was nice to be both; tonight he had no complaints. And, he decided, he would try the morphine. Who knew what tomorrow would bring? He was amazed, though, when she came from her bathroom with her syringe and stuck it in the lower part of body, just at the edge of her orange triangle. He thought they only injected morphine into veins.

She saw his expression and laughed. "Do not be concerned, my love, you just give me your arm and close your eyes and you shall wake up in a dream, a wonderful dream, with me." She kissed him softly on his lips, then sucked on his nipples and went to her bathroom to refill the syringe. "Close your eyes now," she ordered when she returned. He did, and he gave her his left arm.

The result was not what Nata had expected. Alexey at first felt warm, then hot, then nauseated, trembling. He barely made it to the bathroom. Back in her bed, he felt so sleepy that he couldn't move; all his energy was gone, he couldn't lift a finger. The last thing he saw was her concerned face; the last thing he felt were her lips touching his. A tight velvet curtain descended, and the velvet was pleasant enough, but there was too much of it. It was almost suffocating . . . There was nothing he could do. The distant roar of the surf, the boom of the artillery fire, became a melody Nata was playing on her piano.

In the morning, he felt hungry, refreshed, and virile. He woke Nata up and they picked up where they had left off. Time, space, nobody cared until, around noon, Matilda Franzevna knocked. She had breakfast ready. This was Sunday, a glorious blue day. The church bells were ringing. Nata ordered old Semen to get her carriage ready. They would ride somewhere by the river, find a secluded spot, have a picnic. "To the devil with war and death; today we live, Alyosha, today we breathe, we love."

"Let us stop by my house, though, perhaps Lucy is home."

Lucy was not home. She had left a note saying that the field hospital was moved to Brovari, but she would be home all day Monday and she wanted very much to see him.

They stopped a few kilometers south of the city, on a country road, left Semen and the carriage by some bushes with berries which the horses began to eat, and walked across an uncut field of wheat toward the river. The sun was high; there were no people around. Scattered in the middle of the fields were trees full of apples which nobody bothered to pick, and some old houses on a hill, a church without a cross. Nata spread the blanket and they sat and watched the river and two lonely rowboats with a man in each one of them, fishing, near the opposite shore.

"So strange to be in the country." Nata leaned against him. "So strange to be with you, my friend. I almost feel we are destined to part so very soon, perhaps never to see one another again. Will you remember me, Alyosha? Remember me from time to time and remember me with a good feeling?"

"Of course, Nata, no man on this earth could ever forget you."

"You are wrong. There is one who did not even come to say farewell. And he is right: I do not love anybody; why should someone love me?"

"You are not as bad as you think, and I, for one, will always remember you with a good feeling."

"Oh, but I am bad. You cannot imagine how bad I can be. You only saw a glimpse of me as a witch. Believe me, I am a real witch, through and through."

"A bewitching witch." Alexey laughed and embraced her.

"I am serious." Nata's eyes flashed, and for a moment he thought there was lightning in the clear sky. He drew away. "When I was a young girl, I was raised by a warlock. I was in this very exclusive girls' boarding school in St. Petersburg, almost ten when I met this man, this creature. We were well-guarded and supervised and yet he found a way for me to see him and he did things with my body and my mind, and, most important, with my soul, that I do not comprehend even now. In real life, he was a nobleman, a baron, one of the wealthiest men in Russia, and he worshipped Satan. I was completely under his spell. And it was he who told me I was a witch. I never believed him until recently."

"What happened to that man?"

"He was eventually caught. There was quite a trial. He paid whoever needed to be paid, met another witch, and went with her to live in Italy. There he was murdered. I should have believed him sooner; he told me that a warlock can only have sex with a witch."

"What nonsense . . . The witch can have sex with anybody? That's inequality . . . and, please, let's change the subject." Alexey was beginning to feel uneasy. She did look like a witch that first night . . . He remembered the fire in her eyes. *What if she really is a witch?*

"That is an interesting observation." Nata smiled. "But witch or not, I am insane, and you should stay away from insane women." She kissed him, as hard as she had that first day he had seen her. "Let's go."

They stood up and walked toward the river bank. There were two more rowboats near the other shore. From the hill drifted the soft sounds of an accordion accompanied by a voice: *"Eh, my little apple, where are you rolling . . ."* Alexey felt sad for Nata. She had everything and yet she had nothing; she was so lonely, so frightened, and too proud to admit it. He shared her premonition that they were about to part, that the eye of the hurricane was moving closer and their lives would be thrown far and wide across this earth like grains of dust.

He put both hands around her and held her as tenderly as he could, almost as if she were his sister. "No matter what, Nata, no matter what, I will always be your friend, always."

"I am grateful, Alyosha." She looked serious. "And I, too, will be your friend, always."

They walked back, hand in hand, and woke up old Semen, who was blissfully asleep in the carriage. On their way, along with *"little red apple, where are you rolling,"* there were booms of artillery fire. *The sea in the eye of a hurricane is unusually calm and yellow,* Alexey remembered reading somewhere. These large eyes next to him were yellow, golden yellow, and rather calm. Perhaps only on the surface.

Nata spoke wistfully of the films she had made. She did not like *The Star of the Orient*; her favorite was *By Sword Alone*, in which she played a Cossack warrior. She told him that tonight, and perhaps for the next few nights, she had to give her body to some prince who was also a general, incredibly wealthy, and who wanted to take her to his palace in the Crimea, and then to the forests of Brazil.

"Why, Nata, why," Alexey wanted to ask her this for a long time, "won't you leave Russia? If your father is alive, he is on the other side of the front, and you cannot help him. If, God forbid, he is not, that is even more reason for you to leave. Go to Paris, resume your career; you don't need any prince."

"I cannot leave just now. I wish I could."

What a strange, strange woman. Alexey watched her ride off in her carriage. *Almost something out of the Middle Ages. Two gray horses, an old coachman, and inside, possible a genuine witch. And tonight she is giving her body to some prince? She spoke of it as if she were giving a worthless ruble to a beggar. And perhaps she spoke to someone that way about me? 'Tonight I am giving my body to this young man' . . . No, stop it, I must not be jealous, I have no right. A friend, yes, if she wants me to be her friend, I must tell her: 'No, not your body, do not give your body to any prince' . . . Ah, to hell with her. Tonight, I am going to get drunk, really drunk. And come back and sleep in my own bed, in peace. Peace?* He suddenly remembered Kuzmenko and his threat. *Why me?* He groaned. *Stop, don't panic. That dark colonel in counterintelligence is no fool. He probably shot Kuzmenko already. Besides, I forgot to do it yesterday. Somebody else must have told his wife. The whole city is full of Bolshevik spies. Yes, to hell with her.*

He saw Petia Ovcharenko climbing through the hole in the fence and into their vegetable garden. Normally, he would not open the back door. Tonight, even Petia would do, anything but going out drinking alone. Alexey had plenty of money. And Petia was kind enough to lend him some when he wasn't working. "Petuch." Alexey slapped him hard on his shoulder. "Let us go out and have a dinner at some good restaurant and then we drink, we have a wonderful time. The night is young, who knows what tomorrow will bring? I pay."

"Oh, tomorrow will bring nothing good, I fear," Petia sighed. "I hear there is heavy fighting in Irpen."

"What are you saying? Have you read the papers? We are getting closer and closer to Moscow; we just took Chernigov, did we not?"

"I fear the Bolsheviks will come back." Petia shook his head. "Where have you been all day?"

"With the most intoxicating, sophisticated woman, especially in the arts of love and seduction . . ."

"You lucky dog, you've been with Nata! You know, she won't speak to me after I broke her stupid table. I swear it wasn't my fault; I did not lean on it that hard. Perhaps the ghost did it."

"Tell you this—you will be my guide. Nothing but the best.

I am taking thirty pounds sterling. Will that be enough for the two of us, and should we meet some women?"

"Where did you get those?" Petia looked greedily as Alexey counted the new banknotes. "That is real money. Yes, that will be more than sufficient. For theater too."

Sitting in the cozy Café Paris, listening to a small orchestra playing exotic, sensuous tango Magnolia and waiting for their Chicken à la Kiev—Petia stunned the stuffy waitress by adding, "We are in Kiev, of course, are we not?"—Alexey told him of his brief but memorable encounter with the counterintelligence and Kuzmenko.

"So, we go tell the old whore tonight. What is the difference? You may be right, Kuzmenko may already be dead. But what if he is not? Why risk it?"

Happy and only slightly drunk, they climbed the dimly lit stairs of a rather dilapidated building. A narrow corridor, full of boxes and large grotesque masks made from papier-mâché. In an open door, a group of young women in transparent dresses, smoking and laughing.

"Hashish," Petia whispered.

A little man dressed as a clown suddenly blocked their way and said sternly, "Who are you, and what are you doing here?"

"I came to see Antonova. I have a message for her," answered Alexey.

"Antonova? Are you sure about the name? Antonova?" the clown shouted. "Adios, go. Farewell, young wanderers."

"Who is it, Aristid?" came a tired voice from the depths of the apartment. Alexey thought that the voice was very similar to Nata's.

"Two lost souls, oh goddess. I shall promptly send them on their journey. Leva, Vanya," he shouted, "we have unwelcome visitors!"

"Wait, bring them in."

"At once, your highness."

A narrow room, a large dresser drawer with a mirror. In front of the mirror, a well-known vaudeville actress—Solnzeva—was applying cream to her face. She did resemble Nata, could have played her mother. She wore a blue silk slip, the same one she wore on the giant poster in front of Theater Farce. In an old armchair behind her sat a nude young woman, brunette, with a hard, sullen face.

"Antonova is the name on my passport. Very few people know that. You said you have a message for me. What is it? And from whom?"

Alexey had never expected Kuzmenko to have Solnzeva for a wife. Neither had Petia.

"Ah, I have a message from Kuzmenko."

"Oh," she groaned. "What does that devil want from me now? He ruined my body, my soul . . . look." She took down her slip to show scars across her back. "I tried to poison him three times, but he is immortal. I thought with the Whites here I would have a rest. What does he want from me now?"

Alexey noted that her eyes were large too, as large as Nata's, but they were gray, steel gray, and very alert.

"They caught him, counterintelligence, Saturday morning, I was in the same room . . . I was in the Garrison Regiment and he told me to tell you and that you should go to Semen. That is all."

"That is all?" She jumped up and raised her hands in prayer. "That monster is caught, maybe they hung him already." She wrapped her arms around Alexey and kissed him almost as hard as Nata. "Sit, young man, sit! This is the greatest news I have had in my entire life!"

Alexey sat down on a small wooden stool next to her. On her mirror there were several photographs of herself, with and without her costumes. One photograph was different—smiling Kuzmenko wearing a jacket and a tie. *So? She hates him and keeps his picture? Hmm.*

"You did not come here of your own free will, young man. You were probably threatened, frightened; it took great courage for you to come, and your courage will be rewarded. Aristid, a bottle of champagne! Finochka," she waved to the naked woman, "make yourself useful . . . Come." She invited Petia to sit on the old armchair vacated by Finochka, who was now standing, apparently waiting for Solnzeva's further orders. "Do you like her?" she asked Alexey.

"She is lovely, but we really should be leaving."

"And you?" she asked Petia.

"Yes, very much, love her."

"Come on, Petuch," Alexey was getting edgy. "We have other places to go, remember?"

"Do it, Finochka." Solnzeva smiled. The nude woman was not pleased, but she kneeled over Petia and began to unbutton his trousers. "And you, young man, what is your name and what is your pleasure?"

"Alexey . . . Lebedev. I do have a woman I . . ."

"How wonderful! True love? I wish I knew someone who was so faithful. Aha, champagne has arrived." Aristid brought a bottle and four glasses, but since Finochka and Petia were occupied, he filled two glasses and gave them to Solnzeva and

Alexey. He looked with some approval at the rhythmical movements of Finochka's head and filled one for himself. "To love!" Solnzeva proclaimed. "To love and to death. Death of the monster!"

Alexey drank very fast. He was ashamed because Petia was now making noises like a baby goat, and both Solnzeva and Aristid couldn't stop themselves from laughing. Fortunately, Finochka knew what she was doing and it all ended very fast.

"You are a pig." Alexey wanted very much to kick Petia going downstairs. "How will you look my sister in the face?"

"I did not do anything." Petia grinned. "I just sat there."

"And made those idiotic noises."

"Alyosha, these people are actors; it means nothing to them. Finochka is probably doing the same thing right now to that clown, or to Solnzeva. For me, however, this was my first time."

"Where do we go now?"

"Great place. Most exclusive. It is called the Circle of Horrors. Small theater, terribly expensive, and it is run by the Society of the Friends of the Marquis de Sade. Remember?"

"I don't exactly remember, but it sounds good."

"Satanists, they are behind this society."

"Now I remember. They are everywhere, right?"

"Yes they are. And your Nata may even be one of them."

"Let us stop somewhere for a few more drinks first." Petia did not object.

When they finally sailed into the elegant lobby, Alexey had the uneasy feeling that their luck was about to run out. He watched Petia stumble over a couch of red leather and fall, narrowly missing a lamp in the form of a naked woman. *I should just turn around and go home,* he thought. Instead, he stepped toward the table, behind which sat a beautiful blond woman, and said: "Mmm, tickets please." Out of the corner of his eye he saw that Petia was struggling to get up and that a thin, intense gentleman had appeared, possibly a manager.

"Go away," the beautiful blond woman said. Then, seeing a ten-pound note in Alexey's hand, she whispered, "We could meet later, you and I."

"Please." Alexey felt the intense gentleman's hand on his shoulder. "Please come another time. And persuade your friend to leave with you. We have a special performance tonight dedicated to the Great Evil One, and it is already in progress."

"Fuck the Great Evil One." Petia had somehow managed to get up. "Fuck Satan!" he roared, and charged into the auditorium. Alexey belched from sheer astonishment and immediately realized that it wasn't an ordinary belch, and that the Chicken à la Kiev had jumped out of his mouth and was running up and down the cashier's table, alive with feathers and wings. *A thousand pardons . . .* He wanted to explain his position, tell them that he would catch the chicken and put it back where it belonged, only his tongue wasn't moving and no one was listening. *A thousand pardons . . .* He watched some officers carrying Petia out. One of them opened the door and the other two threw Petia headfirst into the street. The intense manager was now screaming for somebody named Samson. *A thousand pardons,* Alexey thought. *I have nothing against Satan or Samson. This is all a slight misunderstanding.* He even gave the beautiful blond cashier the ten-pound note he still had in his hand. *Where did the chicken disappear to?* he wondered. Now this Samson, a tall, evil-smelling man to whom Alexey was not introduced, was lifting him up in the air. The door was opened, and by some magic, he flew out and landed on extremely hard cobble-stones, not far from Petia.

"At least they didn't beat us up," Petia moaned.

"I will never speak to you again." Alexey felt his legs, his head—everything seemed to be in place and he could move.

The rest of the night, the fog was thick, the streets sinister. Devils and vampires appeared and disappeared at random. Petia was whining somewhere and when Alexey managed to get his hands on Petia's throat, he too disappeared, reappearing only when Alexey was trying to unlock his door.

Alexey let him sleep on the couch. *I will strangle him tomorrow.* On the way to his own bed, his mother's easel suddenly came to life and hit him hard on his forehead. Stars, comets. *Comets of empty lives?* He thought he was riding the tail of one of the comets, laughing and crying with the rest of the universe.

The afternoon newspaper headline struck Alexey much harder than the easel or the vodka. He stopped in the middle of the street, in front of one of the many recruiting offices, and almost cried. *No, no, it cannot be,* his whole being objected. Cold headlines in the morning *Kiev Thought:* "MASS MURDERER ESCAPES," and underneath,

> *The top Bolshevik commissar and the former commander of the Garrison Regiment who personally executed count-less soldiers and civilians, Trofim Kuzmenko, escaped while being transferred from counterintelligence headquarters to the city jail . . .*

Two officers moved by him into the recruiting office. The usual posters hung in the window: the white, blue, and red flags on top of the Kremlin walls, the slogans—*"You do not have to be a hero, but you must be a Volunteer."* Why must? Why Volunteer? Another poster, with the minarets and red sun—*"WE ARE ACCEPTING OFFICERS AND VOLUNTEERS INTO THE GLORIOUS TURKESTAN REGIMENT. The goal of the regiment is liberation of Russia and our native Turkestan . . ."*

I will go, Alexey thought. *Lucy,* he then remembered. She had sent him out to get some milk and bread. He crumpled the newspaper and threw it into an alley. A gust of wind picked it up and placed it gently into a gray puddle. *It must have rained this morning,* he thought. Lucy was packing a few of her belongings. The field hospital, along with the two reserve squadrons of Hussars, were being shipped to the front, into the meat grinder.

The great hurricane was moving closer and closer, destroying everything in its path. There was no escape, and even hope, that small streak of blue in the dark red sky, was fading.

central russia
october-november 1919

comrade trotzky, THE PEOPLE'S COMMISSAR FOR
defense and supreme commander of the Red army, had not
slept in several weeks. Mercurial, brilliant, enigmatic, and an
egomaniac, he subsisted on a very strange diet of chicken broth
and cocaine. Frail as he was, his hoarse voice and fiery eyes—
magnified by his thick pince-nez—always produced a mystical,
electrifying effect, and thousands of soldiers and sailors in for-
mations near their troop trains would listen as if hypnotized.

"One bayonet thrust by one Red guardsman will tear the
White front to shreds!" he would scream hysterically, and
thousands would scream with him.

His speeches, important as they were for restoring the
troops' morale in the face of the advancing, seemingly unde-
featable White divisions, were only a minor part of Trotzky's
superhuman effort. The intensive preparations for the Final
Battle, the great Red Offensive, were now over. Every detail of
the attack, meticulously worked out by his staff of over four
hundred former Czarist officers and about the same number
of selected Red commanders and political commissars, was
being put into action. The Whites had been thrown back to
the outskirts of Orel, and that was only the beginning.

Tonight, Trotzky ate two sandwiches with meat and cheese and drank a glass of red wine. He told his orderly not to wake him up for at least twenty-four hours, no matter what, then began looking thoughtfully out of the window of his compartment. His train was standing on the main track of the large railroad station, Volovo. On the other side of the wide platform, crowded with sailors and their bayonets, stood the dark and menacing armored train "Emilian Pugachev." Its turrets and long barrel reminded Trotzky of a medieval castle made of iron. He smiled and poured himself another glass of wine.

The "one bayonet" slogan and the others that he loved to use, like, "All proletariat on the horse!" and "The horse is the tank of the Revolution!" were for the masses. In reality, he knew he had achieved a minor miracle by assembling a force of such awesome strength against the advancing Whites, that Denikin's defeat was almost a foregone conclusion.

The "one bayonet" was a battle-group of shock troops spearheaded by a division-sized unit composed entirely of members of the Russian Communist Party, and commanded by the legendary Frunze himself. Once the front was torn, Budenny's cavalry—twenty-five thousand screaming victorious horsemen—would gallop into the hole to split the Volunteer Corps from the army of the Don Cossacks. On the Whites' right flank, another cavalry army commanded by Zloba, and right behind Zloba, the Latvian Corps—two divisions of fearless, deliberate, well-disciplined soldiers, followed by the veteran Chinese Division, the Estonian Division, and fifteen thousand Kronstadt sailors fresh from their victories over the Whites near Petrograd. On the left flank, the freshly rested and strengthened 13th and 14th Armies, along with the German Spartacus Regiment and the Hungarian Cavalry Brigade.

And that was only the "one bayonet." Four other Red armies were poised and ready to enter the battle. The troop trains stood back to back from Tula to Volovo to Moscow. Long gray snakes of infantry marched across the fields and dirt roads toward Elez and Voronezh. Thousands of artillery pieces of all shapes and sizes driven by exhausted horses and old trucks were followed by endless columns of supply wagons. Well over a million men, one fifth of the entire Red army, were committed to the Final Battle. And to make absolutely certain that nothing remained of the White resistance—the last nail in Denikin's coffin, right after Frunze and Budenny—into the front that would already be torn to shreds, amidst sparks and black smoke, amidst thunder that would be heard throughout Russia and the entire world, a thunder that would freeze the blood of every White soldier—one after one, twenty brown and green and black monsters, giant serpents with their long-range naval guns and mortars, the angels of death and destruction, the very clear vision of the apocalypse—the armored trains of the Red army would race south. Unstoppable!

Led by the fast, deadly "Chernomor," with its crew of Black Sea sailors who were not afraid of the devil himself; followed by "Rosa Luxemburg," with its huge cannons refitted from the battleship "Alexander Nevsky"; then the long brown snake that had strangled the Cossack resistance in the Urals—"The Boa Constrictor"; the newly repaired, victorious "Third International"; "The Bolshevik"; and, finally, "The Proletarian" and the "Stenka Razin." Every crew would be supplemented by an entire company of engineers, six thousand altogether, with all the necessary equipment for repairing railroad tracks and bridges. The Whites would be very foolish if they even thought to slow down this mass of armor and death.

Tonight, Trotzky felt unusually powerful and triumphant. He had defeated General Yudenich and his tanks—after that worm Zinoviev panicked and left the battlefield to hide in his aunt's attic for an entire week—in the heat of the battle for Petrograd. He, Trotzky alone, had vanquished Kolchak's hordes, and now he was ready to grind Denikin into powder. Denikin: the last, the most dangerous.

Tonight, the long-awaited, absolutely secret letter from the Academician Perezvonov had arrived through a trusted messenger. Perezvonov was the chief surgeon of the medical team treating Lenin and he was direct, to the point: *"Lenin is dying, no doubt. Main cause: advanced stages of syphilis. Then, the wound from Fanny Kogan's botched attempt, not quite properly healed. Perhaps the bullet was indeed dipped in cyanide solution. And then, his high blood pressure. I would give him six months to a year, two at most. This is the best I can do, Leva. Let us hope it will be six months. With love and admiration, Sasha."* He then added in red ink: *"Long live our Great Communist Republic and its great present and future leader, Lev Trotzky!"*

I cannot wait two years, Sasha, Trotzky thought. *Lenin has to go. But Denikin comes first. The snake that is half dead is far more dangerous than the snake that is alive and well.* Kolchak, yes, he was dead. He did not know it yet, but he was dead. According to his intelligence, not only was Kolchak fleeing his capital of Omsk and abandoning his armies, but he was only a shell of the former hero Admiral Kolchak, the idol of so many. He had become so addicted to morphine that he was incapable of making even the simplest decisions, and he looked like a living skeleton.

Trotzky used morphine only once in a great while, and did not consider his now-and-then, under-pressure use of cocaine an addiction. He thought of injecting himself with morphine tonight, but decided against it. He felt pleasantly drunk, almost euphoric. His eyes closing, he saw the giant "Emilian Pugachev" roll angrily, flame and smoke coming out of its engines, on the way to the front—the front which was already torn.

Trotzky's orderly waited until he was sure the People's Commissar was fast asleep. He then quickly removed his pince-nez, his tunic, and his boots, and lifted the frail body, placing it like a doll on a comfortable, clean bed on the other side of the spacious compartment. He covered Trotzky with a goose-down blanket, took two revolvers and a grenade out of his pockets, and sat on a sheepskin by the foot of the bed. The orderly was a bear-like Jewish peasant from a village near Gomel. He listened to the strange songs Trotzky's Latvian bodyguards were singing in the next compartment, and looked at the frost-covered window and the darkness beyond. The frost on the window had appeared fast, and in a few minutes covered it completely. From time to time, the wild howls of the wind cried out like thousands of babies in distress. The orderly understood the anguish of the wind, understood what it meant. *Satan itself is walking upon the Russian soil this night,* he thought, *and will walk on it for a long time.*

The sharp point of Trotzky's "bayonet," the unit of the Russian Communists under the command of Frunze, spent the better part of the first day of the Final Battle in fierce, hand-to-hand combat with the second and third regiments of the Whites' Markov Division. In the morning, the Reds succeeded in pushing the Whites back a few kilometers. The Whites regrouped and, aided by two of their armored trains, "To Moscow" and "Our Homeland," counterattacked, throwing the Reds back to their original positions. Instead of pushing the Reds further, however, they stopped, and, inexplicably, began retreating. They retreated so fast that by the late afternoon, the forward elements of Frunze's unit lost touch with the enemy. Their armored trains too left the field of battle.

Frunze himself was delayed by an urgent meeting at Budenny's headquarters in Kazaki, and was not expected to rejoin the unit until the following morning. In his absence, the unit was led by Klimov, formerly a captain in the Czarist army who had joined the Communist Party in 1915, an able and courageous commander. According to his orders, Klimov followed the retreating Whites with his entire unit and the two artillery regiments which Frunze had managed to wrangle from Trotzky at the last moment. As far as Klimov knew, they had to march ten more kilometers before reaching Lesovo, a town composed of seven small villages nestled together at the edge of the forest. This was planned as a unit stop for the night. Then, his orders were to try and break through to the town of Tim. Klimov did not foresee any serious fighting, because the Markov Division had retreated quite a bit to the east, toward the town of Zhigri.

What worried the Red commander much more than the Whites was the sudden change in weather. The light cold rain that had fallen during most of the day was turning now into wet snow. A powerful wind, coming out of nowhere, blew the large, instantly crystallized flakes with such force that people and even horses were thrown off their feet and found themselves lying in ice puddles along the narrow dirt road.

This was not a blizzard, but the beginning of a snow and ice hurricane similar to a tornado or a cyclone—or a Siberian buran—one could not see where it ended or even where it began.

In a matter of minutes, the crack fighting unit became a disorganized crowd of ten thousand soldiers, blinded, help- less, desperately clinging to one another. It was impossible to march, impossible to see any further than one's arm. They were under a wet waterfall of snow. It was as if a black void were opening up: darkness in the afternoon. And the temperature kept dropping. The guides, two local peasants, stood silently and kept crossing themselves, refusing to move or answer any questions, even under the threat of being shot on the spot.

Klimov finally managed to assemble of few of his comman- ders and commissars under an artillery cart. With great diffi- culty, they built a small fire out of some wood and gunpowder. Frightened, they studied the map. It showed clearly that there was nothing at all between them and Lesovo, at least eight kilometers away. But in which direction? There was no road anymore. And they discovered, to their horror, that their compasses and their field telephones did not work. The dreadful conclusion was that this was a magnetoelectric storm of unprecedented proportions. They should have asked the two guides a few hours ago, and the guides would then have told them that this was the infamous Zhigri-Temsko anomaly, something that occurred every two hundred years when the Chort, that *devil*, wished to visit Mother Russia. This was his time, his midnight.

The snow waterfall now turned into torrents of ice. Some of the icicles that fell on the helpless soldiers and horses were as big as daggers and they pierced helmets, fur hats, and over- coats. At the same time, the coldest ice imaginable was crawl- ing through the heavy boats of the Red guardsmen, solidly freezing their ankles. The water in their eyes froze to a stiff glaze. Nasal and throat passages froze. *This is the end, the death,* ten thousand soldiers realized, and nothing in the world could save them. Some optimists still moved their arms and legs, but their movements grew weaker by the second. The commanders, sitting near the fire under the cart, were the last ones to freeze. It is thought that when one is freezing, just before death, one experiences a euphoric sensation of warmth. These poor souls were frozen so rapidly that even that last merciful gesture of nature was denied them.

And the temperature was still dropping. The men and the horses were completely frozen. Some of the gun barrels cracked open. The entire column was covered by a thick sheet of ice. And the ice hurricane, the strange Buran, the Zhigri-Temsko anomaly, raged on, out of control, killing every living being that did not have a shelter.

It only lasted for two days, yet more soldiers perished there than in any battle of the Civil War. Beside Frunze's unit, nearly one-fourth of Budenny's cavalry, an entire division of the Red 13th Army, and two German Spartacus Regiments were frozen into the Central Russian soil. The Civil War came to a complete halt. But only for a few days.

At the railway station of Kursk, in the main station house, a two-story brick building badly damaged by artillery fire with its roof, windows, and the walls boarded-up, the staff meting of the First Armor Detachment of the Volunteer Corps was in progress. The battle situation was serious. The Second Detachment had lost four of its five armored trains in the heavy fighting near Elez a few days earlier and, in effect, ceased to exist. The First Detachment had lost two of its trains and now consisted of "Ivan Kalita," a powerful armored train with two double-barreled, long-range naval guns and two entire batteries of field cannons of various caliber; the lighter, faster "Our Homeland," which had been transferred from the Second Detachment and re-armed with three medium-range naval cannons, four field cannons, six mortars, and a Howitzer; and the light, fast "Officer." The First Detachment also had three support trains, each armed with two field cannons and Lewis machine guns. Two new armored trains were supposed to arrive from the Crimea, but, as General Belousov, the commanding officer, put it, "By the time they get here, the war most likely will be over."

Yet the war had to be fought and, after the great storm, the situation was anything but certain. The ammunition and extra provisions were loaded on the trains during the night. Every train had enough fuel to last for a week—"Ivan Kalita" used coal, "Our Homeland" and "Officer" used oil, and everything was ready to roll.

This morning's meeting was of such importance that only the commanding officers of the armored and supported trains, General Belousov's adjutant, a young cornet, and the commander of the scout train who had just returned from his patrol, were present. The cornet, a nervous, pimple-covered young man, reported, while biting his black fingernails and spitting them out, that the entire railroad line to Zhigri, except for two spots where the tracks had been previously blown up and sloppily repaired, was in excellent condition. The ice had melted and did not present any danger. There were hundreds, perhaps thousands, of dead men and horses along the tracks and four abandoned trains, but this was not a major problem.

"Why did you not go into Zhigri as I had ordered?" Belousov demanded.

"I was attacked by an artillery battery," the cornet lied. He had been chased off by weak rifle and machine-gun fire coming from one of the houses near the station.

"Go and take a bath," Belousov dismissed him. "Well, gentlemen, nothing new here. We knew this last night when two new armored cars returned safely from Zhigri. Is Zhigri still in our hands this morning?" A handsome white-haired man with a mischievous twinkle in his eyes who was, even now, huge and very well-proportioned, Belousov stood and walked to the map on the wall. "Kornilov's division is ordered to defend Kursk. Drozdov's division will be held here, in reserve, so we are covered from the west. Question is, what is happening to Markov's units and Shkuro's Cossack army?"

"No communications whatsoever?" asked the commander of "Ivan Kalita," a tired-looking, unshaven navy captain wearing an old blue tunic with a cross of St. Andrew.

"Nothing. Thin air." Belousov twisted his walrus mustache. "Denikin ordered me to throw all my armored and support trains north to the Volunteer Corps, to Orel. Kutepov just issued an order of his own. He is worried that the Volunteer Corps might be cut off, so he insists that I send at least two armored trains to Zhigri. Now Kutepov, as the commander of the Volunteer Corps, is my direct commander. Denikin is far away. My instinct tells me Kutepov is right, but I only have three armored trains. So these are my orders. Grisha," he nodded to the navy captain, "you go north. Stepa, you take the 'Officer' and roll over to Drozdovs, cover them, and, if need be, blow up the bridges over Seim and Tuscor. Yuri, take a support train along with you, roll over to Zhigri, and then act according to the front conditions. Perhaps you can break through to Kastornoe. There should be at least three armored trains there from the Third Detachment. Explain to them our situation . . ."

"Yuri Efimovich," the adjutant jumped up, so agitated that he did not realize he was interrupting his own general, "please repair the telegraph line, we must get to the Markov units and Shkuro. I apologize, your Excellency—if we do not reestablish communications, all may be lost."

The meeting was over.

"Stay with me, Yuri." Belousov nodded to Skatchko. "Two minutes, and listen." He stood like a mountain over Yuri, a mountain with a white top. His voice had an unfriendly, metallic edge to it, and his eyes were cold and clear. "This is your first command. Remember this—you are not an artillery officer any longer; this entire train is your weapon. And what a wonderful weapon it is. So powerful, it can stop an entire division. Today, forget anything I ever taught you about tactics. In this war, what is relevant is your decision at any particular moment. You are also very vulnerable. Why did we lose three armored and three support trains just last week? Because the commander of 'General Alexeev' panicked, and instead of repairing track, pulled back and let the Red sappers blow up more track. Then, when their infantry attacked, instead of fighting back with shrapnel, he abandoned the train. Of course, they were all captured and killed. Some were mutilated. Did you know that the Reds currently pay fifty thousand rubles for the body of any soldier under my command? Double that for the train's commanders. Should make you proud, at least we're expensive."

Yuri remained silent.

"And so, colonel," Belousov put his large hand on Yuri's shoulder, "you do have a marvelous weapon. But be very careful. Today, be very careful. I can sense something is wrong at Zhigri."

"I will be careful, Ivan Vasilievich."

"Then go with God . . . There is one more thing," the general added as an afterthought. "Last night, I ordered a 'mad' locomotive and had it hooked up in front of 'Our Homeland.'" He saw the worried look in Yuri's face. "No, don't argue, You might have to use it, perhaps sooner than you think. I have a feeling the Reds are attempting something big."

Yuri was not happy with this latest development. "Mad" locomotives were very old, still-working machines, rigged with explosives, pyroxelene barrels, dynamite, land and sea mines, and powder, with a detonating device triggered by several bottles of nitroglycerine. This was a hell machine, and once the steam had built up and the mad locomotive was released at high speed toward the enemy's armored train, or whatever target there was, it was nearly impossible to stop it. The result: one gigantic explosion. The big drawback was, of course, that should the enemy's artillery fire penetrate one of its walls while it was hooked up to the armored train—to the two forward platforms—the whole train might as well become a fireball. But orders were orders.

Yuri stood on the command turret of "Our Homeland" and looked through his Zeiss binoculars at the desolate Central Russian landscape, covered with snow and ice and littered with bodies, dead horses beside their overturned wagons, charred remains of houses, and, here and there, boxcars with black holes in their sides lying by the side of the railroad track like toy trains tossed about by an angry child. *Child?* He thought how very much he wished to be a child again. To fish in the muddy Dnepr with his father, to come home proudly to their house with the blue awnings, lilac bushes in full bloom. To give their catch to his mother who would always laugh and say, "I am not cleaning this Russian fish, it is not fit to eat, give it to the cat." Strange songs she used to sing to him at night. He felt so special then, so loved. Now he was simply a small mechanical part of a giant evil machine, a drop of nitroglycerine in that "mad" locomotive. *Love?* The woman with the golden eyes is probably just waking up. Whose body is next to her this morning? Prince Orechov-Maisky, some young officer?

"Slow down, Misha, very slow," he shouted. "Shultz, to me, at once!"

The armored train was nearing several large buildings and a leaning water tower: the railway car-repair works before the Revolution, the substation called Pyatak. From here, the railroad line split. One went north to Kolopny, the other, the main line, went to Zhigri, Kastornoe, and Voroneth. "Our Homeland" slowed to a crawl one kilometer away from these buildings. Through his binoculars, Yuri could clearly see tiny gray figures with red bands and stars nervously running from one building to another. The substation was in the Reds' hands.

Cornet Shultz, his new artillery officer and temporarily his second-in-command, tore his sharp nose away from his own binoculars. Excitement spread over his boyish face, and he exclaimed, "I saw them all, colonel! They have artillery too, four pieces. Hiding over there." He pointed to a cluster of overturned carts and several dead horses thrown together. *This is dangerous,* Yuri thought. *If one of those cannons hits the "mad" locomotive . . . Of course, the explosives in the mad locomotive were planted well in its belly behind layers of protective steel . . . and yet.* He decided to play for the bank and clear the Reds out, fast.

"Shultz, rapid fire, a dozen rounds, and put the first few to the rear and a little to the left of those carts, just by the water tower. Don't ask why, do it and do it now! Misha, stop the train. Sappers, machinegunners: battle time!"

The armored train, a well-oiled war machine, stood still and silent for a moment. Then the morning was torn apart by the thunderous roar of cannons, brief whistles, and equally loud explosions. Wood from several carts and the bodies of dead horses flew into the air. Another round, and there was an enormous explosion near the water tower. They hit the ammunition dump, just as Yuri had hoped they would. The substation was enveloped in a wall of fire and black smoke.

"Fine shooting, Shultz." Yuri could see even without binoculars that the Red artillery men were tilling out their field cannons from behind the remaining carts in a desperate attempt to save them from being engulfed in the widening circle of fire. Four cannons—Shultz was right—not bad.

"Our Homeland" rolled closer to the substation. Its six long-barreled Lewises and four snub-nosed Maxim machine guns chattered happily, and the few gray figures that did not get cut down by their wall of fire scattered behind the water tower. Several Red machine guns opened fire from two of the buildings, the windows, and the rooftop. Their bullets were like peas bouncing off the armor plates. The third round of cannon fire scored direct hits into both buildings, leaving them smoldering, burning ruins. As the back wall of the larger building collapsed, Yuri saw behind it a long column of retreating infantrymen and a few horse-drawn wagons. They were walking toward the crest of a small hill and the safety of the forest beyond it. They were not in any panic or hurry, retreating in order, even carrying their red banners unfurled.

"Shrapnel, Shultz, rapid-fire, thirty-five degrees, eight hundred meters." He watched as the explosions tore the column apart. Now they were running toward the hill, falling, screaming, dragging their wounded. Another round, and the unit, except for the dead, was behind the hill and out of the effective range of fire. "Our Homeland" rolled ahead a few hundred yards.

"Scouts, sappers!" Yuri shouted. He watched the Volunteers, very familiar with their tasks, jump off the train and run toward the water tower and the smoldering buildings. Sappers, to make sure the Reds had not planted any mines or traps of any kind. Scouts, to find out where exactly the Red column was going, and to set up an observation post at the crest of the hill. The sappers waved, indicating that the tracks were safe. Yuri signaled his support train, which was following "Our Homeland" at a distance of one kilometer, to join him at the substation. He wanted the supply train to pick up the apparently undamaged Red cannons. There was, however, not the slightest possibility of repairing the telegraph line—all the poles were down for at least ten kilometers.

When the armored train stopped by the water tower, Yuri was the first to jump off. "Volunteer squad to me!" Twenty young Volunteers, commanded by a red-haired porutchik called Father Dima, formed a line by the side of the train, then began advancing, cautiously, toward the buildings. Their mission was simple: to secure the substation, see if any Reds were still hiding and whether they had left any supplies, and to check for any surprises.

Yuri waited until the supply train stopped directly behind the armored train and Captain Zenesky, the commander, along with a few of his soldiers, came up to greet him. "Load up these four cannons, Misha." Yuri returned his embrace. "They are almost brand-new, three-inch British; I think they are Royces, very good quality. I wonder where the Reds got them."

Loading them did not present any problems. This was not the first time they had captured an entire battery intact. The

cannons were simply rolled up into a parapet, then transferred to the platforms of the supply train and secured with
chains and pieces of railroad track. Yuri ordered Misha to take
them back to Kursk and not to stop for anything. As the supply train began to pull back, Father Dima ran up to him with
a very strange look on his face—tears rolling down his cheeks,
eyes wide open.

"Dima?"

"Fuck these bastard motherfuckers," the porutchik choked.
"We have it again, in that building. Let the devil take them all;
I should have known. Again! Come, you must see this."

The building was larger than it looked from the outside; it
could easily accommodate ten boxcars for repair. There was
no roof except for a few charred beams, no glass in the huge
windows. On both sides of the long brick walls bodies were
stacked up five or six high, like piles of firewood. Many were
naked. All were frozen, covered by a white dusting of snow.
On closer inspection, Yuri saw that the bodies of White soldiers lay on one side, while the bodies of refugees, women,
and children lay on the other. The refugees had simply been
shot. The White soldiers and officers had been tortured and
mutilated before being shot. The tortures were known to be
favorites of the German Internationalist Spartacus units: the
"iron glove" fitting treatment, the "tree cutting," the "emas-
culation," and some of the more common atrocities, such as
cutting strips of skin off the soldiers' shoulders where their
patches had been and carving red stars on their foreheads.

Yuri stepped out of the building, nauseated. He lit a
papirossa, inhaled, and noticed that his hands were trembling.
The stronger your nerves are . . . So many cellars, barns, catacombs, priests, nuns, children, everybody. *Who are you fighting
for, colonel?* He spit out his papirossa. *For the millions who were*

killed already, for the millions who will die this winter alone? For the
braggart prince and his palace in the Crimea?

There was massive rifle and machine-gun fire.
Immediately, two of Yuri's scouts reported on the situation.
The same Red column that had retreated north to the forest
had run straight into a strong White unit, possibly one of
Markov's regiments, and a Cossack cavalry, and they were
herding the Reds back toward the railroad line.

"To the train!" Yuri shouted. "Battle posts!" He ran, much
relieved, to his command turret. "Our Homeland" rolled a
few hundred meters past the water tower, directly toward the
firing. Very soon, the first chains of Red soldiers appeared.
They were now running, throwing down their rifles, in complete panic. They evidently hoped to escape across the track,
hoped the armored train was no longer at the substation.
Behind them, White soldiers were spraying them with
machine-gun fire from their tachankas; on both of their
flanks were posted the Cossack cavalry. And now they were facing the armored train. Just one volley of shrapnel from the
train convinced them to surrender. They were surrounded by
tachankas with machine guns trained on them and told to sit
with their hands on their heads. A few White soldiers collected
their weapons. Skatchko invited the officers, two Cossack
esauls and the officer of the Markov unit, a very young, sullen
captain, into his staff compartment for vodka and tea.

The Cossack officers gloomily told him that their men were
on the verge of mutiny. They were all that remained of two
squadrons belonging to Shkuro's famed Third Division of the
Kuban Cossack Army. The rest were killed in battle or had
deserted and were on their way home. Their entire division
was decimated yesterday by Budenny's cavalry. Even their
tanks, all six of them, had been destroyed by the Reds. They

were riding back to Kursk, and then they too planned to travel home. Enough of this war! Let the Russians fight it out. Yuri did not try to dissuade them. "God go with you." He gave them whatever provisions he could spare and the Cossacks rode along the railway track toward Kursk. The Markov unit was the first battalion of the First Regiment. They too had suffered terrible losses when Budenny attacked.

The prisoners they had just captured belonged to the German Internationalist Regiment—what was left of it, no more than four hundred soldiers. Markov's units had been fighting with them off and on for the past two weeks.

"They are a part of the Spartacus Brigade, three regiments, and they were trying to break through to Tim. They were just resting here when you arrived," the sullen captain explained.

"Tim?" Yuri was surprised. "That's too far south. Why not Zhigri?"

The captain did not know. He thought Zhigri was still in White hands.

"Do you know what those German bastards did to your brothers here?" Father Dima asked.

"I can well imagine." The captain blinked, took a long pull on the vodka bottle, one of three on the table, corked it, and slipped it into the pocket of his overcoat. "I am a veteran of the Ice March; I have seen it all."

"What shall we do with them? The prisoners?" Yuri asked. He already knew the answer.

"This, colonel, is none of your concern." There was a strange, almost euphoric, smile on the young captain's face. "They are my prisoners. They will get what they have earned."

"I would like to question their commanders first, and their commissars." Yuri did not look him directly in the eyes.

"Whatever for? Listen to me, colonel, we better roll out of

here as fast as we can. There are still at least four Red armored trains rolling here from the north. And Budenny should be here in one hour, maybe less."

"So what do we do?"

"You do nothing. I am going to leave my tachankas and my horses, load up my men and my machine guns, and get the devil out of here. Fast."

"Any chance for me to break through to Zhigri?"

"None."

"How many men do you have?"

"Three hundred and fifty; about fifty are wounded."

"Load them up."

The captain grabbed another bottle of vodka and went outside. A few seconds later, Yuri heard machine-gun fire, screams, howls, and groans. The fire lasted only a minute or two. Then there was silence. Back from the command turret, Shultz now looked very worried. "Colonel, come look."

Yuri focused his binoculars on the farthest hill to the north. He could clearly see four distinct dark gray clouds, moving fast over the white landscape—the Red armored trains. Much sooner than he had expected. He gave the order to unhook the mad locomotive and place it on the secondary track near the water tower. He fixed another surprise for the Reds, ten large British mines, just outside the substation, and had them camouflaged with dead horses. He then rolled out of the substation with Markov's unit aboard and had the railroad tracks set with his five remaining mines. His plan was quite insane: to disable or destroy all four Red armored trains; if possible, to capture one with the help of Markov's soldiers. Then, only then, to retreat. And to hell with Budenny's cavalry. It was insane. But in this war, sanity never seemed to win any battles. Markov's sullen captain, after hearing Yuri's plan, grunted his wholehearted approval.

The first RED ARMORED TRAIN ACTED BRAVELY AND DECI-
sively. Going full speed toward the substation, it opened fire
on "Our Homeland" with its heavy naval guns. Its fire was
deadly accurate and devastating. Yuri had never expected them
to fire without first slowing down. The Reds were firing
armor-piercing shells, and Yuri had misjudged their range as
well—two nearly fatal errors.

The observation tower he and Schultz had abandoned only
seconds before the Red avalanche of fire was blown off completely, and the locomotive suffered a direct hit in its main
boiler. All the machinists were badly scalded by the escaping
steam, and some were killed. Another armor-piercing shell
hit the artillery storage area, and the entire train would have
been blown up into small pieces had the shell not been
deflected by pieces of steel track welded together to reinforce
the area. The oil tank was similarly protected and spared, but
three machine-gun turrets were destroyed, and one of the
main forward cannons was knocked out. Shultz was killed
along with five other artillerymen, and Father Dima was
screaming, bleeding to death from a gaping wound in his
stomach. Two shells penetrated the passenger compartment
loaded with Markov's soldiers and killed many of them,
including their young sullen captain, their doctor, and two
nurses.

Yuri was wounded by two sharp fragments of steel which

lodged in his right shoulder and had to be taken out, immediately, with regular pliers washed in vodka. He lost a lot of blood, but once the fragments were removed he did not feel much pain and could even move his right hand.

The one mistake the Red armored train made was to become too reckless, too sure of its victory. It rolled up almost parallel to the water tower and the mad locomotive, still firing away, ready for the kill. And it was at the mad locomotive, not the train, that Yuri fired his first salvo. The result was astounding.

General Belousov must have put twice the amount of explosives in that locomotive than in any other. The explosion was of such force that the mad locomotive was lifted up in the air several meters, flipped over, and then set down on the command turret of the Red armored train, which was entirely blown off the track and turned on its side, where it lay, burning on the embankment, rocked by strong secondary explosions. A cloud of thick black smoke and fires enveloped the substation.

The second Red armored train also made a mistake: it was following the first one too closely. When the explosion detonated, its commander evidently lost his head. Instead of pulling away, he rolled forward and began firing on "Our Homeland." The shells he fired were not armor-piercing, however, and so did no real damage. Yuri returned the fire. He had only eight armor-piercing shells left and made good use of them. Its main cannons silenced and its command turret blown off, the second train was partially disabled. Two more well-placed barrages and fires broke out in several of its compartments. It too was then rocked by secondary explosions.

The third Red armored train then rolled up to the second,

hooked it up, and pulled it out of the substation and the range of Yuri's cannons. Aside from an occasional explosion and the crackle of the fires, there was now a lull in the battle.

Yuri ran through the compartments once to assess the situation. "Our Homeland" was badly damaged. One of Markov's soldiers sadly informed him that the main boiler was beyond repair. They would now have to rely on their small auxiliary boiler, and that wouldn't give the train much speed under battle conditions.

As far as the artillery, things were not so bad. Only one forward cannon was gone and two side cannons were jammed. There were now twice as many wounded, and with no doctor and no nurses, many of the wounded were simply bleeding to death. The fires had been stopped due to the heroic efforts of Markov's soldiers.

"Our Homeland," now a wounded beast, rolled back, slowly licking its wounds. We probably destroyed their famed "Chernomor," Yuri thought. He could see figures in sailors' uniforms beyond the smoke, dragging their wounded out of the inferno.

On the hill overlooking Pyatak, he saw at least a hundred horsemen, some carrying large red banners. A group of their commanders were looking at him through their own binoculars. *Budenny must be very close,* he thought. And while he had sufficient artillery, all six of his officers and all three of Markov's were dead. He put a few of Markov's soldiers, who were formerly in artillery, behind every cannon. He manned the Howitzer and fired three grenade shells himself. Not much damage, and the cavalrymen quickly galloped into the forest.

His fire was answered by the Red field artillery, well-hidden among the trees. Their first shells exploded several hundred meters behind the train. "Get us out of here as fast as you can!" he shouted to Markov's soldier who was now the machinist. The wounded beast continued to roll slowly. It was picking up some speed, but it was still too slow for any battle. *We will never get out of here.* Yuri saw that the entire edge of the forest was alive with men on horses. Hundreds of red banners fluttered in the air, thousands and thousands of horsemen. Yuri had never seen such a mass of cavalry, not even in the Great War.

The Red field artillery were now following the train, and their shells began to explode closer and closer. Another long line of Red cavalry was entering Pyatak. He could see hundreds of sappers and sailors repairing the railway track and laying the bypass line. *I am still within the range,* he reminded himself. He ran down and manned the main cannon himself. It took him five shots before he hit the British mines. Another gigantic blast. Not as powerful as the first, but he watched the fireball with satisfaction as horses and men flew through the air and the last remaining wall of the building filled with the White soldiers and refugees collapsed, burying the dead.

For some reason the Red field batteries immediately stopped firing. Within five minutes, "Our Homeland" was out of their range and picking up more speed. The battle was over. Yuri sat on the floor by the cannon's feeder and asked the soldier nearest him to get some vodka. Now he could barely move his right hand. His wounds hurt. He noticed that his ear hurt too. He felt it; it was cut, badly. There was no vodka on the train. And no morphine or any medical supplies. He just had to suffer through. And he was mistaken about the battle being over.

Ten kilometers from Pyatak, a frightening, terrible sight: their supply train burning, completely destroyed. The cannons were gone. Bodies were scattered near the track—red armbands and stars, shoulder patches and cockades. And it was impossible to derail the wreck because the track underneath it was a mass of twisted, hot steel. The train had been destroyed by artillery fire and then blown up.

Yuri sent everyone who could walk out of the train to help lay a bypass line. They had to do it fast or they were dead. By now, the Reds at Pyatak should be finished clearing the debris and laying their bypass line. Their two remaining armored trains were fast. And Buddeny's cavalry was not far behind. Thank God for Markov's soldiers. They were calm, not a trace of panic. These soldiers must have seen some sights. Facing death was nothing new. Another stroke of luck, there was no embankment and the ground around the track was still very hard. Working feverishly, they were about halfway through with the bypass when the Red batteries sent their new barrage.

"Our Homeland" retaliated with its guns. Yuri thought he had knocked out one, possibly two of the Red cannons at the edge of the forest. There was a period of silence as they evidently re-deployed the rest. During this time the bypass was linked with the main track.

"Now we go slow," he cautioned the machinist. The armored train moved onto the bypass line like a drunk stumbling into the street. A few pieces of track were uneven, but they held the train, and the dark green caterpillar slithered down and around the burning support train as shells burst over and around it and bounced off its steel sides.

The Red cavalry was in sight again, thousands of gleaming sabers in the air. Ahead of the cavalry were at least two dozen tachankas with their machine guns, ready for an assault. They were trying to cut off the armored train just as it was nearing the main line.

Yuri sent out half of Markov's soldiers to form a perimeter at the crossing, a human shield. When the tachankas came closer, their machine guns blazing, he shot a deadly volley of shrapnel and machine-gun fire and launched several grenade shells from his Howitzer. Many of the tachankas overturned, their horses dying or running away, their machinegunners killed or wounded. The field between the railway line and the forest, which this morning had contained only a few dozen bodies, was now covered with horses and men. The tachankas retreated, but the Red artillery barrage was more accurate, more intense. And the Red cavalry was getting closer; several hundred had crossed the line behind the train. The attack now would come from both directions.

Finally, with great difficulty, "Our Homeland" climbed onto the main track and Markov's soldiers jumped into the armored boxes, dragging with them their wounded. The cavalry stopped their advance. *They can wait,* Yuri thought, *they cannot capture the train now. They will simply wait for their armored trains to finish me, and they might, with their trains and their field artillery. They can wait.*

"Our Homeland" crept at a snail's pace, shooting only when the Red tachankas or cavalry scouts ventured too close. The Red armored trains were coming up fast. Two gray clouds running happily in their direction. Only a matter of minutes now. Yuri swore. In his haste to get away from the cavalry he had forgotten to dismantle the bypass line. It did not matter though, the Reds had so many sappers and engineers. They would have been slowed down for only a few minutes. Yet minutes meant life or death.

He listened with great apprehension to the vibration of the railroad line ahead of him. This meant a heavy armored train was coming, directly at him. He saw the cloud of smoke.

Logically, it should be the White armored train, but then there was no logic in this war. None at all. And by now the Reds might have taken Kursk.

Much to his relief, he saw it was "Ivan Kalita," with its mighty cannons. General Belousov had decided to send it to Zhigri. Aboard the train was a battalion of soldiers from Drozdov's division. The roar of its cannons was sufficient to stop the Red armored trains. The cavalry too had retreated, and the Red field batteries remained silent.

This was incredible luck, because at that exact moment, the auxiliary boiler of "Our Homeland" burst wide open. "Ivan Kalita" pulled it back some five kilometers, where there was a second track, and it sat there, its men listening to the sounds of artillery fire in the distance, a tragicomic finale, until an old locomotive arrived and pulled the armored train back to the Kursk station.

⁂

It was late in the evening when they saw the familiar two-story building, bright lights around it, machine guns and light cannons behind sandbags, soldiers and officers everywhere. There were two long troop trains directly in front of the station, and another train with artillery pieces and tanks on its open platforms was slowly rolling north. Yet another long train, also with artillery pieces, stood a few hundred meters south of the building. Tension hung in the air. A happy, excited tension: anticipation of battle, of victory. The White counteroffensive was about to begin.

When "Our Homeland" finally stopped on the fifth track and the medical personnel rushed to get the wounded off the train, Yuri noticed that another armored train was coming into the station. It was "Mstislav Udaloi," just arrived from the Crimea, well-equipped and majestic in the yellow and white spotlights.

There was happy news for the surviving crew of "Our Homeland"—triple pay, two cans of ham for each person, two hundred and fifty grams of vodka, and new winter uniforms. Medals were also given out. Then there was the usual fly in the jam. No rest for the weary. The trains were to be repaired overnight, given a new locomotive—a more powerful one than Yuri had originally—three extra cannons, and another boxcar with machine-gun turrets. They were also reinforced by twenty-two officers and ten Volunteers.

The commander of the Volunteer Corps, General Kutepov, was in a conference with General Belousov, but they both expressed the desire to see Yuri. Kutepov, thoughtful, exhausted, studied him with great interest and asked only, "Can we break through to Zhigri?"

Yuri mulled it over but his thinking was confused. Budenny's cavalry, the field batteries, the damage to the railroad line, and, last but not least, the remaining Red armored trains. *Yes? No? Perhaps? Impossible?* "Yes," he answered firmly, "but it will take time and you can't do it with just one armored train and a battalion of infantry." Kutepov's tired eyes lit up. *Who are you, colonel?* he seemed to be asking. Yuri's face, dark to begin with, was black, coal-black from the gunpowder. Torn tunic, caked blood, badly bandaged shoulder. *Why you?* Kutepov's eyes seemed to be asking, *What are you fighting for, colonel?*

"I will take you into our confidence, colonel." He grinned and stroked his silvery beard à la Czar Nicholas the Second. "Today, we have achieved a great victory. Our Kornilov Division alone, on its own initiative, counterattacked the

Internationalist Corps and put them to flight. Yes, their famous Latvians and Chinese are still running. We took almost ten thousand prisoners and captured two armored trains, one in excellent condition. Volotuchino is again in our hands. So much for the great Red Offensive. But . . . if Budenny takes Zhigri, and if he and the 13th and 14th Armies break south to Tim, our victory will be useless. We will be forced to withdraw, and the heroes who lost their lives in today's battles will have died in vain . . ."

Yuri did not hear the rest of it. There was an ever-expanding spotlight, an orange fireball in his eyes. In that fireball, there were no generals. For a moment there was a woman's face, so dear, so beautiful. But the grenades were exploding in the small church on Podol, the darkness and the autumn leaves, the snow was like the waves rushing against the houses. The voice, her voice, was crying out, warning him . . . of what?

A kerosene lamp is covered with a thick layer of dust. Boxes of ammunition in the corner. A Russian country doctor who looks exactly like Chekhov smiles and cleans his pince-nez. "Nothing to be concerned about; clean wounds, all three of them. Yes, I found another in your back. And I have stitched up your ear. I will recommend one month's leave." The doctor evaporates.

Another face comes into focus—General Belousov, walrus mustache, another smile. "Yuri, I cannot grant you any leave. Not now. I do regret it, please believe me, but I need you very much."

The following night, "Our Homeland" rumbled across the bridge over the river Seim toward Lgov, and then on to Vorozhba. The night was very dark, light snow was falling, and the railroad tracks, though inspected for mines in the afternoon, appeared dangerous in the bright beams of the searchlight. Instead of the usual two empty platforms ahead of the train, they now had three. And there was a second locomotive hooked up to the rear of the train. No mad locomotives this time; heavy combat was not expected. The railroad line was clear for the next twenty kilometers. There were no Red armored trains or large Red units in the area, according to Belousov's intelligence officer.

Lying on his hard cot and downing his third glass of vodka, Yuri listened to the Volunteers, separated from his compartment by a thin wooden wall, singing:

> . . . a band of outlaws are walking through
> the darkest forest,
> and on their broad shoulders
> they are carrying stretchers.
> Not ordinary stretchers,
> they are made of rifles,
> with steel swords across them.
> And on these stretchers lies
> a young wounded outlaw.
> All clouds, clouds are hanging on
> the treetops and the fog fell in from the sea.
> Oh tell us what you are thinking of,
> oh tell us our Ataman . . . all clouds, clouds.

Why am I thinking only of her? She is probably in Paris, in the Crimean palace . . . Who is kissing her fingers now? He smiled, closed his eyes, made her appear as a wounded young Cossack, falling in love with one of Napoleon's generals in *By Sword Alone.* That was a fine film. *I must get her out of my thoughts, my mind, my heart. She is not for me. The prince, men like the prince for whom this war is just another amusing adventure. Bolsheviks, blood, remote, unreal. Champagne, cocaine, black silk sheets, morphine.*

"Morphine, medic!" Yuri screamed. The shot of morphine that Doctor Chekhov gave him this morning had worn off; the pain, the dull, gnawing pain, was back. Vodka alone would not help.

A young Volunteer assigned as a medic stuck his red pimpled face in the door. "I do not know how to give an injection." He smiled apologetically.

"Give me the ampule and syringe, I will do it myself. You better learn and learn fast. And bring me another bottle of vodka."

The armored train was picking up speed, and the rumbling of its wheels began to make him drowsy. This was morphine too, of course. He had a good officer on duty tonight. Nothing to be concerned with. And the Reds are probably still licking their wounds . . . Women, so many women, trusting, innocent, beautiful, shameless . . . *To the devil with Nata. If she really is a witch, let her find her warlock; fly away with him somewhere, to the end of the earth. Green forests of the Amazon . . . These are Russian forests here, where real Baba Yagas live, and the Chort himself. She is so tormented . . . To hell with her and her torments. I told her her father was dead. Only a question of time before we find his body. They hid him well, for some reason. But all the dead will rise up in Russia. Rise and build a giant bonfire and dance around it and the whole earth will burn. The forests of the Amazon, everything.*

Now his Volunteers were singing:

> . . . *Bravely we will go into battle*
> *for Holy Russia . . .*

Nonsense! Yuri looked carefully at the bottom of his vodka glass as if it were a crystal ball. *A whore, perhaps. Surely. Like Nata, coniving, murderous, loving, caring. Out of my life, God help me, get her out of my life. We are simple outlaws here, carrying on our shoulders our wounded country, deeper and deeper into the darkest forest. And the fog rolls in from the sea . . . fog . . . blood, more fog.*

The early morning was clear, very cold. "Our Homeland" reduced its speed; they were near the frontline—bodies, over-turned carts and wagons, dead horses on both sides of the track. Machine-gun fire in the distance. Another kilometer, and the armored train screeched to a stop. The railroad tracks ahead were taken apart and thrown down the embankment. The officer of the guard was sent to wake up the commander; the alarm was sounded. Yuri, sleepy and groggy, shouted the usual, mechanical words: "To the battle posts! Scouts, sappers, to me!"

Lucy Lebedev ENTERED A SMALL ROOM FILLED WITH the blue smoke of machorka; it felt like a paradise compared to the cold and the icy wind outside. It was warm, and there was a distinctive aroma of Moscow sausage, along with the odor of human sweat. She looked at the table where three candles were burning and the commander of the Second Hussar Regiment, Colonel Vladimir Stepanovich Wolf, was sitting along with his officers, pointing to something on a large map. "You will have to hit them straight in their forehead." He sighed sadly, nodding to Prince Shevshevadse, the commander of the First Squadron. "Ah, Lucy, climb on the stove, get warm."

Lucy stepped up on the wide Russian stove covered with some straw. This was heaven. Her eyes instantly began to close. *No.* She fought it. *I will not go to sleep.* Strange. Now there were two princes and two commanders. She rubbed her eyes. Prince Shevshevadse was leaving. She jumped off the stove and ran toward him. "Little Prince, please, just this once, let me go with you into the battle."

The prince looked her over and smiled. "You want to get killed?"

"I will not, I promise."

He clucked his tongue and scratched his large nose. "Zhigit woman? I like it. I love brave women. Haida!"

She is on her horse, a gorgeous, strong young stallion, Kazbek. The squadron is spread across the wide field; it is their terrifying lava attack. Nothing can stop them. She holds her long, razor-sharp sword, and it does not feel as heavy as when she held it yesterday. She can swing it almost as easily as Volodka Rogovoi, the best swordsman in the regiment. Faster and faster they gallop. A dark building looms ahead, a bloody sunrise to the right. Shots ring out, rifles, one, two, many, then a machine gun. Faster and faster. Little gray figures fall on the snow, fire, then jump up and fire standing, but the Hussars are now upon them. The little figures try to shield themselves with bayonets. The Hussars cut them down. Howls and screams; heads roll on the pink snow. The gray figures that are still alive run in all directions.

The battle is over and I have not used my sword once? Lucy is angry. She sees one tall gray figure running away from her. It is very easy to catch him. Lucy gallops after the running man, waves her sword. Now. But the man turns, covers his head with his hands, and falls on his knees, begging for mercy. There is something very familiar about the man, but Lucy cannot see his face. Suddenly her sword feels very heavy again. She can hardly lift it

"Wake up, Lucy, wake up." Andrei Polenov, the adjutant, tries to drag her off the stove. "Excuse me, but the commander ordered me." Light in the small window, leftover food on the table, smoke. "Great luck," he continues, "Prince Shevshevadse overran the Reds and took the station. We have some wounded."

"Bring them here and get Raisa."

There were five wounded. Four just had scratches, cuts,

and a clean bullet wound, nothing serious. The fifth, a funny, happy young man, the favorite of the regiment, Cat Vaska, had a terrible wound in his stomach. He was coughing black blood and dying. Lucy stuck the large syringe in his hard vein and then, to soften his agony, shot some morphine in the side of his neck.

"We should go ask in the settlement, perhaps there is a doctor here." But it was no use. The doctor could not help Cat Vaska any more than she could. A few minutes later, the man was dead. Raisa, the head nurse and the wife of one of the captains in the regiment, a hard-faced, beautiful brunette with the aspirations of being the regiment's Messalina, rushed in, her large black eyes sparkling with excitement, barely noticing Cat Vaska's last moments.

"Lucy, Lucy, come." She took her under the arm and all but pushed her outside. "We have prisoners; they will be executed. Have you ever seen how we do it? It is so exciting." Lucy hated that woman, but something, some unnatural curiosity, stopped her. No, she had never actually seen anyone executed. Only the known Communists were supposed to be killed, but recently . . .

Outside were several bodies in their underwear, lying next to the wall. Three prisoners were guarded by the Hussars. One of the prisoners was barefooted. Next to a small barn, several meters away from the house, stood Volodka with his sword. He did not have his Cossack hat on. He held it between his legs. It was full of walnuts that he cracked and ate, waiting, grinning.

The Hussars first pushed the barefooted man forward, and he ran toward the barn, thinking probably of some warmth, his bare feet making imprints in the fresh snow. Just as he was a step away from the barn door, Volodka swung his sword, so skillfully that there was no sound. The head rolled clean out of sight into a snowdrift, the body fell down, and the bare feet rubbed one another for a moment or two, as if trying to keep warm.

The next prisoner, a stocky bearded man, resisted every way he could. He bit and struggled and screeched like a pig on the way to slaughter. The Hussars dragged him forward and then pushed him and released him. As he lurched forward, Volodka's sword, swift as lightning, took his head off. The headless body stood by itself for at least three seconds, then sagged, slowly, into the bloody snow.

The third prisoner strained against the ropes that bound his hands behind his back, took a step forward, and stopped. The Hussars tried to lift him and carry him to the fateful barn. He turned his head back to beg for mercy. "Stop!" Lucy shouted, and ran up to the regimental commander, who was watching the executions grimly. "Vladimir Stepanovich, this is a mistake. This man is not a Bolshevik. He is really a Volunteer. I know him; he was wounded in a hospital in Kiev."

"Nonsense," the colonel replied. "He was found hiding with these two Communists, under the hay behind the depot."

"Listen to me, I know him. He is Vanya Zorin . . . Tell him." The Hussars stopped.

The tall man said, "She is right. I was a Volunteer. I was separated from my unit and hid, and when you came I thought it was the Reds . . . Yes, I was wounded and in Kiev's field hospital."

"Are you from Kiev?" the colonel asked.

"Yes, I lived in Kiev all my life. I am not a Bolshevik."

"What unit did you serve in?"

"I was wounded when I served with the armored train 'Our Homeland,' as a clerk."

"Then what are you doing here?"

"I told you, he was in my hospital," Lucy interrupted, seeing that Volodka was almost ready to come up and chop his head off. "He had a leave of absence."

"Yes, I am on leave, my aunt . . ."

"We can easily check it out." The prince scratched his nose. "The armored train 'Our Homeland' is about to join us in a few minutes; it just entered the station. Take him somewhere where it's warm and give him some food. That is, if you vouch for him, Lucy?"

"Yes, thank you, Vladimir Stepanovich."

"Do not thank me yet." The commander turned abruptly and went into the house.

Lucy could not tear her eyes away from the huge dark green snake with its strange brown markings and the cannons and machine-gun barrels protruding here and there from its hard skin, the few black holes in its armored plates that were not completely patched up, the sparks and smoke, and the rumbling noise of its wheels. The snake stopped, stood still, silent, then its doors opened with a screeching sound and a group of officers and Volunteers spilled out on the platform, as if that giant snake had just given birth. The first officer, a tall handsome colonel wearing a dark brown leather coat and an artilleryman's cap with earflaps, embraced the regimental commander, who greeted him on the platform along with his staff. He was then introduced to the rest of the officers and the nurses.

Lucy noticed how Raisa's black eyes lit up, the same excitement as when she had dragged her to see that horrible execution. *She will make her play for that handsome colonel tonight,* Lucy thought. He was handsome though, dark skin, his face resembling the old portrait of Pushkin hanging in the hallway of Lucy's gymnasium. Hanging there, that is, until the Bolsheviks came and the portrait was stolen.

"Lucy Lebedeva?" The colonel had black, velvety, seductive eyes that were watching her with interest, amusement. "Are you related to Vera Lebedeva, the painter?"

"She is my mother . . . *was* my mother." For some reason Lucy felt flustered, embarrassed, and at the same time very excited.

"I met your brother, Alexey, not so long ago, and he informed me about your mother. My sincerest sympathies." He put his left hand up to his cap in a salute, nodded, and went along with the regimental commander toward the station house.

Lucy realized she was breathing too hard. *Am I getting to be just like Raisa?* She was horrified. *So, the colonel is devilishly handsome. And Cat Vaska is dead. Wake up.* She slapped herself lightly on her cheek. *He probably has a wife to whom he is devoted . . . What is that?* She noticed several drops of red blood on the snow where the colonel had stood. He kept his right hand in his pocket, she remembered, and did not shake any hands. *Hey.* She whistled. *The handsome colonel is wounded and bleeding. Now, this is a gift from God.* Lucy held her breath. She hoped Raisa would suddenly disappear, never to be seen again. "Colonel!" she shouted. He stopped and turned, annoyed. "Colonel." She was now a serious, no-nonsense nurse. "I must see you in my field hospital. Please come with me now, for a few minutes."

"What is it, Lucy?" the regimental commander asked, also annoyed. "Colonel Skatchko and I have important matters to resolve."

"The colonel must come with me now. You can resolve your important matters later."

The handsome colonel shook his head. "Excuse me, Vladimir Stepanovich. I was wounded slightly. Perhaps I need new bandages." He pulled his right hand out of the pocket of his leather coat. It was bloody. "Only a few minutes." He walked toward Lucy.

She felt her heart jump up and down and beat faster, much faster even than when Cat Vaska climbed through her window late at night. Outwardly, she was calm, composed. "Follow me, colonel. I will not hurt you."

"No?" The colonel laughed, baring his white even teeth. "In that case, oh sister of mercy, I am all yours."

Go on thinking that way, colonel, and you will be, you will be mine! Lucy saw that his right hand did not have a wedding band or any other ring. *Wonderful.* Lucy smiled to herself. "Here, colonel." She opened the door to the small room with a bed. Her own new quarters. "Sit down and take off your clothing. I shall return in one minute."

Doctor Chekhov had not done such a fine job on the colonel's wounds. He had actually missed one, a rather deep cut which was bleeding. Also, the colonel's ear was badly stitched up and had gotten infected. After Lucy finished bandaging him, she asked, "Why is your skin so brown? I thought at first it might have been sunburn . . . Oh, that doctor of yours is an ass. You could have had a serious infection."

"My dear Lucy. My grandfather led a rebellion in Africa, in Abyssinia, a long time ago. He was defeated and fled to Russia. Same religion, you know, Greek Orthodox, and he was a religious man. Resourceful, too. He founded a small ironworks near Poltava, married a well-to-do Ukrainian woman, and had four daughters. When they grew up, he sent them to Europe to the best universities. Three of them stayed there and one came to Kiev as a companion and tutor to the children of the Homenkos, our millionaires. And that is where she met my father. A simple, uneducated man, but he had dreams, ambitions, charm." The colonel smiled. "And they fell deeply in love, and I was conceived. And I shall bore you no longer with my family history." He stood up, very pleased with her work. "I would like, however, to talk about your family. Your mother was a remarkable artist . . . But another time, perhaps later tonight. I must run to Vladimir Stepanovich; we are planning an important operation. Good day!"

"Until we meet again." *I should pull him in slowly,* Lucy thought. *He is clever as well as handsome, and he has probably had quite a few women. Quite a few. He may even take this for granted, that any young woman who sees him is attracted to him. Perhaps I should pretend to be indifferent and let Raisa do her scheming. She may be older, but she is not as interesting as I. Cat Vaska told me so himself. And he should know, he had Raisa often enough.* Tears wet her eyes as she remembered Cat Vaska. "God rest his soul," she said quietly, and crossed herself.

Today was one of the few rare days where she had nothing to do. Cat Vaska would be buried tomorrow, the rest of the wounded were back with their unit, the seriously wounded in previous battles and the typhoid patients were evacuated to Kiev. There would be, of course, another battle soon; with the arrival of the armored train it would be something big, probably. Another nightmare, and she did not wish to even think about it. She felt very hungry and remembered that she fell asleep so fast last night she did not eat her supper. And they had been served exceptionally tasty pilaf. She hoped there would be some left.

There were loud booms of artillery fire to the north. She watched the green snake come to life and rumble toward the sounds. The station was empty. An old Ford truck stood behind the gray warehouse now used by the Third Squadron. This meant that the mail had arrived. What mail? The last letter she had received from Alexey was when his troop train was in Melitopol, nearly a month and a half ago. Since then, not even a note saying that he was still alive. She wrote regularly, every week, wondering if he would ever receive her letters. She even included one that Nata Tai wrote him from Sumy, of all places, not Paris or Nice but our provincial dreary Sumy, without reading it, a heavily perfumed blue envelope. It was a miracle, in any case, that the postal service was still delivering letters.

The driver of the truck, the blond, young Volunteer Lenka, came out of the warehouse with his carbine. He threw it into the cabin, saw Lucy on the platform, and shouted: "Lucy, kiss me immediately, you have one—a big one!"

The letter was a thick, gray envelope, wrinkled and torn and glued again, with several stamps of military censors: the stamp of a city in Central Asia, the stamp of the ship carrying the letter across the Caspian Sea, stamps of cities in the Caucasus, Ukraine, and finally Kiev, and the stamp of the field post of the Second Hussar Regiment. Lucy examined the letter for some time. She stuck it in the pocket of her green winter overcoat and went to see the cook. There was no more pilaf, but the cook gave her some Moscow sausage and bread and half a bottle of red wine.

Back in her room, Lucy said a short prayer for her brother, drank some of the wine, sat on the bed, and carefully opened the letter. Pages and pages of his small, confusing handwriting. At least he was making up for not writing sooner. It was hard for her even to imagine just how far away he was. Thousands of kilometers and the Caspian Sea separated them now. Would she ever see him again? She drank some more wine, ate all of the sausage, made herself as comfortable as she could, and started slowly reading.

She was on page three of Alexey's saga when the artillery booms became so loud and so intense that she automatically reached for her belt with her faithful Mauser. An explosion just outside her house blew all the veneers and boards off the windows, and a large chunk of ceiling fell, narrowly missing her head. The Little Prince appeared in her doorway, his face red. He was holding his sword and screaming, mixing Russian and Georgian words: "We run Lucy, Haida, Bolsheviks attack!" He pulled her out of the room and the house and they ran toward the gray warehouse outside of which the Hussars were setting up two machine guns. Another loud boom, bright, blinding flame, and the building with her small room folded up and collapsed like a house of cards.

Letter—was all she could think—*Alexey's letter*. The machine guns began to chatter.

There was a different kind of boom now; these were shells fired at something outside the station. The green snake was slithering to the rescue, fire and smoke coming out of its sides. Lying in the cold, cold snow, almost under the Little Prince, Lucy saw many gray figures with red armbands and stars running toward the forest, some cut down by the machine-gun fire. The dark green snake was now firing its cannons at the edge of the forest. There were huge explosions and fire among the trees. The Hussars stopped firing their machine guns, stood up, shouted hurrah, and applauded.

"Great shot, great shot!" The Little Prince clucked his tongue. "We go comb the forest?" he asked the commander of the Third Squadron, a thin, tall Captain Voronov, Raisa's husband.

"Let him comb the forest." He nodded at the armored train just entering the station. "I have one dead, seven wounded."

Lucy looked sadly at the smoldering ruin of the house where she had sat only minutes before. *I should have put the letter in my pocket.*

"Come, Lucy." Voronov gently touched her shoulder. He too had a sad expression on his tired, sensitive face. "I do not think two of my wounded are going to live, perhaps three."

As she entered the warehouse, the world of familiar groans and cries for help, she thought, *Voronov is such a decent man. Why did he ever marry someone like Raisa?*

The wounded were laid out on a large piece of raw canvas, the top of an old tent, in the corner near the wood-burning stove. Sasha, her helper, and two new medics were already bandaging wounds. A large pot of boiling water on the stove, steam, smoke, the neighing of horses tied together at the other side of the warehouse, blood and more blood. Voronov was wrong, Lucy realized by her first glance. At least six will die— one, hopefully two, may survive.

"Call Raisa now!" she shouted to Voronov. "I really need her." Suddenly, the letter from her brother and the handsome colonel and his armored train became unimportant, forgotten objects. The first man had his left arm blown off at the shoulder. Jagged pieces of bone, flesh, and skin floated at the edge of a pool of blood. The man's stomach was also torn open, and she could see his intestines. Only a few minutes left. She gave him a shot of morphine anyway. The second man had a bullet lodged in his jaw. She tried to pull it out—no use. Another shot of morphine. *I hope I have enough.* Out of the corner of her eye she saw two more wounded being laid down near the first dying soldier. Another sleepless night. Raisa ran past her. Sasha began to cry and Lucy slapped him and told him to get out and get some fresh air. Time stopped. It became dark, then light again.

Candles burned as if they were in a church. Several soldiers were singing. Somebody told her that during the fighting, Vanya Zorin, the prisoner, had escaped, and that the regimental commander was very angry with her. *Good,* she thought, *just do not get captured again, Vanya, this time your head will roll.* It did not matter, nothing mattered except pulling out bullets and fragments of shells, cleaning the wounds, stitching, trying to stop the never-ending streams and rivers of blood, closing the eyes of the dead, hoping that at least a few would live to see another sunrise.

Yuri slept BADLY. THE VODKA DID NOT HELP, HIS EAR hurt, he felt angry at himself for nearly botching a well-planned operation by letting the Reds come so close to the station. Had he delayed his fire much longer, the Reds might have overrun it and destroyed the Third Squadron in the process. The Reds had the initiative, it appeared, twice as much manpower, and at least three field batteries. It was sheer stupidity to assign "Our Homeland" here in the first place. *The main front is under such incredible pressure, and Denikin decides to pull me out of action? Over Kutepov's and Belousov's strenuous objections. Why? So many blunders. Perhaps there is something about this third force, the dark force that betrays our cause.*

Even in Kiev, soon after the Whites had arrived, every operation, well-conceived, well-executed, seemed to produce just the opposite result. He remembered his Uncle Egorov telling him that when two players are locked in a deadly game, the third player, however minor, will make a difference. It was true.

When the Ukrainian underground made their infamous raid on the Cheka annex—so inept that they lost most of their own men and gave the Reds pretext for massacring several hundred innocent people—it did tip the balance of the struggle. But the Ukrainians were not the real third player. They were fighting for their homeland, their independence. God knows, his own father might well have fought with them. Yuri believed in the White ideals, fiercely, because they were apolitical. *Let us destroy the Bolshevik oppressors and then let the people decide.* At least that was the goal. Now everything was turning upside down, and the reactionary generals were governors. And the real menace, if there was one aside from the Bolsheviks, remained unseen, undetected. If it in fact existed, it was definitely working against the White cause. Yet it had to have close ties with the key players on the White side.

Masons with their mysteries, other ultra-secretive theosophical mystical societies, charlatans under some spiritual cloak, even Satanists—there were several sects before the Revolution that indeed worshipped the devil. Why not? Yet it had to be a cohesive, determined, coldly calculating group to run an effective conspiracy. He wished Egorov were here so he could talk to him.

He remembered a Sunday liturgy on Podol, the same church where he met Nata. It was not to pray that he had come; he and Shebeko were watching one of Kuzmenko's agents. The sermon and the priest delivering it were unusual. The priest—tall, intense Father Andrei—spoke about a herd of swine. How the Chort promised them their paradise, food to gorge upon, warm mud in which to wallow. So the swines took off and ran across the earth, destroying in their path wonderful orchards that took centuries to cultivate, gardens, other animals, anything that stood in their way. In their mad race toward food and mud, they trampled flowers, fields of wheat. And there really was no food for them at the end of their race, because just before their promised land was a deep ravine with jagged cliffs on its bottom, into which they fell and every swine thus perished. Too bad he could not stay until the conclusion of the sermon, to hear the analogy; he had been on duty. But last night, Yuri thought of the analogy.

Four of his officers from the replacements, probably from the deserters picked up on the streets of Kursk, but officers nonetheless, three porutchiks, and a rotmistr, had stolen all of the medical supplies and a case of vodka and tried to run away from the train. They were, of course, mainly after the morphine. When they were apprehended, Yuri had at first wanted to shoot them on the spot. But that would have been too easy. He disarmed them and dropped them off in the danger zone. He was sure the Reds would mete out an appropriate punishment. Swines, really. And officers—they had taken the oath to Russia and the White movement. Rats, too. So many rats. Not just officers, generals. General Governor Tichomirov has a whole nest around him. *And he himself is the biggest rat of all. Small wonder, the military supplies and the ammunition never reach the front and when they do it is too late.*

Supplies? Right now he had only two armor-piercing shells. Two. And they were the last two shells in the entire Kursk depot. Do you believe in the devil, colonel? He remembered Orechov-Maisky's odd question. *Devil? No. But stupidity and treason and cowardice, yes, and something else, something dark, behind the scenes, in the shadows. The question, what? Enough of these morbid thoughts.*

"Medic, bring some morphine!" he shouted. The same inept, red-faced, pimpled lad. *I need somebody good,* Yuri thought. *In Kursk they did not even have a single nurse, male or female, and no doctors whatsoever. And I have to ride into the battle this afternoon.* Inspiration came along with the pleasant warmth and lessening of pain. *Lucy! Why the hell not?* The Hussars have another nurse and at least five Volunteer medics. And he had to admit he was attracted to that pretty, very young, and courageous woman. *I must talk to Vladimir Stepanovich. For now, only one hour, one hour of precious sleep.*

Even the morphine-induced euphoria was full of recent memories. Volkov was sitting across his desk, cocky, unafraid. "We had a traitor." He smiled. "One traitor. You have thousands of traitors."

"Yes, but you are losing." Yuri blew the smoke from his papirossa into the commissar's face.

"Absolutely not." There appeared to be horns on Volkov's high forehead. He was grinning.

I should have injected myself a few hours earlier. Yuri sighed. *This is so much better than relying on vodka.* "But your Chinese are running, Latvians too, and the Germans and all your Russian workers and peasants of the Red Star are coming over to our side. Soon, you are no more. And in your case, dear comrade commissar Volkov, very soon indeed."

"No, you are not winning." Volkov kept grinning, and his horns were getting larger. "Give me my cocaine, colonel," he pleaded. "I will die in the morning. Let me have my last supper. Let me have the bottle Nata Tai gave you for me."

"Why, of course." Yuri was only too happy, the last act, the noble gesture. Anything for the man condemned to hang in the morning. The entire small flat bottle disappeared in Volkov's mouth.

Now there were catacombs, bodies of the monks and priests, a pentagram in a cavern with a pile of skulls, some with the flesh still on them, wooden buckets of dark brown fermented blood, severed human hands, white candles, black candles. Another cavern, sounds of gypsy songs, women, officers, opium smokers. A figure of a woman running behind a silk curtain. *Nata? Must open that curtain.* "No, colonel, do not go after her!" an officer shouts. Slick hair combed backward, Oleg Baclanov. *So, Shebeko did not kill you yet?* Yuri takes out his Luger automatic and shoots him twice. Yet Oleg keeps shouting, "No, no, she does not love you, she does not love anybody!" And he too grows horns.

⌘

Yuri turns on his back. In the narrow slit of his window, he sees a piece of pale sky with one lonely star. *Shall I make a wish?* he wonders. *Why not? I wish Vladimir Stepanovich will assign Lucy to me.*

The next half an hour is very pleasant. In the blue, almost purple mist of innocence are the people, the objects he knew and loved. The secret place by the river, dreams of adventure in faraway lands with his best friend Seryozha, the gathering of apples after a late summer storm.

⌘

The day was cloudy, cold, remarkably uneventful. The Red units eluded the encirclement by the Hussar Regiment, the Officers Battalion, and "Our Homeland." Only one of their small companies was caught in the net and destroyed. About fifty men were killed, another fifty were captured. There was no loss of life on the White side. There were six wounded, none seriously. It was as though the Reds had decided to avoid the battle at any cost. Even their artillery was silent all day. The reason, it turned out, was simple: During the night, the Red armies had taken Kursk.

This is probably the beginning of the end, Yuri thought. *Christmas will not be celebrated in Moscow this year. Not for a long time to come.* He gloomily looked at his orders. To go with all possible speed to Kiev, to assist General Bredov. With all possible speed? He swore. He should have taken part in the battle for Kursk instead of sitting here. Not that "Our Homeland" alone would have made a difference, but if the White forces were not so spread out, they could have made a strong fist, and the strike from that fist might have made a tremendous difference. At least one victory today. He smiled. He should wish upon the morning star more often. After a long, heated argument, the regimental commander had let Lucy decide for herself whether she wished to serve on the armored train, and she had said yes. She had said yes without any hesitation, looking Yuri straight in the eye. Her expression seemed to be saying to him: *Yes, I will be there for you, but please, please do not ever take me for granted.*

For the first fifteen kilometers, the tracks were supposed to be safe. As "Our Homeland" rumbled on into the darkness, Yuri invited his staff to meet his new nurse at a soldier's supper of borscht and porridge in his compartment. This would be the first time to sit down with his new staff socially. He promoted three of his Volunteers who had behaved so bravely in the battle of Pyatak to podporutchiks and put them in charge of the scouts, the machinegunners, and the supplies. The rest of the officers were new. Only one had worked on the armored train before, the chief machinist, a middle-aged bearded Captain Isayev, who also wore a black and orange knot of St. George on his worn tunic. Altogether, there were ten officers, five at each side of the table, and Lucy presiding. The atmosphere was gloomy. Even after the meal, when they drank vodka and lots of it, the anecdotes, the stories had a false, nervous ring to them. The new artillery officer, a young, very pale ensign, brought his guitar and sang a few old-fashioned ballads. He had a pleasant deep baritone, and he sang well and with great feeling, yet he could not change the mood. One by one, the officers excused themselves and went to their quarters.

Yuri remained sitting next to Lucy on his bed, sitting so close that he could feel her tremble. They listened to the songs that the Volunteers were now singing across the wooden wall—*"Quiet all around, the wind took away the mist, on the hills of Manchuria warriors sleep, and they do not hear Russian tears . . ."*

They sat almost like old friends on the threshold of becoming lovers, both unsure and hesitant, and yet wanting, needing one another. Yuri finally put his hand around Lucy's waist and kissed her. In a moment of time that was forever lost, he saw comets of empty lives, dreams, and desires, and dark wooden buckets of blood, and he saw Nata's eyes exploding in anger like the shells from his Howitzer. He pulled back, took a long deep breath, and kissed Lucy again. Lucy responded tenderly, petting his hair with her hand.

"I am so afraid to love," she whispered, "not just you, yes you, afraid to see you one day . . . I know that every commander of "Our Homeland" was killed in battle—six of them so far. I read your plaque with the names . . ."

He embraced her and held her as tight as he could.

⁂

The armored train began to slow down. There was a discreet knock. They were approaching a small bridge over a creek called Uz. The sentry saw in his searchlight a few figures running away from it. Yuri sent three sappers and five Volunteers to inspect it. There were rifle shots.

Two more searchlights illuminated the gulley from where the shots had been fired. Silence. The sappers found one mine simply lying on the lower cement beam of the bridge and pushed it with a long pole into the creek, where it sank. The Reds apparently had not had the time to set it up properly.

Slowly, the armored train crossed the bridge. There was some more rifle fire, and a machine gun chattered briefly. They were in the danger zone. Everyone moved to their battle posts.

When they reached the territory held by the White units where the rails were safe, it was almost morning. Yuri returned to his compartment and found Lucy asleep in his bed. In her sleep she looked like a child, breathing so evenly, her hand clutching the pillow as if it were a doll. She was fully dressed, covered with her green overcoat. In the narrow slit of his window the sky was getting gray. The window was mostly covered by an iron plate, but there was a piece of thick glass at the very top which had survived every encounter so far. Yuri was so grateful for it. There was still that lonely star, beyond that glass, his morning star. He smiled and made a wish.

That star truly worked wonders. Late in the afternoon, when "Our Homeland" screeched to a stop next to the huge railway station of Bakhmach, there were fifty armor-piercing shells waiting for them, along with a brand new Howitzer, boxes of ammunition, British canned food, and fresh meat and vegetables. The best miracle of all was a small stocky figure with a round face, huge knapsack, and a valise: Porutchik Shebeko, Yuri's old comrade, had been assigned to the train.

After embraces and kisses in Yuri's compartment over a glass of good cognac which Shebeko had liberated in Kiev, they sat and Yuri listened to the dramatic events which had occurred in his beloved city while he was at the front.

Shebeko described in great detail the October attack on the city by the Odessa group. How the Reds had taken most of the city while the numerous staffs escaped and did not stop running until they reached Poltava. How the newly formed Druzhina workers had fought the Reds to a standstill and then how the White storm columns had fought street by street, house to house, and, eventually, had thrown the Reds back into the Irpen forests. More interesting was the fact that Orechov-Maisky had been assassinated shortly afterwards. Actually, Shebeko corrected himself, he had been gravely wounded by another officer who had escaped. The prince was now in his palace in the Crimea. The new commander of Kiev's counterintelligence was appointed by General Tichomirov—Colonel Orlov. Yuri winced at that news. Orlov, then a captain, was a known adventurer, and was suspected of stealing and selling medical supplies to the black market.

The most remarkable news of all was that Nata had disappeared. Completely without a trace. She had not accompanied the prince to the Crimea, Shebeko was sure of that. And Nata's father's body had been found and identified. His body bore the signs of torture. Shebeko did not wish to go into details here. Yuri understood.

"Do you think she was informed?"

"I am sure she was." Shebeko drank his cognac and poured more for both of them. "Perhaps she has taken her own life?"

"She did not go to Odessa or Caucasus?"

"No, I had two men watching the station around the clock. She did not take any trains at all."

"Perhaps an automobile?"

"Perhaps, but I do not think so. Our people were watching every highway. Someone as well-known as Nata Tai? No, I would have heard about it."

"And Volkov, Oleg Baclanov, and our dear Stacy?"

"I regret to say that after you left, the prince stayed Volkov's execution and put him into a special isolation unit at the old prison. When the Reds broke into the city, the guards fled and the prisoners were freed. As to Oleg, I tried to kill him twice, but he is a clever devil. Left shoulder was the best I could do. Now he is out of reach. He is the adjutant to our dear General Governor Tichomirov himself. Anytime Oleg takes a walk, he is surrounded by six Cherkassians. And Stacy?" He shrugged. "She also vanished. Very interesting about her, someone else was trying to kill her too."

"What?"

"Yes, spoiled it for me. I had Stacy in my sights; she was as good as dead. And then four revolver shots. Stacy runs, amazingly fast, and climbs over a fence. And that was the last time I saw her. Forgive me, Yuri, I failed you." Shebeko drank some more cognac.

"You did the best you could. We will kill those bastards yet, when we get to Kiev." Yuri stood up. "You wait. I am going to bring a friend." He walked to the medical compartment, embraced Lucy who was going through the inventory of new supplies, and gently kissed her. "An old friend has joined us. Come, let us celebrate this happy occasion."

Another bottle of cognac stood empty on the table. Shebeko stumbled out of Yuri's compartment. Lucy guided him to her own bed. He dropped onto it and immediately fell asleep. Yuri and Lucy climbed up the command turret to get some fresh air. It was a starry night and it was very cold. Huge, powerful locomotives whistled and, amid clouds of steam and smoke, pulled boxcars here and there for no apparent reason. A very long Red Cross train with the wounded rode slowly toward Kiev, pulled by a locomotive so old and so small, it was a wonder that the train was moving. That train was in quarantine. Typhus, another player, was dealing its deadly cards. There were no medical supplies, doctors, or nurses to stop the epidemic. Not on the White side and not on the Red. But the generals drank champagne and ate their caviar and listened to the gypsy singers. And perhaps a beautiful woman sitting next to one of them in the comfort of his blue luxury Pullman was Nata. Laughing, embracing an old body, on her way to the Crimea, Constantinople, Paris.

Most of the crew of "Our Homeland" was in town on an evening's leave of absence. The guards were trying to keep warm by the fire they had made in an oil drum. *Life is so very strange,* Yuri thought. *And it is getting stranger with each passing hour. Strange? Is madness ever strange? There must be some logic to madness. Descent? Descent into hell? Progressive insanity? Illusion brought on by that evil spirit that Oleg Baclanov was glorifying in his poems? And how will it end? Nata, the tormented Geisha, walking into the silvery water? Nata, the Cossack warrior, giving her life for the French general? Nata, a child prostitute, being killed by her jealous owner? Nata, her long cigarette holder, her veil, her hat of black ostrich feathers, her lips, her eyes. Nata! Stop! No more Nata. No more! Where is my lucky star? There are so many stars out now and they are all sparkling like diamonds. What do they see here? Madness? Illusion?*

Lucy tugged at his sleeve. "I am cold, Yura, let us go down, I wish to feel the warmth of your body."

Khara Khum Desert
Central Asian Front
October-November 1919

Imagination is THE MOST POWERFUL LIFELINE TO those of us who are drowning, falling off the bridge of despair, a ray of hope from the nearby lighthouse cutting across the darkest of all seas. It is the huge orange disk over the cream-colored sand dunes, so soft they appear as the velvet curtains of some forgotten bedroom. Now, this minute, Volunteer Alexey Lebedev, assigned to the administrative section of the First Battalion of the Turkestan Regiment, somewhere in the sands of Khara Khum, now—he not only saw the tents, but could hear the wonderful, seductive music. The palms were swaying in the evening breeze, and several women were dancing by the lagoon where the clear waters were reflecting the setting sun. Imagination. As important as oxygen and love, and that huge orange fireball on the edge of this earth. Alexey was always thankful for his lively imagination. Yet in his wildest dreams and thoughts he never believed that he would be where he was right now. In the middle of a desert and in the middle of nowhere.

To the devil with any imagination. Here I am, at least three thousand kilometers away from my friends, my city. Two points on the atlas, two entirely different universes. Providing, of course, that this is still planet earth and I am still alive, serving in this valiant Volunteer Army and saving Mother Russia from the Red barbarians. Only why here? Because some general drew a line in the sand with his toy sword and said this is the front, you defend it.

A few shots rang out behind the sand dunes, to the left of his boxcar. Not much to be concerned about. Probably some Volunteers on guard duty shooting themselves out of sheer boredom. A pitiful-looking bird, possibly a vulture, flew in the direction of the shots. Alexey stretched, reached for his tin cup, dipped it into the bucket of fresh water by the door, and drank it thoughtfully, savoring every drop. This bucket had to last another two days, and there were four Volunteers and a cornet in the administrative section of the First Battalion of the as-yet-inglorious Turkestan Regiment.

"Alyosha, help me to understand," Cornet Chaikin whined from behind the only table with the only typewriter, in the depths of their boxcar.

Chaikin reminded Alexey of Petia Ovcharenko, and he too was dangerous to be with. Earlier in the day Chaikin had somehow managed to find half a liter of vodka, and he was not sharing it with anyone. Outside the boxcar the orange sun was hanging just above the dunes, simply hanging as if afraid to roll down and disappear in the endless sands. Alexey could still see the camels and the tents, the oasis and the palms. He could hear the music, see the dancing women. *Stop it, imagination! Better yet, do not stop; make Chaikin disappear.* But Chaikin was still crying why was he here and why now, and where was here.

"Give me some vodka," Alexey finally growled at him, "or I will release Suleiman. I gave you my last piece of cheese, you turd." Alexey began to open the jar. Suleiman was a large scorpion he had caught under his bed a few nights ago. He fed him bedbugs which were in abundance and which the scorpion actually ate, with great gusto, much to everyone's amazement. Alexey planned to release Suleiman eventually, but not too close to their troop train. Let some Bolshevik step on him. Of course, there were thousands of Suleimans all around them. "One, two, three. Are you giving it or not?" Chaikin reluctantly pushed the bottle toward him. There were only two swallows left. Alexey finished it off and released Suleiman anyway. Chaikin was shocked. He tried at first to jump on the table, but he was too drunk. So he pulled out his revolver and waved it in the air. Suleiman, however, scurried toward the door and out into the sands.

Bedbugs! Alexey remembered just in time. "The can, Chaikin, move the can!"

This was a sacred ritual. Every evening they had to spread a lethal combination of diesel oil and camphora and kerosene on every floorboard and especially around the walls of the boxcar. It was either that or be eaten alive during the night. Bedbugs. A much more feared enemy than the Bolsheviks. After the two of them finished with that operation, they ran outside and stood inhaling the fresh desert air deeply. *Give me scorpions, snakes, fleas, Bolsheviks, even lice,* thought Alexey, *but the bedbugs, they are the worst.*

"Where did you get the vodka?" he asked Chaikin, and menacingly raised the kerosene canister he still had in his hand.

"From the Frenchmen."

"How much?"

"Two grenades."

"So you were the one stealing them?"

"Me and Sergei and Vanya."

"What are the Frenchmen going to do with them?" This

was a stupid question, since Alexey already knew the answer. *How can I be so preoccupied with my Nata, daydreaming and imagining? This imagination is going to kill me.*

"They are going to stick those grenades into our asses and pull the rings." Chaikin grinned. "What else?"

"Go buy us another bottle. Better yet, get us two, you idiot. Who knows what tomorrow will bring."

Chaikin disappeared with his grenades and Alexey carefully, very carefully, sat down at the edge of the railroad track and watched the sunset. It was so beautiful; the whole horizon was bright pink now with purple clouds above, and below, so blue and transparent and peaceful. The tents and the camels appeared again with the sensuous, melancholy music and the veiled ladies. The palms, the breeze, the water—real water still reflecting the sunset. One of the veiled women danced toward him, took his hand, whispered in his ear, whispered that she would wait for him, naked in her tent, on her silks, that she would show him paradise. She took the veil off for a moment, her golden eyes seductive, inviting. "I shall belong only to you tonight, my beautiful green-eyed prince."

"No!" another woman cried out. This one had a silver dagger in her hand, and she chased the golden eyes away, screaming, "Witch, witch . . ."

A few more shots—they sounded closer than the first ones. I should really get into the boxcar or at least get my rifle. No. Alexey remained sitting where he was, hoping the tents would come back. There were no more shots. In the next boxcar, the home of the Volunteer squad of which Chaikin was the nominal commander, came the pleasant sounds of the harmonica: ". . . *Oh my little apple, where are you rolling, into the camel's mouth, you will fall and you won't come back . . .*"

What am I doing here? Alexey tried paraphrasing Chaikin. *And why? Hmm. I am fulfilling my duty as a Russian who loves his country. I am an honorable man, I must do what I can. But here? Where is here exactly? Hmm, somewhere between Krasnovodsk and Ashkhabad. In the desert of Khara Khum. And we do have new British uniforms and new shiny rifles and machine guns and still almost a box full of grenades.* He began composing a letter to Lucy in his mind. *You see we also have a thousand new, young, strong soldiers with new shiny rifles and bayonets and carbines too. Why are these eagles here and not fighting somewhere near Orel or Kursk where the destiny of the Volunteer Army is hanging in precarious balance? I do not know, no one does except our generals. They know, but they keep it secret. Oh, they are a very smart lot, our old generals. Especially the general who commands this front. Yes, we are called the Trans-Caspian Front. And he is called Koza. He is so old it is a miracle he can still walk. And these thousand healthy brave soldiers, they have arrived from France. They were members of the Russian expeditionary corps fighting the Germans, got stuck over there, and now they are simply attached to the Volunteer Army and to our Turkestan Regiment—the First Battalion, of course. Since there are no Second or Third Battalions anyway. Lucy, Lucy, do you remember us going with Petia to see the* Mysteries of New York, *the whole twelve-part series? How the noble attorney turned out to be the fiendish Black Mask and the Chinese man with the mangled hand was his servant, and they both were after the treasures which the innocent beautiful blond woman had, though she did not know she had them? Forget it. Just think, Petia told me that such adventures never happen in real life. He is wrong. They do happen to perfectly ordinary people. Such as a very clever brother of yours, for example. But when they do, unlike the film, it is not so pleasant to be a part of this sort of mystery. Especially when you have no idea who is doing what to whom.*

The film is very pleasant to watch and you can leave the theater anytime you wish. In real life, or what passes for real life these days, you cannot simply get up and leave. You are a prisoner, a swimmer in a fast-flowing river; you cannot fight the current, you are afraid of drowning, of being washed on some danger-ous shore surrounded by bandits with sharp swords. Stop it. Excuse me, Lucy, my imagination recently triumphs over the rest of my brain. So? Ah yes, the intrigue. The Frenchmen, that is what we are calling the expeditionary-force soldiers, the new ones, are a strange crowd and they are secretive. Will they fight the Bolsheviks or us—that remains to be seen. They do have a strong Communist organization in their companies. And there is another organization, dear sister, much more sin-ister, at work here. An organization that your brother inno-cently stumbled upon. And I wish to dear God I had not. Remember our Satanists? Subjects of many anecdotes—who could ever take them seriously? Here and in Armavir, where we were quartered before being shipped across the Caspian Sea, they were not so amusing. As a matter of fact, my hair begins to stand up when I think back to the first time I had a glimpse behind that fateful black curtain.

A simple flirtation. A young blond nurse on my troop train, Lida Lwovitsh, and a coincidence, of course, she was a classmate of Nata Tai in St. Petersburg. She introduced me to her circle of friends. In the center, a jolly, sophisticated chief surgeon, Doctor Bobrov, another doctor, Sologub, an angry-looking man with a shaved head, medical students, nurses, and the handsome Rotmistr Klenov, cavalry squadron comman-der. Very pleasant people, on the surface.

Evenings of tea and vodka, long conversations, kisses, and embraces . . . and suddenly the earth core did not feel as solid as before. A new nurse arrived, the actress Solnzeva, the star of our Theater Farce, the one who performs au naturel. Oh, she is very attentive to me and pleasant. But Kuzmenko's wife, here? I did not like it. And masquarading as a simple army nurse?

"Hey, Chaikin." Alexey snatched one of the bottles from the returning cornet and climbed after him into their boxcar and onto his bed. He felt he needed the vodka now. The memories? Alexey took a long sip. Back to Krasnovodsk.

Doctor Bobrov was standing over his cot, a bottle of cognac in his hand, his eyes bright red, more intense than the desert sunset, hypnotizing, frightening. "You must tell me, Alyosha, all you know about Nata Tai. I do not wish to harm you, you must believe me. But some of my associates are not so benevolent. Please, I implore you." And he listened as I told him everything, Lucy, Lucy, even the most intimate details. And he was not shocked, but I could detect some disappointment on his catlike face. He let me drink the cognac. He thoughtfully studied me as if still doubting me. How could he? I was completely hypnotized. How could I not tell him the truth?

"Alyosha," he said, and I will never, ever forget it, "you are a Christian. As such, you are my enemy. I and my friends, we worship quite another savior. We are interested, very much so, in Nata Tai because she may have an item which is of no use to her or to anybody else for that matter . . . except us. It has great spiritual value for us. Much more so than Jesus's garments or the Holy Grail or the nails used on the cross, any of your religious artifacts. And we will possess it. For reasons I cannot go into, we must possess it soon."

"What is it?"

At times like this, Lucy, I must force myself to keep my mouth shut, very tight.

"It is possibly a meteorite."

"Doctor"—I could not believe my ears—"you have hypnotized me, forced me to reveal my relationship to Nata Tai, threatened me, told me some nonsense about religious artifacts—and I am not even so religious. And you are looking for some meteorite?" I drank a whole cup of cognac to calm down. "So you believe in the devil. Ask him where it is. And if you do find Nata, ask her, she would gladly give it to you. Why not?"

"It is not as simple as that. Her mother was one of us and then she betrayed us. Her father desecrated this object and the temple in which it was enshrined. He paid a terrible price for his deed. Nata is a complicated young woman. She may try to seek revenge." He sighed, yet there was a worried look on his face. "She may even succeed, in the very beginning. In the end, it would be a pity . . ."

"How can all this possibly concern me?"

"This meteorite, if it is a meteorite, follows a strange path. We do not know for what purpose. If it should cross the path of your life, however, you must contact us. You have to, for the sake of yourself and anyone you love."

"How do I do this?"

"A very simple drawing will suffice. Like this one." He drew with his pencil a crude, funny Chort with horns, hoofs, and a tail, as from some Russian fairy tale for children. "You can draw something like that? Leave it in your room, on a desk in your office, in a book you are reading, on a restaurant table after dinner, in the bedroom of a woman you spent a night with."

"I will," I promised. Just to get you away from me, I will. What a group of lunatics! Lucy, Lucy, this bloody Civil War is raging on, hundreds of thousands of people are being killed, if not millions. And these people are looking for some meteorite?

"You will be justly rewarded. The Lord of all that is dead and living and as yet unborn must be obeyed. Do not ever betray us because the punishment will be a slow and very, very painful death." Now he looked like a vampire instead of a cat. I could have sworn there were fangs under his thin red lips.

"I will tell you if I come across it," I repeated. What does this mad doctor want me to do? Sign something in my blood? Bobrov wished me goodnight and left. A few minutes later, silently as a ghost, Lida entered my room. Her long blond hair, scarlet lips, slender naked body underneath her army overcoat. She told me to turn off the light. Not quite Nata's paradise she gave me, but close to it, Lucy, disturbingly close.

The next day went very slowly. I was rewriting a long order for ammunition, late in the afternoon, when Chaikin ran into my room and happily announced, "They arrested several commissars just now: Bobrov, he was the head of Kharkov Cheka; his nurse, Lida, she was his secretary, shot the imprisoned officers herself; Klenov, he was the biggest one, Lenin's personal emissary; and others . . . I just came from the counterintelligence." Chaikin was still talking when two grim-looking Volunteers carrying rifles with bayonets entered the room and unceremoniously pushed him aside.

"Here." One of them threw a piece of paper on my desk.

"Come," said the other one.

It was a small pink piece of paper. Pink is definitely not my color. It said that Porutchik Makarov of the counterintelligence wished to see Volunteer Lebedev immediately, in his office.

Oh, Lucy, Lucy, I hope and pray that you are still alive. I hope and pray that we shall meet again. So many stars are now above the desert. Perhaps one of them is reserved for us. Alexey listened to Chaikin snoring and put his bottle of vodka aside. *Dear God,* he crossed himself, *take my life if you must, but please, please, spare my sister. What sort of madness are we living through? Are we specks of dust in the strongest of all hurricanes? My country, the people I love, my dreams, dead, scattered, distorted. All I have is my imagination, my carbine, and the grenades which we will probably exchange for more vodka. And the sands, and then the inevitable bullet, hopefully in the head or the heart. Dear God, if you exist, why do you let maggots like Doctor Bobrov scatter about the dying body of my homeland? Please deliver me from these lunatics. Send them all to hell. They worship Chort; that is where they belong anyway. As for Nata, she may be a sinner, she may be a whore . . . but was not Maria Magadalene a prostitute? Yet you forgave her. Forgive Nata too, and if she wants to take revenge on these bastards who probably killed her father, please let her realize her revenge. She does have a soul, don't believe what-ever anyone tells you. She has love in her heart. Let her live wherever she is, let her be happy, let us meet again, at least one more time.*

Every night it was more and more difficult to sleep. *Thank you, God, for this vodka.* It was quiet now. Bolsheviks would usually fire a dozen shots at three or four in the morning, just to keep the Whites awake. They had two cannons, but they seldom fired them. Probably had only a few shells left.

Eh, Makarov, Alexey sipped the vodka and then drank some water, *why did you have to be so proud, so principled? You could have been sitting here with me now, at the edge of the earth, not buried in it. We could have drunk this vodka, talked about God and the devil and why people worship one or the other. And how people change so much with each passing day. Why bother putting the bullet into your head?*

Alexey remembered sitting in Makarov's office so well, answering his questions, lying. He should have told Makarov the truth. Truth? Would it have made any difference? Did he know Doctor Bobrov? Oh yes, but not very well. And Lida? Her body, yes, once he promised to be a good child and behave. Any Communist propaganda discussed? Ridiculous.

"What was discussed? What did Bobrov want from you?" Makarov was playing the game with skill.

"Nothing."

"Come on, Lebedev. Do you take me for an idiot?"

"No, I do not."

"Then talk to me. Did you discuss films, for example, or an actress perhaps, one Nata Tai?"

"Yes—no—perhaps we did."

"I also graduated from St. Vladimir's University, three years ahead of you. Law faculty. Gold medal. I too have lived in Kiev all my life. I was introduced to your mother and your sister, once. I observed you enter Nata Tai's house less than two months ago. And not come out until late the following morning."

"You were spying on me?"

"No," Makarov laughed. "But we kept her house under surveillance because an important commissar was trying to contact her."

"You must have had an interesting time."

"Duty, Lebedev. Now tell me, have you ever seen a drawing

such as this?" He pushed the crude Chort to me, Lucy . . . Lucy . . . *I am going to write all this in my next historical letter to her,* he decided.

"Of course, thousands of times, every Russian child has."

"Recently?"

"No."

"Are you telling me the truth?"

"No . . . Yes, I am telling you the truth."

"You, Lebedev, you have chosen to serve our cause, you took the oath, what are your beliefs?"

"I do believe in our cause, in defeating Bolsheviks, freeing our country."

"And you are Russian Orthodox Christian; do you believe in God?"

"I certainly do."

"And the devil, Lebedev, do you believe in, let us say, a Chort such as this one?"

"No . . . I really do not think so."

"Why not?"

"I just do not think I believe in the devil or in hell, except perhaps for really bad people."

"How interesting; then you do believe in hell?"

"With all due respect, Porutchik Makarov, what does this have to do with me being here?"

"Have you met anyone recently who told you that he or she was a Bolshevik?"

"No." And that was the truth. Alexey could not get Makarov's intelligent face, gray eyes, and close-cropped hair out of his mind. He graduated with a gold medal? Only a handful of graduates in Alexey's memory had achieved this honor. What was he doing here?

"Perhaps someone mentioned to you that they believed in

someone who is the exact opposite of our Lord Jesus Christ? Recently? A Chort even?"

"No."

"What sort of an object were Doctor Bobrov and his companions searching for? Do not be concerned about their reprisals. They are safely in jail and will be shot for something not related to what we are discussing now."

What could I do? I had to reply quickly. Yes, no? To swim or to sink?

"Lebedev, I can order you held in solitary confinement, and after you come to your senses, question you in a way you will not like. Not at all. I will get the truth out of you, believe me. Why not give it to me now?"

"Fine, but you will not believe me anyway. Bobrov told me they were looking for a meteorite."

Makarov was thoughtful, not at all surprised. "Try to remember what else Bobrov told you regarding this meteorite. For example, how large it is, its color, shape?"

"He did not say. But he did say that they had to find it rather quickly."

"For what reason?"

"He did not get into it. He, he actually hypnotized me and I told him everything about myself and Nata Tai. Everything."

"Was he interested in anyone else?"

"No . . . Nata Tai's mother was one of them and then betrayed them, and her father desecrated this meteorite somehow. And Bobrov was a little concerned that Nata might take revenge . . . They did kill her father, I believe."

"Enough of this nonsense, Lebedev. Forget I ever asked you about Nata Tai. Here, read this and sign."

Thank God this was a white piece of paper, a standard form saying that as a member of the Armed Forces of South Russia

I would continue to serve my country with my heart, my body, and my mind until the Bolsheviks were defeated and Russia was free. I signed it, Lucy, with great, great relief.

"You are free to go. Wait, Lebedev, have you seen Kuzmenko recently? Kuzmenko of the Garrison Regiment—the devil, I believe his soldiers called him—have you seen him here?"

"No, and I hope I never will."

"I share your sentiments . . . entirely."

The plot thickened, and Alexey decided to take a few more swallows of vodka. *So quiet tonight. Maybe the Bolsheviks will let us sleep?* The regimental adjutant flew into Makarov's cabinet. He whispered urgently into the porutchik's ear. Something like: "General, vitally important . . ."

"Sit here, Lebedev, I will be right back. There is one more thing I just remembered to ask you." He put the files in his desk, locked it, and told me not to move. Now, Lucy, comes an interesting part.

In front of me was a window looking out on a pleasant yard, with flowers and palms, sunshine, and another white house where our front commander General Koza had lived. Lucy, I will write all this in my neat scholarly handwriting and send it to you the first thing tomorrow afternoon.

Koza's window was wide open, and I heard angry shouts. One voice, a tenor, was Makarov's, another, the deep basso of our battalion commander, a drunkard and a bully who was getting replaced. "Scoundrel, liar!" shouted the basso.

"No, your Excellency, an officer upholding the law and fulfilling his task."

"Liar, bastard," basso.

"I have proof," tenor.

The general himself entered the argument with: "Ba, ba, ba, boo, boo, boo," and, "Children, children, nerves, nerves . . ."

"He sees Bolsheviks under every bush," basso.

"I have proof, and I demand that I be allowed to finish my investigation," tenor.

"The battalion is in the troop train already, and this little bastard wants to endanger the front?" basso.

"The battalion must be delayed or there will not be any front. I demand more time, at least twenty-four hours." The tenor, at this point, had made a big mistake.

"Demand? Baba . . . boo. Porutchik, you are forgetting who you are. I am the commander here and my word is holy. It is the law, baba, ba . . ."

"No, your Excellency, you are not the law. And I am not serving you." Makarov was nearly hysterical. "I am serving my homeland and the Volunteer Army and I shall continue doing so until I die."

"Ba, ba." The window was shut. Minutes later, Makarov returned, red splotches on his face. He looked crushed and dazed.

"Lebedev, what are you doing here? Go back to your duties. Do not be concerned. Go, go."

I, of course, did not argue. Later that afternoon, the adjutant gave me an order to copy. It said that Porutchik Makarov was being transferred, to better utilize his skills, as a junior officer of the Volunteer company of the First Battalion.

Chaikin ran into my office just as I was ready to go eat supper and screamed so rapidly that at first I did not understand him: "Bobrov, Klenov, and Lida Lvowitsh escaped from the city jail, and Porutchik Makarov was shot in the head, an apparent suicide."

The vodka was finally working. There were four shots in the distance. Silence. Alexey placed his head on the softest part of his knapsack and looked at the stars until his eyes closed.

"Stop shaking me." Chaikin was standing over him, fully dressed, holding his rifle with a bayonet, his two revolvers, and his grenades, looking serious.

"Wish me luck, Alyosha. We are going on a reconnaissance mission." Alexey could see the gloomy Volunteer squad, all twenty-seven men standing outside the boxcar.

"Why you?" he mumbled. "What happened to the scouts?"

"They are gone."

Chaikin did not elaborate.

"Wait." Alexey sat up. *I do have this self-destructive streak in me,* he thought. "Wait until I get my tanks tied. I will go with you." He hurried with his stupid British half-boots/half-shoes with long strings, aptly called tanks. He thought about whether he should take his rifle or his carbine, decided on the carbine, took three grenades just in case, and all but ran after Chaikin. Off they walked into the gray, predawn desert.

The plan was to get about two kilometers away from the railway line, then swing south toward the Red positions to where their artillery was supposed to be, and see if the Reds were being reinforced, how far south their front extended, and, if possible, to take a few prisoners. With Chaikin leading them, however, they soon got lost. One big sand dune after another. No sign of the enemy. And the sun was coming up. There were faint noises up ahead: voices, laughter.

They crept to the top of the dune and saw quite a sight: several cooks, large steaming pots, two donkeys standing near two canvas-covered wagons, fires burning under the pots, and cooks cutting meat and vegetables.

"Smells so good," one of the Volunteers next to Alexey sighed.

"Perhaps we . . ." Alexey saw that Chaikin's eyes were shining. He stood up with his revolver and fired in the direction of the cooks, then screamed something incoherent and ran toward them. The herd instinct was strong, and Alexey and the rest of the Volunteers rushed after Chaikin toward the Red's kitchen, shooting mostly into the air.

The cooks were astounded. They dropped whatever they were doing and ran, even their donkeys ran after them. Chaikin threw two grenades after the fleeing cooks. Although the grenades fell short of their mark, the explosions must have woken up the entire Red front. And the White front as well.

As they kept chasing the cooks, another dune and a panorama unfolded. Here was a station in total chaos. The Red soldiers were running back and forth, trying to get organized. From the White side came heavy machine-gun and rifle fire. Apparently, the new battalion commander had decided to attack. The Reds panicked and began to load into their troop train. The train did not remain long at their station. As soon as the locomotive was hooked up, it rolled out fast, leaving scores of their soldiers running after it.

Alexey thought, *No more than ten minutes have passed since the encounter with the cooks and the Whites have taken the station. A glorious swift victory! And a great one at that, because now there is enough water for everybody.*

A thousand buckets a day, the native advisor, a sad-looking porutchik, told them. Everyone was elated. The Reds had also left behind their two cannons and a considerable amount of food and ammunition. Victory.

Only the native, sad-looking advisor was shaking his head in disapproval.

Why? he was asked.

"Because the Bolsheviks have to come back. There is no more water along the entire railroad line from here to Ashkhabad." Upon hearing this, the captain ordered all men to build makeshift showers and to start seriously killing the lice population.

Alexey was told to catalogue all the inventory the Reds had left behind. The captain also asked him to write a glowing report for headquarters.

"Why are you writing that we took only fifty prisoners?" he asked Alexey.

"Actually, Chaikin told me we took only fifteen."

"Put down five hundred." The captain, a pleasant-enough elderly man with a droopy mustache, smiled. "Who is going to count them?" Alexey added another zero. "Good, let General Koza be happy, that old fool."

This was the first night, in the strange Asian land, that Alexey slept soundly. He felt clean after the shower; he washed his underwear. The stars were shining for only a minute or two. His stomach was full of the rice and lamb they had liberated from the Reds. His mind relaxed from a glass of vodka left over from last night. Sleep. No rifle shots all night.

In the morning, after a tasty breakfast of fried pork and potatoes with tea, Chaikin spoiled the atmosphere with his usual hysterical screaming. "They killed them, murderers!" He shook his fist in the direction of three officers, all captains, who comprised the special department of the battalion. "I know," he screamed, "you killed all prisoners last night! I saw the bodies. You fucking bastards!" The officers silently left the table. "Alyosha," Chaikin sat next to him, "these morons are the ones who ought to be shot, not our prisoners. And you know what? More than two hundred Frenchmen went over to the Reds during the night. Our days here are numbered."

"So what can we do? We cannot even run away, there is no place to go. Where can we escape? To Krasnovodsk, and then where?"

"You are quite right, Alyosha, we are doomed. I was thinking of taking my Volunteers and you and two wagons and cutting south to Persia, only it is more than three hundred kilometers over sand, swamps, and mountains. Not possible, because if the Reds don't kill us, the natives will. And do you know what our captain did just now? To show that he is seriously committed to defending the station, he ordered our troop train to roll back half a kilometer and our two boxcars are to be unhooked at the station. That way, he thinks we will not run as fast as the Bolsheviks." *Damn, Damn, I don't want to die right now*, thought Alexey. *I am only twenty-three. It is nice to be fatalistic when nothing immediate threatens you, not so wonderful if you really are destined to die. And in these sands? Without even a white Orthodox cross over my grave?*

To make matters worse, there was no more vodka anywhere. The deserting Frenchmen had taken it all with them. "Do not be so sad, Alyosha." Chaikin grinned. "Where there are soldiers, there will always be vodka. This is a temporary setback. Believe me, before we die, the Turkomans will sell us a few bottles."

"What do we pay them with, our blood?"

"Who knows? Perhaps we will sell them the cannons the Reds left behind."

Among the pitifully small amount of medical supplies that the Reds had left was a small bottle of pure alcohol. Alexey carefully omitted its entry into his catalogue. This bottle was sent from heaven. Three parts water, one part this bottle, Chaikin decided, and they had two half-liter bottles. One for them, one for the other two Volunteers in their boxcar—the medic and the supply clerk.

Another night of bliss. This time no shots at all. Alexey woke up to an eerie silence. Amazingly, the sun was already high and the red brick station house was aglow. But there were no soldiers around. Chaikin and his Volunteers were gone somewhere. *I suppose he didn't want to wake me up.* Alexey was grateful for that. The supply clerk and the medic were still sleeping on their narrow beds. Alexey dressed leisurely, stretched, and went to the station to get his breakfast.

There was no one in the station, and the kitchen looked abandoned. The pots, the porridge, the bread, and the tea were ready and waiting, but not a soul was in sight. A feeling that something was terribly wrong emerged somewhere in the pit of Alexey's stomach. Suddenly he was not hungry.

An impulse, something, made him return to his boxcar, grab his rifle, and wake up the other Volunteers. The three of them peered out with their rifles loaded, cursing the fact that the boxcar was unhooked from the troop train and they were stranded. Silence, so eerie, so frightening, and then sounds of singing. A male chorus singing the "Internationale," coming from the direction of the water tower and moving closer and closer.

Another minute, and Alexey was viewing a very strange procession. Leading a band of about fifty ragtag men with rifles and red armbands was a miracle of nature—an enormously fat, Oriental-looking man sitting atop a camel. How could this mountain sit on top of the camel, and how could the camel carry it? The mountain was wearing a bright red turban, and it was followed by about a dozen horsemen, some with rifles, all wearing red armbands. One was carrying a torn red banner. The mountain rode slowly toward the well and the station house. Suddenly, from the dunes on both sides of the station, at least two hundred Frenchmen appeared. They seemed very happy to see the mountain and his ragtag band. They waved red handkerchiefs, threw their rifles on the ground, and joined in the singing of the "Internationale." The procession proceeded majestically until, near the well, the battalion commander, screaming like a madman and waving a sword, ran in front of the Frenchmen and urged them to fire on the Reds. When they did not, he reached for his pistol.

Three skinny sailors from the ragtag band ran up to him and, before he could fire, knocked him down with the butts of their rifles. At this point, the ragtag gang and the well-dressed Frenchmen mixed together with brotherly embraces. The huge mountain on the camel and his horsemen watched with approval. The battalion commander managed somehow to wrestle a rifle from the sailors clubbing him and shot one, but the other sailors knocked him down again. This time the mountain said something quietly to one of his horsemen, and he in turn relayed the message to the sailors beating the captain. The sailors shouted to the crowd. The soldiers stopped embracing each other and backed off to watch. One of the sailors tore off the captain's trousers, and another forced him to bend down, stuck the barrel of his rifle into the captain's buttocks, and pulled the trigger. But the captain was not killed right away. He screamed and crawled on the ground, and they used his own sword and bayonets to hack him to pieces.

This is the time for us, now or never! Alexey and his friends jumped from their boxcar, fired in the general direction of the mountain, and ran toward their troop train which was

slowly pulling out, rolling north. It was not much of a problem to catch it because the railroad tracks on the north side
made an almost complete circle before turning toward
Krasnovodsk. And they would have escaped, except the mountain sent half his horsemen after them. The horsemen over-
took them less than a hundred meters from the train. Once
caught, they were dragged back. Their wrists were bound
behind their backs with barbed wire and they were put along
the station house wall, where some twenty Volunteers and officers who had been captured earlier were already standing,
glumly awaiting execution.

It appeared to Alexey that it would not be long now, as a
wooden cart driven by a donkey appeared along the railroad
line, and on that cart sat a sailor with a shiny new Lewis
machine gun. Three of the faces of the horsemen surrounding the mountain of flesh looked familiar—Doctor Bobrov,
Klenov, and a lock of blond hair under the Cossack hat with a
red star—Lida. They too recognized Alexey, and Lida even
smiled.

Then Alexey's attention shifted to another man on the
right of the mountain, who said only one word: "Student."
Alexey groaned. "You did not give me away to counterintelligence." Kuzmenko grinned and turned to the mountain.
"Can we spare his life?" Before the mountain had a chance to
reply, a dapper French sergeant stepped from the crowd of
soldiers and walked up to the camel.

"As a member of the Russian Communist Party and the
chairman of the Revolutionary Committee of the First
Battalion, I demand that all White bandits and their officers be
put to death. Volunteer Lebedev must not be an exception."

Kuzmenko whistled loudly, winked at Alexey, and grinned
even wider. His white teeth were shining almost as bright as the

barrel of the machine gun, which was now not more than fifty meters away. The mountain with the red turban made an almost imperceptible motion with one of his hands. It held a curved, very long saber, and that saber very neatly severed the head of the dapper sergeant. It rolled off his body like a head of cabbage. He then wiped the saber with his sleeve. *So much for the chairman.* Alexey thought that to demand anything in these parts was a big mistake.

Some of the Frenchmen did not like it. They stopped embracing their ragtag brothers and rumbled menacingly. Some even picked up their rifles.

"Untie this student," Kuzmenko ordered, still grinning. The horrible barbed wire was gone. Alexey rubbed his hands to restore the circulation. "You smoke, student?"

"Yes!" Alexey shouted.

"Catch." Kuzmenko threw down a portcigar with a naked women embossed in gold on red leather.

Alexey's fingers could barely move. He opened the case slowly and put the papirossa in his mouth. He was now certain that they would shoot him anyway. Kuzmenko was just having the last laugh. As an open act of defiance, Alexey stuck the portcigar in his pocket. *Let the devil retrieve it from me after I am dead.*

Suddenly there were loud explosions. Alexey saw the mountain of flesh slide awkwardly off the camel and fall to the ground. Kuzmenko galloped away with the rest of the horsemen, except for Lida, who also fell on the ground, her beautiful blond hair covered with blood. Bullets whistled and, when another grenade exploded, Alexey saw that the cart with the machine gun was overturned and the sailor was dead.

Several Volunteers led by Chaikin were running toward them. Another miracle, the troop train was rolling back into the station. "Hurry, hurry!" Chaikin screamed.

Alexey untied the men next to him, and they untied others, and everyone ran to the train. Two Volunteers hooked up their boxcars, and the train rolled north before the Reds had a chance to regroup and attack.

Alexey did not realize that he was wounded until they were several kilometers away and somebody pointed out that he was bleeding. He had been shot through the palm of his right hand just below his small finger.

"Good wound," Chaikin approved. "Enough to send you to the Caucasus, out of our trap."

It turned out that Chaikin, the real hero, had had to shoot the engineer in the leg to force the train back to the station. "I was going to shoot him in his testicles next and he knew it." Chaikin laughed. "I do wish I was wounded like you, Alyosha. Now I have to steal a fishing boat and try to get over to the Caucasus and out of this fucking country. Even if I have to shine boots somewhere on the Riviera . . . Beautiful women, blue sea, life. I am through with bullets and lice and bedbugs and Bolsheviks and generals. I want to sniff the flowers, drink champagne. Enough of this bad vodka too . . . What are you going to do? You return to Kiev and it is the Cheka dungeon, and a bullet in the back of your head."

"I have an uncle in Novorossyisk, a dentist. The Bolsheviks will not get that far south."

"You wish to place a wager on that?"

"Oh, Mishka." Alexey seldom used Chaikin's first name, but tonight he felt tenderness toward this brave man who was even younger than he. "I love this woman who is so, so unreachable. I cannot even reveal her name to you. You will laugh and call me a liar. She is so beautiful and so wealthy, and talented and famous. And I am nothing."

"I will believe you, Alyosha, you are not as good a liar as you think."

"Nata Tai. And I feel she loves me too, but in a very strange way . . . I have received a letter from her."

"I saw every film she ever made, all nine of them." Chaikin sighed. "I saw *The Orphans of the Storm* and *By Sword Alone* at least four times. As for the *Star of the Orient . . .*"

"My hand hurts now and I cannot sleep. So tell me something. Have you ever encountered Satanists?"

This surprised Chaikin almost as much as Nata Tai. "I heard rumors. I mean, before the Revolution, of course. And even now, some say that a general next to Denikin, this Romanovsky . . . No, I have never personally encountered any Satanists and I hope I never will."

"I have. They are everywhere in Russia and they are looking for some meteorite. You can sleep with one of them, a beautiful blond woman, and then leave a message, a drawing of Chort—you know, a funny Chort—in the morning. And they are watching me now. Do you see these red eyes, the insane hatred in them, floating just outside our door . . . Do you hear them laugh?"

"Alyosha, I did not realize this vodka was so bad." Chaikin smacked his lips. "Try to relax, please, or I will have nightmares."

At a polustanok where their train finally stopped, a medic examined Alexey's hand. He was a sympathetic Volunteer, a medical student. Nothing was really damaged, and in time Alexey could even move his little finger. But it was a great wound in terms of getting a leave of absence and disappearing. The medic changed the bandage and gave Alexey a shot of morphine to ease the pain. Unlike that first time Alexey tried morphine in Nata's bedroom, he now had quite another reaction. Pleasant, relaxing. He felt warm and glowing and he almost instantly fell asleep.

By morning the train had reached the Caspian Sea. The day was gray; it looked like it was going to rain. Regardless of what the medical student had said about his wound, his hand hurt. It had swelled up and he could not move any of his fingers. He had to open the blue perfumed envelope holding Nata's letter with his left hand. He had received it on the troop train headed to the front. Front? One day earlier and Bobrov would have known where she lives. A lucky coincidence. Or was it? He read the letter at least six times, and each time found something new in it. He almost memorized it.

October 12, 1919
The town of Sumy

Alyosha, my love, my dearest one,

You must be shocked that I am writing to you, that I remember you. Oh, I remember you often and our good moments together. What do I have now? Epaulets and needles, beards and mustaches, sweaty hands and ugly faces. My bed and other beds, morphine and champagne, and the wet, slippery mud. That mud, my heart, my body, my thoughts, and even my dreams are forever covered with that cold slippery autumn mud. You have noticed, of course, the city is not our dear Kiev. Why Sumy? The deepest province. Why not London or Paris or the dives of

San Francisco, as Vertinski sings, and cocaine paints the blizzard? I have millions of admirers, Alyosha, and I am writing only to you, my young green-eyed prince, my love. There was another prince for me in another life, but I have lost him. I am a witch without my warlock. It is six o'clock in the morning. I see the mud slipping through my curtains and that mud now has a reddish color, exactly the color of earth in the graves by the river.

I was en route to Paris. A compartment in a blue Pullman, champagne on ice. A few days in the Crimea, in a large palace. A white French luxury liner.

Ah, the river, gray as a lead bullet. And the graves. The nauseating smell. The reality of madness was there before my eyes. "Your father, beyond any doubt," an officer told me. "You'd better not look." He gave me a papirossa and lit it. I saw the body being pulled out of a reddish mud. I saw everything they had done to him. And now I am here because one of them, one of the people responsible, these horrible, vicious, insane people, is here. He exists today, but tomorrow, the next day, he will be with that funny Russian Chort of yours. What I do to him will be highly unpleasant, but his real suffering will begin after he is dead and will not end for all eternity. They think I am cursed. Foolish people. They have no power except perhaps the power of their own illusion. That little funny Chort, however, is quite another matter. The hapless hero of so many Russian fairy tales? He, or perhaps she, or it, what gender does the devil belong to? Not so little and not so funny . . . but why should you be concerned? In your reality, when you touch someone, it is a touch of summer wind, soft, caring. Everyone I touch, well . . . Enough nonsense.

Do you think I am on a cocaine binge? Not quite, not

yet. How strange when you see your flesh and blood being carried in a gray army blanket, being placed alongside other bodies. And the river is still flowing, people are fishing. I am alone now. Me and a sea of slimy reddish mud. I am lying; I am not alone. One of my lovers here is young handsome Baron Levenvolde. Lately he looks so sad, and when he looks sad he reminds me of you. Soon, soon, I will finish my task here, and on to Paris. Will you come with me, Alyosha? I know you are still alive. Pray that we shall meet again. Pray before this reddish mud and armored trains and evil people drown all the kindness and love. Pray for me. Before someone who is outside my window will laugh and that laughter will tear apart a thousand hearts, torn to shreds within one's body.

I want to kiss you as I did this summer, so very hard, in your Russian fashion, three times on your mouth. So hard, your lips will hurt for a week. Close your eyes, Alyosha, imagine my face, my body, my mouth.

Yours completely and always,
Nata

The provincial Town of Sumy central Russia November 1919

A blinding SNOWSTORM, THE HOWLS OF DEMONS AND whispers of ghosts, frightening, deadly, and overpowering. One night, hundreds of shiny white mountains appeared where the houses once stood. An endless silent polar landscape, where nothing moved. Then a sun came up, an unusually warm sun. *Hope, freedom*, it was saying to the white frozen earth. And the sun melted away the mountains. The roofs appeared again, and the windows. People came out and shook their heads in amazement, seeing the swift rivers of mud and slush. In the evening, it rained. At night, another blizzard once again terrified anything that was alive. It covered the bodies of the dead, and even the fierce, desperate fighting came to a brief halt.

By the cathedral square, the snow and ice had dressed the small trees planted just before the Revolution with angels and stars and diamonds, reflecting some of the lights from the windows of the small shops—mystical designs of tropical forests, of fairy-tale kingdoms, all painted by Grandfather Frost.

Suddenly, a strong gust of arctic wind blew the illusion apart. Everything disappeared and the windows themselves were shattered as the artillery booms, along with the demons and ghosts, once again began their macabre dance. Late-night pedestrians ran toward the warmth of their houses. Warmth, however, was in short supply. There was no coal and very little firewood.

Due to the deep snow, the train from Kharkov was six hours late. The fact that it arrived at all was a miracle. The snow was only one factor. The latest news from the front was about as frightening as the wind and the blizzards. The front was collapsing just like the fairy-tale decorations in the window of a small shop. And the railroad timetables and the railroads themselves and everything that was outside this wind, ice, and artillery fire, was descending directly into hell. This was the last train from Kharkov, the last train from anywhere. Yesterday the news from the front was that the Reds had taken Vorozhba, a key station only fifty kilometers to the north.

The Sumy station, a Germanic-looking one-story building of red brick was well lit. The station clock worked—it was ten minutes past two. There were only a few passengers on the train, and they were all military men, officers. An old coachman with a horse-drawn sled sleeping near the station, covered with ten sheepskins, was overjoyed to see the passengers. He had been told to wait by the town's commandant. The orders were to stay and wait for the train or be shot. The officers ran to his sled as if this were their only salvation. They ran fast.

The first to reach the sled was a tall thin man resembling one of the telephone poles outside the station. He roughly pushed the others aside, ordered the coachman to hurry, and added, "To the Grand Hotel."

At the Grand Hotel—the only hotel in town—the telephone pole strolled into the lobby, awakened the startled hotel clerk, and, holding the clerk by his collar and looking at him with sleepy fish eyes, whispered, "Get me the barber."

In the barbershop, which had somehow managed to retain some of its pre-revolutionary décor—even the leather was not torn off the seats—Monsieur Pierre, a tiny man with a pencil mustache, lathered the dirty tired face and sharpened his blade. "Your Excellency must change and drive to tonight's ball," he murmured sweetly, applying a hot scented towel to the officer's temple. "Oh, of course, it is still in progress. Yes, until dawn. Of course, we have the most beautiful women in Russia. There is Mademoiselle Poplavskaya. Magnificent. Princess Baratova. They are the stars, the moon, yet we have one who outshines them all. Please guess—Napoleon retreats, his wounded marshal and his bodyguards are suddenly surrounded by a band of Cossacks. The bodyguards are cut to ribbons. A young Cossack jumps off and walks toward the French general. Of course, *By Sword Alone,* and the young Cossack is, of course, the one and the most magnificent woman in film as well as in real life—Nata Tai. She is here, and I am not lying. She appeared one day and she is still here, I swear it." He lowered his voice. "For a modest reward, I can arrange a meeting."

The thin officer threw the towel off his face and looked the barber over. Monsieur Pierre felt his knees tremble. The officer not only had the eyes of a dead fish, but there was something fatalistic and frightening in his evil ugly smile. "You can arrange a meeting with Nata Tai?" he snarled.

"Of course. I am possibly exaggerating somewhat, but your Excellency, she is there at the Cadet Corps building, right now. His Excellency can . . ."

The officer silently paid the barber two pound-sterling notes and slowly walked into the icy street. The streets were empty; even the dogs were not barking. An occasional horse-drawn sled carried laughing couples, officers, and their ladies in furs toward the sea of lights, the Cadet Corps building, toward the loud music and the dancing silhouettes in the large windows. The officer coughed and walked purposefully in the direction of the building. It was cold. He put both hands into the pockets of his fur-lined overcoat. The hand in the right pocket still felt cold due to the steel of his Luger automatic. The other hand rested next to a thick envelope.

A dozen steps, and he furtively looked around. His fish eyes were now sparkling, alert. The Bolsheviks did not know about his mission, the officer was certain of that. But that other force, the one that seemed to control everything and everyone in Russia these days, that was quite another matter. He remembered well how the two soldiers of that dark force— Oleg Zorin and Stacy Averescu, the pianist—shot at Prince Orechov-Maisky so skillfully and swiftly that he, Staff Captain Sobolev, his Excellency's most faithful servant and friend, could not shield the prince in time. Destiny alone intervened. The prince's portcigar in the upper left pocket of his tunic deflected three of four bullets.

The prince was recovering rather well. From his palace in Gurzuf, he had sent Sobolev on a mission which could not fail. Outwardly, so simple: to bring back to his Crimean palace a woman, one Nata Tai, a film actress of great renown, a whore, a user of morphine and cocaine, a murderess, and God only knows what else. The one woman the prince was totally obsessed with. To bring her back unharmed, if possible, but to bring her to him, no matter what.

Now Sobolev can hear the seductive waltz from Eugene

Onegin. "Why are you not dancing, Lensky?" Bright lights in the vestibule, warmth, a stairway covered by thick red carpet, well-dressed happy people. "Is there a war to end all wars going on now, Lensky, are we not dying out in the snow? Let us dance. Dance, Lensky!"

The second floor is decorated with tropical palms, white silk drapes, the three-color flags, regimental banners. In the huge ballroom, two orchestras, one from the valiant Drozdov Regiment, the other from the Cherkassian Division. A poet, his face painted white à la Vertinski, screams, "Champagne and pineapples! Pineapples and Irises! No pineapples in Russia? Let us all sail to Hawaii. Irises and lilacs, lilacs and vodka!"

Ah, Sobolev thinks, *this must be Baratova, in the purple gown with black stripes and emerald necklace, and Poplavskaya, a statuesque blond beauty, in the orange dress with rubies. Forget them, the other beauties.* Sobolev is not interested in women, charming, beautiful, even the rich.

Aha. Nata, the mystery. Long black velvet dress with a gold medallion, her eyes fixed on one man, at least for now. He is well-known to Sobolev. He is Baron Levenvolde, a handsome, young, spoiled nobleman. He guides her out of the ballroom. Sobolev follows.

"Champagne and roses!" cries the poet. The Cherkassian orchestra begins with loud trumpets: "March forward, Russia awaits you. Black Hussars . . . fill your glasses." A loud blast from a mortar which was rolled on the stage. The ladies shriek. The mortar's huge barrel is filled with confetti. Pineapples, roses, vodka, oh, give me some vodka.

Two very young porutchiks are sitting on the windowsill watching the floor. A waiter comes by with a tray full of glasses of champagne. One of the porutchiks takes the entire tray.

"Drink Pavlusha!" They drink all twelve glasses and give the tray and the empty glasses back to the angry waiter.

"Pavlusha, there is our idiot baron with Nata Tai. I swear it. I know; I have seen all her films. She is incredible, she is my love, my dreams."

Another waiter approaches, but turns away rather quickly. "Drink this Kolka." Pavlusha pulls out a metal flask from his pocket.

"What is it?" Kolka's body is exploding and drifting away.

"What is the difference? Live. Here." Pavlusha opens a matchbox and drops some white powder into his friend's palm.

"I want a woman, Pavlusha. I know I am going to die in the snowdrifts. You too." He embraces his friend. There are now real artillery booms close by, north of town. "Inhale, Kolka, and leave some for me."

Cold, invigorating, soothing white powder. In the dark classroom, Baron Levenvolde whispers tenderly, "Natochka, I love you; Natochka, be mine, here, now, anywhere." He too pours the powder on Nata's fist. She inhales it. "Nata, I want you so much, please."

"Do not be so boring."

"Natochka, I have the premonition. We are moving to the front tomorrow." The baron clutches her wrists, pushes her down on the floor.

"Not here, not here."

"Where?" His eyes are shining, his hands are moist. Dreams? Perhaps they do come true.

Nata laughs, her laughter is dry and ten times more intoxicating than cocaine. "In the gentlemen's room, with your officers, all of them, and you will be the last. These are my rules. You will be the last . . . yet satisfied."

The baron roars, his face contorted; he is on top of her.

"You are strangling me!" Nata screams. "Let go, I was joking; I will do what you wish."

Suddenly, Levenvolde rolls off her and lies motionless on the floor. Another officer's face, looking at her with some concern.

"Who are you?" She stands up.

"What did you do to this boy?"

"Nothing serious. You do not recognize me, Natalia Vladimirovna?" He turns on the light.

"No, wait . . ." The fish eyes are familiar. Where? Yes, the prince, his portable bar, Chateau Rothchild, beluga caviar, pastries, fruits, and behind the bar is the fish-eyed captain.

"Staff Captain Sobolev, at your service. I have a personal letter for you from his Excellency Prince Orechov-Maisky."

"But his Excellency is dead. I read the newspaper accounts. And I have talked to witnesses. Stacy and Oleg, these Bolshevik agents . . ."

"They are not Bolsheviks, as you well know. They are practicing Satanists. However, the prince is recovering, and it would speed up his recovery so very much if you would accompany me to his palace in Gurzuf."

Baron Levenvolde is beginning to move.

"Staff captain, please give me a papirossa." Sobolev gives her one and lights it. Nata sits on a desk, tears open the letter, and reads it.

"Are you familiar with its contents?" she asks.

"Yes, to a large extent."

Nata gives him back the letter and blows smoke in his face. "Staff captain, I do not wish to go."

"I beg you to reconsider."

Nata throws her papirossa away, opens her gold medallion,

and pours cocaine on the back of her slender hand. She inhales and looks once more at the fish eyes. "My decision is irreversible. I love it here in this provincial forgotten town. I have my house, my servants, my friends. And it is not as dull as you might imagine. There are concerts, balls, every night, another excitement . . . and as much cocaine as I need. No, I will not be a concubine, I do not wish to see Japan or Nizza or the Hawaiian Islands. Please inform the prince."

"Natochka, I apologize." The baron stands up and wipes the blood off his forehead. "Who are you?"

Sobolev ignores him. "So you do not pity the sick man?"

"Pity? I would imagine the prince would be horrified if he knew that I came to him out of pity. Now, staff captain, I and my friend, Baron Levenvolde, are going back to the ballroom. Would you care to accompany us?"

"In two days, our army will leave Sumy." Sobolev's voice is as hollow as the sound of artillery fire. "I shall remain at the Grand Hotel, in the event you should need my assistance."

Light snow. It is getting gray. A small, boarded-up house on the edge of town. A wooden sign on the front door:

E. Bobrov, Surgeon
S.E. Bobrov, Dentist

"Wait for me, Baron. I will not be long." Nata jumps off the sled leaving Baron Levenvolde and the two heavily armed Cossacks who are their escorts.

She has the key. She opens the door. There is no one in the house. She strikes a match and lights one of several candles on the table in the waiting room. Appropriately, a black candle. The trap door to the cellar has a heavy lock on it. Nata has the key for this lock as well.

There is an old wooden table, an open surgeon's leather case with various knives and scissors on top of it, some dentist tools. On the floor lies the body of a man, bound and gagged, in a pool of blood.

The man is barely alive, his rounded blue eyes pleading for mercy, anticipating more torture. Nata sits down on the only chair, searches in her handbag, takes out her portcigar and a papirossa, and lights it. She smokes, and notices that her hands tremble. What nonsense!

One of the gleaming knives she has not used as of yet. She picks it up, bends over the man, and cuts the scarf over his mouth—his gag. The man's lips are moving, but only some hoarse whispers escape, no other sounds. He cannot speak. Tears roll down his cheeks; he knows this is the end.

Nata puts her ear next to his lips to hear what he is whispering. "Prosti, forgive," over and over.

"I forgive you, Sergei." Nata closes her eyes for a moment, then slowly cuts his throat.

The clock next to Nata's bed rang four times. These sounds were louder than the artillery fire. Four in the afternoon and it was already getting dark. Heavy snow was falling. Nata got up, washed her face, combed her hair, and turned on the lamp on her night table. A miracle—the electricity worked. She sat on her pillows and opened at random a book she was reading. Ralph Nickelby was carefully plotting his moves. She could well learn from him. She heard the sounds of her doorbell, angry voices of men, and the cold replies of Matilda Franzevna.

"Who was it today?" Nata asked when Matilda Franzevna brought her a cup of black coffee and a piece of toasted white bread, Nata's usual daytime diet.

"Baron Levenvolde came six times. He pleaded and cried about some premonition. I was almost tempted to let him in, he is such a beautiful young man."

"Who else?"

"An ugly, very thin officer, Sobolev, four times."

"He expects me to leave with him to Gurzuf; he is the prince's servant."

"We should leave, Natochka. Let us depart. There are rumors that the town is about to be evacuated. If true, and if the Bolsheviks arrive . . . you know what they did to your father."

"Yes." Nata choked on her coffee. "But they will do nothing to me. I am destined to live. You see, Matilda Franzevna, they need me, my name, more than the Whites. The Whites have Vera Holodnaya and Tamara and Maya, and who do the Reds have? Faina, and who else? Believe me, any commissar who discovers that I am still in Russia will get an extra gold star. And I do miss the cameras, the excitement . . ."

"You can have it all in the Crimea. They are making films there too. Or in Paris. New York. The Bolsheviks, they are truly beasts."

"They are not very much different from our generals. But you may be right. I had unfinished business here in Sumy. Now it is complete. Nothing really for me to do here now. Yes, there is something—go prepare my red dress. There is a ball tonight in honor of the Wild Kuban Cossack Division. General Shkuro himself will be there. Hurry."

"I think, Natochka, you should let that ugly captain know that you wish to leave, first. So he can make arrangements."

"Go, Matilda Fanzevna. The night is young."

Nata leaned back and closed her eyes. She felt now that her temples were inflamed. She was hoping her headache would not come back to haunt her. Yet the familiar fires of hell began to dance in her head; someone faceless beyond the flames was laughing, or was it really laughter? *You did well, witch, it was a good beginning, yet you still have a long journey. Ten more. Ten! You may think there are eleven, but I know. I know everything, my child. Laugh with me, dance in my fires!*

Nata opened her eyes and threw the book in the dark corner of her bedroom. Laughter. Artillery fire. Charles Dickens on her polished floor.

Matilda Franzevna came in. The ball in honor of the Wild Division was cancelled, and it looked certain that the evacuation had begun.

"We must leave, Natochka," she pleaded. "God help us. The Bolsheviks promised to massacre half the town when they come back. Do you wish me to get your captain?"

"No. Not yet. Matilda Franzevna, dearest, could you prepare for me your Russian herbal mixture? I am suffering and cocaine does not help very much. Nothing helps."

"Oh, Natochka." Matilda Franzevna shook her finger. "You live in sin night after night. I swear, if your dear father was alive, he would cut a bunch of twigs from our rose bushes and beat your white bottom, and you would not suffer and not have your headaches."

"Matilda Franzevna, dearest, please."

Half an hour later, Nata drank the steaming, dark brown, very bitter mixture. She drank the whole glass without stopping and immediately felt better. She picked up Charles

Dickens, found Ralph Nickelby, and read a few paragraphs. She thought she should eat something, yawned, pulled up the goose-down blanket, and fell asleep.

She woke up several times during the night but had neither the strength nor the desire to get out of her bed. She saw that Matilda Franzevna was curled up on a sofa by the door and wished to thank her for that wonderful, magical brew. A mixture she learned to make in faraway Manchuria, as a servant to her father and mother, long before the Revolution.

From behind the tightly drawn curtains Nata could hear shouts of commands, the muted thunder of carts and carriages, the neighing of horses, and the dull thuds of artillery fire.

The morning was exceptionally bright, the snow a light blue reflecting the clear sky. After a week of storms, there was not one cloud. After weeks of artillery fire, there was total silence.

A barely visible wisp of smoke hung in the air—the uncertainty, the fear. People stood outside their houses and spoke in whispers. On Cathedral Square, the sheepskin overcoats with the golden shoulder patches of the officers were conspicuously absent. From time to time, a large horse-drawn sled loaded with household items and civilians in fur coats would race toward the Kharkov highway.

A tiny white-bearded postman in a torn brown overcoat carrying a leather pouch slowly made his way along the snowdrifts of Goncharnaya Street. He stopped to chat with a janitor of one of the houses, a younger man with a reddish beard also dressed in an old brown overcoat. The two leisurely smoked a Goat's Leg.

"Left?" asked the postman.

"Clean out. Only at the station, they say, are some Cherkassians."

"Bastards," the postman grumbled softly, and shook his head. He thought of tossing away his pouch and going home, where he had two bottles of vodka hidden for just this sort of occasion. Foolishness, pride, or perhaps just old habit urged him to go on. He left the Goat's Leg with the janitor, walked up to Number 20, and rang the bell.

When Matilda Franzevna unlocked all the bolts and chains, he handed her a crumpled gray envelope. "Registered." He grinned. He thought it was amusing. The world had just ended, and here he was delivering a letter to these bourgeoisie who would be shot a day or two after the Reds took the town.

Matilda Franzevna carefully signed his logbook and gave him a ten-ruble note. Out of old habit, the postman raised his cap with rabbit-fur earmuffs.

"Who was it, Matilda Franzevna?" Nata shouted from her bedroom.

"Only a postman, Natochka. A letter for you, from Kiev."

"Letters, letters. I shall be so happy if I never read another letter in my entire life. Who is it from?"

"It is smudged. Read it yourself. Some breakfast?"

"My coffee and bread." Nata tried to read the return address but then impatiently tore the envelope apart and read the signature: Petia Ovcharenko. *Why would he write me?* The letter was brief.

> *Dear Natalia Vladimirovna,*
>
> *Only recently, I found out your address from a mutual friend. I feel a moral obligation to bring to your attention two things that may be of interest to you. One, quite by*

*accident I found a clue as to where your esteemed father hid
his valuables, including a certain item which has more than
just monetary value. If I understand my sources correctly,
it must be retrieved by you and taken out of Russia. Two, I
also know of three people who are your enemies, and where
they can be found. Of course, I cannot discuss specifics in a
letter, but should you ever return to Kiev, I would be most
honored to . . .*

"Matilda Franzevna! Hurry! Send someone to the station to
buy tickets. We are leaving on the very next train!"

"Natochka . . ."

"Why are you standing like a statue? Go, go!"

"Natochka." Matilda Franzevna had a sorrowful expression. "Natochka, we cannot leave today or . . ."

"Why not? We must!"

"Natochka, there are no more trains and no more Whites.
Last night they all left."

"What?"

"Last night, the entire night, supply columns, the whole
army. The Bolsheviks are expected within hours, perhaps
sooner. God forgive us."

Nata bit her lip. Thousands of thoughts ran through her
mind melding into one—*fool, fool, idiot!*

"Wait. Not all is lost, Matilda Franzevna. There is still
hope. Run to the Grand Hotel. No, I will go myself. Start
packing." She hurriedly dressed, threw on her sable fur coat,
and ran into the bright morning.

At the Grand Hotel, the clerk looked at her with open hostility. "Their Excellencies, fuck their mothers, already rolled their asses out of here last night." He spat in her direction. Nata cursed herself for not bringing along her Browning. *My acting ability better help me now.* She stuck her hand deep in the pocket of her coat and screamed, "Where is Number 16?"

The clerk paled. "Down . . . corridor."

Holding her breath, she knocked on the heavy oak door. A quiet, confident voice called out, "Please enter."

A fully dressed thin body was sitting on the bed. Empty bottles, cups, and dishes were piled on the table next to him. Long bony fingers held an automatic pistol pointed at her.

"Excuse me." Sobolev stood up, still holding his pistol aimed at her. "Are you now ready to leave?"

"Yes, I am quite ready."

"Excellent. I will be at your house in half an hour."

Monsieur Pierre's razor is shaking. He steadies his hands—dare not cut fish-eyes now.

"Your Excellency wishes some lilac water? I will have to get it myself. My boys are all gone, run off. Such little bedbugs and already Bolsheviks . . . His Excellency met Nata Tai, I understand . . . Hmmm, there are rumors the Reds are already in Sumy. Nonsense, of course. How can the Reds be here when I am shaving his Excellency in my barbershop?"

Half an hour later, Sobolev looked at the dozen leather suitcases Matilda Franzevna had packed. He picked out the smallest one, opened it, and threw its contents on the floor. He told Nata to leave her sable coat behind and get into three sweaters, an ordinary woolen overcoat, and a heavy scarf. He gave Nata a nurse's cap with a large red cross on it. Next, he walked into the kitchen, took the fried chicken meant for that evening's supper out of the oven, and grabbed a few tin cans. He wrapped the dripping chicken in a towel and deposited it into the smallest suitcase.

"Do you have any alcohol?" he asked.

Matilda Franzevna reluctantly nodded toward the liquor cabinet. He put the entire contents of it—all five bottles—into that same suitcase. He looked at Nata again and shook his head. "Take off your boots and put on woolen snowshoes." Nata did so with great reluctance. She loved her red riding boots. "Now we are leaving." Sobolev placed the small suitcase on his shoulder.

"Natochka, you are leaving me?" Matilda Franzevna pleaded, standing by the door, dressed and ready to go.

"I am afraid we are." Sobolev's voice was cold. "Had you agreed to leave yesterday morning, I would have delivered you both in comfort. Even last night. Today I can take only Natalia Vladimirovna. The trains are not running. The bridge over the river Psel is mined. We have to walk almost nine versts and then, hopefully, hopefully . . . We must hurry. The Reds could arrive here at any moment."

After less than fifteen minutes of walking through the snow-drifts, Nata stops, out of breath. "Staff captain, I must rest. I cannot keep up with you. You have such long legs." The fish eyes sparkle. There is even a semblance of a smile on his face.

"I can drop this suitcase and carry you, if you wish . . . but, I believe, it will not come to that." Fast approaching them is a light sled driven by one horse. On the sled, two soldiers are singing and waving their bottles. "Stop!" Sobolev shouts.

The sled races past them. Three dry shots. The driver falls backward out of the sled; the other soldier jumps out and runs back toward the town. The horse stops.

"Get in, Mademoiselle."

"You killed one of your own soldiers?"

Sobolev drives on.

They pass a small crowd of refugees all pleading for a ride. A few kilometers out of town, a funny figure is struggling down the road carrying two huge suitcases. The man's face is made up as a circus clown with a red bulb for a nose. His checkered overcoat and his laquered boots are not made for this weather. There are tears around his blue eyes. The small clown is crying. He waves his arms in desperation. He knows he will never reach the station.

"Staff captain, please stop." Amazing things are still happening. Sobolev stops.

"In the back," he growls. "Leave the suitcases." The clown jumps in. He leaves one suitcase but hangs on to the other. Sobolev pretends not to notice.

Three or four more kilometers down the road, a black military wagon without horses is blocking the way. Two Cossacks sit on the wagon, about a dozen more with their horses stand around a bonfire, drinking bottles of champagne and then throwing them into the fire. Their commander, a rosy-cheeked young esaul, raises his enormous black fur hat, waves it, and screams, "Halt!"

Sobolev stops.

The esaul puts his hat back on his head, reaches into one of the wooden boxes for another bottle, and pops the cork. He tries to stand straight and look serious. "Staff captain." He salutes. "I have to ask you and your lovely companion and this thing in the back . . . to, to disemba . . . disengage, because I am requi . . . sitioning your sled for . . . military needs." He breaks down and laughs. "Here, captain, drink champagne."

Sobolev is not amused. He reaches for his Luger.

The esaul shrugs, drinks the champagne himself, and throws the bottle into the fire. Sobolev notices that the two Cossacks on the wagon are folding back the thick oilcloth and that underneath is a shiny new Lewis machine gun, with its barrel pointed directly at him.

He puts the Luger back in his pocket, helps Nata down, and reaches for her suitcase. "Three more kilometers." He winces. The comic too climbs out. They begin to walk around the military wagon toward the station.

"Wait!" the esaul shouts. "For you, beautiful girl. A bottle to make travels easier. From the cellars of local merchant Poplavsky and the heart of a Kuban Cossack, Esaul Nagornyi."

"I am so grateful, esaul." Nata has an idea. She walks toward him, closer, closer, closer. "Do you not recognize me, esaul?"

"Unfortunately, no . . . Wait. No, it is simply impossible. You look like . . ."

"I am Nata Tai." She kisses him on his lips. He is speechless. The other Cossacks stand around gaping at her.

"A thousand pardons." He slaps his forehead. "What an idiot. Of course you are Nata Tai . . . How can I be of service?"

"You can give us back our sled. We are traveling on a special mission. One of great importance to our cause."

"Stepka!" he shouts to one of his men. "You will accompany these people to Bashi and bring back the sled. Hurry." A Cossack with a carbine climbs in.

Sobolev drives on. "The Reds are in Sumy." He nods to Nata. "Listen."

Behind them are the exploding firecrackers of rifle shots and the drumbeat of machine-gun fire.

⚜

At the Bashi station, in a filthy smoke-filled hall with boarded-up windows, a sea of humanity on the floor. Wounded soldiers, officers, civilians with small children, the elderly. Outside the building stand two long freight trains without any locomotives. Hours go by, slowly.

Nata, finished with her champagne, is asleep next to a ticket counter. Sobolev sits nearby. In her dreams, she is as light as a feather, dancing with Baron Levenvolde on a fast-moving sled driven by three black stallions, racing into a forest which is on fire.

Sobolev's fish eyes are half-closed, watchful. From time to time he takes a long pull on one of the bottles of liquor. From time to time he cannot refrain from coughing.

Evening arrives. There are still rifle shots and machine-gun fire in the distance. No artillery fire.

Nata feels an insistent jabbing in her ribs and opens her eyes. Sobolev's hand is now on her mouth. "Please be very quiet," he whispers. "Follow me."

They carefully navigate among the sleeping bodies. Outside, they walk across the snowdrifts and railroad tracks, climb under some platforms. Another miracle: a passenger train. The door opens as in *Arabian Nights*. They are in a first-class compartment. It is dark and full of people, and here too people speak in whispers.

Nata is guided by Sobolev to an empty seat. As soon as she sits down, there is a slight movement of the train. A little faster, the train is picking up speed; the train is leaving the station. Someone lights a kerosene lamp. From the station house, small figures run out. They are screaming, outraged that they are left behind. Some run after the train. Faster and faster, the screams fade in the distance. Nata looks around.

Across from her sits the elderly General Borovik, the town's former commandant, with a white beard to his waist and mischievous blue eyes. Next to him is his wife. In the corner, Father Evdokim and his wife. Madame Poplavskaya, stunning in her furs, and her teenage daughter. All faces are made of white porcelain. *We are on the way to Dante's inferno.* Nata sighs. *So be it.*

"Ah, and who is this?" General Borovik is amazed to see a small body under his couch. "Why, Monsieur Pierre, what are you doing there? Come, old friend, sit with us, there is enough room."

Pierre sits in the corner, trying to take as little space as possible. "You realize," he explains, "my clientele was exclusively their Excellencies . . . With the Reds there may be unpleasantries . . . Of course, the Cheka."

"Mademoiselle Tai." Borovik finally recognizes Nata even though her face is wrapped up tightly in a scarf. "What a great honor. And who are you?"

Sobolev does not reply. He opens Nata's suitcase and unwraps the fried chicken. He looks at the two remaining bottles of liquor, gives one to Nata, and climbs on the upper berth with the other.

"Not a sociable chap, is he?" smiles Borovik.

Everyone looks greedily at the chicken.

"Please," Nata invites them, "please join me."

The train is now rolling rather slowly. Behind them is a wall of flames where the Bashi station once stood. The train rolls slower and slower. Twice during the night, the male passengers get out and chop wood for the locomotive. Staff Captain Sobolev, however, never moves from his berth.

In the morning there is a catastrophe.

A troop train carrying a fresh infantry brigade to the front unhooks their locomotive because the brigade's own locomotive is too small to pull the endless boxcars. All the screaming by General Borovik and pleading by Nata and the lovely Mademoiselle Poplavskaya, who also offers a generous bribe to the brigade commander, do not help. And they will not leave their own locomotive, because they need it in case the Red artillery knocks out the big one.

General Borovik sends one telegram after another to Kharkov. At noon, the conductor happily informs them that there are no more locomotives available, and there will not be. "It is ten kilometers to the nearest village," he adds, "but I doubt that you will find any form of transportation there. Sleds, carts—they have all been requisitioned by the army. Everything that can move."

In the evening, a long Red Cross train carrying the wounded and soldiers with typhoid fever stops by the water tower. "Staff captain, get me on that train." Nata is serious.

"You are insane."

"I am certain you know this by now. Get me on that train."

Sobolev disappears into the darkness and the snow. He returns looking grim. "You will have to ride with the typhoid patients for the first ten kilometers. After that, you will ride with the medical personnel. This is the best I could do under the circumstances. I myself will have to ride between the cars. I beg you to reconsider."

The heavy iron doors opened into an inferno such as Dante could never imagine. Vomit, coughing, human waste, there was no air. Around the coal-burning stove, in the middle of the boxcar, wallowed a mass of groaning, delirious bodies covered with rags. Nata immediately felt lice crawl across her hand. She turned and rushed back toward the door, but it closed with a bang more ominous than any artillery shell. She heard a heavy bolt thrown across it. The train began to move. Holding her breath was no use. She cautiously breathed through her nose and tried to find a place to sit down. Bodies lay everywhere on the floor—some were dead, others still dying. She backed up to where there was a tiny crack between the door and the wall, where she could lean her face and inhale the icy-cold fresh air.

She watched, in horror, as a skeleton stood up near the stove, and holding his long naked arms in front of him, walked in her direction, stepping on bodies along the way. *He wants to strangle me,* she thought. She covered her eyes. *Ten kilometers. Ten eternities. Ten? Did not someone faceless mention that number? No, that was another nightmare. This is reality.*

"Nurse, sister, please, please give me a cup of water. I cannot do it myself. I do not have the strength." The skeleton collapsed on someone who was already dead.

Nata forced herself to move toward the bucket of water to her right. She found a metal cup, dipped it in the bucket, and gave the water to the skeleton. Now she could see his face—square, gentle, with a dark tangled beard—so Russian, perhaps very young, a peasant or a worker.

"God may look after you, sister." He closed his eyes and lay on the floor. It took Nata some time to realize that the man was dead. For some reason, she took the cup out of his hand.

A body next to the skeleton moved, and the head appeared.

This one was not young. His face was black and his eyes shone, reflecting the red coals in the stove. "There is a little room here, sister. Sit down. Sit with a man who will not see another sunrise." Nata sat down and looked into these eyes reflecting the red coals. There was kindness in those eyes, and, for the first time in a long time, there was also sanity.

"You are not a nurse. Who are you?" The man smiled. "It does not matter much. To me you are a princess out of a book. And I regret I never learned to read. I am a peasant and I will die a peasant, very soon. Listen to a Russian mujik, princess. Do you think this war we are fighting is an ordinary war? This is a slaughter. The fires of hell are breaking through the Russian soil from the very depths of the earth. Like a giant sword cutting the world from the inside toward heaven: Satan's own sword. And he will appear too, victorious, and spare no one. Not us and not the Bolsheviks. All the earth will be the Chort's kingdom for a hundred years . . . then a woman will appear. She may look like you, my princess. She will have the flame in her heart, a stronger flame than all the fires of hell that the Chort can muster. The name of this woman will be Russia, resurrected and holy. She will banish the Chort and will reign until the end of time . . ."

He was still talking, but Nata held her hands over her face, feeling more lice crawling across her body, hoping, almost praying, that these ten kilometers were over and that the train would stop. She drifted off into a semi-coma and was on her back, on the floor, when the train did stop and Sobolev's strong arms pulled her out of the boxcar.

She spent the rest of the night sitting on hard boxes with medical supplies looking at the darkness and the snow, thinking about Yuri and also about Alyosha, the two men who had somehow found their way through the hard layers of her defenses and touched the inside of her heart. *Yuri is definitely dead,* Nata thought. *Armored trains are equal to a death sentence.* The prince had told her that. *Perhaps Yuri has a death wish. But it is interesting, people who have a death wish often live longer than people who wish to live.* She wanted so very much to see him now, to be next to him. He was such a great lover too, the best she had ever had. *But being a great lover is not all-important. It is when the two hearts come together—that is when life becomes special. And Alyosha? He is probably alive. Good, innocent, talented. Why do I love these two so much and no one else?*

Morning came, with it the gray shapes of factories and large buildings. The train was nearing the Kharkov station. And the weather was still insane. She saw that the snow was melting again. The many lice crawling on her body did not disturb her anymore. Later in the day, she would be taking a long, sooth-ing, luxurious bath at her aunt's house. At that time she would decide how to escape from Sobolev. She had no intention whatsoever of continuing with him to the Crimea. She had some unfinished business, some scores to settle in Kiev. On her father's grave, she swore to avenge his death. A long jour-ney? So be it!

Getting away from Staff Captain Sobolev proved more diffi-cult than Nata had imagined. That fish-eyed officer stuck to her like a leach. He insisted that he too would sleep at Nata's Aunt Annie's, and when the aunt refused, he calmly laid his thin body on the dining room divan, shut his eyes, and did not move until dinner was served.

He then sat at the head of the table, uninvited, cut himself off a huge slice of baked ham, ate it without uttering a word, took an entire bottle of cream sherry off the table, and, with the bottle, went back to his divan, drank the sherry, and fell asleep. Aunt Annie offered to call a few of her friends and throw him out.

"No." Nata smiled. "Let the sleeping dog, or, in his case, sleeping pig, sleep." She listened to him snore. *I do need a good night's sleep.* She felt extremely tired. Tomorrow Sobolev could go to hell for all she cared.

The ham and cream sherry notwithstanding, in the morning Sobolev did not look well at all. He had hollow rings under his eyes which were unnaturally bright. He coughed more often, and for a long period of time he was unable to stop. He did not touch the breakfast that Aunt Annie offered him. He asked if there was any more alcohol in the house.

Fortunately, there was none. Sobolev had to go out and get some, and this was Nata's opportunity. A few minutes after Sobolev had left, Nata packed some fresh clothing and ran down to the railroad station less than three blocks away. At the ticket counter, a great disappointment. No trains to Kiev. None at all. Nata saw the station commandant, a heavyset, red-faced colonel, who offered her some exceptionally tasty oranges, but no help. He did not know if any trains would ever go to Kiev. And even if there would be one, it would surely be a troop train.

"Perhaps they will take an army nurse?" Nata asked.

"No, my dear. All nurses are needed right here. There is a horrible typhus epidemic. Hundreds, possibly thousands, are dying every day."

Nata paused to rest among the confused, depressed humanity at the station waiting for nonexistent trains. She put her suitcase on the floor and immediately two small boys snatched it and vanished into the crowd. There was no use calling gendarmes. And there were no gendarmes in sight. Nata was relieved that at least she had her purse under her overcoat and her Browning in her pocket. She was angry and frustrated, contemplating her next move, when she heard, "Natochka, darling, is it really you, my love?"

"George!" she exclaimed. She was embraced and kissed by a tall handsome blond man in a captain's uniform: George Forster, one of her oldest and best friends and, of course, a one-time lover. George, whose father had been an American engineer serving under Nata's father at the European-Russian railway system, and whose mother gave Nata her first piano lesson. George, the happy mischievous boy and handsome cadet. He was now so serious with a mustache and a red scar across his cheek. What luck.

"Natochka, it is a miracle." He tenderly kissed her eyes. "Let us not talk here; I have another two hours, come." He dragged her to a small café, found a secluded table, and held her arms, afraid that she would vanish. "Waitress, a bottle of vodka and some caviar . . . What? No caviar? Some pickled herring then. No pickled herring? Pickled cucumbers? None?"

They only had vodka and tea.

George's parents had both been killed by the Bolsheviks in the infamous massacre of engineers in Moscow in 1918. George had escaped south and fought with General Kornilov. He was wounded four times, decorated, and was now company commander in a special officer's battalion being sent to the front. After he heard Nata's saga, he triumphantly raised his vodka glass. "You always were lucky Nata. More so today than you realize. Your life is a superb adventure film, superb and with a happy ending. At least for now. I am your knight in shining armor, happy to be at your service." He drank the vodka and threw away the glass. "As it happens, my troop train is leaving for Poltava in less than an hour, and I guarantee you a place of honor in our officer's Pullman."

Nata laughed. She imagined for a moment the face Staff Captain Sobolev would make when he realized that she had escaped.

***

The ride to Poltava was extremely comfortable. George's unit was a crack battalion of veterans of many battles who were quite fatalistic about the outcome of the war and their own lives. In the compartment of company commanders were boxes of various expensive liquors and wines which they had liberated somewhere along the way. There was a bag with fifty grams of cocaine, cans with tasty British ham, and music, of course. And the inevitable Russian seven-string guitar with a beautiful dark-haired porutchik singing in a low baritone about Hussars and gypsy nights.

***

There was a fistfight between George and the battalion adjutant in the beginning of the journey. Jealousy ran high for the first twenty kilometers, but as the officers became sufficiently drunk, and as Nata's strange tastes and desires were explained to them, they realized there was no need for any jealousy. The compartment became the scene of one happy party which lasted until the train arrived at Poltava West station late the following morning and it was the time for the battalion to disembark.

George decided to desert his battalion and travel with Nata to Kiev. He had a score of his own to settle with a railroad mechanic he thought was responsible for his parents' arrest and who now lived in Kiev. He promised to help Nata too, and then perhaps to try to get out of Russia through Poland. Enough of this war, enough of this dying country.

The news at Poltava was bad. There was no direct railroad link with Kiev because of heavy fighting with the advancing units of Budenny's cavalry; they had to take a freight train to Kremenchug. From there to Znamenka they rode in a train carrying livestock. Along the way, another man, Ensign Klimenko, who was traveling to Kiev on some mysterious business of his own, joined them. They rode the last leg of the journey in the armored train "Ivan Grozny," sitting between heavy armored plates, listening to the hail of bullets bounce off the sides as the train fought its way through the territory controlled by Ukrainian anarchists.

Finally, they arrived at Kiev's main station, and the first thing George said after looking around and seeing the depressing crowds dragging suitcases and children was, "Smells like evacuation."

"Smells?" Ensign Klimenko wrinkled his nose. "More like stinks."

Nata and her companions reached her house late in the afternoon. The front door was open and there were two carts in front of her house loaded with her furniture. Four huge soldiers were trying to get her Steinway through the front door.

"Who gave you permission?" she screamed.

"Colonel, here," answered one of the soldiers. They put the piano down. The colonel, a small fat man, was defiant. "And who the hell are you?"

"I am the owner of this house."

"Hmm, yes." He softened his tone when he noticed Nata's

friends glaring at him. "You see this house. This was the division's supply headquarters, and since we are leaving . . . You would not leave all this to the Bolsheviks?"

Nata's old coachman, Semen, climbed over the piano. "Natochka," he cried, "these bandits cleaned us out!"

"Silence!" the fat colonel shrieked. The soldiers stood to the side, uncertain of the outcome.

"Start putting everything back," Nata ordered. The colonel and his soldiers did not move. George took out his Mauser and pointed it at the colonel's stomach.

"One, two, I am counting to three," he said. The ensign also took out his revolver. The soldiers pushed the Steinway back into the house. Semen went to one of the carts and began unloading it.

Just then, a military patrol, consisting of about a dozen soldiers with bayonets and an officer, appeared. The colonel and his soldiers saw the patrol first and ran swiftly in all directions. George and Ensign Klimenko were a few seconds too late.

"Halt!" the officer of the patrol screamed as his soldiers raised their rifles. "One step and you are dead."

"Motherfucker," the ensign swore. "Amba!" They both had their revolvers still in their hands. "George," the ensign whispered, "let us shoot and run."

As if anticipating just such a move, three of the advancing soldiers put their rifles to their shoulders in the firing position and the officer screamed again, "Drop your revolvers and put up your hands!"

The patrol officer—tall, dark—reminded Nata of Yuri. He courteously saluted her and said sternly to her companions, "Your documents, gentlemen." When neither George nor Klimenko could produce anything substantial—

although they both talked rapidly and a great deal—the patrol officer marched them at the point of a bayonet toward Kreschatik.

"Are they going to be shot?" Nata asked.

"Nothing to worry about, Mademoiselle Tai. Yes, I did recognize you, it is an honor. These two will simply be assigned to the unit composed of other deserters and sent to the front."

The entire first floor of Nata's elegant townhouse was empty except for some discarded tin cans and bottles of all sizes and shapes. The walls were a sickly yellow with layers of dust where her father's paintings once hung—his favorite Renoir, Degas, Levitan, Popova—the entire collection, gone. It was cold and damp. The soldiers evidently had burned anything they found. There was a mountain of ashes in her fireplace.

The second floor, however, was safe. Semen and his wife Olga had barricaded the stairway and the doors and had managed to keep the looters away by threatening to shoot them with Father's huge shotgun.

"Natochka." Olga embraced and kissed her. "Child, you cannot imagine what we lived through. Where is Matilda Franzevna?"

It was warm on the second floor. Semen had installed a wood-burning stove in Nata's bedroom. Soon there were pots of boiling water on the stove, water for her bath. When her tub was filled and she cautiously slid into a cloud of steam, it was a real paradise, total euphoria. Nata thought it must have been at least five centuries since she had taken the bath at her aunt's house, and her aunt's tub had been so small and uncomfortable. She immersed herself as much as she could and thought that this was ten times better than having sex or taking any narcotics, and so relaxing.

When Olga came in and began to wash her back, Nata began to cry. A nervous reaction, of course, yet she could not stop. She cried for her father, for everyone who happened to cross her path. Yuri and Alyosha, and even her friend George, and Klimenko. They too would perish on the front, killed somewhere in the blizzard. Olga put some Valerian drops under her nose. Nata continued to cry uncontrollably. *Valerian drops are not what I need. Cocaine? Morphine? Sex? I think I had enough sex on that officer's train to last me for quite awhile.* She so seldom cried, it was a great relief. And as Olga continued washing her, she sobbed quietly, then purred like a kitten, and finally sighed and yawned.

Her bed was very near the wood-burning stove. Yet this was such a friendly, playful fire in the stove, so unlike the fires of hell, so unlike the coals in the inferno. Her bed felt incredibly soft, and her body felt like silk—as light as a feather. A few seconds later, she was fast asleep.

In the morning, over strong black coffee and fresh white bread, Nata discussed the situation with Semen and Olga. The news from the front was, of course, depressing. After losing several key battles, the Reds, who vastly outnumbered the Whites, had finally broken through and taken back Chernigov. They were now advancing toward Kiev. It was rumored that an order to evacuate the city already existed. The city itself was riddled with criminals and filled with Bolshevik agents. Last night, for example, as one supply column was moving north, there were rifle shots from the rooftops and some soldiers were killed.

"A very bad time for you to come back, Natochka," Olga concluded. "You must leave—the sooner, the better. Semen and I have relatives in Zmerinka. We will take the silverware and whatever else is left of value, and sell it to survive these times. But you, my child, must flee. The Bolsheviks will kill you just as surely as they killed your father. And that witch Stacy came looking for you. She frightens me. Leave as soon as you can."

"I have some important matters to finish here." Nata sighed. "It will not take me long. Afterwards I will leave. And once I am established abroad, I will try to get you out." She put on her black Persian-lamb overcoat, slid her flat Browning in the right-hand pocket, took some money, and, just in case, asked Olga to wash her Red Cross hat, which was almost as black as her overcoat after her travels.

She had to walk some distance from Luteranskaya to the university. The air was clean, fresh. On the way, she encountered several familiar faces, all asking, "Why, Natochka, why? Everybody is leaving and you have to be an original? Now is not the time. Get out while you still can, at least to the Crimea." At the faculty housing complex, she found a simple green sign on one of the doors—*Professor V. Ovcharenko*—and knocked.

Petia's father, a tall man with rumpled white hair, peered at her from behind thick glasses. "Natalia Vladimirovna? Of course, come in, come in. Forgive the disorder. We are packing. My son wrote to you? Hmm. I regret he is no longer living here. He was drafted. He is in the Caucasus. Wait." The professor found a letter amidst the papers. "Here, this is his address . . . last address. Turkestan Regiment, Mozdok."

"Turkestan Regiment?" Nata exclaimed. "That is where Alyosha . . . Alexey Lebedev is serving. Is Alexey still alive?"

"He was a few months ago. He was wounded and Petia saw him in Kislovodsk. That is all I can tell you. Please take the envelope."

"Petia did not tell you about any valuables belonging to my father?"

"I am afraid not. He did act strangely the last few days before he left. He bought me and his mother warm camel-hair coats and new boots. But he never mentioned anything about the money or valuables. Perhaps he told Lucy Lebedev. They were good friends."

At Alyosha's apartment, another disappointment. His Aunt Sophia was living there now with her three children. And Lucy, that shy, almost mousy sister of his, a typical gymnasium teacher who said that she abhorred all violence and did not like extramarital sex, had suddenly joined the Volunteer Army as a combat nurse serving with the Second Hussar Regiment, fighting to the north of the city.

The next house on Nata's agenda was very familiar. As she neared it, her heart beat faster and faster. She now desperately wished she had some cocaine, a lot of cocaine. She held onto her cold Browning automatic to reassure herself and rang the bell.

A flight of stairs, the same comfortable red leather sofa. She sipped a glass of sherry and listened to a small man with an energetic, intelligent face—Pavel Sergeevich Rosanov, her father's attorney for many years. "What on earth . . . You always have to be an original? When everybody is leaving . . ."

"Pavel Sergeevich." She smiled with her lips only. "Please give me some cocaine. I know you have it. Please." After inhaling some, she felt a surge of energy, purpose. She could think again. She finished her glass of sherry, stood up, embraced the small man, and kissed him three times. He kissed her hand, then they both sat down and looked at one another. "I am such a sinner, Pavel Sergeevich." Nata sighed. "You have no idea."

"Excuse me, Natochka." The small man was getting a little nervous and impatient. "I am your attorney, not your priest or psychiatrist. Get to the point. How can I be of help?"

"Remember how you used to take me to the circus when I was still in pigtails and had the terrible braces on my teeth?"

"Of course I do. And I also took you to see *The Night Before Christmas,* among other spectacles." He smiled, yet his eyes were now watchful.

"Ah, *The Night Before Christmas* and that funny little Chort in the burlap sack. How we all cheered when the blacksmith flew on the back of that St. Petersburg Chort to give Catherine the Great's boots to the girl he loved in his village!"

"Natochka, I am a busy man. Do you need any money, advice? Do you need a first-class seat on the train to Odessa or the Crimea? A visa to France?"

"And I remember that you did not like the part before sunrise, before releasing the Chort—because we all know that the devils and witches must disappear on Christmas Day—when the blacksmith gave him a few whacks with his belt. You did not like to see the Chort whimpering and running off the stage to the laughter of everyone." Nata looked at him seriously.

"No, I did not." He was very serious now, even grim.

"Why did you do it? My father thought of you as one of his best friends? Always."

"I have no idea what are you talking about, Natochka. Of course Bill was my best friend. God rest his soul."

"Pavel Sergeevich, shame on you." Nata laughed. "Perhaps next you will cross yourself? Oh, but where are your icons? I know, in that round room at the back of your apartment."

"How?" He turned ashen.

"Do not move a single hair, because if you do you will go to your eternal suffering in that same moment." She took out her Browning. "I finally killed Sergei Bobrov, oh, seven days, seven eternities ago—what is the difference. I think I did to him everything that was done to my father. So draw your own conclusions as to what I learned, and how, and think carefully before you answer just two of my questions."

Rosanov nodded his head.

"Stacy?"

"She worked here in the Red underground. Two weeks ago she was transferred to the Caucasus." Nata raised her Browning. "To Sochi, and then she will travel to Novorossyisk. I swear it is the truth."

"Oleg?"

"He is here, but you cannot kill him. Someone else attempted and failed. He is surrounded by bodyguards. He is the adjutant to General Tichomirov."

"And Bobrov, Klenov, Lida, Kuzmenko and all the others are also in the Caucasus . . . How interesting."

"Not Lida, she is dead."

So that was what it meant by ten, not eleven, Nata thought. So far, she had killed two. And someone else killed Lida. And the ritual was done, appropriately enough, by the devil's dozen. Not anymore. *After I leave, there will be only nine of them left.* Still a long journey to travel.

"Natochka, I beg you, give it up; you cannot win. We will forgive you if you stop now. You cannot even imagine what awaits you."

"Speaking of forgiveness, Pavel Sergeevich, I understand that should you drop to your knees and beg me to forgive you, your master may take perhaps some pity on your soul. Or am I wrong?"

"No, no, you are not wrong." He actually began to tremble.

"Do it then, and do it quickly." She stood up.

"Prosti, forgive." Now Rosanov was terrified. He kept repeating these words and he tried to kiss her boots. Nata did not utter a word. She shot him three times in the back of his head and ran out of his apartment.

There was some confusion in the street, but it was not related to the pistol shots. More people, agitated, hurrying, gloomy. A trolley went by, followed by a small infantry unit. She entered Café Paris and ordered coffee and a napoleon. Another cup of coffee, and her nerves were under control. She decided to walk home by way of Kreschatik. Two more familiar faces, saying, "You are still here, Nata? How amazing . . ."

Directly in front of her house stood a shiny gray Packard limousine with a soldier at the wheel. As Nata entered her house, Semen whispered, "Natochka, some officer is waiting for you upstairs. Very unpleasant type." Across her clean bed lay a filthy and smelly familiar body. It stood up with some difficulty, coughed for a minute or two, and clanked its spurs. The face was red and swollen, the fish eyes bright with madness, the voice hoarse and barely audible. And the smell around him was that of a decomposing corpse.

"Good evening, Mademoiselle, or is it morning or afternoon? Or are we all dead already and this is the great hereafter? I certainly hope so . . . Now, I have a limousine to take you to the station, or," he coughed for another two minutes, pulled a flask out of his overcoat and drank something which smelled as bad as his body, "or should you chose to play tricks . . . I can telephone to hmm . . . competent officials. It is even now against the law to shoot a prominent attorney . . . It does not matter if he happens to be a practicing Satanist. Murder is murder. Which do you choose?"

"There will not be any tricks. Can I pack a few items?"

"You have five minutes." Sobolev coughed, spat pink phlegm on the parquet floor, and sat down on her bed.

∽

When the driver of the limousine delivered Nata and Sobolev to the station, it was dusk. The sky was crimson between the railroad depot and the gigantic, dark repair shops. Sobolev carried Nata's new suitcase with some difficulty toward a train consisting of six first-class Pullmans and one yellow fourth-class car. There was a giant locomotive being hooked up to the Pullmans. In the doorways of the Pullmans could be seen the Cossack fur hats and slanted eyes of the Cherkassian guards and the bayonets of junkers with their blue and gold shoulder patches. Inside, beyond the cream-colored drapes, thick carpets, soft leather seats, crystal chandeliers—silence.

"All this for us?" Nata asked, as they entered an empty compartment. She was impressed.

"Not quite." Sobolev yawned. "I have to ride in the fourth-class car. All this is for you. And General Governor Tichomirov, your great admirer, wishes to relay through me his best wishes for your journey. This is his train, and he hopes that you will dine with him and a few officers of his staff later tonight. I was not invited. Now please excuse me, I can hardly stand up."

"Staff captain, I do hope you feel better. At least wash yourself and change your clothing. Small wonder you were not invited for dinner. You look and smell like a vurdalak." A few minutes after Sobolev's departure, a young junker brought a tray with a bottle of champagne on ice, a small plate of black caviar, and one glass.

"Compliments of General Governor. Dinner will be served in approximately one hour. The dining car is at the head of the train. Should you need anything, call the guard." Nata noticed that the glass began to tinkle very softly. The train was moving.

In the spacious dining car, General Tichomirov, a small-eyed pink behemoth, sat Nata at his table to his right, and treated her like a long-lost daughter. He had seen all her films, and especially loved her as a geisha in *The Star of the Orient,* a print of which he had on the train. As the dinner drew to a close and the staff officers emptied every bottle on the long table, the general spoke to Nata in French, relating amusing, bawdy anecdotes and stories. Suddenly he stopped midsentence. A new officer stood in the doorway, a porutchik. His face sent shivers through Nata's body. That face—so familiar and hated—pock-marked and scarred, with tiny blue icicles for eyes, thin red lips curled into a sneer, the large cruel mouth. Oleg of many names, a self-proclaimed poet of Satan. Nata had known for some time he was with Tichomirov, and yet she was still startled when she saw him.

Oleg was startled as well. Especially seeing her next to the general. There was a worried look on his angular face, but only for a moment. He lowered his head toward her and said mockingly, "Mademoiselle Tai, a great honor."

"My personal adjutant, Porutchik Nezvanov." Tichomirov introduced him as if in a trance. He lifted his massive body and, bidding everyone a good and restful night, left the table and the dining car. Oleg once again lowered his head, smiled, and walked out behind the general.

"Do you know this officer?" the commander of the guards, Cossack Esaul Bubnov, who was seated next to Nata, asked.

"Vaguely. I've met him a few times." Nata knew that Oleg

would move fast. He would try to kill her, perhaps tonight. He was decisive, that she knew.

Bubnov continued to look at her, his bushy black eyebrows raised in a question mark. He was a wild-looking man, for a moment he too reminded Nata of Yuri. "Why are you looking at me so?" she asked.

"Excuse me . . . Nata." The Cossack smiled. "I can see that you are worried, and early in the evening you were so happy, so carefree. This porutchik, he threatened you?"

"No! He was only associated with my circle of friends, some of them. He is a poet, a mystic."

"Yes, I have heard." Bubnov was now thoughtful. "It appears that this adjutant, who only joined us a few weeks ago, is now giving orders to our general. Strange. In any event, can I be of service to you?"

"Thank you. I really must go. I am so tired." Nata stood up. The Cossack also stood and kissed her hand.

"Please walk me to my compartment, esaul."

"With great pleasure."

She walked in front of Bubnov into the corridor, then another corridor. In the narrow passage near her compartment, the Cossack placed his hands on her shoulders and drew her close to him.

"I was not joking, Nata," he said quietly and calmly. "I have lost count of the men I have killed in combat, and I have personally hung at least a hundred Bolsheviks in the Caucasus alone. Say one word—yes, wink one of your beautiful eyes—and I will cut this porutchik's head off with one clean sweep of my saber. One life, more or less, does not matter to me. I am on my way to hell."

She looked at his face and again was reminded of Yuri. Another calm, professional soldier. He would do it too, this

Cossack whom she had met only two hours ago. He was willing to kill for her, and the amazing thing was, he did not expect her to sleep with him, he expected nothing in return. "Yes, Cossack," she whispered, and winked.

She really was exhausted. The lower berth was made up and comfortable. Her door was bolted, her Browning was under her pillow. No dreams, no nightmares.

In the morning, the train stood near a small station. There was rifle and machine-gun fire in the distance. The sky was beautiful, not one cloud.

Nata looked out of her window at the snow-covered steppe and the long snakes of trains rolling past them somewhere south. Some were cattle cars with red crosses painted on their sides, some were yellow, some were gray. All were pulled by small toy locomotives. It must have been very cold, yet the refugees sat on the roofs of the cars, between the cars, on the open plat- forms, and even on the tenders. It looked as if the toy trains were covered by swarms of black flies.

The junker who had brought her champagne last evening brought in a tray with breakfast: tea, fried eggs, sausage, and pastry. After placing the tray on a small table, he stood by the door and watched her. He had a pleasant aristocratic face, very thin, very young. Nata sat up in her nightgown and drank her tea. "What are you waiting for?" She smiled.

"I am here to guard you. I was outside your door most of the night."

"Thank you, junker; what is your name?"

"Victor Bittenkopf. I, I do have a revolver." He pulled a large Mauser out of his galif. "And I do know how to use it."

"Victor, I am not hungry. Please sit down and eat my breakfast." He ate everything in less than a minute. "Thank you, we seldom get eggs or sausage." He grinned. "And I have long forgotten what a pastry tastes like."

"Now tell me, why must I be guarded like a Bolshevik spy?"

"Strange, tragic events transpired during the night. I am not at liberty to tell you," he lowered his voice, "but you will know soon enough anyway. Our new adjutant has lost his head. Literally. His body is on the train . . . but not his head. It was not found. This part does not bother me. But then, our commander of the guards was found with a bullet in the back of his head, and another officer, some staff captain, was shot the same way. We believe there may be Red assassins aboard the train. But I am not simply here to guard you. The general personally ordered me to entertain you, amuse you, do anything to make your trip a pleasant one. Anything."

"How old are you, Victor?" Nata smiled, seeing the junker turn bright red.

"I mean . . . for example, I thought, it is such a great winter morning and we will be standing here at Boyarka for another three hours, we can venture out for a sled ride. I can arrange it. But then," he sighed, "anything. I am almost seventeen. The general explained to me that you may make requests of a personal nature."

"And if I do, will you be simply following your orders?"

"Of course not! Just being here with you, Mademoiselle Tai, for me, this is the greatest honor."

The idea of a sled ride appealed to Nata. *If only this boy could find a sled so fast it would take me out of Russia,* she thought. Oleg was dead, but his people were clearly at work. Sobolev was gone. So was the Cossack esaul. There was real danger now, the dreadful part of it, not knowing who would strike or when. But then, she had been in grave danger before. And she did have this boy to protect her. "A morning sled ride? I like it. Not dangerous?"

"That rifle and machine-gun fire we are hearing, that is in the village. A Jewish village, and it is in the hands of Ukrainian anarchists and, I am afraid . . . they are killing the Jews. But we control the railroad line and around the station. And there are no Reds anywhere."

"I am going to get dressed now. No, do not turn away, I like men to watch me getting dressed, or undressed."

They got no further than the platform. The officer of the guard had an order not to let anyone off the train. They watched a group of men in fur hats and black overcoats being chased away from the station by Cossacks waving swords and whips. "The Jews," the officer of the guard expained. "They found out that this is the general governor's train and sent a delegation to ask him to stop the massacre."

Nata saw one of the Cossacks strike an elderly man with his sword, the red blood exploding on the snow, the man falling gracefully, his bearded face peering at the beautiful sky.

"Come," Victor forcefully pulled her back onto the train.

"Why?" She kept looking at the dead man.

"Because we have the brontosaurus Tichomirov in command. We raised our three-color banner in the Caucasus for justice. Look at this justice now. Fucking generals! He could easily stop the massacre. Send a company of Volunteers and throw the bandits out. But he won't lift one of his fat fingers. Pity that it was not his head cut off last night." The boy was so upset that red splotches appeared on his face.

Back in her compartment, Nata's feeling of danger, impending doom, death, became so strong that she used up all the cocaine she had left in her gold medallion. Next, she used the boy until he was exhausted. Still her nerves were on edge. "Victor, put your uniform back on and go get me two bottles of champagne and something good to eat. Now I am hungry."

"I cannot leave you, but I will call the guard and pass along your request."

The bottles arrived, on ice, and a large plate covered with black and red caviar, sliced ham, pickled mushrooms, smoked sturgeon, and a loaf of white bread. There were two glasses this time and a note from the general governor. Victor was astounded. Nata calmly opened one of the bottles, poured herself some champagne, drank, and read the note. The general apologized for not being able to see her tonight—"military matters, my dear"—but said that he would definitely dine with her in Fastov. Love, devotion, hope that she was enjoying herself on his train.

"Eat, Victor, drink. I will teach you a few interesting things later on. They may be useful when you find a woman you love, but for that you will need all your strength. Eat."

"Mademoiselle Tai . . . Nata, I love you so very much." He tried to embrace her, but she pushed him away.

"I am a whore. Remember that always. I do not love . . . What is this?" When she had pushed the boy away, a napkin was knocked off the table. Underneath the napkin was a folded piece of paper, and on it, a familiar drawing of a silly, grinning, hapless Russian Chort. Underneath, in red ink, a child's scribble: *Witches die also.* Nata crumpled the paper and threw it in the corner.

"What is it?" Victor was suddenly very alert, his Mauser in his hand. He retrieved the paper, studied it, shook his head. "I do not understand."

"It is better that way. It is not important. Just someone's idea of a joke." She drank some more, ate, and finally began to relax. The note, if it intended to frighten her, had produced just the opposite effect. *They must be very upset if they are sending me this,* Nata thought. *And not ready to act. Otherwise, why bother? They will probably hold a special service, pray for guidance.* Now her nerves were steady. She felt sleepy; it was time for a pleasant nap. The train began to move again.

"Can you sing, Victor?"

"A little."

"Sing me a Cossack lullaby."

Victor had a nice tenor: *"Sleep my beautiful baby, bayushki bayoo, quietly the moon is shining into your cradle . . . I will tell you a fairy tale, I will sing you a song. Sleep while you do not have a care in the world, bayushki bayoo . . ."*

⁂

Strange. Now a mighty chorus is singing: *"Beyond our window, Terek is flowing, splashing muddy water . . . angry Chechen is crawling ashore, sharpening his dagger . . ."* Arkadi Lubimov, Nata's favorite director, has two cameras rolling at once.

"Natochka," he screams, "pay attention, please, you are dying, not dead! Roll your eyes and part your lips and move just a little on your stretcher."

Why are they carrying me through these snowdrifts? Ah, this is only cotton. This boxcar and the stove are decorations. A shot of morphine? Arkadi knows what I like. But why the unpleasant nurse with the round face? Why is she taking off my gold medallion?

"Natochka, raise your head," Arkadi cries.

Where is the camera now? The wind sings the lullaby: *". . . I will give you a holy icon to take with you on your journey . . . going into the battle, remember your mother . . . now sleep, my tiny baby . . . bayushki bayooo . . ."* The sad, distant mother kisses Nata on her forehead. Another camera. It is rolling, everyone is excited. Her father appears in his railroad uniform. He whispers, he shouts. She cannot hear him. The doors of the boxcar open with the thunder of an exploding artillery shell. The bearded face of Rasputin is screaming into the camera, "Brothers, there is a woman here! Vanya, load the horses. Misha, take her to the station." The neighing of horses. Arkadi is working from an unfamiliar script. No need for pantomime. Station house. One room. How realistic. The makeup man dusts more powder on Nata's face. It is warm, comfortable. The camera pans. An officer snores not far from her on the floor. He wakes up. He speaks to a civilian. They argue about vodka. The officer gesticulates, explains that he went to get some in the village and missed his train.

Nata wonders what she must do next.

"No vodka in the hereafter!" the civilian screams.

"Let us break for five minutes," Arkadi announces.

"Wait!" Nata screams, but no sounds come out. This is a silent film, it does not matter. *Wait. What is Oleg doing here on this set? He is carrying his own head. He found it.* His head snarls, tries to bite her.

There are firecrackers exploding near the cameras. The officer is now waving his revolver; he is diving into the door like a swimmer into a lake. More firecrackers. The room is filled with new extras. They are carrying rifles, bayonets, a field telephone, wearing red stars and red armbands. They spread maps under the kerosene lamp and look at them. One soldier screams, "Yes, yes, this is the unit of Comrade Tuhachevski!" Interesting script, good acting. A face of an intelligent, sensitive young man leans over her, his eyes wide with concern. Her love interest?

What are they screaming into that telephone? "You are

insane! I have a large cavalry force and an armored train? You want me to commit suicide?" And again, the parrot, "This is the unit of Comrade Tuhachevski . . . yes . . . yes."

"Here is some hot tea." The man with the sensitive face, somehow familiar. "Drink it; it is my own cup. It is clean." Ah, from *Ruslan and Ludmila*. The good wizard pouring the water of life on the dead Ruslan.

"Action," Arkadi screams, "we are rolling!" An earth-shattering, ear-splitting explosion. The cup falls out of Nata's hand. All the boards fly out of the windows and the ceiling disappears. Dark starry sky. Sparkling champagne. Poison, stars, and the crescent of the moon. Nata's sad mother glides toward her, kisses her on her forehead, and covers her with a purple blanket. Chorus: *"Sleep peacefully, my tiny baby, bayushki bayoo . . ."*

A small electric bulb near a wooden ceiling. Iron walls. The room is filled with mist. Somewhere a man's face appears. A dear, familiar face. *If I open my eyes wider,* Nata thinks, *it will be gone forever.* The face moves closer and closer to her own. It is unshaved and bloodied, but the eyes are calm, concerned, filled with love. These incredible black velvet eyes that made her heart stop beating dozens of times, the eyes she thought she would not see again in a million years. She tries to touch them but cannot move, cannot raise her hand. The mist is so thick now. *Bayushki bayoo . . .*

The trains ROLLED SOUTH IN A NEVER-ENDING LINE: cattle cars with red crosses on their sides, sleek blue Pullmans of the generals, yellow cars and green, and the open platforms filled with refugees. Along both sides of the railroad tracks stood columns of carts, sleds, trucks, and automobiles, and soldiers and civilians walked stubbornly through the snow. Some soldiers carried their wounded comrades.

This was an exodus unparalleled in Russian history. The people—nobility, peasants, workers, monks, priests, university professors, children, and the elderly. All with one desire—to escape the inescapable, the darkness which was about to descend on their native country. There seemed to be no end to this mass of humanity, and yet, there was an end. The end does come for everything.

When the last boxcar, the last sled, the last group of refugees disappeared over the snowdrifts, nature itself breathed a great sigh of relief. The railway tracks stood empty and shiny. From the forest, a pack of stray wolves ran toward a small burning station house, where they smelled human blood. Behind the wolves, cautiously moving along the edge of the forest, rode horsemen in dark green overcoats and huge white fur hats. A few at first, and then more and more, until the entire field between the forest and the railroad track resembled a white tablecloth onto which someone had spilled a plate of green peas.

This was the Second Hussar Regiment covering the retreat of the army. The Hussars rode some distance toward the railroad track, to where a tired monster, a giant caterpillar with cannons and machine guns, with a torn white, red, and blue Russian flag flying above its command turret, was awaiting them. The armored train, "Our Homeland," also covering the retreat of the Volunteer Army.

BOOK TWO

odessa
january 1920

The days WHISTLED BY WITH THE SPEED OF MACHINE-gun bullets flying above the snowdrifts and ice-covered rivers. In these snowdrifts and under the thick ice, countless bodies lay waiting, praying for the eternal spring. Those who were still alive had only twenty-four hours to live in each God-given day. And those twenty-four hours had to be enjoyed to the fullest. In two, three weeks at most, death and darkness would descend on the beautiful southern city, and all who arrived here in the luxury of generals' Pullmans, in horse-drawn sleds or in armored trains, in old Ford trucks or on foot, and even those who had always lived here in the comfortable spacious apartments, they all knew—darkness and death.

Everyone tried to live each day as if it were their last. Just as a condemned man savors his last meal, each hour of sunshine, each soft moonlit night had to be enjoyed and enjoyed. Beyond the chalky white powder, moist lips, and tears as transparent as vodka, nothing mattered, nothing at all.

No one could save the condemned. Not the clean-shaven General Governor Shilling who paced aimlessly back and forth in his huge empty headquarters, not the faraway General Denikin who himself was fleeing swiftly with his elite Kornilov and Markov divisions, not the treacherous and indifferent allies, not the countless Volunteer units made up of old professors, young schoolboys, and retired colonels.

And not the estimated sixty or seventy thousand well-dressed, well-armed officers roaming the streets, filling every restaurant, theater, and bordello. And certainly not the few hundred soldiers who, with rags and old blankets covering their uniforms, waited patiently on the giant piers.

The fortunate few who had invested their money in the Bank of London or the Lyons Crédit, were puffing on their cigars and embracing their wives or mistresses at the captain's table of some luxury liner on its way to Marseille. In the windows of their cabins, cigar smoke covered like mist the distant shore of a country gone mad, a country once known as Russia.

Some still nurtured a spark of hope that the Whites could hold out in the Caucasus and the Crimea. After all, the Bolsheviks had taken Odessa in 1918, but they had broken their teeth on the Caucasus. These people wrote long letters to their relatives and friends, paid bribes to various officials, and waited. But the vast majority had given up waiting. They drank, made love, inhaled cocaine, injected morphine, and remained quiet. Being Russians, of course, they cursed their fate. And the generals, the allies, the speculators charged incredible prices for a gram of Merkov's cocaine or a half a liter of homemade vodka.

Nearly everyone sniffed cocaine. Officers and prostitutes, the elegant refugees from St. Petersburg and Kiev, bankers, doctors, thieves, and generals. And nearly everyone wanted love. All the bordellos were filled at any time of day or night. The madames could not supply enough flesh. But if the traditional prostitutes of this port city could not meet the tidal wave of demand, the wives of bankers and doctors and attorneys, the countesses from St. Petersburg and Moscow, the wives of the officers and generals also knew that the end was near. And they gave themselves freely, without reservation, to just about anyone who would touch a knee in the dimly lit theater or the backseat of a limousine, anyone who would send a bottle of champagne to their table or simply brush a hand in a crowded vestibule. There were only twenty-four hours in each given day. And the days were flying like bullets.

At night, the city was brighter than it had been before the Great War. Long lines formed in front of every theater, cabaret, cinema, and restaurant. Even after the great Vertinski departed to Paris having sung for the last time his "Cocainette," about a street waif crucified by cocaine on the wet boulevards of Moscow; even after Tamara Gruzinskaya stopped singing about Russia forever buried under a blizzard, and sailed to her native sunny Georgia; even after Utesov disappeared in the Red underground and Vera Holodnaya sailed for Yalta, the nightlife was as bright as ever.

The lines grew longer. There were more officers; officers with unshaven, exhausted faces, their uniforms torn and infested with lice and reeking of sweat and blood. There were also many more soldiers. The soldiers did not stand in lines. They walked slowly past the cabarets, in small groups, dragging their rifles and machine guns toward the piers to join with their brothers in waiting for the nonexistent transport ships.

Nearly everyone prayed. In churches, synagogues, mosques, Buddhist temples, the privacy of their homes, on the giant piers. Jesus Christ, Allah, Iegova, Buddha, saints, prophets, angels, and even the Russian pagan gods like Perun and Dazhbog, all heard the same plea: *I DO NOT WANT TO DIE!*

At the elegant palatial villa of the Greek merchant Popondapolo, in a well-appointed basement with round walls painted black, thirteen people sat in a semicircle in front of a large figure cut in reddish marble, a grotesque and almost funny shape with a golden trident in its long claws. The trident signified that the creature depicted in marble was the master of all things alive, dead, and as yet unborn—on earth, in the sea, and in the sky. In front of the statue stood a silver vessel decorated with precious stones resembling a sarcophagus, and in that vessel lay a small body that, earlier that evening, had been sacrificed.

The heart had been carefully removed and cut into even parts which were placed on small silver plates and eaten while still warm. The blood from the body was collected into a large golden chalice and passed along so everyone could partake. There were almost one hundred incantations during the service. These people did not pray to get something or to extend their lives, they prayed only that they would be allowed to serve their master, in any way they possibly could. And to die while serving the master was their greatest pleasure, their supreme achievement. Although the religion of the people in the basement predated Christianity by more than ten thousand years, they scrupulously followed the later Babylonian rituals of sacrifice, incantation of the dark spirits, and communication with the devil, Velsevul, Satan, or the one known in Russia simply as Chort.

The ritual was over and the people sitting in the comfortable leather armchairs were beginning to awaken from the slumber induced by a special brew imbibed after the intake of human blood. That brew, secrets of its ingredients known only

to the priests, created visions and revelations in the participants' minds, and was supposed to instantly kill all those who
were not true believers. A tall woman wrapped in a black cape,
her face hidden behind a veil, walked up to the statue and
embraced one of its scaly legs. "I must address this gathering
first," she announced in a deep nasal voice.

The gathering included, among others: two generals and a
captain, a wealthy industrialist, a well-known actress, a
madame of the most fashionable bordello, the secretary of the
revolutionary committee of the Russian Communist Party, his
deputy, and the present mayor of the city. They were almost
evenly divided between men and women.

"You may speak," proclaimed a huge bald man,
Popondapolo, the host. "There is no need to cover your face,
Mademoiselle Averescu." He grinned. "We are here of one
spirit. Please begin."

"I came especially for this gathering and I am leaving
tonight for Novorossyisk. I have an urgent message. Our Kiev
congregation made a terrible blunder. A man who was our
enemy for many years and who had desecrated and hidden a
large part of the sacred scroll was questioned by us, but died
from a heart attack before revealing to us what we needed to
know. What is much worse, his body was discovered, and his
daughter, the well-known film actress Nata Tai, saw the body
and the results of our interrogation, and swore on his grave to
avenge him."

"Kill her! Death to her," several voices cried.

Averescu ignored them. "So far, she has killed four of us,
including one especially dear to me and known to all of you,
Oleg Zorin." The huge Greek, his face a mask of hatred, stood
up and shook his fists in the air. "Sit, Gregory!" Averescu
screamed loudly. "We made an attempt to kill her and that was

the biggest mistake of all. She has a certain power; she too communicates with our master."

"How can that be?" the Communist Party secretary asked.

"I am not certain. Her mother was one of our high priestesses, perhaps she is still protecting her daughter . . . In any event, we are not allowed to touch a single hair on her head. If one of us kills her, it is the end of everything. Should she die of some other cause, then it is different. Furthermore, the object we all are searching for can only be returned to our master freely. Perhaps by Nata Tai alone. We tried to acquire it by force and we failed. We must be very cautious. There is more. We cannot kill anyone she loves. Any man . . . or woman she is truly in love with."

"She is planning to marry one of my colonels." A heavyset general spoke. "Yuri Skatchko—he commanded the armored train 'Our Homeland' before I ordered it decommissioned. But I know Nata personally, and I do not think she loves anyone except herself."

"I know her personally too, and rather well. I agree with you, general . . . Yuri Skatchko?" Averescu took the veil off her face and raised her black eyebrows. "Here in Odessa?"

"Yes, we are trying to kill him, and I cannot interfere in that particular operation," the Party secretary said. "It is directed by an agent from Moscow."

"As long as it is not one of us."

"Anything else you wish to say, Mademoiselle Averescu?" the Greek asked.

"We will find the scroll in the Caucasus." She nodded her head and moved back to her chair.

The Greek stood up again and walked to the statue. Standing next to it he was almost as tall, menacing in the flickering light of the black candles. "Our enemies must die!" he cried out. "And our spirits must be set free! I now bid farewell to many of us. Not an easy task." He poured scented oil over the body in the sarcophagus, lit a torch, and ignited the flame. Dark smoke and the smell of burning flesh filled the basement. The incantation and chanting grew in intensity, people rose from their chairs. Some fell on the ground and rolled near the sarcophagus, some kissed the hooves and other parts of the statue, others wandered aimlessly, rocked in one place, or embraced one another. As in Babylon, thousands of years ago.

The alarm clock rang at a quarter to six. Yuri reached and turned it off. He tried to turn on the electric lamp on the night table, but Nata embraced him and pulled him away.

"Not today," she whispered, and kissed him on his ear.

"Natochka," he tried gently to push her away, "today I must go. Very important."

"Today, tomorrow, yesterday. Always so important. Am I not important? Stay!"

"For a little while." He kissed her on her lips, her breasts, her body. *She is such an addiction,* he thought, as he entered her again and again and again. Their lips and bodies were one, together in a rhythmical, wonderful dance, one with no beginning and no end, one that could go on forever. Resting inside of her, Yuri felt the warmth of her tongue licking the sweat off his chest, sucking gently on his nipples, driving him hard, invigorated. And the dance began anew. This time she was on top and he was catching the drops of sweat rolling off her breasts. Then her lips again, her mouth, forceful, demanding.

"Stop," he finally cried out. "You can wear out a tiger. More of this, and I will not be able to walk."

"Good." She jumped off his stomach, reached for a papirossa, lit it, smoked some, then passed it to him. "I do not want you to walk. I want us to get married, and I solemnly promise that as soon as we are married I will become a perfect wife. I will not sniff cocaine, not use morphine, and I will always be faithful. Always. We can buy a house somewhere in the south of France and look at the sea. I have at least a million of those pretty green dollars in the Bank of Zurich alone. With my father dead . . . it is all mine . . . and it is all yours. We can go to Africa, land of your forefathers, to Hawaii, anywhere in the world. Raise a dozen children and make love ten times a day, every day, every year."

"Very tempting. And we will get married, in less than a month. Then I have a leave of absence. We will go to Sevastopol. I was assured it would be safe in the Crimea."

"Not to France? Yura, listen to me. For you I am ready to give up everything. Ready to break a promise I made to my dead father, give up my vendetta, and you, you still wish to fight this senseless war? I could see it before, when you had a chance to win. Your cause is lost. You have been hopelessly betrayed. There is no more of that *most important* thing in life for you. I am the most important thing in your life. Life itself is the most important thing, and love. I learned that when I was poisoned and dying. I simply want to live and love, with you."

"We will talk about it tonight. I really must hurry."

"Fuck their mothers, Yuri Efimovich," Porutchik Shebeko growled. He was driving the gray Benz down the

Deribasovskaya and was forced to slow down because a large group of officers were having a heated argument in the middle of the busy street. "Let me drive straight through those bastards." He glanced at Yuri and at General Egorov, who was next to him in the backseat.

"No. Pull over and stop. We can walk from here."

"I have a better idea." Shebeko grinned and continued toward the crowd. As he drove, he lowered the window and stuck the barrel of his Marusia out. This was a weapon of his own invention, a cross between the large-caliber shotgun and a small cannon. A young blond officer, whose red pimpled face happened to be closest to the Marusia's astonishing barrel, smartly jumped to attention and squeaked, "A thousand pardons, your Excellencies." He then vanished into thin air with most of the arguing officers. The street was clear. Shebeko reluctantly put his Marusia back in his lap and continued driving.

"Really, Yura." General Egorov was amazed as they passed another large crowd of wandering officers and then another standing in front of a theater whose giant marquee announced the "au naturel" appearance of thirty of the most beautiful women in Russia. "There is indeed an entire army of them here. Why are they here and not at the front?" General Egorov had just arrived aboard the destroyer "Gnevni" as a personal representative of Denikin.

"Wait until we are at the conference." Yuri was thoughtful. "A few more minutes." *Nata was right, we were betrayed.*

"I know why," Shebeko growled. "Because nobody had enough courage to put a few hundred of these bastards to the wall."

"Next week, Shebeko," Yuri smiled, "I will personally give you two machine guns and a detachment of my workers. And you can go shoot as many of them as you wish."

"Next week it will be too late. Perhaps now it is too late. Anyway, why waste bullets? When the Bolsheviks come, they will put them to the wall, every last one of them. Here we are." He stopped the Benz by the old post office building which was now the headquarters of the Odessa Military Region.

At the entrance, half a dozen officers carefully checked their credentials and told Shebeko to get back to Yuri's Benz and wait. That order did not sit well with Shebeko, who had recently begun to consider himself Yuri's personal body-guard, and who carried his Marusia with him everywhere, even to parties. "Go fuck yourself," he told the officer in charge, and raised the gun. "We are all going in."

The officers guarding the entrance proved to be quite different from the ones in the street. Four of them raised thier own rifles to firing position and two took out their revolvers. "One step forward, porutchik, and you are dead," the officer in charge said. "Colonel Skatchko, please be good enough to order him back to the automobile."

"Go, Shebeko, take a nap, get something to eat, visit a bordello. This will be a long conference."

There were seven colonels and four generals in a huge room. Skatchko and Egorov were the last ones to arrive. On the wall-sized map of southern Russia, the red pins were stuck ominously close to Odessa. As Skatchko introduced him, Egorov whispered, "We have a good quorum, exactly the devil's dozen."

"I will come directly to the point." General Governor Shilling looked everyone over through his monocle, then for some reason looked at the ceiling as he began. "After General

Bredov's battle group, our main force, so shamefully left the front and retreated toward the Polish and Romanian borders, leaving our front vulnerable, to say the least, to the overwhelming Bolshevik forces . . . hmmm . . ." He poured himself a glass of water from a crystal decanter on the table and drank it. "We have been retreating like a proverbial snowball, faster and faster, downhill. This, sad to say, is but one of our problems. As most of us know, the Bolshevik underground within the city, which is very powerful, is preparing an uprising to coincide with the final push of the Red army. So the purpose of this conference is to find ways to stabilize the front, and to eliminate, or at least temporarily render harmless the Bolshevik organization within the city. General Kruglov, our front commander, will have the first word."

A well-preserved, energetic general on Shilling's right stood up, sighed, and attempted to smile. "You can see for yourself." He pointed to the large map. "The situation is critical. The Bolsheviks have at least fifty thousand rifles and about eight thousand sabers. They have four armored trains, a strong artillery presence, two tank units, even planes. And I have less than ten thousand rifles, about fifteen hundred sabers, no artillery to speak of, five tanks, and seven planes. But my planes are useless because we have no bombs. And I have no armored trains. For some reason, General Bredov lined the Zmerinka railroad line for fifty kilometers with armored trains, back to back—trains loaded with artillery and ammunition—and, of course, just left it all there for the Bolsheviks. One armored train that fought the rearguard action until recently, 'Our Homeland,' was ordered decommissioned and stripped of its armaments by General Tichomirov," he nodded toward the fat small general at the end of the table, "just when we needed it most."

"I had my reasons," Tichomirov barked back.

"I am certain of that. So, unless I receive substantial rein-forcements, substantial winter uniforms and ammunition, the front, which is now collapsing, will be no more." He sat down.

In the uncomfortable stillness that followed, someone said, "And here we have sixty thousand healthy, well-armed cowards whom no one dares send to the front."

"That number is an exaggeration." General Shilling banged on his glass with a pencil. "We do have thousands of officers here, hmmm, but certainly not sixty thousand. And they should all be sent to the front, I agree. Now I will intro-duce Colonel Kashin, our chief of counterintelligence."

Colonel Kashin, who sat in the middle of the long table, almost across from Yuri, tried to get up. His skeleton-like frame wavered back and forth. He opened his mouth wide, but no sounds came out. Then his body collapsed back into his armchair.

That clown, Yuri thought, *is either totally drunk or sniffed so much cocaine he does not know where he is.*

"Colonel Kashin." This time Shilling knocked his pencil on his pewter ashtray. "Please be good enough to go on with your presentation." There was no movement in Kashin's arm-chair. "Colonel Kashin, please stand up and share with us your plans to eliminate the internal threat."

This time, Kashin managed to get up. He looked the gath-ering over with a strange euphoric expression on his thin tired face and suddenly screamed, at the top of his lungs, a high falsetto, a woman's cry of agony: "No, I will not be good enough to disclose my plans for eliminating the Red under-ground, because I believe that in one or two hours after this conference my plans will be known to the key members of the Red underground!" He dropped back into his armchair.

General Shilling impassively knocked again with his pencil. "Please clarify your statement, colonel."

"I believe the Bolshevik plague has touched several of our staff." Kashin sneered.

"All our staff," the angry front commander retorted, "perhaps even the counterintelligence."

"Of course, of course." Kashin laughed. "True, quite true. However," he rose again, "your Excellency, around each and every one of us the Red agents are buzzing like flies. Most of us, nevertheless, continue to serve our cause with honor and dedication. For example, a Bolshevik agent sits right under Colonel Skatchko's own nose. Yet the colonel would never say anything to him that would harm our cause. Some of the old and distinguished generals, on the other hand, cannot keep from wagging their tongues, especially in the company of a young Bolshevik whore, and sometimes even a not-so-young Bolshevik whore." His strange gaze was fixed on the hippopotamus-like Tichomirov.

"Are you insinuating?" Tichomirov lifted his massive body. "You are a liar and a scoundrel." His face was now dark red, as if he were going to have a stroke. "I, who served my lord the emperor as a full general with such distinction. I am insulted here by a debauched bastard? Beware, colonel. I am sailing for Novorossyisk tomorrow, and I will talk about your behavior with Denikin himself. I am going to destroy you."

"Do not threaten me, your Excellency, I am not afraid of you or your devil."

"What? You are mad; I will see you court-martialled."

"Do not overburden yourself, your Excellency. As you well know, I will be dead by the end of this week."

General Tichomirov breathed heavily and glared at the mad colonel. Suddenly, he put a handkerchief to his eyes and ran out of the room. General Shilling, a gracious host, hurried after him.

An uneasy silence hung once again in the room. The gray army colonels were afraid to move. The generals puffed on their pipes.

Shilling returned rather soon. Unperturbed, he sat down and banged his pencil. "Please, Colonel Kashin, we are waiting. And, colonel, please refrain from theatrics. We have had enough drama."

This time Kashin stood up without any difficulty. He walked to the general's seat, took the water pitcher, and poured and drank six glasses quickly. Then he walked back and began speaking. At first he spoke so quietly that everyone had to lean forward to hear him. As he went on, his voice became stronger and calmer. Yuri was aware of the nightmarish picture the colonel was painting. And yet, he could not help but admire Kashin's brilliant presentation and his wide knowledge. At this moment, according to Kashin, the Bolsheviks controlled ninety percent of all factories, and all the railway yards. They were organized into small fighting units and had stockpiles of weapons and ammunition. They were organizing the dockworkers and had begun a strong propaganda campaign aimed at the soldiers on the piers. They were about to launch a general strike and then an uprising. "Of course," Kashin concluded, "we are in a most difficult situation. But we do have at least three battle-ready units. Colonel Skatchko's battalion is one of them. Then, a special officers unit and a battalion of German colonists. Together this is a force of over two thousand men. More than enough to eliminate the underground threat. But, but," he rolled his eyes and once again was a mad colonel twitching uncontrollably and wavering back and forth, "all is useless. And my operation will not bring the results we need." He sat down and covered his face with his hands.

"Clarification, colonel?" Shilling asked.

"No, your Excellency, I have said enough."

Yuri spoke briefly about the readiness of his unit. Other commanders spoke too, some briefly, some not. The last to speak was General Egorov. He was an excellent speaker. "It is sheer nonsense that the Bolshevik forces are invincible or overwhelming. On the Odessa front, besides the Latvian and Chinese divisions and Kotovski's cavalry brigade—put together, not more than twelve thousand rifles and two, three thousand sabers—they have nothing. One strong, well-placed blow will throw them back hundreds of kilometers. The overall situation of the Volunteer Army is improving daily. Once we left Rostov, we were holding the fortress town of Bataisk firm. The Bolsheviks have lost the initiative. They are far away from their supply lines and will soon be cut off and annihilated. We, on the other hand, are near our traditional base of support, the Kuban region. We are also beginning to receive more weapons, uniforms, and other supplies from the allies. Our overall position is stronger than last year's. I believe the main problem facing the Odessa Military Region is the low morale of its fighting units. We must lift the morale and we will. We are not able to send reinforcements at this time, but we must organize and send to the front most, if not all, of the officers loitering in the city. Even if we send to the front six instead of sixty thousand officers, that will assure us victory. I am leaving for Sevastopol later tonight and I will personally supervise the signing of contracts for delivery of artillery, ammunition, and winter uniforms to Odessa."

"Such tender care . . . to supply the Bolsheviks," Kashin murmured as he looked at Egorov.

"As to the internal threat, we must act swiftly and decisively. Once the Red underground is eliminated, the front will breathe easier and more units can be sent north."

There followed a lengthy discussion about the thousands of officers who had flooded the city, and what to do with them. No decision was reached. No one spoke about preparations or contingency plans for evacuating the city.

After the conference was over, Yuri caught up with Kashin and asked him about his remark that all was useless.

"Who do you suppose we are fighting, colonel?" Kashin was playing the fool again, his mouth twitched, his eyes rolled.

"Bolsheviks, I believe."

"You believe?" Kashin laughed. "If only it were so, colonel, if only it were so." He quickly walked away.

"Interesting character." General Egorov watched him disappear. "One of our best counterintelligence officers. You and I are but amateurs compared to this mad colonel. Now you must take me to a good restaurant. I have not eaten today. Come."

It was already after five. *My God,* Yuri thought, *Nata will be furious.* And he had not even had a chance to telephone her. He hated this conference, and yet he was forced to sit there and watch it and its participants like a rabbit watching a boa constrictor, as if hypnotized. These generals and colonels would be gone in another week at most. The only man in the room who offered something concrete was the mad colonel. Perhaps he was the only one who was sane. "Uncle Petia, I will drive you to my apartment first. I want you to meet someone."

"Yes I know." Egorov smiled. "Good news travels almost as fast as the bad news. So you are engaged to the most beautiful, and certainly one of the most fascinating women in all of Russia. By all means, let us go. I am eager to meet your happy bride-to-be." They woke up Shebeko, who once again had to plow the Benz through throngs of officers on Deribasovskaya. The crowds were festive and three times larger than during the day. Around every light officers stood drinking, dancing, singing. A huge, boisterous carnival.

At Yuri's apartment, their landlady, Sara Borisovna, shook her finger at him. "Natochka waited for you and waited and finally went out."

"Where?"

"You had better ask with whom. With that handsome Count Zagorski. You had better not neglect her with working late and other nonsense. Or you will blink and the paradise will be gone."

"Perhaps we should wait a bit." Yuri was getting angry. *Damn it. That postcard aristocrat knows that we are living together and planning to get married, and every time I turn around, there he is, inviting her to operettas, plays, sending her flowers, rare champagne.* This had to stop.

"I cannot wait. I simply have to eat something." Egorov was firm. "Perhaps another time."

"Shebeko, drive us to the Bear and, I regret, you will have to stay in the automobile—these bastards will steal it in ten minutes."

In the private room of the comfortable, old-fashioned restaurant, after several glasses of good Chandon, Egorov became melancholy. His very clear blue eyes became clouded, lifeless. "Kashin is right," he sighed, "there is no use. Our cause is lost."

"Uncle Petia, I simply cannot believe that you are saying this. You, of all people. You, who less than two hours ago said that our situation is better now than a year ago. I know you are not a liar. You have organized the entire Kiev underground and risked your life a thousand times. You, who brought me into this struggle, as well as hundreds, perhaps thousands, of others. And you, who saved my life twice and the lives of hundreds of officers waiting to be slaughtered. I cannot believe my ears."

"What I said was true. And we should be in Moscow right now. We had the will and the means to defeat the Bolsheviks even after their offensive. But . . ." He shrugged and cut himself a piece of steak. It was rare, and he studied the reddish sauce on his plate. "We made a stake on the ace, and someone or something substituted our ace for the queen of spades." He ate thoughtfully and drank some more wine. "Let us not talk of war. So, are you happy?"

"With Nata? Yes, yes I am."

"Good. Then take her out of here. Go to France. I will get you visas. Your future bride, I happen to know, is a wealthy woman. I knew her father rather well. He made his millions in Manchuria long before the Revolution. And, wisely, he invested most of his money abroad. You two could live like a king and a queen."

"An excellent evasive maneuver, Uncle Petia." Yuri grinned. "But not completely successful. Let us get back to the queen of spades. You are a collector. Rare spiders, rare stamps, rare watches . . . rare people. Tell me straight, as one soldier to another, who has substituted our ace?"

"I have heard many rumors and have listened to many tales." Egorov paused. From the main dining room came the sounds of a gypsy violin. "I believe it all goes back to the beginning of the twentieth century, perhaps earlier. You have people in St. Petersburg, Moscow, Kiev, wealthy beyond belief. Noblemen who own more land than a medium-sized country in Europe. Decadence, arrogance, evil that comes with enormous power. On the other side of the coin, poverty—humble, terribly oppressed people praying to Jesus Christ just to help them survive. And hardly anyone in between. So the nobleman who owns a country within a country and has everything doesn't have to pray to someone like Jesus Christ, the humble Son of Man. Hence, the time was ripe for mystics and healers, the occult—the more mysterious, the more frightening, the more hideous, the better. Am I boring you?"

Yuri smiled. "I too have heard stories about our Satanists; everyone has."

"Good. I know that they were quite in vogue right after the war of 1905. The Assyrian Babylonian faction was extremely fashionable among the intellectual elite. Then came the Great War which, I think, brought on their decline. Only a few wanted to indulge in metaphysics; there was more than enough real blood spilled. And their sacrificial rites too lost their charm. Now, I believe, they have resurfaced again, and perhaps there is a new dimension to their ideology. Pardon— faith. I have no solid proof just yet. Perhaps Kashin does. Ask him if you have an opportunity."

"I will," Yuri promised. "You said you had known Nata's father. Who was he?"

"An American engineer, a genuine soldier of fortune, and he certainly found one, perhaps two or three. A good, decent man. He was tall, about a head taller than you, Yura. A passionate gambler. He married a Russian actress. I met her only once. I thought she was a very strange lady."

"In what way?"

"She looked so sad, so forlorn . . . I cannot explain."

"And have you met Nata?"

"No, but I have seen all her films. And once I saw her in a play." He looked at Yuri and waited.

"What play?"

"A loose parody, actually of Sollogub's *Petty Devil,* a porno-graphic interpretation. She played Sasha, the geisha boy. It was presented in an intimate theater in St. Petersburg by the Society of Friends of the Marquis de Sade."

"Nata told me about her past."

"Let us then drink to the future. Waiter, a bottle of vodka." They drank to the bride-to-be, to the groom-to-be, and to the victory, the deliverance of Russia, against all odds and all forces. "My destroyer leaves in less than two hours, Yura, drive me to the harbor now."

Yuri, however, gave Porutchik Shebeko another command: "To the freight station, you know where."

"Yes, I do." Shebeko was grim. "I certainly do."

In the back of two empty warehouses—still guarded by Volunteers around the bonfires, although there was nothing to guard—stood empty boxcars, their doors open wide, some of their walls torn open for firewood. Snowdrifts were rather high here, covering the railroad tracks, sometimes reaching the black doors of these skeletons.

"Where the hell are you dragging me?" Egorov protested, but he followed Yuri and Shebeko to where the tracks made a curve and went toward an open field. On that snow-covered field stood a dark, frightening castle made of iron. Its turrets were empty of machine guns and there were black gaping holes in its armored plates where the barrels of the mighty cannons had once protruded. There was no Russian tricolor flying from the command turret. There was something awesome about the armored train, and pathetic at the same time. This once-proud monster, left unarmed and forgotten in the snow.

"Here is proof for your theories, Uncle Petia. The most powerful advanced weapon—there was not another armored train in the entire Volunteer Army like 'Our Homeland.' Destroyed not by Bolsheviks, but by General Tichomirov. The old fool did not want General Shilling to have it. Or perhaps he had another reason."

There was a flickering light in one of the empty iron boxes. Both Yuri and Shebeko took their revolvers out of their holsters. As they came closer, they heard a woman's voice and a man's voice singing: *"Silence surrounds us, the wind carried off the mist, on the hills of Manchuria warriors sleep and they hear Russian tears . . ."*

The woman's voice was so painfully familiar, Yuri stopped. He wanted to turn around, to run back. But Shebeko was already by the car, climbing in and shouting, "Lucy, give me an embrace and a kiss, pretty girl! God, I thought you were in the Crimea. Vanya?" He saw the man whose life they had saved and lowered his voice. "You Bolshevik bastard, you better get out of here. The colonel is coming with some general, they can arrest you."

"I will not, Vanya." Yuri was already in the doorway. He put away his revolver. "But you should be more careful. Once the counterintelligence grabs you, they will shoot you." Vanya did not wait. He hurried out of the armored train and into the snowdrifts and was gone.

"Be healthy, Vanya." Lucy was still wearing her green overcoat and her huge white fur cap. Same as he last saw her, walking proudly away from the train after they arrived in Odessa. She was sitting on some boards they were using as firewood and did not stand up, although she let Shebeko embrace and kiss her. "I came here to, to get drunk and remember, and you frightened poor Vanya away."

"Lucy." Yuri could not think of anything to say. "Lucy."

"Who is that general with you?" Lucy laughed derisively, waved the bottle she was holding, and spat in Egorov's direction. "Fuck all generals, all colonels too! Get out of here! All of you. You too Shebeko, go lick his Excellency's boots."

"Lucy!" Yuri had wanted to say so many things to her in the smoke-filled days of the battles, after they had found Nata in the small station, and later in Odessa. Hundreds of thoughts, feelings, all of them disjointed, many of them so strong, many so false. "Lucy!"

"Go, Yura, go to your rich, beautiful whore, enjoy a rich, wonderful life. Do not remember me, please. Not even in your dreams. Not even when she throws you out with her garbage. Leave!" she screamed so loudly that the three of them stepped back into the snow.

"She is drunk, Yuri." Shebeko tried to console him as they walked back. "She does not mean it. She . . . likes you."

Yuri was silent. He heard Lucy singing again, *". . . On the hills of Manchuria warriors sleep . . ."*

"I will leave you at the battalion," he told Shebeko. "I will drive the general to the harbor myself."

As they were nearing the harbor, Egorov broke the long silence. "I believe you love that very young woman on the armored train—Lucy, whoever she is." Yuri did not reply. "That is not a great sin, not an aberration." Egorov patted him on his shoulder. "A man can love two women. It happened to me once. Question is which one you love most." Yuri remained silent.

On the dark narrow pier, a detachment of sailors and

marines with rifles and machine guns guarded the perimeter of a sleek new destroyer. A bearded bear, the naval officer of the day, shook his head in disapproval as he checked their credentials. "The colonel should know better than to drive the commander-in-chief's personal representative here without an escort. Every house surrounding the harbor is filled with Bolsheviks."

Yuri embraced his uncle, held him for a few moments, and kissed him three times. Then they both crossed one another. No words were spoken. Yuri waited until the general disappeared under the blue and white banner of the St. Andrew's cross which looked gray in the yellow searchlights. He watched the frantic activity aboard. The destroyer was apparently waiting for Egorov and was to depart immediately. "Until we meet again, Uncle Petia," Yuri said quietly, raising his hand to his cap in a last salute. He felt certain he would never see his uncle again.

The sailors formed a line and marched onto the destroyer. Only the marines were now guarding the pier. The naval officer approached Yuri. "I have the honor to inform the colonel that I have summoned a detachment of Cossacks to escort you back to the city. They should be here within an hour. You can wait in my quarters until they arrive." Yuri ignored the naval officer. He jumped into his Benz, made a wide turn, and pushed the pedal to the floor. He had to get back to his unit fast, and to Nata. There was not a minute to lose.

A full moon was already hanging over the harbor. The Black Sea was unusually calm, and on its shiny surface, every single ship, every fishing boat, and even the British dreadnought "Marlborough" were toys on the floor of some child's long-forgotten bedroom.

As he drove back, Yuri cursed himself for many things. He did love Lucy, his uncle was right. And he loved Nata. What he did not have was the time to think, to try and understand his feelings. The events had moved so fast ever since he joined the Kiev underground this spring, he felt almost like a piece of driftwood in a river full of rapids and whirlpools. He had never had a chance to think about what he really wanted to do. It was always this operation or that, fighting just to save his own life, loving and not knowing whether the next day would be his last. Now too, everything was crashing, flying into a bottomless canyon, the only moments, hours of happiness, were the moments stolen, torn from life, so rare. He felt badly wounded by what Lucy had said. *Oh, Lucy, if I could only explain, if I could only take you once more in my arms.*

I should have waited for an escort. The realistic thought flashed through his mind. Even Shebeko with his Marusia—anything seemed better than this racing through narrow streets where every house looked at him like death, grinning with machine guns from the black windows. Another minute, no more, he could see the bright lights and wide avenues in the distance. *I am safe. No.* Just as he was about to make the last turn and drive toward the center of the city, three loud explosions in rapid succession blew out his windows and propelled the Benz through a wooden fence, into a yard and an outhouse. Another grenade thrown shortly afterwards found its mark, and the Benz exploded into a bright fireball. By that time, Yuri was running alongside a ditch. He climbed over a fence and sprinted across another yard, toward a well-lit tall building. He knew that at least four, possibly as many as six men were chasing him. He stopped for a few seconds to empty his revolver. He thought he killed or wounded two, maybe three. Not enough.

Why are they not shooting? He knew the answer immediately. *They want to take me alive. Damn. I forgot to leave the last bullet for myself.* He jumped over another fence, but a new group of men was waiting there. One of them knocked him in the mouth, another hit his head. As he went down, more men jumped on top of him. "Tie him up, comrades," someone said. "Semen wants to question him first."

The ropes hurt. Yuri fought furiously, but they tied his hands behind his back and stuck some rags into his mouth, and one of the men lifted him up, threw him over his shoulder, and carried him a few steps. Suddenly, the man fell down. There was a volley of revolver shots. Someone smashed Yuri's head with a heavy object. The last thing Yuri heard was the chatter of a machine gun.

When he came back to life, he discovered that he was lying on top of some burlap sacks in the corner of a very large, warm room. The ceiling was decorated with pink cherubs looking down from the four corners as if in some museum. Besides the burlap sacks, the room contained several buckets filled with kerosene, a few mops and brooms, a flickering fireplace, many metal cabinets, an enormous wooden desk, a chair in front of that desk, and a machine gun standing on a tripod in the opposite corner. A familiar skeletal figure sat behind the desk, his face hidden by a dark shadow—the mad Colonel Kashin.

On the chair in front of Kashin's desk sat another familiar figure: Vanya, a very decent young man whose life Yuri had saved at the tiny station, who unfortunately happened to be a Bolshevik. Vanya was chained to the chair, hand and foot, and the chair was nailed to the floor. To one side of him stood an officer with a revolver pointed at his head. *I told that boy to be careful.* Yuri tried to sit up. He felt bandages on his head. *Just how long have I been unconscious?* he wondered.

"Ah," Kashin noticed him, "welcome back, Colonel Skatchko. Our doctor assured me you were in no danger of dying. You did not even lose very much blood. Those Bolshevik beasts, however, should use chloroform, as we do. Less problems." Yuri slowly stood up. "Speaking of Bolsheviks," Kashin continued, "you will have to excuse me for a few minutes. Your former clerk here claims he is as pure as a Sleeping Beauty, foolish boy . . . Listen, Vanya," Kashin raised his voice, "it makes no difference to me whatsoever whether you live or die. The choice is yours. Only, please, please," Kashin made a grimace of distaste, "no revolutionary rhetorics. I have heard so much. Simply say yes or no." Vanya was silent.

Yuri noticed that Vanya's gentle, sensitive face was bruised. His glasses were broken, there was a big red bump in the middle of his forehead. Vanya looked bewildered, confused, hurt, and yet there was a dignity and stubbornness on his face, and hope too. "They are all the same, colonel," spat out the officer next to his chair. "Swines. They are only brave when they are killing unarmed men and women."

"We do not murder civilians," Vanya quietly replied.

"Vanya!" Yuri exclaimed. "You honestly do not know? In Kiev, as God is my witness, when we took the city and, and saw . . . in Cheka dungeons, hundreds of civilians, women and children too. I was sick for a whole week afterward."

"We do not kill civilians."

Kashin yawned and poured himself and Yuri some cognac. "Drink, colonel. It is a miracle you are alive. Well, not exactly a miracle. I knew for some time the Reds had organized a team to kidnap and kill you. Even sent a commissar from Moscow to carry it out. So I too knew of your whereabouts. But I did not expect to get you back in such good condition . . . Now talk, Vanya," he shouted, "or I will shoot you here and now!"

"I am a member of the Russian Communist Party," Vanya said calmly. "You are going to shoot me anyway. Do it. I will tell you nothing about my comrades. And the victory will be ours. Long live our great socialist Revolution! Long live Comrade Lenin. Long live Comrade Trotzky."

Kashin nodded to the officer. The officer placed his revolver to the young man's head and fired. Some of the blood splattered on Kashin's desk and his tunic. Yuri was furious, but before he could do anything, the limp body flopped in pain, and Vanya groaned. His head, minus a part of his left ear, jerked up. His mouth was now wide open.

He will tell everything he knows now, Yuri thought. There was a look of a hopelessly trapped animal on Vanya's face, longing to live a moment, a minute, an hour longer.

"Take him away," Kashin sighed. "Deposition and the usual."

After Vanya and the officer had left, Yuri sat down in Vanya's chair. He asked for some more cognac. "I knew Vanya's father, a decent man, taught arithmetic in my gymnasium. Let Vanya go, Kashin. What difference does it make now?"

"What difference?" Kashin screamed. "Perhaps I should place him in his mother's custody? This is not a game we are playing, colonel. We are fighting for our homeland." He searched among the scattered papers on his desk, found a silver box with white powder, and held the entire box to his nose for several long seconds. He then leaned back into the shadows. "You are right, of course, Yuri Efimovich. What difference does it make, especially now when everything has collapsed, oh yes." Kashin scribbled something on a blank piece of paper and affixed his stamp. "Enter!" he shouted, and a soldier who was as young as Vanya and even looked somewhat like Vanya walked into the room and saluted. "Take this order to Captain Zicht. Hurry."

After the soldiers left, Kashin sniffed more cocaine. "I wrote an order to bandage Vanya's head and release him."

"I am grateful." Yuri drank the last of his cognac and felt much better. He stood up, ready to go home.

"Not so fast, colonel." Kashin laughed and there was an unpleasant hollow ring to his laughter. "We still have serious matters to discuss. No, not the operation we spoke of. That was cancelled by order of General Shilling. Do you find it so difficult to believe?"

"Yes, I do. I think it is criminal on his part and, well, it is treason, in my opinion."

"Treason. Yes, that is the word I used in my memorandum to the supreme commander."

Yuri held on to the sides of Kashin's desk until his knuckles turned white. *Those bastards!*

He felt he was once again encircled by the Chinese, fighting with Lucy by his side, firing volleys of shrapnel, everything he had, laying the bypass line, and finally breaking through. "We must stop it, Kashin. It is our duty. Place General Shilling under arrest. If you do not have enough men, I will give you as many as you need."

"I was about to do just that, Yuri Efimovich. And I do have enough trusted officers and soldiers at my disposal. Only," he sniffed more cocaine and this time offered some to Yuri, "only remember what I told that pig Tichomirov earlier? That I only have a week to live. Apparently, I am an optimist. Look at this." He pushed toward Yuri a crumpled piece of paper on which some child had scribbled in red ink: *"You will die before sunrise."*

Yuri shrugged. "When I was in the Kiev counterintelligence, I received these anonymous threats every day."

"Anonymous?" Kashin laughed again. "Look on the other side." There was a crude drawing of the Russian Chort. Yuri knew he had seen a drawing such as this somewhere. Where? He could not remember. "Funny, helpless Chort?" Kashin's body suddenly shook. He lifted his glass of cognac to his mouth and spilled nearly all of it. "Funny? Yes, helpless? Really funny Chort?"

"Get ahold of yourself, Kashin. You are spilling good cognac. You said you have something serious. Let me use your telephone, at least."

"By all means."

Yuri called his apartment. No one answered. He let it ring a dozen times, no answer.

"Perhaps your beautiful bride-to-be is fast asleep." There was something evil in Kashin's smile now. "So, colonel, you are telling me to get ahold of myself; now I am going to ask you. How good are your nerves?"

"My nerves are quite good." This was a lie. *Nata was not home. Where? With that Count Zagorski? And Lucy, Lucy, why can I not get you out of my mind? . . . The stronger your nerves are . . . Why is this madman here? What sort of game is he playing?*

"No games, colonel, we are beyond playing games. Since I am as good as dead and you are the only officer with similar experience and the only one I can trust, you are a logical choice to be my successor."

"Nonsense. I have my battalion, and whatever fighting I will do, it will be in the open air, not in some basement." Yuri stood up again.

"Please, please hear me out. Give this fool a few more minutes. Then you can decide."

Yuri sat down very reluctantly. Kashin had saved his life. Whether it was worth saving or not was debatable. A sudden thought: *Perhaps the orders cancelling the operation were just a figment of Kashin's sick imagination. Perhaps Kashin himself staged the attck on him?*

"This ambush, the blow you have suffered, was not of my doing." Kashin rubbed his temples. "The operation was really cancelled. I am not a traitor, and not as insane as you imagine. So, your nerves are strong?"

"Strong enough."

"Who are we fighting, colonel?" Kashin screamed hysterically, and rose from his seat. "Not the Bolsheviks, no, no, no, colonel. The Bolsheviks are like fleas. Someone touches them and they jump. They are trained. They are circus fleas. Have you ever seen a flea circus? Does not matter. We are all fleas. We jump when our masters touch us. You too, colonel, you too, the whole world, everyone. Oh yes, the entire world must obey, every living creature . . . the dead and those not yet born." He paused, poured the last of the cognac into his glass, drank all of it, opened one of his desk drawers, pulled out another bottle, and set it on the table.

"No cocaine for you, colonel? Good, I will have some more. It is only an hour or two before sunrise. He reached into his desk drawer again and pulled out a large red folder. With mock surprise he threw the folder into the air, caught it, then put it in front of him. It was stamped with the usual *ABSOLUTELY SECRET TO BE KEPT FOREVER* stamp. There were some numbers on the cover and underneath the numbers, the same crude drawing of the Russian Chort. "Look familiar, Yuri Efimovich?"

Skatchko sipped his cognac. He remembered Sara Borisovna's warning: You blink and you will miss paradise.

Paradise? Nata has millions and wants a house in the south of France and a dozen children. Perhaps Count Zagorski would jump at such an opportunity. Perhaps he already had. At least jumped on her. "Yes, so the drawing looks similar. Get to the point."

"Do you think, Yuri Efimovich, that I am crucified by cocaine, and drunk, and so paranoid that I am seeing devils?"

"Colonel, I do not think of you or any devils or that you are being paranoid. I just want to go home. I am simply too exhausted to think."

"I took only one, but I have them all," Kashin continued solemnly. "Yes, I have them all. It is all here in this red file. And now, as I am about to die, I am saying to you, my son, like some baron from a Spielhausen novel—you can have all my castles and riches, but our name carries a terrible curse . . . Do you, Yuri Efimovich, believe in God?"

"Yes, I do."

"Good, then you must believe in Chort. Good and evil. Day and night?"

Why doesn't somebody kill him now? Yuri thought. *Perhaps I should do it and put him out of his torment.* "Give me some of your cocaine, colonel, perhaps it will wake me up. You are really boring me now."

"Boring you? Oh no! Icons, fairy tales, devils? Boring? I will do something after you finish sniffing . . . something that . . ." He rose again and leaned toward Yuri. His eyes reflected such terror that Yuri moved away. "I will . . . Would you like, Yuri Efimovich, to meet the real Chort, right here in this very room?"

Yuri laughed. He did not know exactly why he laughed. Kashin's face was deadly serious, and the room was a depressing enough place for meeting the devil, if there indeed was one around. "I think, Kashin, your work . . . Look, why do we both not end this?" But he was curious now. Just what kind of a game was Kashin playing, and why, why?

Yuri did not see Kashin press the buzzer on his desk, but out of the corner of his eye he noticed that the door opened and two officers entered the room. "Yes, the real Chort, Yuri Efimovich. The co-creator of this world of ours and everything in it, including you and me. Oh yes, one part of everyone of us belongs to it and always will. Do you wish to see what no human being should ever see? To look beyond the curtain? Beyond what we are allowed to see, beyond fear, beyond death, beyond anything imaginable?"

So that is what it was. Yuri felt perspiration on his face. He was not the least bit frightened, just very uncomfortable. Kashin was too far gone. Yuri looked into the rounded, red-blue holes of his eyes and said as coldly as he could, "Listen, Kashin, if you do have the Chort somewhere, bring him over. But afterwards, I must go back to my battalion. Agreed?"

"Wonderful." Kashin applauded. "Yes, bring that . . ." He shouted to the officers, "Chains, of course, double chains on . . . legs! Wait outside until I call you in. Understood?" The officers silently departed. "Now, Yuri Efimovich, we wait. Oh," he was carefree, smiling, "getting back to the Bolsheviks, that they are persistent fleas and creative too. I was amazed to discover, just recently, that they have managed to bribe the entire command of our dear allies. Three French generals, one British general, and several naval officers. The British general was bought for a mere pittance. Twenty-five thousand pound sterling. We could have doubled that had we known in time. Do you think it is a coincidence that every second cannon we get from them blows up in our faces? And every tank, every plane, develops engine problems? Are you not interested?"

"No, and I do not think you are either."

"Wait, I think I hear something. Now, Yuri Efimovich, I urge you to sniff more of my cocaine. You will not be able to ride this one on cognac alone." He watched Yuri more intently than ever. "You are thinking, of course, that I am another addict. True, I certainly am. I take cocaine and inject morphine and drink vodka and cognac by the buckets. And yet I still think of myself, even now, as an honest officer performing my duties, serving our cause. Wait, perhaps not so honest anymore. I think my honesty followed my sanity into the dark void from which there is no return. And love? Not now. Another time, another life, I too was in love. Come, have some cocaine. It is the very best. We confiscated it from a Greek merchant we shot last night."

Yuri inhaled some. It felt good. He inhaled some more. Now Kashin did not seem to be such an idiot. Chort? Amidst this insane slaughter anything was possible. Devils, angels. Yuri thought that he would not be surprised if Jesus Christ Himself suddenly appeared in this room.

There were definitely strange noises coming from the corridor. Uncertain, desperate shrieking sounds, like that of a very large bird. Heavy thuds, guttural moans. "The moment of truth." Kashin smiled. He had his hand over the buzzer. "Just think, Yura," he winked, "you will see something, someone that . . . Forgive me for calling you Yura, colonel, you are so young, you could be my own son. You have so much to live for. In the south of France, for example, on the Hawaiian Islands. Once that door opens, it will be all over." He drummed his fingers nervously around the buzzer.

The moans, thuds, and shrieking noises subsided. But suddenly, there was an indescribably terrifying growl just outside the door, followed by a clanking of the chains. "You have a beautiful bride," Kashin continued, as if unaware of the sounds. "You have your battalion, your war, your ideals, friends. You can look at the sky today, tomorrow. Love a woman, kiss a child. Once this door opens, it will be all over. *Oh, my Agnes,*" he sang, *"my dear Agnes, lift the curtain, your black curtain . . ."* He raised his forefinger over the buzzer and held it there.

Now there was another soul-tearing screech, more thuds, clanking of irons, and a very loud roar. The walls began to shake. Yuri jumped up. Kashin too rose from his seat. The door opened just a crack, and a frightened officer's face peered in. "Colonel," the officer stammered, "I do not believe we can hold it much longer."

"Now, colonel?" Kashin reached down with his finger to press the buzzer, but Yuri grabbed his hand. He could not believe he could be so frightened. He heard himself begging Kashin not to press his buzzer. Kashin sat down, breathing heavily. Yuri too sat down. "Take it away!" Kashin screamed. The noise in the corridor began to fade. Kashin's entire body shook as he looked at the door. "Yes, colonel, you were right," he finally muttered, and drank directly from the bottle. He caught his breath. "And I should be horse-whipped for playing tricks such as this."

"Tricks?" Yuri jumped up and shook his fist. "A joke?"

"I am a debauched bastard and an addict and an alcoholic. I have no right to live." Kashin reached under the *ABSOLUTELY SECRET* folder for a small Browning which Yuri had not seen before. He raised the pistol to his temple. "Say the word, Yuri Efimovich, and I will shoot myself right now, this very second. Otherwise, accept my profound apologies."

"You staged all this for my benefit? Why?"

"Simply to test you. And what better way to do it than to

bring a certain metaphysical element into it? Please, Yuri Efimovich, if you are still angry, tell me to press the trigger and I will obey. Otherwise, let us drink what is left in that bottle and get out of here. It certainly was a long night. Oh, and I did save your life."

"Put that pistol away." Kashin put it down and refilled their glasses. They drank in silence. "Such an elaborate production. Or was it a production?" Yuri asked.

"Of course it was." There was flicker of worry in Kashin's eyes. "Did you think this was real? This file? Here." He took the *ABSOLUTELY SECRET* red folder off his desk, walked with it to the fireplace and threw it into the smoldering fire. A few seconds and it ignited and burned brightly. Kashin's thin figure, with his reddish eyes and pointed black beard, was outlined against the dancing flames. Yuri thought for a second that the mad colonel himself looked like Mephistopheles.

"What time is it?" he asked.

"Time? Oh yes, Yuri Efimovich. That is why I saved you. Time. A present for your bride-to-be." He reached into the pocket of his galif. "Here." He gave Yuri a woman's bracelet watch of exquisite workmanship. "I sincerely doubt I will attend your wedding. Unless as a vurdalak." He returned to his seat. The watch was gold with emeralds and had a little impression on the back of . . . that same crude Chort. Five-thirty in the morning.

Yuri hesitated, then dropped the watch into his pocket and stood up. He shook the mad colonel's weak hand and resolutely walked out of the room. As he opened the door, he thought he heard Kashin's voice telling him that he could give this watch to anyone he wished, except to a woman he genuinely loved. He turned back, but Kashin was bent over his desk, sniffing his cocaine.

In the vestibule downstairs, Yuri was issued a new Colt automatic, a holster, a belt, and a box of cartridges. His battalion was only a ten-minute walk from counterintelligence, quartered in the former Young Women's Conservatory. The walk revived him. He noticed though that the streets were deserted. Normally, even at this hour of the morning, there were some signs of life in this big city: the peasants with their carts on the way to the markets, the officers and their whores staggering out of the closed restaurants, the railway workers on their way to the yards, the French and British sailors. Now there was not a single person in sight. As he was approaching the conservatory, however, he saw a beehive of activity.

Fires burned brightly around the building. Both officers and soldiers were loading ammunition onto trucks at the entrance. "Where have you been?" Shebeko, clearly worried, ran up to him. "Half an hour later and you would have missed us. Here." Shebeko introduced a small infantry colonel simply as Saveliev.

Saveliev wasted no words: "During the night, Bolsheviks took Voznesensk and by now have certainly taken Beryzovka. Our front has collapsed. They have three armored trains, tanks, armored cars, cavalry, and the Latvian division. We have nothing . . . except what you see here."

Yuri could not believe it. "Cherkassian cavalry?"

"Galloped to the Romanian border."

"Preobrazensky Regiment?"

"Fought to the last man. Gone."

"No one?"

"Remains of the Second Hussar Regiment. No more than

two hundred sabers. Perhaps some small units. Nothing, really."

"So they want us to die to the last man?"

"Exactly. And if we do not, the Bolsheviks will be in the city in a matter of hours, perhaps sooner."

Two limousines screeched to a halt a few steps away from them. Out jumped a dozen colonels and generals, led by Shilling. He was unshaved. His red eyes looked just as insane as Kashin's. "What are you doing here, Colonel Skatchko?" he screamed. "By now, you should have been halfway to the front. This delay is treason. I will relieve you of your command. I will have you shot!" The general stopped screaming when he saw Yuri and Shebeko take out their pistols and motion the other officers to surround the limousines. "What are you doing?" he gasped.

"Your Excellency will have to walk back to your headquarters," Yuri glumly informed him. "We are requisitioning your automobiles."

"What?" Shilling paused just long enough to see the hatred on the faces of the officers and soldiers who surrounded his entourage. He shook his head; there were tears in his eyes. He sharply turned and walked back, followed by his staff.

"Break the front windows," Yuri yawned. "Put the Lewises on the front seat and the Maxims in the back." He did not need to give these orders since his officers were already smashing the windows and dragging out the machine guns.

"Yuri," Shebeko took him aside and whispered, "you have problems on both fronts, both are terrible. Last night I stopped for a few glasses at The Gypsy Earring, and there was your beautiful bride, so entwined with that Count Zagorski that she did not even notice me. And it was not simply a friendly conversation. As a matter of fact, later on, they took one of the private rooms in the back. I hate to be the one to say this. Do you want me to go strangle the count? Or shoot him?"

"You think they are still there?"

"I think so."

"Strangle him?" Yuri's voice was hoarse. "No, if she wants her fucking count, she can have him."

He stopped, feeling nauseated, leaned against the side of a limousine, and threw up.

"Yuri, get hold of yourself. She is a whore, your bride. Lucy was right. And Lucy, she came back last night. She is organizing our medical unit." Yuri tried to hit Shebeko, but the porutchik deflected the blow and held his hand. "Get hold of yourself, I beg you."

"Why, Shebeko, why?" Yuri felt it would have been better if the Reds had killed him last night. He must think, however, Shebeko was right. *The stronger your nerves are . . .* not just for himself, for others.

"I can take our small truck, drive down to the Earring, kill the fucking count, and get back in fiteen minutes."

Yuri saw Vanya coming out of the bulding, his head bandaged, carrying his knapsack. *So the mad colonel was honest; he did let Vanya live.* "Come here, Vanya," Yuri said firmly. Vanya reluctantly came over. "I saved your life twice now. Are you willing to pay me back a part of your debt?" Vanya nodded. "Good. You will ride with Shebeko to The Gypsy Earring. You two will pick up Nata, drive her to the harbor, put her on a ship, any ship. After that, I do not want to see you, and you too Shebeko, ever, ever again. Shebeko, get the old Ford. Hurry!"

Shebeko did not protest. He embraced Yuri, then ran to the small automobile parked by the side entrance. Vanya followed.

Yuri watched the automobile roar down the empty avenue.

It was time to move out. The three large trucks and the limousines were ready. Lucy and four soldiers were loading boxes of bandages and stretchers into a requisitioned city bus standing on a side street.

The sun broke through the morning clouds. For a few seconds, everything was very still. Yuri was planning to say a few words to his men before moving to the front. Suddenly, very clearly, they heard the familiar song:

> *Bravely we will go into the battle*
> *for holy Russia.*
> *And all as one will spill our young blood . . .*

A strange unit was approaching. It consisted of about thirty youngsters, led by a middle-aged man in a civilian overcoat. He had a rifle, as did three of the boys. The rest were unarmed. The civilian came up to Skatchko, saluted, and said, "Professor Pelshe, at your disposal. These are some of my students from the Odessa Maritime Institute. We are your reinforcements as per orders, here, signed by General Governor Shilling."

Yuri looked at the boys. The oldest one was no more than fifteen. *We are killing our best,* he thought. *For what?* Slowly, deliberately, he tore the orders in half and threw them in the nearest fire. "I regret to inform you, professor, that I no longer require any reinforcements. As the acting front commander, I order you to disband immediately and leave your weapons by this automobile. Go back to your houses. Hurry." The professor looked at Yuri, as if seeing him for the first time. He understood. He dropped his rifle. The boys walked dejectedly back.

"Battalion, listen to my command!" Yuri shouted. "Everyone into formation. I am going to say a few words." He climbed onto the hood of one of the limousines. "Brothers, I am giving each one of you a choice. Our situation is hopeless. Those who follow me to the front have little chance of survival. Those of you who wish to live, go back to the harbor and try to board a ship or a boat. And go with God, I will not think of you as cowards. We are all fighting a just cause and sooner or later our cause will prevail. God save each and every one of us. God save Russia!"

There was a murmur of angry, excited voices. Arguments broke out, but only for a minute or two. About a third of the soldiers and half of the officers decided to go to the harbor to try to get evacuated. Lucy and her four helpers wanted to stay, but Yuri ordered them to go to the harbor. There was no need for medical personnel where he was going.

As the remainder of the battalion, now numbering less than two hundred men, began to walk north followed by trucks and limousines, an armored car rolled by and stopped alongside Yuri. Inside the car were four totally drunk officers from counterintelligence. Yuri recognized one of them as Captain Zicht, the one who had shot Vanya's ear off.

"We are rolling ahead, colonel. We will clear the road for you. All the way to the Kremlin!" the captain shouted, waving his bottle.

Another bleary-eyed officer slapped the barrel of the machine gun and growled, "Ah, colonel, we saved you yesterday. Why do you wish to die today? You know," he lowered his voice mysteriously, "our Kashin is dead. He saw the Chort and he will burn in hell." The armored personnel carrier picked up speed and was gone.

There was a loud explosion ahead, and fire. Several horsemen in green overcoats and huge fur hats raced toward the battalion, the Hussars. One of the riders was the regimental commander, Vladimir Wolf. "The Reds are right on our backs!" he shouted. There was no sense in going to the front now. The front was here. Yuri ordered the battalion to set up defenses around the conservatory and in the nearby streets and houses.

He did not have to wait long. In a few minutes, the horsemen appeared again. This time they wore red stars and armbands. Several machine-gun serenades chased them away. Silence. Only for a few minutes. A column of five armored cars, their machine guns blazing, rolled down the avenue, followed by hundreds of infantrymen and the cavalry. The side streets and the yards too were overrun with hundreds more gray figures wearing red armbands. The Whites did not have enough grenades and machine-gun bullets to stop this avalanche.

Yuri and his officers disabled two armored cars by throwing boxes of grenades under their wheels. Yuri ran to one of the limousines that was now blocking the street, pushed aside the dead soldier behind the Lewis machine gun, and got hold of the weapon. In the window of the limousine, in the sights of his machine gun, Yuri could see only dark smoke. Suddenly, in the middle of that smoke loomed the shape of a tank, the black barrel of its cannon only a few meters away. And just as when he took Lucy in his arms an eternity ago, Yuri saw Nata's golden eyes before him, exploding in helpless rage.

In the DEPTHS OF A SUBBASEMENT WITH A BLOOD-COVERED floor, a tiny madman in a colonel's uniform was shooting, reloading, and shooting again. His pistol danced in his hand and the bullets did not do any damage; they instantly dissolved, and the chains were melting away. A cry of terror sent the madman scurrying into the corner, covering his face.

This was no ordinary terror, nothing that any man had ever known.

The flesh of the madman began to crawl away from his bones, his body swelled up, his eyes fell out of their sockets, and his head popped off like a cork on a bottle of champagne.

There was an eerie silence in the subbasement—an empty void—and then the walls crumbled.

The Black Sea
January 1920
Leisure Ship "Catherine the Great"
En Route to Sevastopol and Novorossyisk

Nata always REMEMBERED STANDING ON THE EDGE OF Niagara Falls when she was almost seven, on her one and only trip to America. Her father held her tight in his big hands and yet she wanted so much to be one drop of water amidst the torrents of the waterfall, one drop, just one, travelling at a fantastic speed into the mist and the rainbow, disintegrating and being reborn and flowing toward another mystery, another adventure, another endless wonder. One drop of water, just one. Now she was one drop of water flowing in this gigantic Russian waterfall, thousands of times higher than the mighty Niagara.

One drop could never be found, but whatever created the waterfall directed her drop to travel at a certain speed, in a certain direction. Through the torrents, the mist, the rainbow, untouched, not disintegrating and not reborn. Something, its hoofs implanted in the sea of reddish Russian mud, angrily pointed at her with its sharp claws and ordered her to do it. Its eyes were burning coals—bright, shining orange sunsets. They burned; they brought pain.

Nata shivered and opened her eyes. The small room reeked of tobacco smoke and alcohol. The blanket was down on the floor. The body next to her was chalky white. Almost as white as the cocaine on the bottom of her matchbox. She inhaled what remained and threw the matchbox away. A volley of rifle shots, firecrackers, exploded right outside the window. On the wall, next to the window, hung an elaborate print depicting a Roman orgy. *So close,* Nata thought. A loud explosion shattered the window and blew in a gust of icy air. The print fell to the floor. This was serious; she quickly began to dress. The body too sat up, a revolver in his trembling, elegant hands. He pointed the gun at the door, which flew open as an officer and a soldier entered the room.

"Put that down." The officer had a frightening sawed-off barrel in his hands. He calmly walked to the body holding the revolver, yanked the weapon out of the man's hand as one would take a toy away from a child, and, looking with great contempt at the man's well-fed, milky body and aristocratic face, smashed the man on his forehead with the huge iron barrel. The blood splattered on the soiled sheets. The man's body fell backward on the crumpled pillows.

"Shebeko, you killed him!" Nata shrieked. "You killed Count Zagorski."

Only now did she notice the young soldier. "Vanya? What are you doing here?" This was the middle of the waterfall again. *When will it end?*

"I did not kill him," Shebeko sighed, watching Zagorski's body move. "Now listen, cunt, put his boots on and this nurse's cap and get your fucking ass out of here. Come on. Or we will all be dead."

"Nata . . . Natalia Vladimirovna," Vanya stammered, "do hurry, please, we must take you to the harbor."

"Harbor?" Nata did not understand. "Yuri said we have at least two weeks." Shebeko helped her put on the riding boots with the spurs, threw the count's gray overcoat with the fur collar over her, and dragged her toward the door. "I do not wish to go with you!" She fought Shebeko with her fists. "I will wait for Yuri. I have to explain to him . . ."

Shebeko set down his Marusia, slapped her twice—not too gently—and threw her over his shoulder. "Follow me, Vanya, do you wish to die over this whore?" Rifle and machine-gun fire was now everywhere. Nata stopped resisting as soon as she was in the backseat of the automobile and Shebeko slammed the door. "Keep down," he warned. The automobile leaped forward, amidst explosions, and picked up speed.

Nearing the harbor, Shebeko tried to ram his way through hundreds of stalled and abandoned vehicles—trucks, buses, limousines, and armored cars. It was finally of no use, a major intersection was jammed and a few vehicles were burning. He tried to drive on the sidewalk. It worked for a few blocks, but then the sidewalk too was blocked by a burning cart filled with boxes of ammunition. "Vanya, you escort Her Highness to the ship. You two will have to run from here on. I am returning to the battalion."

This was not meant to be. The entire street suddenly erupted with machine-gun fire and grenade explosions. Now every vehicle on the street was burning. The black acrid smoke turned the bright morning back into night.

Shebeko's body slumped over the wheel. A dark red stain was spreading on his fur cap, blood dripping on his gold shoulder patches. Vanya helped Nata out of the automobile and they both ran in the general direction of the sea. They sprinted across yards and orchards, climbed over two fences. Vanya's knapsack, which he did not want to leave at the battalion, was his undoing. Just as they glimpsed the piers, figures with red armbands appeared and fired. Vanya fell down awkwardly, near a wooden fence. "Ours," he whispered, "these are ours." And he was gone. The figures fired again.

I am not running anymore. Nata stood up. *If they are going to kill me, they are going to kill me.* But the figures with the red armbands ran away. A young Volunteer, his head and his hands bandaged, appeared next to her.

"Do not cry, sister," he consoled her. "Let us go down this path, perhaps we can still get on the ship." They hurried past a factory building. From one of its windows someone shot at them, but missed. Another ten minutes, and they were at the end of a giant pier, and a new nightmare unfolded. A crowd of thousands of refugees, including many women and children, was trying to push its way toward a large white ship about to set sail. The crowd was held at bay by no more than a hundred Volunteers with bayonets. In the middle of that bayonet fence was an entrance guarded by a few officers who checked documents and, from time to time, let a few chosen people pass and board the ship.

"Come." Nata resolutely pulled her wounded Volunteer along, shouting, "This hero is dying, let us pass!" They wound their way through the crowd, helped along by the Volunteer's moaning and groaning, as if he was indeed about to expire. When they reached the entrance, the nearest officer, a young porutchik—bleary-eyed, pencil mustache—did not even bother to look at them. His attention was focused on an odd group roughly pushing their way through the crowd and nearing the entrance. First, there were four large Cherkassian cavalry men with carbines and swords. They were followed by two men in black overcoats carrying expensive-looking leather suitcases. Following them was a small man wrapped head to toe in a mink coat, accompanied by three young women, also in furs. Four more Cherkassians made up the end of this procession. As the small man walked through the gate, the pencil mustache jumped to attention. The man in mink waved his pink hand and continued toward the ship.

This was the last straw for the angry, frightened crowd. Although the Volunteers shouted that they had orders to shoot, the crowd pushed at them with such ferocity that the bayonet fence collapsed in seconds and the race began toward the two main ramps a hundred steps away. Nata and her Volunteer were caught up in this human whirlpool, but by the time they reached the ramp, there was already a bottleneck. Hundreds of bodies were pushing desperately through, but very few were actually getting onto the ship. And there was a detachment of sailors too, who were blocking the way.

"Here." Nata saw that some dozen steps away was a much smaller ramp, guarded by just one Volunteer, which had been so far unnoticed by the crowd.

"Halt!" The guard was young and frightened. "Or I will shoot."

"I am accompanying a gravely wounded hero," Nata said, and simply walked past him, dragging her Volunteer. Several dozen people in the crowd saw the maneuver and ran up the small ramp, pushing the kid aside and spilling onto the ship. Nata was shoved toward some lifeboats and was stuck amidst several boxes; her Volunteer was pushed in another direction.

There was a loud cracking sound, a chorus of agonizing screams and curses. The ship was moving. More screams. Beyond the boxes, Nata could see that the ship was now some distance away from the pier. Dozens of bodies splashed in the water, screaming for help, going down and not coming up. There were still hundreds of people left on the pier.

The ship moved rather slowly. Nata saw several trucks arrive at the end of the pier. They were decorated with red banners and slogans, and they carried gray figures with rifles and machine guns. The first truck stopped near the crowd of refugees, and a thin bearded man with a huge red armband climbed on top of the truck's cabin. He had a revolver in each hand and he fired into the crowd. The machine guns from other trucks and the gray figures with rifles also began firing. People began falling down. Some tried to run, some jumped off the pier; women shielded their children with their bodies. But the machine-gun fire was methodical and deadly. In less than two minutes, most of the people on the pier were dead or dying. Nata closed her eyes.

A few more minutes, and she was able to step out of her corner. The deck, which had been crowded with people like ants on top of an anthill, was now almost completely empty. Inside, it was crowded. Bluish smoke hung in the air. It was not as crowded, however, as she had imagined. The unfortunate few hundred left on the pier could have been easily evacuated. Nata read with some amusement the ship's name on the wall: CATHERINE THE GREAT. She had sailed on this very ship just before the Revolution. And not just once, at least three times. Of course it was always in the summer and always first class. And now, just one day away from her twenty-eighth birthday, she was standing in a crowd of refugees, sailing once again for the Crimea.

Perhaps it is just as well, she thought. *I shall get off in Yalta, telephone the prince, and tell him to take me to Marseille. Once I am out of Russia, I will not need any princes.* She saw an empty space near a small round window and cautiously sat down. She felt drowsy. *This marathon running across yards and alleys is not for me. I am not an athlete.* She wished desperately for a papirossa and something to eat. Another few minutes and she leaned her head on the shoulder of an elderly military man sitting next to her and fell asleep.

She awakened when the man shook her gently. He was smiling. He had a square, wrinkled face and question marks in his small blue eyes. She must have been a strange sight. Overcoat with a fur collar, nurse's cap, and Count Zagorski's boots with spurs. *And even stranger underneath,* she thought. An evening dress, the flimsiest lingerie, and black stockings. At least Vanya had the foresight to stick her small purse into the pocket of the overcoat. Otherwise, she would not have had any money. *Poor Vanya, dying so very young. He probably wasn't older than Alyosha. It was good for Alyosha to leave Kiev. Had he been with me much longer, he too would be dead. Everyone next to me dies. Yuri too is better off without me. He will probably go back to Lucy, fight his war, and die in some snowdrift. And this is what he wants to do. I was foolish to hope . . .* Nata felt tears roll down her cheeks, and a feeling of emptiness, great loss in her heart. *Perhaps he is dead. No, I must not think of death.* She wiped her face with the sleeve of the overcoat.

The man with the blue question marks unwrapped a paper bag and offered her one of the two pirozhoks his aunt had prepared for his journey. That pirozhok with cabbage and onions was delicious. He then offered her a hard-boiled egg and salt; that too was wonderful. Somewhat revived by the food, Nata decided to explore the ship. She had known it was huge, but she had had no idea that it was a real floating country. It was endless. Some officers playing cards on the floor invited her to join them and drink vodka. A passing sailor told her that they were giving out soup. "Hurry, nurse." He pointed to a long line of refugees. Everyone had a container in their hands—an old pot, a plate, or a cup. Nata smelled the delicious aroma and moved past the buffet counter. As she was about to leave the third-class deck, she heard a stern voice.

"Nurse, why are you not in the hospital?" The speaker was an ugly colonel with medical insignias. "I demand an answer." Before Nata could think of one, the colonel was summoned by a naval officer and they both walked downstairs.

Hospital? Nata thought it over. "Where is the hospital?" she asked an old bald man, obviously a doctor, his white jacket covered with blood, who was hurrying by.

"Why do you wish to know?" His face was tired, concerned. "Nurse, I advise you to take off your cap and become simply one of the refugees. In our hospital," he rubbed his eyes, "we have mostly typhoid cases. You will be in quarantine. Please excuse me." Nata took off her cap; the bald doctor was right.

She remembered another life. Soft music in the ship's main ballroom. Popping corks. Her first-class cabin. The moon over the Crimean mountains. The film cameras, lights, wardrobe, and decorations. Arkadi running back and forth, screaming at everyone. Runich, so concerned with his looks. Max Linder and his two male lovers. And Nata's own true love, Lola Gerdt. At night, meaningful glances, broken ampules, hopping in and out of different beds. And filming in the Tartar villages scorched by the sun. Mosques and palaces. This was her last film, *The Rose of Bahkchisarai,* a lukewarm love story about a shipwrecked beauty, Nata, and the leader of a band of smugglers, Runich. Max played the villanous Russian gendarme. *Ah, those were wonderful times.*

She cautiously opened the door to the first-class section. The thick carpet was still there. For a moment she wanted to fall on that carpet, to sleep for at least a century. To wake up in a world without wars and blood, surrounded by green plants and smiling, friendly people.

"Halt!" At the head of the stairs stood a tall Cherkassian with a cruel face, his hand on his saber. "Turn back!" he screamed when she remained standing there.

I am just too tired to turn back and run. It was pleasantly warm in the corridor, and the air was clean. No cheap tobacco smoke or sweat. *That race toward the pier wore me out more than I realized. Plus the night with the count and all that cocaine and wine.* No, Nata decided, she was not moving. The Cherkassian started toward her.

"Goddess, is that you? What a miracle!" The voice belonged to a funny little man dressed like a clown with a red nose—a circus clown from some provincial circus. A checkered purple and orange suit that was five sizes too large, red shoes, a yellow hairpiece. The man's gray eyes looked at her with such genuine astonishment and adoration that Nata smiled and said, "Good day . . . I am . . ."

"Oh, I know, I know. How? When? But forgive me, first things first. Please allow Aristid to escort you to your cabin." The little clown confidently led her past the unfriendly Cherkassian guard and halfway down the silent carpeted corridor. "Aha." He bowed his head as he unlocked one of the cabins and held the door wide open for her. He saw Nata hesitate and interpreted it in his own way. "I took the liberty of hanging your dresses and your furs here." He opened the closet. "I cried for you; I could not think. But you are safe . . . here . . . We were all so terribly worried." He removed a large ring from his index finger and placed it on the night table. "Open it whenever you wish, precious. Two grams, Merkov's best . . . and, of course, anything else you should desire." He winked. "Anything or anyone. I am aware of your exquisite taste."

"Aristid," Nata smiled again, "I am very tired. Please leave me for now."

"Anything you wish, just shout Aristid and I shall appear, as a warlock from the mist." The little clown backed out of the cabin. Nata looked at her new wardrobe. All the dresses, very expensive, her size, as were the boots and the high-heeled shoes. The furs were black sable and white fox. Not bad. Her taste exactly. She took off her overcoat and Zagorski's boots. *I hope Aristid doesn't discover his blunder soon,* she thought. She really needed at least a few hours of sleep. This bed was softer, infinitely softer, than her bed on the "Catherine the Great" during the filming of *The Rose.*

She woke up and there were already many stars in her window. The Black Sea was calm. In another cabin, a wonderful baritone was singing, *"Comrades, we are sailing so far, far away . . . far away from the Russian soil . . ."* There were sounds of clinking glasses, laughter, piano music.

Perhaps all I just lived through is one singularly unpleasant nightmare, and this is the beginning of the reality? Far away from the Russian soil? Oh, how I wish to be far away from the Russian soil, as far away as humanly possible. Nata stood up, examined her new wardrobe once again, selected an almost transparent black silk dress, slipped it on, and shouted, "Aristid!" A few seconds later she heard a polite knock on her door and the clown's head appeared.

"How can I serve you?"

Good, excellent, he has not discovered his mistake yet. Or perhaps it was no mistake? It does not matter; I am so hungry. "Aristid, bring me my supper. You know my taste. Go!"

Charcoal-broiled thick slices of lamb, tender and rare inside. Mushroom sauce, fluffy white rice with almonds. Thick red Crimean wine. Black coffee and a napoleon pastry. She devoured everything. That little clown definitely knew her taste in food. *Perhaps I should see just how much more he knows.* She opened the large ring and inhaled the cocaine. It was of a far better quality than the stuff she and the count were sniffing last night: strong, clean, not mixed with quinine.

Bath! She remembered that every first-class cabin had its own private bath. She tried the gilded knob. Yes, how amazing, the water was hot. Soap, perfumes, towels. She went back into the cabin and called Aristid. When he rolled in, she removed her silk dress and stood naked before him. He did not turn away. *So he knows that part too, good.* "Aristid, I am about to take a bath. I want you to come with me and wash my back." The clown was very good at it. He also massaged Nata's tired shoulders and the back of her neck. She felt invigorated and was getting aroused. She thought over several possibilities and variations and decided on a relatively simple one. "Aristid, bring me a man and a woman. Make certain they are clean and know what is expected of them. Oh, champagne, caviar, and a box of papirossas. I wish to begin celebrating my birthday at the stroke of midnight. Do you know how old I will be?"

"Of course, goddess, twenty-eight."

"Remarkable." Nata laughed. "Perhaps you might know what I sometimes love to wear underneath my dress while entertaining a woman . . . or a woman and a man?"

"Certainly." The clown was very serious.

"Bring it now."

He returned with the familiar-looking oblong box. The same Paris manufacturer. The only difference—this box was covered with purple velvet; the one that Nata had among her exotic collection of toys in St. Petersburg was blue. She examined the exquisitely made replica attached to the black leather panties and lined with red silk. "Now bring the guests. Do not make me wait long."

The guests were a dark-haired, sufficiently handsome and trim cavalry officer who introduced himself as Eugene and a very young, pretty blond woman who introduced herself as Luba. *Luba is an aspiring actress,* Nata thought. She hated all actreses. Also, this one reminded Nata of Alyosha's empty-headed sister Lucy. *Simply too innocent. Will not do at all. My clown magician finally made a blunder.* "Aristid!" she shouted angrily, and when the clown came in, she slapped him. "How dare you send me this woman? Bring me another." Both the clown and Luba disappeared.

The second woman was more to Nata's liking. Not too pretty, large amoral gray eyes, full lips, and a knowing smile. Best of all, she did not remind Nata of anyone. Her name was Toni and she immediately removed her dress and her undergarments and sat down on the bed stroking her slightly oversized breasts. Nata too took off her dress and exposed what she was wearing underneath. Toni did not appear to be startled. She had evidently been told by Aristid what to expect. She climbed on the bed, face down, got on her knees, and raised her backside.

Nata entered her hard, pushed all the way, until Toni moaned, and, as Nata worked herself into a wild frenzy, she began to squeal. The cavalry officer was next. Nata rode him long and hard, until he too begged her to stop. She had to rest in any event. Now, after champagne and caviar and cocaine, the two of them would do anything she told them to her body. *This,* she thought, *might be almost as pleasant as releasing my own anger.*

After her guests had finally departed and her body felt soft as silk and relaxed as jelly, Nata's own Russian Chort came to pay its greeting. Not exactly the funny Chort in the innocent Gogol story. He could have been a clown from a provincial circus, except for his eyes. They burned through Nata's mind until her entire body was on fire. She felt like she had died during the night and this fire of hell was going to consume her, along with everyone she had ever known and the only two people in the entire world whom she loved. And she would burn forever, there was no escape. She shrieked and covered her face, and when Aristid tried to console her, she shouted obscenities at him, slapped him, scratched his face, and continued screaming long after he fled her cabin.

The Chort remained at the foot of her bed, its face unseen, its eyes no longer burning her body. It might have laughed. At least she thought she heard laughter. It invited her to see a film directed by the Russian Chort itself. The first scenes were of a Manchurian shrine and Russian soldiers killing a very tall Chinese priest. The next few scenes were of an officer and a soldier breaking apart a statue that indeed looked like a Chort. The shrine was now burning. Cut, to a tension-filled card game. Round table, sweaty faces, smoke. Her own father, still a young man, at the head of the table. He was dealing the cards. A mountain of money lay on the center of the table: paper, gold coins, rings with rubies. Nata's father was turning toward a pale, unshaved officer, the same officer who had killed the Chinese priest. The officer was frightened. He took something wrapped in a white handkerchief out of his pocket. He placed it on the card table and began to unfold it. Darkness.

End of the film? No, that Chort of mine is a far better filmmaker than even Arkadi. One night, it will show me the rest. Darkness in the cabin. The ship was gently rocking in the waves. The stars were not so bright. Another hour and it would be morning. Her eyes closed, Nata felt her mother's presence, felt cold lips on her forehead. *Bayushki bayoo. . .*

The morning, bright turquoise outside her window. So bright she had to turn away. The ship was still moving. As she pressed her face to the window she saw the familiar sights of Sevastopol, and even recognized one of the large houses as that belonging to Kamski, her father's friend and business advisor. *He will certainly help me get out of Russia,* she thought. *Help me? How can he help me when we are sailing away?* The houses and the old fortress were getting smaller and smaller. *Why was I not awakened? What happened to my faithful Aristid?*

"Aristid!" she shouted. There was no response. She noticed that all the bottles and plates, the purple box, the dresses, furs, the ring with cocaine, everything was gone. The cabin was clean. In the closet hung Count Zagorski's overcoat and her evening dress, and on the floor stood the count's boots with spurs. Everything had been a dream. She dressed and walked into the corridor. No Cherkassian guards, of course; they had been a part of the dream. She walked up to the bridge. There were fewer people; the ship was almost empty. The captain, a large handsome seawolf with a salt-and-pepper beard, expressed concern.

"I am greatly surprised, Mademoiselle Tai. I assumed you left the ship with your friends, General Tichomirov, industrialist Homenko, and their entourage. How can I be of service?"

"It really makes no difference." Nata asked for a papirossa. The smoke cleared her head. "I will simply get off in Yalta. I have two friends in Gurzuf. Prince Orechov-Maisky and General Edelli." She stood up, ready to leave.

There was more concern in the captain's blue eyes.

"What is it?"

"I regret to inform you, we are not stopping in Yalta. We are sailing directly to Novorossyisk."

"But, this ship, 'Catherine the Great,' always stopped in Yalta . . ."

"Yes, my dear, but those were different times."

"Dear, dear captain," Nata smiled as seductively as she could, "please stop in Yalta, for me, please. It is so important. And I will never forget you."

"For Nata Tai, I would sail this ship to hell itself." The captain smiled back. "But I am not even in command. I am under the jurisdiction of the army. They have a colonel here who is really in charge. Go ask him."

The colonel did not respond to Nata's charm. He had a terrible cold and, in between coughing and sneezing, said only, "No, my dear, no, no, no."

Novorossyisk? Stacy, Bobrov, Kuzmenko, Ahmed, Klenov, the entire cabal? she thought with great distaste. *On the other hand, Alyosha might also be there if he is alive, and Petia Ovcharenko with his clue to my treasures. I suppose I was dealt a new set of cards. To hell with cards! The first thing in Novorossyisk, I will seduce some colonel or general and make him drive me along the Black Sea highway to Sochi and to Georgia. General Edelli's family in Sukhumi will help me get abroad. Farewell, Mother Russia, that whore of all whores!*

She returned to her empty cabin and sat by the window. The magnificent Crimean shoreline was fading, the sea and the sky became one light blue canvas.

No, I will not simply flee Russia leaving Stacy alive. I must kill her! My destiny itself is moving me closer toward her. I missed her in Kiev; I will not miss her now. If I knew then what I learned in Sumy from Sergei, she would be dead already. Oh, how I want to hear that witch scream, what I will do to her! Nata took a deep breath. *The rest, they will go to hell soon enough. Of course, if I can put them there sooner, so be it. And it is so strange that General Tichomirov is travelling with Homenko and they did not even stop by to say good day.*

Wait! Nata sat up straight and laughed. *That old dog!* She remembered that the general had faithfully seen almost every performance she had given in those small cubicles in a certain villa just outside St. Petersburg. The honorable member of the Society of Friends of the Marquis de Sade. And Homenko too came from time to time to that Villa Aspasia. *So, the two friends watched the great Nata Tai perform? Where? What looks like a mirror is not necessarily a mirror at all.* She remembered that so well, from her nights at Aspasia. She moved the mirror over the dresser aside and examined it. Not this one. There was an unobtrusive watercolor depicting a birch tree forest hanging over the bed. This was their observation post. Two holes, each the size of a silver ruble, burrowed in the wall from an adjacent cabin. The print in the frame was cut out in such a way that it was difficult to see, even looking at the picture, that anyone could be watching from up there. And she certainly was not looking.

That sly hippopotamus and the little weasel! Nata shook her head in wonder. *Hopefully those two old swines saw what they wanted. If I had had the slightest suspicion . . .* She laughed again. *That woman and that cavalry officer will not be able to sit down for at least a week. And that clown? Strangle that clown! Scratch the nose off his face!* Nata did not feel gloomy anymore. *I am going back to that seawolf,* she decided. *Tell him that today is my birthday, to sit me next to him at the captain's table.*

Birthdays are not celebrated as much as name days in Russia, but to Nata, her birthdays were special. That was the only day she was sure she would see her father. Even if he was working thousands and thousands of versts away, he would come. With wonderful, unusual presents, his laughter, and his love. She never knew, never could guess what he would give her. One year it was a Renoir, another year an antique emerald bracelet that used to belong to an Indian princess. And his gifts were not nearly as precious as he. This would be the first birthday without him. A part of her flesh was torn away. The wound was so gaping, no amount of cocaine, of sex, of love could fill the void. *And that is why revenge is so important. It is worth living for.* And yet, with Yuri, she had been willing to give it up. So strange. Perhaps love does conquer everything, even hatred, even a quest for revenge.

Now the love was no longer there. It had retreated to the farthest corner of her heart—not dead, but not nearly so powerful.

The captain reminded Nata of her father. He was funny and clever and his clear blue eyes had seen the world from many different angles. Physically too. He was very tall and handsome, and he even moved in the same manner.

"Do you like to gamble?" she asked him.

"Oh yes, my dear, that is definitely one of my vices."

The captain had assembled an interesting group of characters at his table, no doubt reflecting his sense of humor: a huge, sullen Greek merchant with a shaved head, Popondapolo, who was sailing to Novorossyisk on business; a famous blind violinist, Istomin; and a young singer of gypsy romances, Alena Piontkovskaya. There was also an odd elderly couple. She, Zagorulko, had a wrinkled apple of a face—a typical babushka selling vegetables in the market. He, Brandt, wore a black suit and black hat with wide lapels which he refused to take off, and held a fancy walking stick. He looked exactly like a Protestant minister, and that was what he was.

Nata thought for a moment that this gathering could well have included her little clown. There was one empty chair too. And just as the soup was served, the clown appeared. He nodded his head to everyone, sat down, and quickly began to eat. His face was puffed up. Nata could see that he had tried to hide her scratches with makeup and powder. They were still quite noticeable though, especially the one across his red nose. "Aristid Michailovich Simonov," the captain introduced him, "a man of many talents." Aristid kept eating.

I will teach that rat a lesson he will not soon forget, Nata decided. *A goddess? Good, I will show him what this goddess can do.* She glared at him, but he pretended not to notice. Right after the main course of stuffed cabbage, the huge Greek abruptly excused himself and left. Aristid too tried to leave. "Stay, Aristid," Nata smiled sweetly, "we have so much to discuss."

"Yes, Aristid Michailovich, you must stay," the captain supported her. The clown seemed highly uncomfortable, but he did stay.

"You have seen the horns on Popondapolo?" The wrinkled apple, Zagorulko, smiled at Nata. She had lively blue eyes, and was watching Nata with great interest. "I can see the horns on all of them. That violinist, he too is one of the Babylonian cabal."

"Excuse me, I do not know what you are talking about."
Nata felt uneasy. She drank some wine.

"You too, my dear. I can see your horns very clearly. And
yet you are not one of them. Most unusual." Nata thought of
moving away from her to the captain's left, the empty chair
where the Greek had sat. Fortunately, a group of officers from
a nearby table approached and begged Alena to sing a few
songs. The entertainment part of the evening had begun.

A large torte in the form of a heart with Nata's name in the
middle was wheeled in. Champagne corks popped. An orchestra played the "Tango Magnolia." A tall Hussar lifted Nata into
his arms and carried her to the dance floor. There were thunderous hurrahs, applause. Long live Russia's greatest film
actress, Nata Tai! Embraces, kisses. She was lifted on the
shoulders of another officer, thrown up in the air a few times
and caught, and almost pulled out of her evening dress.

Breathing heavily, she managed to get back to the captain.
He was now sitting by himself. All the characters, including
the clown, were gone. "Boisterous crowd." He laughed,
observing the dancing officers and civilians. "Nata, do you
wish to accompany me to the hospital? Istomin is giving a con-
cert to the wounded . . . Do not be concerned, my dear. The
thyphoid patients were taken off the ship in Sevastopol. These
wounded are very fortunate. They are discharged from the
army, on their way home."

Nata was not a great admirer of serious music. When Istomin
finished tuning his violin and announced that he was going to
play a hymn to Satan, she was startled, along with the rest of
the audience. Two minutes later, she was simply astounded. As

Istomin's violin sang—of love and torment, of cruelty, tenderness, and again of love—she felt tears roll down her face. Quickly she turned to look at the faces of the soldiers and nurses, and they too were crying. The only one who was not crying was the captain. Istomin played with such incredible power, such passion, Nata felt that the walls of the ship and the people had disappeared. She was a little girl, somewhere in the middle of a dark sky, and the wind was carrying her to some unknown yet wondrous destination.

Istomin played, and everyone forgot about the war, their wounds, their sorrows. After he finished there was silence. He lowered his violin and nodded his head. Above his dark glasses, at the very top of his high forehead, for a moment, Nata thought, she saw two small gray horns.

That night she slept with the captain. She was happy and relaxed in the arms of this hairy bear of a man. No visitors, no dreams, and no clowns dared to intrude, dared to disturb her peace.

In the morning "Catherine the Great" stood outside the Novorossyisk harbor. There was much activity in the port. All five of its giant piers were busy. The British transports were unloading cannons, tanks, and ammunition. The French warships were getting ready to sail.

The captain lived in Sevastopol, but he also owned a small house in Novorossyisk that was boarded up and looked after by a good friend. He gave Nata the keys and a note to his friend, because he had to sail back immediately with an army unit. He also gave her a letter for another friend, an attorney who worked for a British firm and could be helpful in getting her a visa and money from her various bank accounts. "Be well, my dear." He kissed her and held her tenderly. "The sooner you leave this cursed country of ours, the better."

"Leave with me, Dimitri." She squeezed his hand. "I have so much money, I will buy you a house somewhere near Marseille, wherever you desire."

"Tempting, my dear. But I am an old sailor. I have seen many sights and I have known a few women. You are a whore, my dear, but you are a magical whore. You are every man's fantasy come true and a nightmare as well. And I sense you have something on your mind, some mission you wish to accomplish before you leave Russia. Revenge? If so, I pity the object of your revenge. You are a lover, my dear, such as no other. And you will find your love someday. Until then, you are a sailboat without a rudder. A magnificent, proud, lonely sailboat. I am so very happy to have known you, Nata." He kissed her lips, then kissed her hand and walked away.

"Goddess, wait! Wait for me, please." Nata could hardly believe it. The little clown was following her, carrying two large suitcases. Now she remembered where she had seen him first: the snow-covered field outside Sumy. Sobolev, their sled.

"Aristid, you have deceived me. For your own sake, go away."

"Please let me explain. They threatened to throw me overboard. I had to do what I did. And they betrayed me. Now, now, I need you, but you need Aristid even more."

"I do not need anyone, go away."

"Please, I know so much, I can be of great help."

Nata stopped. "You know what?"

"I know who they are, I know where they are, I know how they think and breathe."

"Why do you wish to help me?"

"They have betrayed me. Tichomirov promised me a visa to Constantinople and he left me on the ship."

"They left you?"

"Yes. It was I who cleaned out your cabin while you slept."

"And these suitcases?"

"This is your wardrobe . . . plus a few other things."

"Continue." Nata was now interested.

"Good. I once worked for Solnzeva; you know her, of course."

"I saw her once or twice."

"She is Kuzmenko's wife. And she is in this fair city."

Nata was even more interested. "And you, Aristid, what do you wish from me?"

"A shelter, a visa to France, a modest sum in pound sterling to help me begin a new life."

"Do you know every one of them?"

"Every last one, goddess."

"Why did they not simply kill me? They had many opportunities on the ship. They poisoned me once already. Why?"

"They are not allowed to do that, goddess. I overheard Tichomirov himself. The Greek merchant wanted to strangle you, to tear your heart out with his bare hands."

"Tichomirov?" That revelation somehow shocked her.

"You do need me, my dear, at least for awhile. You cannot possibly murder all of them without my help."

"Do you still have that ring?"

"Oh yes. It is refilled and waiting for your beautiful nose. And anything, anyone you desire, I shall procure for you, I am good at it, as you know. I am also," he grinned, "a very good cook."

"Get us a carriage, Aristid. I will give you what you want and I will be generous. But you had better not betray me, ever."

"I will never betray a witch such as you."

"A witch and a clown?" Nata smiled. What a combination. Where was Arkadi with his cameras and his sense of the macabre? Trying to make a few worthless rubles cranking out his cheap Vera Holodnaya and Runich films somewhere near Yalta? Sleeping with the dark-skinned Tartar boys and still dreaming of his days of glory? Of the time when he directed the great, the only Nata Tai?

The captain's house was very comfortable. Nata took the large bedroom, Aristid the small one. There was an inside bathroom, a kerosene water heater in the basement, and a wood-burning fireplace. An upright piano in the living room, cans of meat, and jars of sugar in the kitchen. "We can entertain, oh goddess." Aristid found a bottle of wine, poured two glasses, and started playing the piano, singing, *Silence is surrounding us, the wind took away the mist . . ."* And the happy song, *"Oh, my little apple, where are you rolling, in Nata's mouth you will fall and you won't come back."*

Another universe, Nata thought. The Caucasus. The land of Pushkin, Lermontov, and Hadji Abrek. The highest mountains in Europe: Elbrus, Kasbeck, and Beshtau. The treacherous Empress Tamara who always killed her lovers at daybreak, only at daybreak. The noble knight in the tigers' skin. The land of waters in clear springs that could cure any illness and, some said, give eternal life. A land where, under the cover of mist, God and the devil are locked forever in their mortal struggle. A land of the mountains and valleys from which all humans came and into which they will all return. A land of magic and mystery, love and hatred. Of the forgotten ruins of Babylonian ziggurats and Genovese castles, and the buried treasures of so many empires. Of the people with skin as black as coal, and the fair-skinned Cherkassian women and Terek Cossacks. A land of Muslim and Christian people and Kalmyk Buddhists and a lost tribe of Israel. And, not so far from Novorossyisk, by the Black Aul, a tribe of devil worshippers who had lived in the mountains for thousands of years.

Nata knew that because back in 1916 Arkadi Lubimov had wanted to direct a film about them, starring Nata, of course, as their high priestess. Nothing had happened with that project. Arkadi had suffered a nervous breakdown, and Nata had been persuaded by her father to enter the Sevarius clinic for her morphine addiction.

The Caucasus. Romantic, proud, and exotic. Nata had never been to the Caucasus in her life. *Exotic? Yes, but damn it, it was still Russia!*

The Town of Armavir,
North Caucasus
January-February 1920

The church BELL RANG TWICE. IT WAS TIME TO GET UP. Alexey Lebedev scratched his head, tied his tanks, looked at Petia Ovcharenko who was blissfully asleep on his cot, then locked the door of their tiny room and walked down the narrow cobblestone street to the Café Venetia. This was his ritual: one pastry, one cup of black coffee, one newspaper.

The national news today was rather gloomy, as it had been every day for the past month and a half. Apparently, both Odessa and Krasnovodsk, two opposite points of the collapsing White front, had fallen. *Good,* he thought, *the sooner this bloody comedy ends, the better.* He saw that across the street, in the window of a stationery store, the large map of Russia—with a white, blue, and red line covering half the country—was being replaced by a map of North Caucasus. *Good. Damn all the White generals and officers and the bourgeoisie. Damn them all to hell!*

The local news was not much better. Yesterday, in broad daylight, some unknown persons attacked a branch of the Russian-Asian bank with small firearms and a machine gun. After a fierce firefight with the bank's employees, during which three pedestrians were wounded, the bandits fled empty-handed. So that was the shooting he had heard as he tried taking his nap.

Alexey stepped out of the café and made his way back to his Uncle Stepa's house to collect Petia. After greeting his uncle with a quick embrace and a kiss on the cheek, Alexey hurried back to his room. *Only three more hours. Too bad I unpacked my knapsack. Why do I need it at all? Just my historical letters and, of course, the one in the blue perfumed envelope. All else are assorted rags.*

"Three more hours, two-and-a-half-hours!" he shouted to Petia as he opened their door. But Petia was not on his cot. This was highly unusual. Petia worked at the regiment at night and slept during the day, from at least noon to about five or six. Petia's knapsack and valise were gone. Alexey felt very uneasy. For some reason he bolted the door. His own knapsack was in the middle of his bed, not at the foot of it. Alexey lifted it. There was a folded piece of paper underneath, a note from Petia hurriedly written in pencil.

> *Alyosha,*
>
> *They are waiting for me in a truck. The whole regiment is leaving now for the mountains to fight some Greens. I fear I will never get out alive. Under the floorboard next to the window is a leather briefcase. Please take it with you. Its contents belong to Nata Tai. Do not open it yourself. If you ever see her, give it to her. If not, throw it into the sea, or bury it, or burn it.*
>
> *With love and hope that we will meet in a better world,*
> *Petia*

The briefcase did not look like an ordinary briefcase. It was small, black, and square—more like a case for binoculars. It had a shoulder strap and it was locked. It was also unusually heavy for its size. *Nata Tai?* Alexey laughed bitterly to himself. *That idiot Petia! Me, ever meeting Nata Tai?* Still, he owed Petia a few things and quite a bit of money. *I will keep it for him. The regiment will probably go to Tuapse,* he thought, *and then to Novorossyisk. Where else can they retreat to?*

Greens? What next? Purples? Oranges? He threw out two pairs of his summer trousers, some socks that were mostly holes, and his useless raincoat. Who needs summer clothing? Will there ever be another summer? He had heard from the Volunteers and Cossacks who escaped across the front that the Bolsheviks were massacring not just the White officers and soldiers but entire villages and towns they perceived as being friendly to the Whites, anybody who had a relative in the White army or held some official post, and priests, monks, and mullahs. Lenin's famous decree abolishing the death penalty was the greatest propaganda coup and the biggest lie of this century.

Oh, it would be so good to get out of Russia. Chaikin was right, even shining boots somewhere on the Riviera was much better than some commissar shooting you in back of your head in a cold dungeon. *Oh, Nata, if you are a witch, use your powers. Take me on your magic broom any place you want. Somewhere so far over the oceans that the people have never heard of Russia. And I know you are a real witch. I can feel it. And I know you are alive, I can feel that too.* "Yours completely and always." Alexey closed his eyes for a moment. *Enough of that!*

He hoisted his knapsack onto his back, slammed the door, and walked back to the station. *I will wait in Uncle Stepa's tiny office,* he decided, *and drink my last bottle of red wine.*

"Still in uniform?" Uncle Stepa shook his head in disapproval. "I brought my brother's clothing, even his boots. They are about your size. You still have time to change."

"Let me think about it, Uncle Stepa."

"Alyosha, what is there to think? You are a wounded soldier and demobilized."

"I do have my medical certificate." Alexey drank some more wine.

"You are a fool." Uncle Stepa left.

Alexey drank about half the bottle and untied his tanks. Stepa's brother's Russian boots felt good. Almost as if they were made for him. So much more comfortable than the Oritish tanks. This was a sign from heaven. Alexey took off the rest of his uniform and put on civilian clothing. There was a hole, not very big, in the upper left side of the jacket. *So the bastards shot Stepa's brother?* He wondered whether it was the Whites or the Reds. He sat in the leather chair behind Stepa's desk, his feet with the new boots on the desk, trying to dream, trying to imagine that he was on a beach somewhere on the Riviera, palms, warm breezes.

With a mermaid's mysterious laughter, her eyes Klondike gold, reflecting the sun, Nata runs to his table under an umbrella. She is naked, her body is so perfect, so familiar. She embraces him and kisses him hard, so hard his lips hurt . . . Enough of that! His bottle was almost empty when Uncle Stepa returned.

"Good lad." He smiled, but then his face became serious and concerned. "Listen, there will be no train. And yet you must get out, flee."

"Why? No train, so I will go back to my room. It is paid for by the army."

"You cannot go back. While you were drinking your wine here, your room was ransacked from top to bottom. Mattresses slashed, floorboards torn up, walls gutted. The gendarmes are still there. And they want to ask you some questions. "Also," he lowered his voice, "there were two men, one officer, one civilian, looking for you in the waiting room. Thank God you were in my office and not with the rest of the crowd. They looked menacing."

"I am trapped. Is that what you are trying to tell me? They are probably these Satanists that follow me around. I swear it, I slept with a woman and she is one of them, they are every-where . . . And Petia Ovcharenko must have given me that thing, that meteor they are searching for. And now I am as good as dead. And tortured before I die. Here is to quick death!" Alexey raised the bottle, but Stepa pulled it away from him.

"Alyosha, no more drinking." He poured what was left on the floor. "Listen good. Take your knapsack and follow me." Stepa unlocked the back door. They walked across the tracks in the darkness, toward the water tower. "Wait here." Stepa stopped. "There will be one locomotive here soon. A single engine. It will stop for no more than one minute. The machinist is a good friend of mine. He knows about you. This is your last chance to get out of here. Take it!" They embraced and Stepa walked back to the station.

I wish I had more wine. It was cold. Stepa's overcoat was not as warm as the British overcoat Alexey had left behind. Every minute was an eternity. Torture. He tried hopping up and down to keep warm, but it was no use. His feet were beginning to freeze. *Oh God,* he prayed, *don't let me die now, now that I have crossed the Caspian Sea twice and survived in battle and am only two hundred versts from Novorossyisk. I am so young. So young? After what I have been through, I feel as if I am thirty. But I still want to live. Petia, Petia,* he marvelled. *You did act so strange and mysterious. And you did have an unlimited supply of money. So now you give me this briefcase, this shoulder bag, and Bobrov told me specifically . . . Oh, to hell with Bobrov!*

That was all a nightmare, is a nightmare. Oh, Nata, please use your powers now. Ten more minutes and I will simply freeze to death. Help me now!

He saw Nata's two golden eyes moving toward him out of the darkness. Closer and closer. Now there were three eyes, three lights coming down the track. The small hissing locomotive stopped not too far from him. A machinist and his helper jumped off. "Hurry, lad!" the machinist shouted to Alexey. "We did not come for the water, it is frozen solid. We stopped for you. Climb in."

It was so wonderful and warm by the furnace, as the wheels sang into the night. From one extreme to another. Alexey was pleased. This extreme he loved.

"Drink this. You can sleep over there." The machinist's helper directed him to a pile of rags a bit further from the furnace. The brandy he gave Alexey was sweet and smooth and the rags were soft. So soft that the next few songs the wheels sang were to a child who was fast asleep.

In the morning they passed Kavkazkaya, once again taken from the Reds, and Alexey was one of the last sardines to squeeze onto a passenger train en route to Novorossyisk. Victory! Escape! Temporary insanity prolonged, undiagnosed. The executioner was sick today. Live, rejoice!

It was not too bad. After Ekaterinodar, Alexey was even able to sit down on his knapsack. He was now counting hours. The hours went slowly, but not as slowly as the minutes in the snow, waiting near the frozen water tower. Eventually, after an endless tunnel, the train slowed down to a crawl. Another night. Many, many stars. He could hear the whistles of the ships, see the harbor. The last time he was here, it was before the

Revolution, so many centuries ago. Yet the Black Sea was still here. And so was the small wind-swept city on the hills. And, most important, there was his uncle's house, warmth and peace.

Alexey smelled the fresh sea air, remembered the seaweed and the pebble-covered beaches. He took a deep breath and walked confidently toward the city.

novorossyisk
february-march 1920

NATA SAT ON A SOFT COUCH LOOKING THOUGHTFULLY AT the fire. A piece of birch tree produced a pale orange, almost yellow fire. The pines dripped sap and hissed; their fire was bright red. The smoke, both blue and gray, rose from every branch, every piece of wood, up and up into the darkness of the chimney, toward the roof, to be blown away by the howling northeaster. The heavy iron poker, its end sharpened and curved like a thin crescent of the moon, lay on top of the red fires; the crescent was already turning dark red. A few more minutes. Aristid moodily played a waltz from Eugene Onegin on the piano. "Why are you not dancing, Lensky?"

"Goddess." He drank from a glass of vodka that had been sitting on the piano, his hands trembling. "Goddess, give it up, simply kill the bastard, quick and clean, and be done with it."

"If it were only so simple, Aristid." Nata opened her ring and inhaled directly from it. For a moment, she thought she saw her faceless visitor in the fire, heard his laughter. This time she was mistaken. It was the wind howling over the roof, the whistles of ships in the harbor. The log of the birch tree exploded, shooting off a handful of bright sparks that landed just short of where she was sitting.

"Goddess." Aristid poured himself another glass of vodka and drank it all. "Give it up."

"Do you want to watch?" Nata's eyes narrowed. "I can make you watch."

"You can make me do anything, but please, please, no." He dropped the empty glass.

"It will not take me long. Play something gay in the meantime." Nata stood up. The tip of the poker was now bright red. She took it out of the fire. The rest of her tools were already in the cellar, along with Rotmistr Klenov's body, bound and gagged, but still very much alive.

This cellar was smaller than Sergei Bobrov's in Sumy. Nata put aside the hot poker and cut a pentagram on Klenov's forehead, then tore off the skin. She thought for a moment about whether to go ahead as planned. Yes, she had to be firm. She pulled his eyes out of their sockets with a pair of pliers. This was the first time she had ever done this and it felt almost like a small glass of cognac, a warm, pleasant glow in her stomach. She put the eyes on the wooden box where her black candle flickered and picked up the poker. Klenov's galif was pulled down to his knees, exposing his genitals. Even in the candlelight, Nata could see that this part of his body had already been ravaged by some venereal disease. She used the poker to singe another sign on Klenov's chest and burned off his nipples. He was squirming and groaning. Nata pushed the poker, still red hot, straight into his heart, again and again, deeper and deeper. There was blood all over her hands now, her dress, her face. Klenov's body stopped moving. To make certain, Nata threw the poker aside and slit his throat with a straight razor.

Aristid was ready for her when she emerged from the cellar. He had a wet, hot scented towel to wipe off the blood and a syringe full of morphine which he expertly pushed into her vein. She calmly changed into her black silk nightgown. "I am frightened, goddess. I am terrified."

"Why?" She was beginning to relax, the distasteful part was over. For now. "I have your visa, Aristid, and I took fifteen thousand pounds out of the bank which I have decided to give you. You can sail tomorrow night on a Greek trawler to Batumi . . . after I finish with Solnzeva . . . or you can stay another two days and help me with Kuzmenko and I will give you another five thousand. And book you a cabin on a French liner. Once I am out of Russia, I may never see you again."

Aristid drank another glass of vodka. "You cannot just leave him in the cellar."

"No, you will carry him to that abandoned church they like to gather in. Let them find him and see. Let them know that I have not forgotten . . . Oh, do not be so frightened. I will go with you. We will do it just before morning."

⁂

Nata now felt a bit tired. She enjoyed the morphine to the fullest. She also poured herself a little vodka and drank it. It had taken her two days to lure Klenov to a café where he could be drugged. *They are getting so careful,* she thought. *It will be so much more difficult to kill them now. And they are very frightened. Perhaps even desperate.* She remembered her father saying that she should never underestimate them. And she never would. Under her pillow rested a shiny new Browning. Just in case.

In any event, she was not doing so badly. Klenov was the sixth. Only seven left. Almost half are gone. Now Nata focused her attention on Solnzeva, Kuzmenko's wife. After she was through with Solnzeva—unlike with Klenov, Nata would thoroughly enjoy this session—Kuzmenko might be drawn out in the open and even . . . Stacy. The rest, they did not matter. Bobrov, she could just put a bullet in his brain, not worth torturing. Khan Achmed, yes. He was the one other exception. She wanted to do things to him just to pay him back for the Marquis de Sade days and nights in St. Petersburg. And then, farewell Russia, *bayushki bayoo*. There was something else and someone else. But that would either come together or it would not. She hoped it would.

"Aristid, come rub my back."

The clown, drunk as he was, his hands still trembling, did his very best.

"Do not wake me up until oh, an hour before dawn."

"No, goddess." There were tears in his eyes. The clown was crying. Just like the first time she had seen him. Nata went into her bedroom. She closed her door, checked the bolts and chains on her window, and lay down. The Browning felt comfortable under her soft pillow. *I am skating on very thin ice,* Nata thought. *Hopefully, not for very long. If I could only get Stacy, I would gladly forget about the rest. Let them live. But Stacy is just as clever as I am, and just as resourceful, perhaps more so. And she has her cabal, or what is left of it. She definitely has the advantage. But not for long.*

When she awakened, the sun was already coming down over the gray-green sea. A flock of noisy seagulls flew over the yard. Nata sat up. It must be late in the afternoon. It was half past three. "Aristid!" she shouted. No answer. She took the Browning from under her pillow, pulled back the safety, and cautiously opened the door of her bedroom. The house was empty.

He had left her a note. The little clown had good, clear handwriting:

Goddess,

I carried Klenov to the desecrated church and placed him under the wall. I am terrified of you and so I must leave you. I took my visa and the fifteen thousand pound sterling which you promised me. Please forgive me and please do not look for me. You are insane, my beautiful goddess, hopelessly insane, and only true to your own madness. May the Almighty in His wisdom take pity upon your soul.

With love,
Aristid

Nata angrily crumpled his note and threw it into the ashes of her fireplace. *That little rat has lost his nerve. I should have known.* He had also taken her sable coat. *Still, he did carry Klenov. So Stacy has probably gotten my message.*

She now felt almost as hungry as when she had boarded "Catherine the Great." She sliced several pieces of ham and pushed them into her mouth one after another. *Eyes,* she remembered, and descended into the cellar. *Damn!* Aristid had taken the eyes along with the body. So much blood she was repulsed, sticky dark blood. *The rats will feast on it, clean it up, the real rats.*

She did not like her face in the mirror. There were definitely two, perhaps three wrinkles under her magnificent eyes, and the eyes themselves looked tired, reddish. She could fix all that. Aristid's ring was still on her night table. There was some white powder in it. She would buy more in the city, later on. Nata inhaled and her eyes gradually became golden once more. She walked to the tripod with the looking glass pointed at the harbor.

"Catherine the Great" was still on the outer raid. Another hour and it would be coming to the pier. Enough time for me to get there and meet my handsome captain, as every old sailor should be met: by a beautiful young woman waiting for him on the pier with a bouquet of flowers. She felt confident the captain could be persuaded to sleep with her in his cabin on the ship. It would be infinitely more romantic, and much safer too. Underneath her bravado, though, Nata was worried about Stacy's first reaction.

According to the captain's letter, he would only be in Novorossyisk for this one night. "Catherine the Great" these days was like a ball bouncing constantly between Sevastopol and Novorossyisk carrying army units, the wounded, and typhoid patients. She leisurely dressed, put on a rather nondescript but warm gray overcoat she had bought here—there were far too many robbers in this city and going out alone in her black fox coat was out of the question—slipped her Browning in the outer pocket, her money and small pocketbook in the inside pocket, and carefully secured the locks on the front door. For a second, she thought she saw a face just above the wooden fence. *Very possible. They will probably be watching my every step from now on. Let them.*

At the pier, flowers and all, a great disappointment awaited her. The captain had taken ill, typhoid, and remained in Sevastopol in grave condition. Nata saw a woman kissing a wounded soldier and gave her the flowers. She slowly walked back to the city.

My first plan of action was probably correct, she thought glumly. *Get some old General to drive me to Georgia. Oh, to hell with Georgia!*

To hell with Stacy too; she is becoming a boring obsession. I do have a French visa now. The "Adriatic" sails tomorrow and I know I can get a first-class cabin. In the meantime, I am still very, very hungry.

Before long she was on Serebryakovskaya. The lights came on from one end of the street to another. Crowds, officers, ladies appeared, well-dressed civilians. More bright lights in front of theaters, cabarets, cinemas, restaurants. This was not on the scale of Odessa, but it was a feast in the time of the plague. Nata walked past one of the theaters advertising naked young women in a hilarious new farce, *Poor Lambs.* In the main role, after triumphs in Kiev and Odessa, the one, the only star of vaudeville, N. Solnzeva.

Nata stopped and smiled. *Poor Lambs?* Solnzeva had always annoyed her, although she could easily have been her mother and did bear some resemblance to her, especially at a great distance. *Poor Lambs? And I am as hungry as a wolf. Who knows, perhaps we are destined to have a private meeting, you and I, the lamb and the wolf.*

The one exquisite restaurant in this small city was The Bear. Nata entered it, slipped the maitre d' a twenty-pound note, and asked for a private room. "Are you expecting anyone, Mademoiselle Tai?" he asked in French.

"No, Paul, but then . . . miracles do happen, do they not?" She smiled. "And the evening is still young."

"Young and beautiful, but, alas, not as beautiful as you are, Mademoiselle Tai. Please let me know if I can be of any assistance."

Nata was escorted to a room in the back of the restaurant. She ordered her usual charcoal-broiled lamb, rare in the middle. *Poor lamb? How appropriate.* A sauce of wild mushrooms, preferably boroviks. A bottle of local red wine. And she wrote a number on a piece of paper for the maitre d': *10.* Ten grams of cocaine, enough for now.

The lamb was delicious and so were the mushrooms, served in a bowl, whole, in a spicy, buttery mix. She devoured everything, drank the entire bottle of wine, and still felt very hungry. When the maitre d' brought her a small, soft envelope, she said, "Paul, amaze me. I am still very hungry. I am at your mercy."

"Any entertainment to help you enjoy your meal, Mademoiselle Tai?"

"Only if he or she is young and beautiful and can sing. Nothing else."

"Any preference as to he or she?"

"None."

Paul did amaze her. Never before had she eaten smoked bear meat in a sauce that looked and tasted somewhat like gooseberry jam. Not sweet at all, but tart and wonderful. A large mushroom stuffed with tiny pickled snails. And more conventional delicacies: black and red caviar, steamed sturgeon covered with incredibly delicious white sauce. At least ten dishes and small pots, on two trays. And two more bottles of red wine. The entertainment part was also excellent. A very young Ossetinian girl, Bella, sang in a deep alto some of her native songs and played on a seven-string guitar.

Nata invited the girl to join her, to finish the feast. She was not hungry anymore. She was feeling sleepy now. She lay down on the couch with a glass of wine in her hand. "Can you sing me the Cossack lullaby, Bella?"

"'Terek Cossacks'? Of course."

"Come here." Nata gave her two twenty-pound notes. "When you finish singing it, please leave. Tell Paul I am taking a nap, oh, at least an hour."

"Beyond our window, the Terek is flowing." Bella sang so much better than the pale junker on the train to nowhere. *"Sleep*

while you do not have a care in the world, bayushki bayoo." Bella sang so beautifully, it was so heartfelt, Nata gave her another twenty-pound note and sent her out. Very sleepy and yet alert, Nata took out her Browning, put it beside her on the couch, and covered herself with the overcoat. *Bayushki bayoo,* she thought. *The last time they poisoned me. What will they do to me this time?*

Death. Is it really the end? On that train rolling into the cold void, the end was complicated, even beautiful. It depends when the real darkness, real emptiness arrives. And beyond darkness, beyond the end, is there another beginning? The soul? The singing in a small Russian church on Podol, another life in another dimension, one that goes on forever? *Everyone must die. I am not an exception. Will the Almighty take pity on my soul, as Aristid hopes?*

And is there one Almighty or two? If so, which one has jurisdiction over my soul? And the current life, the insanity? Aristid is right, I am insane. Insane beyond the help of any psychiatrists, any priests. True to my madness? I hope he is right, I do not know what my madness is. Damn! Now with these thoughts of death, I am not so sleepy.

She had to go to the bathroom anyway. This was a good restaurant, but in the deepest province. In Kiev or Odessa, or even in Yalta, the private rooms in elegant restaurants always had their own bathrooms with a bidet. Not here. She had to walk down a long corridor and then downstairs. The bathroom was simple and very clean.

On her way back, she discovered a curious thing. Along the carpeted corridor there were about six numbered doors on one side, six on the other. She had no idea what the number of her room was or where it was. There were voices and music behind some doors, silence behind others. Reason whispered to Nata that she should simply go to the main hall and ask the maitre d'. Nata seldom listened to reason. She stopped by a door where a heated argument was taking place.

"Nothing we can do?" cried a man's voice that sounded familiar. "We are like lambs led to a slaughter!"

Lambs again. Nata smiled. A waiter hurrying by with a tray showed her where her room was. She ordered some black coffee and a napoleon. She thought about opening her envelope with cocaine, but decided to wait awhile. Not being able to recognize the man's voice disturbed her. The voice now seemed very familiar. The maitre d' came in with the waiter.

"A young man, rather shabbily dressed, says he has something to give to you personally. That he knows you."

"I do not know any shabbily dressed young men." Nata yawned. "What is his name?"

"Alexey . . . Lebedev, I believe."

Several grenades exploded in the small church on Podol, "Catherine the Great" had broken in two and dropped to the bottom of the Black Sea, the Chort with his trident danced in the flames, and the armored train rolled through a forest at an incredible speed as skeletal subhuman creatures clung to the barrels of its cannons.

"Shall I chase him away, Mademoiselle Tai?"

"No, bring him right now, and bring food, plenty of good food. And more wine, the best you have. Hurry."

"Oh, Alyosha, Alyosha!" Nata was nearly hysterical. Kissing him, embracing him, clinging to him, almost raping him on the spot. *No, there will be time for that later.* She tore herself away, allowed him to sit down, catch his breath. Between eating and drinking and more kisses and embraces, Alexey told her that for almost a week now, he had known that she was living in the city, but he had not known her whereabouts.

"I have an uncle here, a dentist, and an aunt. The only relatives I have left, I fear. My aunt, Emma Ottovna, has a nephew, Niks, about my age. It took me a few days to learn that Niks is a speculator and a cocaine seller, a very untrustworthy type. As soon as I mentioned that I wished to see you, he nearly jumped out of his skin . . . and that same night we were burglarized. Thank God I had a premonition and had hidden that bag of yours, here, behind my uncle's books. I think that this was what the burglars were looking for. They went through my knapsack so thoroughly, but did not take anything. Petia Ovcharenko gave me this bag . . . he thought he would be killed . . . and told me if I could not find you, I should destroy it. I think I am being followed by somebody because of the bag . . . So, I was walking along Serebryakovskaya and met Niks, and he told me you were at The Bear. I ran home and brought this bag for you. It is heavy."

"Do not be concerned about anything, Alyosha. This bag indeed was my father's and now it is mine. Have you opened it, seen what is inside?"

"No, it is locked. I do not have the key. Besides, Petia told me not to open it. He was so mysterious about it . . . I believe that this is the very meteorite a . . . group of Satanists I have encountered is searching for . . ." He saw the amazement on Nata's face. "Bobrov, Klenov, Kuzmenko, and Lida . . . Lida was killed . . . and they are interested in you . . ."

"Stop it, Alyosha! We will not talk of them tonight." Nata was thoughtful. Now was the time for her cocaine. "Sometimes it is better not to look and not to talk. I will open it tomorrow." She sniffed long and hard. When the waiter arrived with another tray she told him that she wished not to be disturbed.

There was a small bolt on the door. Nata slid it shut. She undressed, sat naked in Alexey's lap, and began to undress him. "You are so skinny, Alyosha," she exclaimed, "and what happened to your hand?"

Skinny? That is Emma Ottovna's dietary meals . . . Hand? Sands, scorpions, Turkestan. His body was on fire. All was in the past. Something he had dared not even think about was happening now. He held Nata and she pressed into him so hard that he felt as he had in Kiev. Their bodies merged into one, and not just their bodies, their hearts, thoughts, everything. He was just a tiny speck in her huge eyes, summer ponds of warm water painted gold by the sun. He was drowning, only to be reborn, again and again.

Sometime later, they sat in an embrace, sharing the last glass of wine. Nata pressed her lips to his ear and whispered: "I wrote you once, Alyosha, so very long ago. Have you received my letter?" Alexey nodded his head. "I meant everything. Now, too, I am yours, completely and always."

There was a knock on the door. The maitre d' politely informed them that is was now seven in the morning and the restaurant would be closing soon. It was time to leave.

"You come with me, Alyosha. I let you go once, I am not letting you out of my life ever again."

They walked hand in hand to Nata's house and slept until just past noon. Nata decided to put aside her vendetta and go back to the French consul, whom she knew personally, to offer him another bribe—this one for Alexey's visa. She then had to stop at two banks and also needed to find out if she could still book a cabin on the "Adriatic." They did not speak about the black shoulder bag. Nata did not open it. She did hide it, however, in a niche behind bricks near the kitchen ceiling. Alexey left to pick up his knapsack with his historical letters and to say farewell to his uncle and aunt. He felt so weak for some reason, he had to stop a few times just to catch his breath. He attributed this to the wild night with Nata. "Emma Ottovna, Uncle Stepa," he shouted happily. "I am leaving for France! Nata and I, we are getting married!"

"Congratulations, Alyosha." His uncle embraced him and kissed him. His aunt also beamed and gave him a hug and a kiss.

Niks shook his hand and said, "Do not forget your poor relatives."

There was one other person in their living room who remained sitting in his chair, next to the bookshelves: a young cornet with a sour expression on his face. When Alexey turned to him, the cornet stood up, clicked his heels, and said, "Alexey Lebedev? Please follow me. Counterintelligence." He showed Alexey his credentials. "Nothing to worry about. A few pro-forma questions. Good day."

Alexey noted that his historical letters, which were usually locked inside the book cabinet, were missing. "Do not worry, Alyosha," Uncle Stepa whispered, "I know General Semenov, he is in charge of the counterintelligence here; he is my patient."

As soon as the cornet and Alexey were in the street, a black automobile drove up, the door opened, and Alexey was pushed inside. The cornet sat next to him. It was very cold in the automobile. Alexey's teeth began to chatter. They stopped in the yard of a gray two-story building. Alexey was ushered into a room with a couch, two leather armchairs, and an oak desk with a vase filled with flowers.

A white-haired general with a friendly smile stood up from behind the desk and stretched out his hand. "Egorov," he introduced himself. "Sit here, Lebedev." He opened one of his desk drawers and took out Alexey's historical letters, along with Nata's blue envelope. They were now neatly tied together with a red ribbon. He put them next to the vase with flowers and looked thoughtfully at Alexey. He had unusually clear blue eyes, the eyes of a much younger man. "So," he said quietly, "do you wish to tell me something?"

I wish to tell you to go directly to hell and take all the other generals with you, thought Alexey. He took a deep breath.

"Your Excellency summoned me here, I was told, to ask me a few questions."

"First let me convey very good news to you. Your sister Lucy was able to escape from Odessa and is now safe in Sevastopol. Second, I would like to congratulate you, Lebedev. I just heard that you are about to marry Nata Tai. Not many mortals are so fortunate. She is so beautiful, so wealthy, so . . ." The telephone on his desk rang and he talked very quietly for a minute or two. "Ah, questions, questions, and so few answers. Tell me something about yourself, Lebedev. Who are you and how do you happen to be in Novorossyisk? Are you feeling well? You look so pale."

"Your Excellency read my letters . . ."

"Yes, but indulge me anyway." Alexey spoke briefly about his background and his odyssey of the past three months. "So you only met Mademoiselle Tai the day before we took Kiev?" Egorov seemed genuinely surprised.

"Yes."

"I am," Egorov rubbed his forehead, "the chief of the counterintelligence department that works directly for the supreme commander. I do not wish to pry into your personal life. But you, Lebedev, have encountered certain people . . . an organization of sorts, a society that is of great interest to us. And that is why you are here, and that is why I have read your letters."

"General." Alexey could stand it no longer. His head was throbbing now. *If that old swine is going to let me out, he will let me out. If not, he will keep me, whatever I do.* "General, your interest is rather belated. Everything is falling down on your head like a house of cards. The Reds are at Ekaterinodar, if they have not taken it already. And you are questioning me about Satanists?"

"Not only Satanists. I have a little problem regarding your future wife."

"Nata? Why not ask her yourself?"

The general ignored him. "I have a problem that King Solomon himself should have. On the one hand, I have people who are so vicious, so frightening, so terrible, that they all deserve to be shot on the spot. For what they did to Russia, to our cause, to so many innocent people. These Satanists are responsible for monstrous deeds, such as you could never imagine. Some tea, Lebedev?"

This is going to last awhile, Alexey thought. *What the hell is he driving at?* "Yes, please." He wanted tea so very much, anything to drink. The tea arrived with delicious ham sandwiches. The general stirred the sugar in his cup.

"Suddenly," he lifted the spoon in the air to emphasize his point, "these terrible people, murderers every one of them and worse, began dropping dead like proverbial flies. Good?" Alexey nodded. Sounded good to him. The general shook his spoon. "Oh, partly good, partly not so good. One was shot three times in his head, for example. That was good as far as I am concerned. Another was stabbed a few times in the back. This too is not so bad. But there were instances . . ." He stopped and pursed his lips, watching Alexey's reaction.

"I do not understand you. How in the world does it concern me or Nata?"

"Not you, Lebedev. As for Mademoiselle Tai, she is a lady of many mysteries."

"I love her and I ask you not to make insinuations about her when she is not present."

"Quite so and I apologize." He smiled. "She is a lady of many wonderful mysteries. You are from Kiev, Lebedev. Tell me, have you ever met Yuri Skatchko? Dark complexion, rather handsome, a colonel?"

"Yes, once, I was arrested for violating the curfew and he questioned me briefly."

"He is my nephew. *Was* my nephew. He was killed recently, defending Odessa. In fact, he died in your sister's arms. They both served on the armored train 'Our Homeland' and loved each other rather deeply, I believe."

"I am sad to hear it." *Lucy? The dark-skinned colonel?* Now the bells were ringing in Alexey's head and as hard as he tried to listen to the general, his words sounded far away.

"Oh, I think Yuri knew he was about to die. It was a miracle he lasted as long as he did . . . I have only one more thing to ask you, Lebedev, and then you are free to go. Please give me the names of all Satanists you have encountered and also of anyone you or any of your friends suspect of being a Satanist. Please think carefully and try to remember."

"Hmm, Bobrov, of course. Klenov."

"Rotmistr Klenov?"

"Yes. Lida, she is dead. Kuzmenko, his wife Solnzeva . . ."

"The actress?"

"Yes. There is this porutchik Sologub; Petia thought he was one of them." *God, let me get out of here fast.*

"Petia Ovcharenko, your friend?"

"Yes, and of course Stacy Averescu and Oleg Baclanov. That is about everyone. Wait, Petia thought that both General Tichomirov and General Romanovsky . . ."

"Good day, Lebedev, you are free to go. Take your letters. My warmest regards to your beautiful wife-to-be, and best wishes for the future. In the meantime, rest up a bit. You look as if you are about to collapse." He walked Alexey to the door, shook his hand, noticed the wound, and asked matter of factly, "You have given Nata Tai the meteorite?"

"Yes." Alexey said it without thinking and then felt like a complete idiot. What a cheap trick, and he fell for it. The last moment, the crucial question, of course, and he took the bait. Yet the general kept on smiling, not at all surprised.

"Do not be concerned, Lebedev. I have no interest in objects, however unique or whatever symbols they represent. I, more or less, collect people. Besides, it does belong to her. Again, good day and my very best."

The northeaster was especially nasty and cold today. Alexey's head was now split in several parts and, by the time he reached his uncle's house, every last one of these parts had developed its own splitting headache. Everyone was greatly relieved to see him back so soon. Emma Ottovna noted that he did not look well, and Uncle Stepa gave him a spoonful of pain-killing powder to swallow that was not cocaine. And it did not do any good. Hot and cold needles began running up and down his spine. He hurriedly said goodbyes, promised to write, and picked up his knapsack, which was now at least three times its former weight.

When he stumbled into Nata's house, he was completely

exhausted. The needles were running wild across his entire body, his head was full of demons frying his brain on a bonfire, and sweat was pouring down his face. He dropped the cursed knapsack in the corner and poured himself some brandy. Nata's business took more time, apparently, than she had anticipated. Alexey cleaned the fireplace, gathered the wood, and started the fire. He moved the couch as close to the flames as possible and lay down. And yet the needles were still running wild all over his body, and now they were all very cold needles. His body shook. He poured himself some more brandy and drank it, but that did not help his headache and did not stop the needles.

It was already getting dark. He undressed, climbed into the bed, put all the blankets on top. On Nata's night table was the torn envelope with some cocaine still in it. Alexey inhaled. That seemed to help ease his headache. But now he began to hallucinate.

He was a boy of ten and Lucy was seven. Uncle Stepa was taking them on a mysterious trip just outside of Kiev. On a ship? Alexey tried to guess. On a train? squeaked Lucy. On an automobile? shouted Alexey. On a troika? cried Lucy. None of these. In a big field, in the middle of it, was an orange hot-air balloon. Oh, how high it went, and how frightened and thrilled Alexey and Lucy were seeing the tiny houses and trees. Then the wind picked it up and whirled it, and the balloonist screamed at them to sit down in the basket and remain absolutely still. They flew over the river, far into the sky, so far, Alexey could no longer see the earth. Amidst the clouds he heard Nata's voice, felt her face next to his, her lips. But he was told to be absolutely still. He must obey the balloonist. And Lucy was no longer in the basket. Where was she?

Nata was sobbing. Another voice belonged to a man. It was

calm, soothing. For a few moments Alexey could actually hear some words. "Poisoned? No, my dear. Typhoid . . . fever, fever . . . typhoid. Out of the question . . . fever . . . typhoid . . ."

"Water," he groaned, and opened his eyes.

Nata's face was close. "Oh, my love, Alyosha, my love." She held his head in her arms and carefully poured the water into his open mouth. His eyes closed; he listened.

"He could have picked it up from anyone, even from you, my dear. It is a strange illness. Many succumb to it, some do not. For him, this week will be crucial."

"This week? I have just come from the French consul. He told me the Reds took Ekaterinodar two days ago and are force-marching here, virtually unopposed. We have only two, three days at most. All foreign nationals are leaving tonight. I have a visa for him and we booked a cabin on the 'Adriatic' . . ."

"Go, Nata," Alexey whispered, "leave, flee, leave, for God's sake. I love you so much, save yourself . . ."

"Be quiet, Alyosha." Her eyes flashed. "I will not leave you! You are going to get well. Sleep."

The balloon was now flying through a narrow canyon with jagged cliffs on both sides. So fast, toward the brightest blue sky he had ever seen, so fast, he could not breathe. Oh God, he prayed, do not let it rip on one of these cliffs, let it fly into the blue.

The time?

Months, years may have passed, centuries. The cliffs are made of iron, sabers, and bayonets. There are repulsive, frightening creatures now climbing up, reaching for his bal-loon, tearing at it with their claws. The blue opening is still there, but much smaller and so far, far away.

Part two of the Manchurian film.

Close-up: Nata's father's face. Calm, confident. He is dealing cards. A queen of diamonds, a ten of spades, a queen of hearts. In the middle of the table, a mountain of gold coins, paper money, and a shining object the size of a billiard ball, in the form of a human eye.

Close-up: The strange officer is hypnotized by its shimmering glow. He is not looking at his cards. He is frightened, horrified. He slowly pulls out a revolver and shoots himself in the right temple.

Close-up: Kuzmenko's face, the enraged young devil in a soldier's uniform. He is trying to strangle Nata's father. Other players jump up, wrestle him down on the floor. Pink mist covers the room. Melancholy piano music.

Close-up: Nata's mother sitting on her bed, tears rolling down her cheeks, she is gasping for air, her arms are outstretched, she is trying to reach someone. Mist again.

The familiar laughter. The end perhaps? What is the end? The theater is now empty, yet the faceless director remains behind the piano. Melancholy, haunting, Scriabin.

Boom, boom! The artillery fire in the hills. Red glow in Nata's window. So many warehouses are burning and exploding, sending flames hundreds of meters high into the starry night. Amidst the warehouses, near the piers, tens of thousands of demoralized, terrified soldiers are storming the few old transport ships. Boom! boom! The end perhaps? In the red glow of her window, Nata sees the faces in the yard of silhouettes, some familiar, all hateful. And they are unable to harm her—Stacy, Kuzmenko, Achmed, any of them.

During the day, Nata had drawn a circle around her house, a very special circle into which they could not enter. Pathetic, evil creatures, insatiable in their hunger and lust, and already in pain. One who could enter would do so just after midnight, amused perhaps that she had thought of that particular device to protect herself. Nata defiantly opened her window. A gust of warm, smoky air from the harbor blew into the room.

She could now hear the murmur of thousands of voices, shouts, whistles of the departing ships, rifle shots and machine-gun fire. She peered into the darkness of her yard, raised her Browning, shot at a shadow that moved along the fence, and screamed, "Give up, Stacy, give yourself to me and the rest of you flee, run, I curse you all! Run while you can!"

To her amazement, there were several rifle shots in the street just outside her gates, a blinding white flash, and a very loud explosion. She saw Stacy leaping over the fence like a cat, firing at someone in a sailor's uniform who pursued her. There were more sailors. One stopped next to Nata's window, a thin young boy. "Robbers? Eh, lady? We will catch them!" And he too was gone. Another giant warehouse erupted in flames by the piers. The hills, the sea, and the dark, tense city turned orange for a few minutes.

Nata closed the window and sat back on the sofa. *Alyosha, Alyosha.* She thought of him lying motionless in her bed. *Now I must pray, really pray.*

Novorossyisk, Naval pier
March 1920

one kilometer AWAY FROM THE BURNING WAREHOUSES was a narrow, brightly lit pier, at the end of which rested two proud destroyers, "Zharki" and "Gnevni." A single-track railroad line ran like a small stream from the main station and ended a few dozen steps from the pier. Three blue Pullmans and an open platform with a searchlight and machine guns stood behind sandbags at the very end of the line. Guarding the Pullmans were the tense figures of sailors and marines with their carbines. These three Pullmans, the pier, and the destroyers were the last tiny speck of White Russia about to be covered by the Red flood.

There was a light in one of the Pullmans. The supreme commander of the Armed Forces of South Russia, General Denikin, leaned away from the window and turned to a few of his generals sitting in the compartment. It was almost three in the morning. Denikin sighed, his puffed-up, apathetic face devoid of emotion, and asked General Egorov whether there was any vodka on the train.

Egorov was somewhat startled. Denikin seldom drank, even wine. He walked into the hallway and asked one of the officers of the guards. There was no vodka on the train. "Anton

Ivanovich," he reported, "everything was transferred to the destroyers, and I think, your Excellency, that you too should board one of the destroyers immediately. Within the past two hours the situation has completely deteriorated. Had it not been for the armored train 'General Kornilov' and a battalion of Markov's Volunteers who came God only knows from where and took up the defense of the city, the Reds would have been here hours ago. They know from their agents, of course, that we are on this train and may organize an attack aimed at taking your Excellency alive. The local Bolsheviks are well-organized and well-armed. And we have a relatively small unit guarding us. Anton Ivanovich, for your own safety, leave the train now."

"No." Denikin closed his eyes. "I shall remain here until the last White soldier is evacuated."

He has totally lost control of himself, Egorov thought. "I regret, this cannot be done, your Excellency, the last two transports are overloaded and about to cast off. Tens of thousands are being left behind. Perhaps as many as fifty thousand."

Denikin sighed again. "Please send someone for vodka, Petia," he almost implored. "In the meantime, select a small unit, say one third of our guards, and send them beyond the perimeter to clear the neighboring streets of possible Bolshevik infiltrators, and to stop the incidents of looting and rapes, if such incidents are taking place."

Denikin's voice was weak and unemotional. Egorov shook his head. The man was completely out of touch with reality. He felt it was useless to argue. He walked outside and gave the order. The orange glow was intense, overwhelming. Fires of hell were breaking through the Russian soil. The last two transport ships were moving away from the piers. For a second, Egorov saw small figures falling into the black water. He turned toward the sea.

On the outer raid stood the impassive observers: a flotilla of British and French warships. Their multicolored signal lights jumped playfully from one dreadnought to another like larks in the middle of a storm. Another warehouse exploded. Egorov felt a hand on his shoulder. An officer whispered that Denikin urgently needed him. *Perhaps that tub of lard wishes to commit suicide, as he had promised. That would be a very decent thing to do under the circumstances. Letting his army be betrayed in such a monstrous way! He knew that every Volunteer, every officer, every soldier or Cossack left behind would be killed by the Bolsheviks. I showed him Lenin's own secret orders that not only every White soldier who surrendered was to be killed, but every close relative of that soldier had to be liquidated, and every civilian who worked for the Whites in any capacity, and their relatives. I pleaded to have every available transport brought here for the evacuation. And he practically ignored me,* Egorov thought. *He left his soldiers to die! Was it done deliberately? Of course. Was it done by Denikin himself or one or two of the generals sitting with him in the Pullman? Generals who perhaps tasted pieces of human heart? It did not matter now. The White movement died tonight in these gigantic fires of hell.*

Not a single sailor or marine in the small detachment liked the idea of leaving the perimeter and going into the dark, menacing streets. They moved out though, ten groups of five men each, slowly, cautiously. Every man was armed with a pistol, a carbine, and two grenades. Dima Grivzov, the gunner's mate who had recently turned eighteen, liked this assignment less than anybody else. He was deeply in love with an army nurse he met last month in Sevastopol. A few nights ago they had decided to get married. Dima had three weeks' leave coming to him. Three weeks! Three lifetimes! Now, walking the dark street, lit only by the huge fires near the harbor, all he could think of were her lips, her blond hair, her slightly upturned nose. Of how very sad she had been the first time they met, a man she loved had been killed in a battle. And the first time he had made her laugh, her wonderful, infectious laughter. And the first time they had slept together.

He walked near his boatswain, Grigori, a middle-aged sailor who kept urging his group to walk as slowly as they possibly could. "That way, we will remain closer to our destroyer. Who knows what will happen in this fucking city. Be alert lads, something happens, we will just run back. There is no shame in running back. Not now."

The streets were deserted. Silent, except for an occasional explosion near the harbor and the booms of artillery fire in the hills. At one intersection the patrol met six very drunk Cossacks. The sailors took away their rifles and sabers. One of the sailors was sent back with these weapons. *Why not me?* Dima thought. *Grigori knows that I am a good shot and he is a very bad shot. That is why.*

On another corner they encountered at least ten strange, thin figures. These apparitions were wrapped in white sheets and blankets. They were patients released from one of the hospitals, wandering the streets, looking for a warm place to spend the night. "All the doctors and nurses fled and we lost our belongings! Everything was looted, even the beds," complained one of the apparitions. They were escorted toward the destroyers by another sailor.

"Fuck your mother, Denikin!" Grigori thoughtfully scratched his head. "Enough fighting for one night, lads. Let us roll our asses back to our ship!"

A pistol shot rang out from one of the dark houses. It was

followed by several carbine shots and a grenade explosion. More shots. A sailor from the group to their right ran up screaming for help. "These bastards killed Boris, but we have them in that yard!" The sailor himself was wounded in the shoulder and collapsed. The group to Dima's left, all five sailors, were already running toward the yard. Dima and Grigori followed them. One sailor stayed with the wounded man.

"You two go around the house," the second mate, who was in command, ordered, "and behind that little toolshed. Be careful, we thought at first they were robbers, but they are Bolshevik agents. All wearing red bands. When you get close to that shed, throw your grenades and we will finish them off."

As they slowly crept along the side of the house, Dima noticed that one of the windows was open. A light from a candle flickered in the room. The candle was black. For a second, he saw the pale, ghostlike face of a beautiful young woman. There was something familiar about that ghost.

They crept silently across the yard and approached the toolshed. There was more shooting from the enemy. Grigori was hit in the leg. He threw a grenade and the blast illuminated two figures crouched with revolvers behind a tree. One was a woman with a face resembling a vampire. The man screamed and rushed at Dima. He too was frightening in appearance, like a charging bull. He held a huge revolver, which he emptied, firing wildly and hitting no one. In his other hand he carried a long curved dagger. At first, bullets could not stop him. Dima and the other sailors shot at him and hit him several times before he finally fell down, just a step away from Dima's feet. Dima shook from fright. He threw one of his grenades in the direction of the woman and shot at her. He thought he hit her, but then saw that maybe his aim was off. She disappeared, and three sailors ran after her.

"This one looks like the devil himself," the second mate whistled.

"Must be an important commissar." He searched the dead man's pockets and tore the man's gold star off his overcoat. "How many do we have so far?"

"We got six of them, all gone to the kingdom of heaven. Five men and a woman, a pretty woman at that," one sailor reported. "I searched the bodies. No wallets, nothing in their pockets. What do we do with them?"

"Leave them where they are. And ours?"

"We lost Boris. Vassili and Vanya were wounded."

"Where the hell were the marines? And stop shaking, lad." The second mate turned to Dima and slapped him on the shoulder. "It is all over, we are turning back."

The three sailors who had run after the commissar whore returned, empty-handed.

"I think I hit her twice. Once in the leg and once in the back," one sailor said. "She is either dead or hiding somewhere nearby. She is the one who killed Boris. Give us five more minutes, mate, we will find her."

"Three minutes only. And you, Dima, help them. Three. Count to one hundred and eighty and roll your asses to the ship as fast as you can." They quickly searched the yards and the sheds, looked into every ditch in the street and the alley. Nothing. When the time was up and they trooped by the house where Dima had seen the beautiful, familiar ghost in the open windows with her black candle burning, he stopped. He was stunned.

Damn! On the wooden wall just under the window, Dima saw a trail of blood—fresh dark blood shining in the orange glow. And under his feet was a small puddle of blood too. The window was now shut, a tight curtain was drawn. *So, that com-*

missar whore must have doubled back and climbed into the window while we were looking for her near the toolshed.

He thought of breaking down the door of the house, but there was a loud machine-gun burst. The sailor behind him screamed, "Let us run!" And Dima ran. The sailors ran all the way to the pier, dodging a hail of bullets fired at them from the darkened windows of some factory building. They dropped their carbines and raced as fast as they could. They reached the pier when the destroyers were already casting off, with no seconds to spare.

Dima jumped on the iron deck, lost his balance, and fell, hitting his head against a very hard object. It did not matter. He felt the movement of the ship and saw that they were now in the middle of the bay. He felt so incredibly relieved, he stood up and looked at the sky. It was getting light; the horrible night was over. He was safe, safe, and he would see his beloved Lucy again. *Thank you, oh God.* Dima tried to cross himself but his arm felt stiff.

Next to him, Grigori was smiling. "They got you too, lad?" He rolled up Dima's sleeve up and looked at the wound. "It is nothing. Clean wound on your wrist. Medic!" he shouted. "One minute later, a few seconds later, and you fellows would have been left behind. These generals, fuck their mothers, only care about their own fat asses."

The medic washed Dima's wound and gave him a shot of morphine. In his hammock, Dima remembered where he had seen the face of the beautiful ghost. It could not be, of course, and yet the face was that of Nata Tai. Or of someone who could pass as her twin. He wondered why Lucy refused to go with him to see Nata Tai's best film, in his opinion, *By Sword Alone,* when it was showing for free on the naval base in Sevastopol.

So, that commissar whore who looked like a vampire is in that house?

But there was too much blood under the window and on the wall; she could not have climbed into the window by herself. Had the ghost helped her? Maybe the ghost, Nata Tai, her twin, whoever, was also one of the Bolshevik agents? And why the black candle? Dima had never seen a black candle before. *Such an adventure! At least we got six of those bastards for sure. And that devil that rushed at me, we must have shot him twenty times before he fell. What a face!*

Dima began to feel drowsy. The destroyer did not sail for the Crimea, as he had hoped. It stood on the outer raid, rocking gently on the clear surface, and watched the burning harbor.

I am going to sleep as long as I can, Dima thought. *And when I wake up, all I want to see are Lucy's beautiful green eyes.*

The serpent HISSED THAT SHE WAS UNARMED AND MORtally wounded. When she saw the black candle burning, she smiled. Her lips, thick and always ruby red, were now as black as the candle. Those lips that Nata loved so much to kiss, that knew so well every crevice of her body, were parted, sensually, waiting, hoping.

Unarmed or not, mortally wounded or not, Nata sat with her Browning trained on the serpent's lips and told her to take off her bloody clothing. There was no need for garments; the room was warm. Nata herself wore nothing. The birch logs burned brightly in her fireplace and the poker's sharp crescent on top of the logs was already pink.

"Lie down on the floor, Stacy," Nata said wearily when the serpent was naked. "Face down." She was wounded. In the right leg, below the knee, a small wound. In the left arm above the elbow—nothing serious—the bullet had passed through the flesh. There was also a dangerous-looking hole in her left shoulder, and that wound was still bleeding.

Perhaps she really is dying, Nata thought. *Why not? Everyone around me is dying, why not her? I would not let her live in any event. And she knows it.*

Nata tied her wrists together, then her ankles. The rope was strong, the same rope she had used on Klenov, it even had his blood on it. The little clown had untied his body when he carried him away. She did not tie her as hard as Klenov; she wanted to see Stacy squirm and wiggle and struggle, in terrible agony. Nata was proud of the fact that no one had ever escaped her bonds. After she finished tying, Nata turned her over and put the pistol away. She opened her ring, held it under Stacy's nose, and watched her hungrily inhale all of the cocaine.

"Why did you come?" Nata asked. "You know what I will do to you, what I have to do to you."

"Natochka, give me some water first. Better yet, some vodka." Nata poured her a glass of vodka and Stacy drank it all. Nata poured herself some. She felt so tense, so anxious.

"Two witches, you and I." Nata smiled, but her eyes narrowed. She leaned over Stacy and put her index finger on the serpent's tail, just inside Stacy's black shiny triangle. She slid her finger up, following the back of the serpent as it slithered along Stacy's white body to her left breast, poised with its fangs just above her nipple. Nata once considered getting a tattoo exactly like this one. A snake coming out of her vagina. A snake? So primitive. What she had decided on were two dragons, frightening dragons with wings and claws, one climbing out from her front, another from the rear. The deal was made. The artist was paid. But then she had agreed to go to the sanatorium . . . *Life, death, serpents, dragons, are they really so different?* Nata playfully squeezed the nipple, watched Stacy part her lips even wider.

She then stroked Stacy's hair. She knew that once, Stacy had shaved her head just to put the tattoo of the Chort on her skull. Each one had an image of the Chort which they had to carry at all times, she knew that. It was the only thing that could give them away. Kuzmenko had the Chort tattooed on his chest; Solnzeva carried the image on her bracelet. Now they were gone, all of them, and she was denied her revenge. Except for Stacy, the one she really wanted. One of her prayers had been answered. "Why did you come to my window?"

"To confess, to ask your forgiveness, to touch the one thing that is more precious to me than even my soul."

"I cannot forgive you, Stacy." Nata thought she should start torturing her right now. The poker was bright red. Nata also knew that they all feared the fire much more than knives or pliers or any instruments made by human hands.

"Please, Natochka, hear me out. I loved you once and I was your friend. In the name of that love, that friendship, hear me out . . . and then do with me what you wish."

"You have betrayed my friendship and you murdered my father." Nata picked up the poker and watched the fear light up in Stacy's black eyes. *I will burn her lips off first,* she decided, *and her tongue.*

"I have betrayed you, but I did not murder your father. I arrested him, yes, but he was forewarned. I had to arrest him. He was on the 'A' list. All wealthy people in Kiev, all we could find, had to be shot that night. Your father was wealthy, but he was also a valuable specialist who had a mandate from Lenin himself. So Commissar Volkov stopped his execution and wired Moscow for instructions. In the meantime, he was held in the Railroad Cheka . . . Kuzmenko somehow found out. He and Oleg took him away, to Darniza. They tried to force him to reveal . . . You know the rest. We cannot obtain it by force. I killed many innocent people and tortured many before they died . . . and tasted human hearts while they were still warm and drank so much blood . . . Tonight, we did not expect you to draw your circle . . . we were waiting for it to weaken. I would have killed you tonight, and . . . your heart . . ." Stacy's eyes were beginning to close.

She really is dying. Nata noticed that the pool of blood under her was growing larger. She put the poker back on the logs, went to her hiding place, removed the bricks, and pulled out the black shoulder bag. She looked into her bedroom. Alyosha had not moved. Not once this evening. She was too frightened to confirm his death. He did not seem to be breathing. Her main prayer remained unanswered.

Perhaps I will forgive Stacy, she thought. *Let her touch that thing, nothing matters anymore.*

"Stacy." She shook her gently. "Here is what you want; you may touch it." She turned Stacy on her side so she could feel the object with her fingers.

"Forgive me, Natochka, you cannot imagine what your forgiveness means to me now."

Nata could not open the lock, so she simply cut the top of the shoulder bag open with a straight razor, and the object rolled out on the floor. The room was suddenly bathed in the bright, pleasant, multicolored glow of a thousand rainbows, so bright that Nata had to close her eyes. She thought she heard sounds too, sounds such as she had never heard before, reminiscent of seagulls flying in her yard, only so much more tender, seductive, musical. As if the blind violinist had begun to play his sad enchanting song right here in this room.

Stacy moaned as she touched the shining object, first with the tips of her fingers and then with her lips. "Natochka," she sighed deeply, "I will be dead in a few moments. Do you forgive me?"

"I forgive you, Stacy." Nata could not believe she had said it. Yet with this magical feeling surrounding her like a warm cocoon, she could forgive anybody, the entire world. And this room was not a part of this world anyway. It now stood in an entirely different time and space.

She noticed that Stacy was not breathing. Her eyes were wide open and there was a happy, almost euphoric expression on her face. Nata bent down and picked up the shiny object.

As soon as she touched it, she knew what Stacy had meant, that she would give her soul just to feel it.

She is falling through the air, not as fast as a stone, more like a feather blown by the wind, a child's kite, the years and the days and the hours. And this life is filled with wonders, her life, yes, but only the good side of it, the way her life might have been, a song of love and devotion. She sees herself in the church, but there are no grenade explosions. She is a bride wearing white and Yuri is standing next to her, looking at her tenderly. He is wearing his brown tunic with the golden shoulder patches and decorations. His side won, the three-color Russian flags are everywhere, and the bells are ringing. She notices her father and mother standing behind them, feels the heavy gold ring on her right hand. Yuri kisses her and carries her outside through the lilac bushes, into the spring. A house appears with blue Ukrainian awnings, white lace curtains, and sunflowers near a wide misty river. Nata sees her child, a girl with blond pigtails running toward her; another child, a boy, cries from the cradle.

Purple mist covers the river; Yuri steps out from that mist. He is wearing a white Russian shirt and carrying the fish he has caught. The moon looks into their bedroom, smiles at their passionate embraces. The morning comes and another day. Her girl is a young, beautiful woman, thick brown hair falls on her shoulders and her eyes are golden, her mother's eyes. Yuri is teaching the boy to ride a horse. The boy is handsome, black hair, black eyes, looks like his father. A short train ride to a city. Her father, an old man, lies in a bed, surrounded by priests and icons. Her mother greets the four of them, ushers them in. The purple mist from the river gently covers their house, the sunflowers. Another morning perhaps, another life?

This church is different, no icons of the Russian saints, no people. Only a priest and three elderly women who are the choir are present. Alyosha stands beside her, his green eyes are filled with joy. He gives her the ring. Outside the window, blue sky and dark green palms . . .

Nata shut her eyes, grasped the object as hard as she could, and cried out, "Oh, let it be, please, please make it come true!"

Epilogue

The sea OF BLOOD THAT COVERED MOST OF RUSSIA PARTED briefly, and Nata escaped. She made films abroad. One was *The Eagle*, with Valentino. In it she once again played the Cossack warrior. Not quite as big a part as in *By Sword Alone*, and not about giving her life to save one of Napoleon's marshals who later betrayed his emperor. As the great Vertinski sang in Odessa during the time of madness: *"The last time you were seen so very close, down the narrow streets your limousine carried you away . . . Perhaps, perhaps in the dives of San Francisco . . ."*

Some White army survivors driving taxicabs around Marseille believed that in a large seaside villa in Antibes, Nata, a near hermit, lived with only one servant, a younger man, and an old wrinkled German housekeeper, along with her two children, a boy and a girl. The housekeeper, who insisted on being called Matilda Franzevna, was loved by the local merchants who delivered only the best food, wines, and whatever else she happened to order. She gave them generous tips, but never let anyone in the house. Rumors in the small Russian émigré community along the French Riviera flew back and forth. Within a few years, however, the villa stood empty.

Legends live longer than people. Even now, there are possibly a handful of elderly people who, as children, used to sneak into the cinemas to see Nata Tai films, hear the sounds of an old piano, and dream for a little while.

And that is what anyone's life is really about—only to dream for awhile.

As for the strange meteorite—or whatever it was and whatever it caused—it lies among the yet unknown undersea weeds that give the Black Sea its dark appearance.

The Black Sea, just like Russia itself, is a place of mysteries and wonders.

Also available from Akashic Books

ONCE THERE WAS A VILLAGE
by Yuri Kapralov
163 pages, trade paperback, $12.00

"The street riots of 1966, the break-up of his own stormy marriage, poignant or amusing but always memorably etched stories of the Slavs, Russians, Puerto Ricans, blacks and artists young and old who were his neighbors, his own breakdown—all of it makes a 'shtetl' experience that conjures up something of Gorki and Chagall."
—*Publisher's Weekly*

"[*Once There Was a Village*] is the authentic account of a period by a survivor . . . Kapralov's background—and gifts as a writer—make him the right annalist for the East Village."
—*Village Voice*

JOHN CROW'S DEVIL
by Marlon James
226 pages, hardcover, $19.95

"*John Crow's Devil* is the finest and most important first novel I've read in years. Marlon James's writing brings to mind early Toni Morrison, Jessica Hagedorn, and Gabriel García Márquez. While he writes about the travails of a small Jamaican town still struggling to unfasten the yoke of its colonial past, the issues and themes James raises are universal, and hugely relevant in the world today. Under the guise of self-righteous religious fervor, much evil is done here; but as Mr. James so wisely points out, true imprisonment is the self-imprisonment of the mind—perpetuated through ignorance and fear."
—Kaylie Jones, author of *Speak Now*

BROOKLYN NOIR
edited by Tim McLoughlin
350 pages, a trade paperback original, $15.95
*Finalist stories for EDGAR AWARD, PUSHCART PRIZE, and SHAMUS AWARD

Twenty brand new crime stories from New York's punchiest borough. Contributors include: Pete Hamill, Arthur Nersesian, Maggie Estep, Nelson George, Neal Pollack, Sidney Offit, Ken Bruen, and others.

"A stunningly perfect combination . . . The writing is flat-out superb."
—Laura Lippman, winner of the Edgar, Agatha, and Shamus awards

SOUTHLAND by Nina Revoyr
348 pages, a trade paperback original, $15.95, ISBN: 1-888451-41-6
*Winner of a LAMBDA LITERARY AWARD & FERRO-GRUMLEY AWARD
*EDGAR AWARD finalist

"If Oprah still had her book club, this novel likely would be at the top of her list . . . With prose that is beautiful, precise, but never pretentious . . ."

—*Booklist*

"*Southland* merges elements of literature and social history with the propulsive drive of a mystery, while evoking Southern California as a character, a key player in the tale. Such aesthetics have motivated other Southland writers, most notably Walter Mosley."

—*Los Angeles Times*

ADIOS MUCHACHOS by Daniel Chavarría
245 pages, a trade paperback original, $13.95, ISBN: 1-888451-16-5
*Winner of the EDGAR AWARD

"Out of the mystery wrapped in an enigma that, over the last forty years, has been Cuba for the U.S., comes a Uruguayan voice so cheerful, a face so laughing, and a mind so deviously optimistic that we can only hope this is but the beginning of a flood of Latin America's indomitable novelists, playwrights, storytellers. Welcome, Daniel Chavarría."

—Donald Westlake, author of *Trust Me on This*

HAIRSTYLES OF THE DAMNED
by Joe Meno
290 pages, a trade paperback original, $13.95, ISBN: 1-888451-70-X
*PUNK PLANET BOOKS, a BARNES & NOBLE DISCOVER PROGRAM selection

"Joe Meno writes with the energy, honesty, and emotional impact of the best punk rock. From the opening sentence to the very last word, *Hairstyles of the Damned* held me in his grip."

—Jim DeRogatis, pop music critic, *Chicago Sun-Times*

These books are available at local bookstores.
They can also be purchased with a credit card online through www.akashicbooks.com.
To order by mail send a check or money order to:
AKASHIC BOOKS
PO Box 1456, New York, NY 10009
www.akashicbooks.com, Akashic7@aol.com

(Prices include shipping. Outside the U.S., add $8 to each book ordered.)